# FRONTIER PASSAGE

*A Novel by*
ANN BRIDGE

THE BOOK CLUB
121 CHARING CROSS ROAD
LONDON W.C.2

THIS EDITION 1944

To
G. H. K. C. O'M.

PRINTED IN GREAT BRITAIN BY
EBENEZER BAYLIS AND SON, LTD., THE
TRINITY PRESS, WORCESTER, AND LONDON

# CONTENTS

## FOREWORD

THIS story is pure invention. Though the places and scenery described are real, and though the larger background of events in this novel bears some relation to historical fact, the characters are wholly imaginary, and their actions and adventures have, and had, no sort of counterpart in real life, with one exception—the nameless Republican soldier who threw the packet of cigarettes into the car on the road to Cervère. Since however characters in novels are people, they must live and move, and speak and hold opinions; and in the world of the imagination these characters do so. But the reader is asked to remember that the words and sentiments attributed to them are theirs rather than the author's, who could not possibly hold so many differing points of view simultaneously—and belong solely in that strange place, the world where Fancy is bred. There is no subject on which outsiders are more ready to pass moral judgements than the Spanish Civil War; and no subject on which the judgement of outsiders is liable to be at once so categorical, so illfounded, and so harmful. For my part, in writing this book, I have been determined to leave it to the Spaniards themselves, and to history, to appraise the true meaning of these tragic years, while attuning my heart and mind to the indestructible significance and nobility of the Spanish attitude to life—and death.

ANN BRIDGE

# CHAPTER ONE

## *The Far Side—Madrid*

IN each generation, and everywhere, there are always a few people to whom public circumstances are important, not only as they touch them personally, in their individual lives and fortunes, but as they affect the whole character of their time, and the hopes and destinies of mankind at large. Such people are not common; there are women among them as well as men. One knows them by a certain preoccupied look—sometimes a haunted look, almost —and by their speech, of which they are apt to be sparing; when they do speak it is slowly, and with restraint; they are never voluble or violent. Usually they have some historical knowledge, but there are not many of them among the ranks of historians proper, because historians recognise facts without emotion, while these people recognise with satisfaction or dismay, or even despair, the probable tendencies of the events going on about them.

James Milcom, shaving gloomily in his emergency bedroom in the Telephone Company's Building in Madrid, during the second winter of the Spanish Civil War, after a night noisy with artillery fire, was a very good example of this type of person. He was a journalist, and represented that mighty daily, the *Epoch*, in Republican Spain—a job he did admirably, as he did most things to which he set his hand. Foreign assignments had been his specialty for some years past; he had been in Italy and in Germany for long periods since 1932—but here in Republican Spain his work lay where his heart was. He wrote at all times like an angel, but in his long, thoughtful, well-considered articles from Madrid a hidden passion flowered sometimes into passages almost lyrical in their intensity—in the sedate pages of the *Epoch* they produced an effect as startling as flowers in a Bishop's hair. As he ran his razor over his lean angular jaw, with the two deep lines running down from the nostrils, round the wide close-lipped mouth to the cleft chin, he stared at the lathered reflection of his big ugly intelligent face with a sort of ferocious desperation, from under his jutting black eyebrows. The grey eyes under the great corrugated forehead were so brilliant and set so deep that they looked penetrating even when he was sleepy, and passionate when he was tranquil. But in fact he was seldom either sleepy or tranquil—he was much

more often passionate, burning with a fierce intellectual flame
about something: passionately finding out, passionately endeav-
ouring, passionately admiring or contemning. It was that passion
which gave him the look of desperation, and sometimes of gloom
—the look that had made the Spaniards nick-name him "El
Melancolico." It was also what made him an unusually good—if
difficult and individual—journalist. But the *Epoch* valued him as
he deserved; the editorial staff recognised the tremendous quality
both of his stuff and of himself, and put up with his eccentricities.

His thoughts as he shaved were as gloomy as his face. He liked
the Spaniards as a race enormously, and hated to see them subject
themselves to the worst of all evils that can befall a nation, civil
war. But even more he hated and feared the implications which
he recognised in this particular civil war. He saw in it the first
open threat to humanity at large of that new theory of tyranny,
the tyranny of ideas, which he had watched with dismayed
repugnance developing, first in Italy and then in Germany,
during his years in Rome and Berlin. Then already he had
realised that the theory in itself menaced everything that was
most admirable and worth preserving in human life, in the
countries immediately affected by it, but his hope had been that
like a fever it would burn itself out within the organisms that it
had attacked. But here in Spain he saw the infection beginning
to spread beyond its own borders. Ideas—false, doctrinaire, un-
related to all genuine human values—were what men were fighting about here; the Marxian nonsense of Communism, the even
more false, silly, and destructive nonsense of Fascism and Nazism
were responsible for the bombardment that had kept him awake
last night. Men had fought for foolish things enough in the past,
he thought, wiping his razor on a dismally dirty scrap of ragged
towel—but frontiers and trading rights and colonies had *some*
sense in them; even dynasties had some degree of actuality. Nothing so madly unreal as this theoretical lunacy had ever before
thrown down solid useful buildings, and sent healthy laughing
lusting men, with work to do, to their profitless death. He
fastened his collar and tie, hitched his braces up over his shoulders,
drew on his jacket, stuffed passports, papers, pocket-book, notebook, pipe and tobacco into his pocket, swept some loose change
off the dingy cover of his toilet-table and pocketed that too, and
pulling on an overcoat, grabbed up his hat and left the room.

It was still early, barely light, when he emerged into the street;
a bitter wind sent little swirls of cold dust round his ankles as
he walked. Though he had a car, he used it mostly for longer ex-

peditions, outside the city. Fires and bursting shells seen from the eighth-floor passage-window during the night had given him a rough idea of where the main damage was to be expected, out in the direction of the University City, and towards that he made his way, walking fast. Here and there queues were beginning to form outside the shops—thin lines of women, mostly bareheaded, but a few with shawls drawn over their heads against the cold, bags and baskets on their arms, standing patiently; in the harsh grey light they looked like exhausted ghosts. Oh yes, queues, he thought angrily—that was all part of it, the final fruit of these high-sounding ideological speeches: queues, and lack of clothes and eggs and butter, and pellagra rampant everywhere—he had seen women killed in Madrid in the street during bombardments, because they refused to leave the line to take shelter, fearing to lose their chance of buying what food they could. This was the reverse of the medal, the other side of building jimcrack empires overnight, and screaming about *Lebensraum*; those were the symptoms, but this was what the patient looked like when he had really got the disease.

He came after a time to the area of damage. In several streets of medium-sized houses, and round a square, there had been a lot knocked down; heaps of rubble lay where houses had stood; a church had had the end blown off and then had burned out, the grey sky looked in through the charred and still smouldering rafters of the fallen roof upon the blackened ruins of the altar. He made a few notes, and started to walk round to the far side of the church. There were few people about as yet, though some of the usual fuel-scavengers were out already; up by the chancel he passed close to one of them, a woman, prowling among the wreckage, gathering wood for firing. This was a common enough sight in Madrid that winter, desolatingly common; the shawled figure excited no particular interest in Milcom—she was just another of the weary ghosts, like the women in the queues, quietly keeping life going in the most impossible conditions. She was tugging at a piece of wood that was stuck under a block of masonry, and he noticed as he passed that the hand thrust out from under the shabby black shawl was surprisingly white and shapely; with one of his habitual impulses he went over, grasped the piece of timber, wrenched it loose and pulled it out. "There you are, Señora" he said in Spanish, and made to go on.

To his immense surprise he was answered in English—"Thank you so very much; that is very kind of you."

It was very good, very pretty English, but it was not an Englishwoman's; he turned and stared at the woman with genuine curiosity. She put back her shawl, and he found himself looking into the most beautiful face that he had ever seen. James's Spanish was more than adequate, it was very good; but it was not *amour-propre* that prompted his next remark, it was a desire to prolong the conversation and find out who this lovely creature was.

"De nada," he said. "How did you know I was English?"

"Oh, not your Spanish," said the shawl, swiftly—"but your look; and I saw you writing. You are a journalist, no?"

James said that he was.

She looked full at him. Her eyes were a clear grey, under reddish-bronze hair and dark brows, very unusual and very beautiful. She let the piece of wood fall, and drew her shawl together across her breast with that very white hand with a curious gesture; holding it so, she continued to look at him. "May I ask you something?" she said at last.

Of course, James said.

"I see that you are kind," she said hurriedly, "or you would not have helped me. It is milk, tinned milk, that I want so much. I have a little child"—her voice dropped. "It is so hard to get, and she is getting so thin. Even one or two tins—it is easier for foreigners. I know it is a lot to ask," she added deprecatingly.

Milcom was embarrassed. He was not in the habit of buying tinned milk, and his English defensive mechanism caused him to say, almost automatically—

"Could you not get that from the Quakers?—or the relief people?"

She continued to look at him steadily.

"That is not so easy for me," she answered. "I am a White."

"Surely they pay no attention to that," he said, faintly irritated by his embarrassment, or her persistence, or something.

"*They*, no—Los Quaqueros are quite impartial," she said, with a sort of judicial calm which struck him. "But others are not. It is—it is not a very good plan for us to be seen too much in the queues."

A White—what was she doing here anyway? And her beauty, and those lovely hands. Curiosity and compassion got the better of Milcom's negativism.

"Come and show me where you live," he said—"and I will see what I can do."

He picked up the piece of wood which he had pulled out for her; hastily, she gathered up some other fragments which she had collected—Milcom took these too, and they set off through the ruined streets, under the grey harsh sky. He eyed her as they went. She walked beautifully, with a light rapid graceful step, an unusual thing in Spanish women. She was an aristocrat, obviously—got caught here somehow, he supposed. There were a few Whites in Madrid living "under supervision," and on the whole they had a pretty thin time of it.

"Why do you speak English so well?" he said, asking the first question that came into his head.

"My grandmother was Scottish."

"Indeed! And have you been in Scotland?"

"Twice I was there," she said—and a little smile, the amused smile of a very sophisticated person at an entertaining recollection played for a moment over her face. "We shot grouse, walking for miles in rows, and killed salmon, sitting in boats. And always it rained."

"It generally does," said Milcom, whom this faithful description of Scottish country-house life caused to smile too. "Have you had breakfast?" he asked abruptly, as they passed a small café.

"No, not yet."

"Nor have I. Let's come in here and have some."

The drab little restaurant was practically empty at that hour; it was not warm, even in there, but it was warmer than outside. The woman took off her shawl before they sat down at one of the small bare tables, and for the first time Milcom got a thorough look at her. She was tall and very slight, with a long slender neck rising finely from rather too narrow shoulders; her hips were narrow too, so that when she stood without her shawl the whole effect was that of an arrow or a wand; her face was long and pale, with a high-bridged delicate nose—the vigorous modelling of the cheek bones and eye-sockets, and the very high square forehead gave it a Gothic look, like a mediaeval statue on the front of a cathedral. In spite of this rather peculiar countenance, she was, undeniably, fantastically beautiful. Her face was vaguely familiar to Milcom; as they began to eat the small hard rolls of white bread—throughout the civil war bread remained white in Madrid —and to drink the milkless, sugarless coffee which a shabby woman set before them, he wondered where he could have seen her before. He asked her how she, a White, came to be in Madrid?

They had got caught, she said, she and the child, when they went to visit her husband in hospital at D——, in September '36; he was in the Navarrese Division, was wounded and sent to hospital. It had seemed safe to go and see him, but there was a surprise attack by los Rojos, and they had been taken there. She had a brother in Madrid on the Republican side—"we are so mixed up; it is very complicated," she said, with another of those little sophisticated smiles—and she had somehow managed to get to him. "While he was living, it was really all right; he managed things for us," she said simply; "but he was killed six months ago, fighting, and now—it is rather difficult."

"And where is your husband now?" Milcom asked.

"Still in prison, at Almadera—so far as I know. I have heard nothing from him directly, of course, but the last news that my brother got for me, he was recovered, and well."

In spite of his antipathy to the cause of General Franco, and therefore to Whites, Milcom found himself rather liking this woman. She was so quiet and direct, and her gift for under-statement was almost English. He made some more enquiries into her circumstances, most of which she parried with a gentle courteous skill which indicated a high degree of social training—she was giving nothing away that she could help, he realised, and asking for nothing but his aid in getting some tinned milk for the child. Now that he was able to take her measure, to place her, more or less, the pathos of that first appeal came home to him with fresh force. And why the devil did he feel so sure that he knew her face?

At last, straight out, he asked her name.

"Raquel de Verdura," she said.

Milcom was uncomfortably certain, afterwards, that at that softly-pronounced name he must have jumped like a shot rabbit. The Condesa de Verdura! The legendary beauty, acclaimed everywhere as the most beautiful woman in Spain, if not in Europe; the great heiress, married to a husband twenty years older than herself, of almost equal wealth and of even more legendary infidelity. No wonder her face was familiar—before the war the social papers had displayed it whenever she appeared in public; and her portrait, by every European artist of note, had adorned the main picture-shows in Madrid, Paris, London, Berlin, for years past. He looked at her again, thoughtfully, while the stories about her husband and his amours flowed back into his retentive journalist's memory. At that moment he thought less about how strange it was that this woman, of all women, should be sitting with him in a dirty little café, after he had helped her to scavenge wood like any beggar, out there by the ruined church, than about her herself, and her own life. What had she made of her husband's so blatant and publicised unfaithfulnesses? Had she minded? Had she in any way recouped herself? With that matchless face before him, and the soft voice still in his ears, confronted with her still dignity and quiet uncomplaining acceptance of intolerable conditions, those were the questions, the personal, unwarranted questions that sprang into his mind. They were to trouble it again and again in the time to come.

When they had eaten, he went with her to her home, still carrying the load of wood—which now seemed the most improbable of burdens for the escort of the Condesa de Verdura. It should have been a mink coat, or flowers! And he remembered how she had said, when she begged for a tin of condensed milk— "I know it is a lot to ask." A lot!—well, in Madrid that winter, a tin of condensed milk *was* a lot, at that. The "home," when they reached it, was a wretched place. All that could be said in its favour was that it was in a cellar, which in view of bombardments by night and aerial bombings by day was a definite recommendation, since it made frequent trips to the public shelters less necessary. But it was dark, damp, carpetless; there was a rickety table, one chair and one stool—a rather tumble-down stove in one corner, with a few pieces of wood beside it, a single palliasse on the floor in another; a minute mirror on the wall, a few clothes hanging from nails. It was perfectly neat; one or two cups and plates, and a few jugs and dishes were ranged tidily on an old wooden tea-chest by the stove; there was a tin basin for washing, and a bucket of clean water on the floor; a towel on another nail above. An unshielded electric bulb gave light; the window was of course broken, and had been patched partly with wood, partly with sacking. One thing Milcom found peculiarly touching. In a common earthenware jar on the table some dried wild grasses, and the seed-heads of various common weeds were arranged like a vase of flowers with great taste and skill—in every shade of fawn, beige and deep brown, they made a charming and striking decoration in that miserable room.

And he could not help being touched by the child. She was a little thing of about seven, russet is colouring like her mother, but fairer, and not beautiful; only the same immense blue-grey eyes looked out of her small, pitifully thin face. She sprang up at their entrance, and went towards her mother with an illuminated face of greeting, but without a sound—then checked at the sight of the stranger; when she was introduced she curtsied, and then busied herself in stacking the wood neatly in a pile beside the stove, and in stoking that up with a few small bits. It was bitterly cold in the room. This done, she sat down on the corner of the palliasse and went on knitting at a small sock, which she had put down when they came in. The Condesa sat on the stool and gave Milcom the chair with the imperceptible gracious finality of the accomplished hostess, which it would have been ill-bred to disobey. He did his best to conceal his dismay at their surroundings, and talked as well as he could; most of the time he watched the child. She was unnaturally quiet and discreet in all her actions, it seemed to him—and she looked horribly fragile. Sometimes she raised her eyes and rested them on her mother with a look which went right through Milcom—the look of a person holding to their only life-line, their one security. And they had been living together like that, in that room, for a year!

Before he left he got the name of the Republican brother, who had been killed fighting before Madrid. Milcom was on the best of terms with the Republican authorities, and had some excellent connections in high quarters; being a foreigner, he could befriend even a White, if he chose, without much risk, but the brother's name would be a help. As he walked away he realised that he had definitely decided to befriend this pair to some extent—that look in the child's eyes had clinched the matter.

Food was his first concern. The child looked half starved. He, like most foreigners, had a very small reserve of such things as chocolate, sugar and cigarettes, presents brought in from outside, which came in handy on occasions like the present. He went and talked to one of the relief organisations, explained the situation, and raised a couple of tins of condensed milk; from the proprietor of a restaurant where he had eaten regularly for months he managed to obtain some tinned soup, and, for a vast price, four eggs and a small lump of butter; later he made an expedition to a very shabby indeterminate little back yard down by the Manzanares, from which he emerged with a small and ancient hand-saw wrapped in newspapers, and three more eggs. Milcom had all sorts of odd friends and acquaintances all over the city, who were useful to him for a variety of purposes; the late proprietor of the hand-saw was one of these. But he knew better than to take all these stores at once to the Condesa's cellar residence; that would merely be to invite trouble. His room contained a wall cupboard, with a good lock, and in this he stowed away all but one tin of milk and two of soup, the four restaurant eggs, the butter and the saw; these he made up into a parcel with some sugar and some chocolate, and again on foot, he set off to carry them to the Condesa. A car outside her door might have excited comment, and anyhow the government requisition chits for petrol were strictly limited, even for journalists. All these

activities had taken some time—nothing can be done quickly in
Spain—and a harsh coppery glare, interpenetrating the heavy
clouds, showed that the day was nearing its end as he strode
rapidly through the streets, his hat pulled down over his gloomy
face against the savage wind, his coat flapping round his long legs
as its ragged garments flaps round the single leg of a scarecrow in
a field.

As he went he was thinking, oddly enough, about his mother.
She had been in his mind all day, though he had not consciously
thought of her for years. She had had the same unusual blue-
grey eyes as the Condesa—Irish eyes, he had always imagined
them to be; it must be the Condesa's eyes, and that little child's,
that had brought her back into his mind like this. He rammed his
hat farther down over his head, as a gust caught him at a corner,
and hurried on.

The fact was that life had always been difficult for him, and
tragic; less in the sense that he had any immediate personal
tragedy than that he was deeply imbued with what Unamuno
calls the Tragic Sense of Life. For this his mother was at least
partly responsible. James Milcom was very far from being what
a wit has called "no more than the remains of a mother's meal";
but he had been deeply and sensibly devoted to a beautiful and
gifted mother, and on her tragedy had laid its hand. She was
Irish, married to a Yorkshireman, the reasonably wealthy owner
of a wool mill outside Bradford, and her wit and the sparkling
quality of her mind, the queer dancing logic of the Irish mentality
had been in perpetual gay conflict with his father's dour, hard-
headed, and wholly unenthusiastic common sense. That in itself
didn't amount to a tragedy, though tragic potentialities are
always latent in such a combination; but it was sufficient of itself
to produce a certain effect on a child. Too sharply contrasted
characters in the parents, however well they may manage to get
on, have a very marked effect on the development of their off-
spring; the children's minds are unnaturally sharpened by living
in two mental climates simultaneously, their own inherited
tendencies force them instinctively to take sides, to move in one
atmosphere rather than in the other; they become wary and
sensitive. All this had happened to the child James. But this was
not all. The elder Milcom was implacably opposed to Home Rule;
his youngest brother-in-law, over in Ireland, became an ardent
Sinn Feiner, and was eventually shot by the Black-and-Tans in
1922. Between Milcom's mother and this brother there had existed
a very close link of affection and understanding—in her own

words, he was the world and all to her; and with his death tragedy had unmistakeably come into that household.

James, then a boy of twenty, had watched his mother's agony, and his father's rigid and stubborn refusal to compromise with his political principles even to ease the sorrow of a wife to whom in his own stolid way he was devoted, and on whom he was in fact absurdly dependent. He had seen then, with eyes sharpened by pain, the cruel tyranny which love exercises over duty and compassion, as he watched her struggles to adapt herself to an emotional situation which was really impossible of endurance. That lasted for about a year; then she died—apparently of influenza, really, the desperate boy realised, of a broken heart: a heart broken less by the loss of the brother she adored than by that interior struggle, the attempt at an impossible degree of self-suppression and self-control. At his father's quite genuine despair at her death he had not known whether to laugh or to rage—within himself he did now the one, now the other.

All this had had a profound effect on him. The wary sensitiveness of the child who is brought up in two conflicting mental climates had been extended and developed into the man's attitude towards adult personal relationships. It was almost timidity—but not quite; rather a cautious, almost harsh avoidance of what could cause such horrible pain. From love and marriage he had definitely averted his face; the passion that might have gone into them he deflected onto the affairs of mankind at large. Beginning as an instinct, this had turned into a deliberate rule. He had allowed himself a few brief love-affairs, in which the spirit was in no way involved—and thoroughly unsatisfying he had found them, apart from the immediate physical satisfaction. But rule his life as he would, from his sensitiveness there was no escape; any human suffering or distress or generosity or beauty moved him instantly—he was helpless, defenceless in the face of such things. That child in the cellar, to whom he was now hurrying through the windy streets, and her quiet-voiced uncomplaining mother—to such he would always be accessible, would always have to waste the better part of a day on doing something to help them out.

They were sitting quietly at the table when he arrived, under that horrible unshaded bulb; the child still knitting at her little sock, the Condesa mending a small dress. When he undid his parcel, putting down the tin of milk, the two tins of soup, the butter and the eggs beside the graceful vase of wintry flowerheads, the child opened her mouth, silently, while the delicate colour flooded her thin face—then, without a sound, she shut it again.

No words, no gesture, could have moved Milcom so much. To escape from his own emotion, he finally drew out the little hand-saw.

At that, the Condesa exclaimed.

"Oh, how clever you are! No, but it is wonderful that you should have thought of that. We needed one so much—but it is so difficult to get them, now." She looked full at him. "I do thank you—so much."

Of course she wanted to pay. James had expected this, and prepared for it. He had friends, he said, who were under an obligation to him, and sold to him unreasonably cheaply; the eggs and butter were so much, the saw a loan; the milk, soup, sugar and chocolate were a distribution from Los Quaqueros. He had absolutely no compunction about lying to her about this, and to his relief she accepted his lies. She counted out a few pesetas from a shabby little despatch case, which lived behind the stove, and, gravely thanking her, he took them. There was more milk already given, and more soup, he told her; but he had locked it up at home. "I shall bring it round in a day or so." The child's face, as he spoke, caught his eye; she shivered at his words, and then broke into a fit of coughing. The room was still very cold. He glanced at the small heap of wood by the stove, and took his leave. Outside the house, he did not turn homewards, but instead walked rapidly towards the burned-out church where he had met the Condesa that morning. There, in the icy dusk, he spent half an hour grubbing among the ruins, till he had collected a large pile of wood; this he tied into his overcoat, and bore it back to the cellar.

The Condesa raised her delicate dark eyebrows when she opened the door to him a second time within the hour.

"I found some more wood, so I brought it along," Milcom said apologetically—her face made him feel apologetic. And, awkwardly, he set down his overcoat bundle on the floor, untied the sleeves and the tails, and began to pile the wood on the heap by the stove. She stood watching him, an unfathomable expression on her lovely face; she had risen from the table, where the little Pilar still sat, eating that unwonted treat, bread and butter, and a helping of omelette.

"I'm disturbing you at your supper," James said, uncomfortably. "But if you would just go on, and eat it while it's hot, I could saw some of this up for you." His face and voice were almost appealing.

At that, the Condesa smiled, a brilliant smile.

"That would be very kind," she said. "I shall—take you at your word; is that how you say it?"

So while the Condesa and the child finished their meal, Milcom, kneeling on the palliasse, sawed up his wood into lengths suitable to the capacity of the stove. Concentrating on his task— it is a job to saw wood without a sawing-horse, when one must hold it steady with the left hand—he was nevertheless aware of what they were doing; the child clearing the table and setting the things aside on the tea-chest, her mother making coffee on the stove. It was all very domestic, and rather charming—poor as the room was, it was a home, and feminine, and pleasant. When he had done, and had re-stoked the stove and stacked a fine pile of wood beside it, she invited him to a cup of coffee; Pilar meanwhile curling herself up on the palliasse. He sat on the stool this time; he took out a packet of cigarettes, and offered one to the Condesa—she took it, and when he had lit it for her, inhaled with an air of profound satisfaction.

"That is *wonderful*!" she said, with a natural fervour which touched him.

"Do you smoke a great deal?" he asked.

"I used to," she said. James realised the whole world of deprivation which those three words contained. He wished to God he had thought to bring cigarettes too. Shamefacedly, when he left, he offered her his packet—"I am going straight home, and I have plenty; people bring them to me."

"Thank you," she said. "I shall enjoy them." Then her face changed, the expression seemed to deepen, though her soft voice remained quiet and unemphatic. "And thank you, so very much, more than I can tell you, for all that you have done for us. You are very good." She held out her hand in farewell.

But the child was, for once, emphatic. "Buenas noches!" little Pilar cried, springing up from the palliasse and running to him. "Oh, muchas muchas gracias!" And she dropped her discreet little curtsey.

"Buenas noches, you little popinjay!" Milcom said, patting her small russet head in an awkward caress—and took his hat and went. As he climbed the dark steps he heard her high voice asking her mother what a "popinjay" was.

During the next few weeks Milcom became a regular visitor at the cellar. Two days seldom passed without his dropping in with something—a tin of milk, a screw of paper with sugar in it, a packet of cigarettes, a spot of butter, some tinned soup or corned beef, one or two precious eggs. Usually he went in the evening, after dark, so that his visits might arouse the least attention from possibly hostile neighbours; he generally sat for a little, talking, while the Condesa sewed and Pilar, small and silent, knitted at her socks, curled up on the palliasse. Their subjects of conversation were rather limited, since Milcom from the outset made no secret of his Republican sympathies; politics were therefore ruled out, and even comment on the latest bombardment was limited to details of how it had affected this street or that shop. Those hearty expressions of detestation or satisfaction, which so nourish a population in time of war were denied to these two. They had no mutual acquaintances to talk about, their lives had no common background—even the background of books and literature was extremely restricted in their case, since the Condesa had read very little in English, and Milcom's Spanish reading had been chiefly among the modern Liberal philosophers, like Unamuno, whose books were on the Index for Roman Catholics, and in any case were rather outside the Condesa's intellectual range. He did get some idea of what that was, bit by bit—how, he hardly knew, for she never spoke about herself, her family, her husband or her past life, except in the briefest allusion; sometimes, when James mentioned a place that he had visited in the course of his work she would say—"Oh yes, I know that"; and then would go on to ask if he remembered this bridge or that church or village. On such occasions she would slip back into recollections, very vivid and clear: "There is a little valley, where the river makes a bend, so" —her hands shaped the bend—"below some rocks, and three olive trees are in a very pretty group by the river, and a little chapel, very much ruined. There used to be white goats there. And in autumn the pink cyclamens, the very very little ones, grow on the bank. Did you go there?" Nearly always, flowers figured in these memories of places, he noticed. Or she would tell stories of the peasants, funny things they had said, touching things they had done. And sometimes she would ask the child if she remembered this place or that.

Even out of these slender materials, he managed to form some sort of idea of her as a person—but it was a curiously abstract, disembodied idea, wholly detached from all the externals of her own life; thinking about it once, he was reminded of a friend's description of Virginia Woolf's characters—"souls swimming about, waving their tails, in a vessel of crystal prose, like goldfish in a bowl." Like goldfish too he and this woman, he felt, swam about, not in a bowl of crystal prose, but in the shadowy, cold, hunger-ridden, death-menaced city, a form of existence which had something ghostly about it. He had first met her prowling like a shawled ghost among the ruins; and their continued relationship had this same ghostly quality, as of a foregathering of discarnate spirits. From her speech and voice and aspect he did, in these frequent meetings, inevitably gather some impression of her character—overshadowed as this was by the shattering fact of her extreme beauty, a thing which tends to dwarf personality; and not only in the beholder. Very beautiful people, he had long since decided, had almost as much of a job to become or remain fully human as great artists. "I sometimes wish people were not so beautiful—it distracts one from the conversation." That quotation from George Mallory's private diary was often in his mind as he sat with Raquel de Verdura; the cast of his mind was such that as he grew to know her more, and like her increasingly, he felt her beauty to be almost a disfigurement, a distortion of her real self.

What was that self? More and more frequently, his mind asked that question. Simplicity ruled by sophistication; naturalness governed by social training; spontaneity allowed by a rigid self-control—of all these he was aware; but she really *was* simple and natural and spontaneous; she had, he was certain, a nature in itself happy, trained for enjoyment; she was vividly aware of things, gave a quick ready response; she had a seeing eye, as her little verbal sketches of the places she loved showed; and she had an odd shrewdness—though her education and intellectual interests appeared fairly limited, she was not stupid. As to her relation to the child, it was charming; it seemed to him perfect. Pilar brought the one element of human actuality, which could not be suppressed or disguised, into the picture. There was between them a mutality of understanding and tender devotion which, visibly, made every moment together a separate happiness, and every parting, even when she only went to stand in the street to wait for rice and chick peas, a dismay. (For wood the Condesa no longer went searching—by one means or another, he kept the cellar supplied with that.) He found this relationship infinitely touching; as for the child herself, he soon became quite devoted to her. "Es nuestro Meelcomm!" he would hear her little voice say, as he clumped down the cellar steps, with a gladness, a welcome in it that warmed his unattached heart.

Slowly and methodically, too, he busied himself in getting better quarters for them. The cellar was intolerably damp and draughty, and the child's cough, which got only slightly better under the influence of condensed milk and occasional eggs, worried him continually. He would have liked to get them into the

Telephone Company's Building, which had central heating, but that was impossible. However he eventually found another and a better room, drier, and with fewer draughts, and persuaded the Condesa to the move.

Of course he came up then, as before, against the question of money. About this one private circumstance of hers, her situation forced the Condesa into an unwonted and reluctant openness. Her own and most of her husband's estates were in Republican Spain, and therefore brought in nothing any more; she knew nothing of what had happened to his investments. Her sole source of income at the moment, what produced that scanty store of pesetas in the little despatch case behind the stove was a small allowance brought to her once a month by her dead brother's old steward—acting, he said, on his master's orders. Where the money came from she had no idea. But little as it was, it was regular, and it was all she had. She said it was sufficient. But the new room was rather more costly than the old—and since she would have to pay the landlord herself, James did not dare in this instance to lie about the price. He told her what it was, and urged her for the child's sake, at least, to let him pay the difference. On that occasion he went, by appointment, quite late at night, when the little Pilar was already asleep on the palliasse. The vigorous argument which ensued was conducted in whispers, by candle-light. It was the most direct human contact he had yet had with her; whispering, he fought down her reluctance, fairly scolded her. "You are letting your pride, your silly pride, stand in the way of her health," he hissed, pointing to the bed on the floor in the corner. "I don't understand you. It is wrong. Why should you care who pays, so long as she is in better conditions? I am nothing, I am someone you barely know—but what does that matter, so long as she has her chance?" She bowed her beautiful head at this attack, the tears standing in her eyes.

"You are right—I agree. It is that I am not accustomed——" her whisper trailed away into silence.

"Of course you're not," he whispered back, more gently; "we're none of us accustomed to war. Spain is upside-down." He had been bending towards her; he straightened up and murmured briskly—"That's settled, then; and I shall come with the car for you on Tuesday, at eight."

## CHAPTER TWO

### *The Far Side—Madrid*

THE new room was a great improvement on the old. Milcom, through his odd friends and by devious means had produced a second bed complete with bedstead, a largish rug, and even a small arm-chair, and had fixed a shelf and a row of coat-and-hat pegs, acquired from his friend down by the Manzanares, on the wall; the same friend had furnished an old packing-case to stand by the stove and hold the wood. When it was all arranged it looked quite homely and pleasant; James, who had not only transported the Condesa's effects from her old abode, but had helped to install them, looked round him with a certain satisfaction. As for Pilar, she moved delicately about with a face of delight, examining everything—sat quietly in the arm-chair, patted the pillows on the new bed, stroked the rug with the toe of her little shoe, all without a sound; only when Milcom left she did what she had never done before—after dropping her little curtsey she pulled him down by the arm, put her own small arms about his neck, and gave him a kiss. James was both charmed and embarrassed; when he raised his head he saw that the Condesa was watching them with an expression that was at once sweet and inscrutable.

The landlord of this new abode was for some reason in Milcom's pocket, so that it was no longer necessary for him to restrict his visits to the hours after nightfall; indeed occasionally they all went for a walk together, he and the Condesa and Pilar, and took coffee or a meal at a restaurant—when he was aware, with a mixture of pleasure and embarrassment, of the very domestic picture which the three of them presented. He continued to bring food, and to produce and saw up wood; both he and the Condesa settled down more and more into a very simple acceptance of this odd, limited relationship—even into a sort of dependence on it. He realised that he was the only support, and the nearest thing to a friend that she had in the strange hostile city, since her brother's death. But she preserved her delicate remoteness; he still knew nothing about her but what he saw: her beauty, her love for the child, her social perfection—which persisted even in a single room, and ruled it as a great hostess rules a salon. All that, and her extraordinary fortitude. He recognised that as a very Spanish thing in her; what the crude sentimental Anglo-Saxons have christened "Spanish pride" is really fortitude, an amazing detachment from material circumstances, a sort of spiritual fortification against any practical humiliations of poverty or hunger or inconvenience. How little he knew of her!—that was one of the constant burdens of his thought; he had no idea, even, if she ever speculated about him as he, so constantly, did about her—whether she had any curiosity as to what manner of man he was. For, infected perhaps by her withdrawnness, he told her nothing of himself, of his experience, save what was of international, of European import—and little enough of that.

At the end of February a fresh offensive broke out in the mountains to the North-East of Madrid, and James had to go and cover it. He was surprised to find how much it bothered him to leave her and the child alone. He did everything he could think of for their well-being; he filled the box by the stove with wood, and made a complicated arrangement with the landlord and the man in the back-yard to maintain the supply; he brought a quantity of condensed milk and other tinned foods, and fixed up something about eggs and butter with another individual who was for some reason in his debt.

"I hope you'll be all right," he said rather nervously to the Condesa at parting—"I ought to be back in ten days; a fortnight at the outside."

She smiled at him—her wonderful smile that made her lovely face still lovelier, as a sudden burst of sunshine irradiates a landscape already classical, already faultless, with astonishing magic.

"I am sure we shall be all right," she said; "you have been so good to us—you have thought of everything."

But the little Pilar, for once, did an odd thing—lost her tiny, demure, unnatural self-control. She ran to Milcom, where he sat in the upright chair, and fairly flung herself on him, her little face all distraught.

"Oh, do not go!" she cried, while unwonted tears, tears he had never seen, poured down her small cheeks. "Oh, please do not leave us! Some evil thing will happen if you do. I feel it! Oh, do not! Do not go! Remain, remain!" And when her mother, disturbed by this astonishing exhibition, rose and tried to calm, to remove her, her childish voice rose to a minute scream.

"*No!* I am right. He should stay! Oh Meelcomm, *please* stay!"

He couldn't stay, of course. He kissed, caressed, tried to console the funny mature adorable little thing, but in the end he had to depart, leaving her in her mother's hands. This small episode made a most painful impression on Milcom. All through the cold, dismal, snowy campaign Pilar's face and voice, and little clinging claw-like hands were with him, and her unconsolable sobs, and her presentiment of evil; he worried; his nights, short and uncomfortable anyhow, were broken and troubled by dreams of her, of them; his days, busy, hurried, and dangerous, were nevertheless filled with anxiety about those two lonely creatures, friendless ghosts in a city of ghosts, of forlorn and half-starved women— Madrid.

He was kept away longer than he expected, and on his return went at once to the cellar. To facilitate his bringing in wood and other supplies, Milcom had actually, with the Condesa's concurrence, got a duplicate key; he knocked on the door first, and getting no reply, let himself in. It was late, and he was a little surprised that they should still be out; usually Raquel brought the child in early, because she thought the air towards sunset was bad for that cough. It was chilly in the room, and getting dark—the fire was nearly out; James stoked up the stove, but did not turn on the light; he sat waiting, as the twilight deepened. At first he was quite content; glad to be there again, directly happy in the expectation of seeing the pair of them—at any moment now they would come, he would hear their voices outside. Pilar's little high voice and her mother's soft but very penetrating and resonant one, with that indefinable male quality that there is in the voices of many Spanish women—and then they would walk in. He pictured their surprise at finding him; Raquel would either smile that brilliant smile, or put on her enigmatic face that so intrigued and charmed him; and Pilar—he was not sure what Pilar would do; run to him confidently, almost certainly, and perhaps give him the salute of her arms round his neck, as she had given him at parting.

But they didn't come. It grew darker and darker; James got first impatient, then restless; he turned on the light, and looked at his watch. What could they be doing? Now he became anxious; something must be wrong; they were never as late as this. He got up and moved about, studying the room, now that the light was on, noting all the familiar objects, as if to reassure himself. Something was missing—at first he was not sure what. Oh yes— Pilar's little cap hanging on the wall. But she would be wearing that anyway, if she was out. He moved along the row of pegs, lightly touching the garments that hung there, in an unshielded intimacy that always half-touched, half-embarrassed him. But where was Pilar's other dress, the tidier one that she wore on Sundays? And—he turned to the table—where was her little knitting, that usually lay there below the brown winter vase of flowers, when it was not in her small hands? It was not there. He went to feel under the pillow on the bed of his providing, the one with the bedstead, in which the child slept—sometimes she tucked it away there. No—not there either; but as he replaced the faded quilt he noticed that the pillow had no pillow-case on it. A horrible anxiety, that turned him physically cold, overtook James; he pulled the quilt down, exposing the thin blanket. No sheet either. But what was this? Under the quilt was the hem of a little tartan woollen dress, Pilar's day dress—neatly folded. As panic seized him, he heard the click of a key in the lock; he turned, still holding the edge of the quilt in his hand, as the door opened and the Condesa came in. She was alone.

They stood looking at one another—then she shut the door, and came a couple of steps into the room.

"Yes," she said, looking at his hand which held the quilt. "Yes."

"Oh, God!" Milcom said. He dropped the quilt, and moved towards her; then, as if he felt her somehow unapproachable he turned aside and sat down, unthinkingly, in the arm-chair. For a moment he said nothing, did not even look at her—then, with an effort, he raised his head.

"What happened?" he asked.

She sat down, slowly, in the upright chair, and pulled the shawl off her head before she spoke; she looked extraordinarily tired.

"It was a pneumonia," she said. There was very little tone in her voice. "It began two days after you left—indeed I have thought since that perhaps she was already ill that day, when she behaved so strangely with you."

"The poor little thing!" James said. "In a way, you know, I loved it, her running to me like that." He was taken quite off his guard by all this. "Oh, God!" he said again, and sank his head in his hands. After a moment or two he raised it and said—"Go on."

"There is nothing to tell," she said, still in that voice without tone. "She was so small, and so thin, she just had not enough strength. With a pneumonia, it is all a question of strength, and hers was insufficient. She had had the cough so long."

"Did you have a doctor?" James asked.

"Yes. I sent a letter to Los Quaqueros, and the doctor came, a lady, a wonderful woman. And she gave her a *piqure*, and they sent medicines, and did everything that could be done—but she had not enough strength."

"Oh, God!" he said, for the third time. "No wonder I was worried."

"Were you worried?" she asked, looking faintly surprised.

"Frightfully. The whole time. I dreamt about her. I couldn't get it out of my head—how she had begged me not to go. But I had to go," he said, looking at her almost pleadingly.

"Of course you had to go," she answered quietly. They sat silent then for a time, James looking at his knees, the Condesa watching his great black head and lined gloomy face. He was thinking what this meant to her, the loss of hourly sweet companionship, of occupation, of a reason for living; and of her complete and utter aloneness, now—with that bad hat for a husband, and anyhow in prison—and of how little he, James, could do for her; and of how much he wanted to do. What she was thinking, her face when at last he looked again at her gave no sign.

"What are you going to do now?" he asked.

"Stay here, I imagine. What else can I do?"

What indeed? There was nothing she could do, and nowhere that she could easily go—and no one, save him, James, and the old steward whom she could even call friend, to whom she could turn for anything. It all came in on him, her utter desolation, and her exhausted uncomplaining quiet in the face of it. And it was almost more than he could bear.

She stayed on, where she was. He tried to find her another room, which would be less filled with memories, but it was not easy, and she said she didn't want to move, in any case. The room was a sort of companion, she said once. He saw her practically every day, and went on doing for her all the things he had done before—supplying wood, eggs, cigarettes, butter occasionally. Only after the child's death she would not accept any more tinned milk; that ought to be for children, she said. As the days lengthened and the weather grew warmer they went out more and more—took walks, ate in small restaurants in the legthening spring evenings, sitting outside on the pavement, or in tree-shaded courtyards. It remained a strange, ghostly comradeship, curiously impersonal; only her sorrow and her fortitude taught him steadily a little more of what she was—and the memory of the child, and his patient attempts to occupy and distract her, drew them closer and closer together in their isolation. Knowing almost nothing about her, he yet came to feel that he knew her very well. But he asked himself no questions as to what was happening, and where all this was taking him—ghosts in a city of ghosts do not need to concern themselves with the practical day-to-day problems which personal relationships raise in more normal circumstances. He let it all ride. There was he and there was she; she needed him, simply because she had no one else; and he was there, at her service, with a completeness of which he hardly allowed himself to be aware. So the spring deepened into the long hot arid summer, and still under the brassy sky of Madrid they walked, and ate, and talked, and built a relationship of whose strength and intensity neither was fully aware, until something happened which jeopardised the tranquil sober-hued routine of their companionship.

On the whole the women of the Franco persuasion were quite decently treated by the Republicans; indeed the Spanish war seems to have been remarkably free from any definite persecution of women. A Franco sympathiser in Madrid had rather a harder time getting food than other women, as the Condesa had told Milcom at the outset, and it was advisable to do as she did, to stick pretty closely at home, and to remain as inconspicuous as possible to avoid the irresponsible hostility of neighbours. Normally, that was all it amounted to. But from time to time, when some plot or piece of sabotage had disturbed and frightened the city, a burst of White-hunting would occur—sometimes one would occur for no assignable reason, even.

In the late summer following Pilar's death such a spasm broke out. The Condesa was re-examined, threatened, harried. It was always difficult, in such circumstances, to decide in what degree of actual danger the victim stood; Milcom made all the enquiries he could, intervened on her behalf, and came to the conclusion that she was probably fairly safe. But it was also borne in on him that this time Raquel, in spite of her courage and endurance, had had all that her nerves and strength would stand; more, he suddenly realised that he himself could not stand any more of this sort of torment for her. He decided at all costs to get her out of Spain. When he told her of his decision, she said "Very well— Yes, thank you," with a curious listlessness; she asked no questions, showed no curiosity as to where she was to go, expressed neither satisfaction nor regret. Then there began the usual dreary round of bribery, intrigue, and forged papers. Milcom's good standing with the Republican authorities helped him in this, so did the fact that the Condesa had a cousin on that side in Barcelona; but it was a slow business, and it was late in September before he finally got everything in order, down to the special requisition for extra petrol for his car, and drove her off.

At Barcelona there were fresh delays. James suffered the usual discomfort of the Englishman in Spain in such circumstances in not being sure whether these were deliberate and therefore dangerous, or merely the result of dilatoriness and incompetence. The Condesa was taken over by the cousin and remained hidden away in a small room—James stayed in a hotel, and hardly saw her till the moment when, with the cousin's connivance, she was got onto a boat. There was an air-raid as they left the harbour; the bombs of the Savoias missed them by a matter of feet. To James's great surprise, this seemed to upset her very much. Raids and bombardments in Madrid she had always treated with the indifferent calmness of most Spaniards; but whether it was that the strain and suspense of escape had affected her nerves, or for some other reason, she started and trembled at each explosion, and went on trembling long after the poor little steamer had lurched out to sea in safety, and was well on its way to Port Vendres. It was a rough uncomfortable trip; the accommodation was of the poorest, and Raquel was very sick. They were both completely exhausted by the time they reached port.

Port Vendres—Portus Veneris—is the first harbour on the French side of the Spanish frontier. They put into it one afternoon early in October, when the clear bright colours of the houses which climb the dark green slopes round the harbour glowed like enamel in the rich Mediterranean sunshine. James got a car, his suitcase was stowed in the back—owing to the secrecy and other difficulties attendant on their getting away from Madrid, the Condesa had been obliged to leave all her poor possessions behind; she carried the little shabby attache-case that used to hide behind the stove in the cellar, and that was all. They drove off to Perpignan.

It was the fashion some years ago, without much point, to refer to modern hotels as "vast caravanserais." But the Hôtel de l'Europe at Perpignan really does recall the old oriental caravanserai, since it is built round a central court onto which, for its whole height of four or five floors, the bedroom windows open. This court is roofed with sparrow-wire and glass, and the effect is to make it look like an enormous parrot-cage in some zoo; the echoing properties of the tiled floor and glass roof make it as noisy as a parrot-cage too—it is also very stuffy. There are small tables for light "consommations" in the centre, and two rows of arm-chairs on either side of the gangway leading from the front door to the Bureau constitute the only public sitting-room provided by the management; they are usually occupied by wine-merchants or commercial travellers, sipping Dubonnet or Amer Picon, and silently watching the entry of other clients.

In one of these chairs the Condesa sat while Milcom went to

take rooms for them. Whenever the door opened, (which it did with an explosive bang, after first sticking), or a car back-fired in the street outside, she started violently, then sat back again, try-ing, by folding them together, to control the trembling of her bare hands. It was evident that she had not got over her reaction from that air-raid as they left Barcelona at all; she looked com-pletely exhausted. Now and then she muttered to herself—"I must stop—I must stop being so silly." But it was clear that she could not stop—at the next bang or crash she started and trembled as before, and put out her hand to the shabby little attache-case which reposed on the chair beside her.

Presently Milcom came back to her.

"I've got a room for you," he said abruptly—"would you like to come up? You must be tired."

"Thank you." But she made no move. "Are the shops open still?" she asked, glancing half-doubtfully at her little case, and then at him.

He looked at his watch.

"I expect so—yes. Do you want something?" His tone was not encouraging—it was almost brusque.

She gave a little laugh. "I want almost everything! But soap and powder most of all."

"All right—shall I go and get you some? Anything else?"

She said nothing for a moment—again she sat looking up at him doubtfully. At last, with a visible effort, she said—

"Mr. Milcom, when you have done so much for us, it seems absurd to make a fuss about little things. But you see now that Miguel no longer brings me my allowance, I really have no money at all—for the present, whatever you get me, you must give me."

James was embarrassed by this. He had been embarrassed by taking the two rooms, on two different floors—and had taken refuge in that brusque abruptness to cover his embarrassment.

"Of course, of course," he now said hastily; "it's only a long loan." He was hearty, with the blatant heartiness of an em-barrassed man who is also tired out—his eyes were like sockets in a skull with fatigue.

"Just say what you need, and I'll bring it," he went on, very business-like—"it was stupid of me not to remember that you've no luggage. Soap and powder—and what else?"

"I would like a sponge—and a nightgown, if I could." Her voice was rather faint; his change of manner to this chilly business-like tone was making these difficult requests more difficult still, was routing what was left of her courage and self-control.

2

Poor James, however, was rendered still more embarrassed by this last commission.

"What sort of a nightgown? I don't know much about these things. Pink? You wouldn't rather come and choose it yourself, would you?"

At the word "pink" the Condesa suddenly began to laugh—and soon it was clear that she could not stop. "Yes, yes, pink!" Her words came out almost in a scream. "Pink, pink—oh, it is so funny!" She laughed louder and louder, till she was sobbing with laughter; the noise echoed up the parrot-cage, till the whole building resounded with laughter and sobs. Even to Milcom it was evident that this was raging hysteria. Before he could remember what to do she rose to her feet, really screaming now—"Yes, yes; I will come. I will choose." A waiter came running from the bar, the manager hurried out of the Bureau, gave one look, and sent a page flying for the *femme de chambre*; then, with admirable promptitude, he sat the screaming woman down in her chair again, and dashed a glass of water in her face. When the maid came, with smelling-salts, he pressed them firmly under the Condesa's nose.

"Madame is overtired," said James sourly, in excellent French —the little crowd of gaping attendants melted away, he was so stubbornly sour and dignified. "Her room is No. 153—take her up," he said to the *femme de chambre*. Soused and gasping, but now silent, the Condesa was borne off. James called for aspirins, and followed; the maid had removed her coat and shoes and had laid her on the bed. James sent for tea, gave her some aspirins and a cup of the hot watery stuff; he closed the curtains, put the dingy quilt over her feet, and telling her to try and sleep, he left her. Then he went out into the town and resolutely bought a box of powder, a sponge, a white nightgown, six pocket-handkerchiefs and a cake of soap, which he had sent up to her, later on, together with a light dinner.

This whole episode brought Milcom up sharply, for the first time, against the realities of his situation vis-à-vis Raquel de Verdura. It made him realise abruptly that they were no longer what they had been in Madrid, ghostly comrades in a city of ghosts, but a man and woman back in normal human society, involved in all the complications which human society normally imposes on relations between men and women. His embarrassment—which he now realised had actually, more than anything else, driven her to that burst of hysteria—made him worriedly aware of all this, and of something much more profound, which for the moment his mind shied away from. To protect himself from that disturbing certainty he began to concentrate on what he was to do with her, now that he had got her out of Spain. He thought about it a lot, alone that evening in Perpignan, dining in the big café built out over the river. He sat looking out through the plate-glass windows at the strings of lights along the two embankments, with the dark perspective of the house-fronts behind them, and the dark half-empty bed of the river between. It was a little like Dublin, Perpignan, he thought, with its river running slap through the town—and how nice that made a city, the interrupting river, breaking up the continuity of streets and houses, with the spacious embankments where you could see the sky, and the linking bridges forever to be crossed. Still, it was no good thinking about Dublin, he reflected gloomily; the point was what he was to do about Raquel. There she was lying, at that moment, on her dingy bed in the hotel, in the nightgown he had bought for her; beautiful, penniless, her husband in prison, and she herself, so far as he could judge, utterly incapable of doing anything whatever to earn her own living. But he had got to go back to Spain. She must be parked somewhere. He knew that she had a sister, the Duquesa de las Illas; she had told him for certain that the Duque de las Illas had been killed, but she believed her sister had been at Santander, so she might have escaped. She had spoken occasionally of her brother too, Juanito Torre de Modero, whose name was well known to James—but James himself had heard from sources as good as most that Juanito was almost certainly dead. God, what a war!—in which no one knew for certain where or how any of their kith and kin were. Anyhow the Duquesa seemed to be the best bet—and if she had got out from Santander she would probably be at San Sebastián or Biarritz—they seemed to congregate over on that side. He'd better ring up someone at Biarritz and find out—what a curse it was that there was no telephonic communication between Spain and the outside world. It made one more difficulty for newspaper correspondents. He paid his bill, strolled back along the embankment under the plane trees to the hotel, put a call through to a friend in Biarritz, and sat in the parrot-cage waiting for it; people were drinking and dining at the little tables in the centre, the noises of speech and crockery echoed up to the glass roof, as her terrible laughter had echoed a few hours before—she would never, he reflected, be able to sleep.

After several false summonses to the telephone box, which seem an inevitable accompaniment to making a long-distance call in France, he got through. Yes, the friend believed that the Duquesa was at St.-Jean-de-Luz, but he was not sure, nor did he know at all at which hotel. Yes, he could find out to-morrow and let James know. Yes, by six o'clock for sure. Any chance of seeing James at Biarritz? There might be? Oh, good. "Bung-ho!" said the friend, and rang off. James went wearily up to his room, ordered a last *fine à l'eau*, propped his portable type-writer on the rickety little table, and switching his mind dexterously off the Condesa and her affairs, began to write up a message about Barcelona for the *Epoch*.

They passed the next day waiting for the telephone call. James had no great confidence that the Duquesa would really materialise, and still less that if she did, she would be in a position to support the Condesa; his anxiety made him if anything rather exasperated by Raquel de Verdura's touching certainty that if only she could find her sister, all would be well. This certainty made the suspense the more painful to her, so James filled up the day as much as he could. In the morning they went shopping, in the rather inadequate shops of Perpignan, and bought shoes, a dressing-gown and slippers, some underclothes, and stockings— Raquel could not get over the abundance of silk stockings, a commodity which had by that time almost vanished from Spain. Then after an early lunch James hired a car, and they drove out into the country for the afternoon.

They drove rather aimlessly at first, westward along the high road that leads towards the Pyrenees, and the pass into Spain at Le Perthus; here the planes were golden and the mulberry-trees yellowing along the roadsides, and on either hand, all over the gently broken country stretched the vineyards, dusty and withered now; the lowland vineyards of the Mediterranean coastal plain, from which comes the heavy sugary wine, full of alcohol and tasting faintly of caramel, which goes to the making of Dubonnet and Quinquina and Amer Picon. Along the dry beds of streams great belts of reeds stood up, their feathery heads already pale with autumn. It was a misty day, with light uncertain sun, but warm; the mountains rose blue and vague before them, and on their right the great mass of the Canigou towered huge and rather lowering under the clouds that, as usual, swathed its head. James drove gently, sensitive to the pensive quality of the season and the light, glad of the pause between the strain and effort of the past few weeks and fresh anxieties to come; and the Condesa, to whom peaceful drives in sun and open fields had become a strange and wonderful thing, sat quietly by his side.

Near Le Boulou she caught sight of a signpost with the words "Amélie-les-Bains, 16 kilometres."

"Oh, what a charming name! Can't we go there?"

Of course they could, since there was no real reason why they should go to one place rather than another; they turned to the right, heading across open country towards the mouth of the Vallespir, the valley through which the rive Tech runs southward, parallel with the frontier range of the Pyrenees and close under it, till it reaches the open plain and crosses it towards the sea. Now the country became more broken; the white rocks stood out through the rich yellowish soil, covered with a scrub of myrtle and juniper and wild mimosa. They crossed the Tech by a slender stone bridge which leaps the river in one superb single span; it was so narrow that they had to wait till a solitary laden donkey had finished its passage before they could drive across—this is not surprising, since the bridge was built in the year 1340.

Beyond the bridge the road followed the river itself, upstream along the valley; to their right they looked out across it to lower hills, and a turn of the road brought into view a lovely small town perched on the steep opposite slope, the brown roofs and creamy walls huddled together in a charming symmetry, the whole dom nated by two tall towers. It looked completely mediaeval and rather Spanish. Could that be Amélie-les-Bains, Raquel speculated? But it was not; it was Palalda, as another sign-post presently informed them—and in a few more minutes they ran into Amélie itself, that rather absurd little piece of rococo 19th century building, squashed in sunlessly and uncomfortably between the high jagged cliffs from which gush the waters which give it its name, its *raison d'être*, and its smell. Even as they drove across the first bridge, through whose plaster balustrades the green water could be seen steaming and swirling below them, the smell met them, as of a thousand rotten eggs. And it filled the whole town—the steep narrow main street, the tilted square outside the Thermes Jadis, where the fountain below the ancient plane trees runs with hot water from one spout, with cold from the other, the terrace in front of the Café which adjoins the square, where the wireless was braying out music from Radio Toulouse among the empty chairs and little tin tables. James would have liked to linger; he was amused by the graceful ridiculousness of the architecture, a bad Victorian copy of Bath, made by Frenchmen, and intrigued by the incredible abundance of the sulphurous waters, running recklessly away down the rocky gorge in an open river—but the Condesa, one of her new handkerchiefs held to her exquisite nose, said that the smell was intolerable and the music worse, and that there was no sun—which was true. So they got into the car again and drove on up the valley, once more informed by sign-posts that they were heading for Arles-sur-Tech and Prats-de-Mollo. James, happy, commented idly on the names; no prick of foreknowledge warned him, on that soft autumn day, of how well he would later come to know both these places.

After the chilly rock-shadowed gorges of Amélie-les-Bains the valley broadens out again into the open level stretch in which Arles-sur-Tech stands, with orchards now bordering the road instead of vineyards, and sloping down to the grey rushing river—James and the Condesa, emerging gladly into the sunshine, drove slowly between the bright-leaved, bright-fruited orchard trees, with their background of wooded mountains golden with autumn, rich on the lower slopes with the deep glossy green of wild box. They told one another, truthfully, that it was a pretty place. In Arles they left the car and strolled about in the sunshine; they examined the Church, so jammed up against other buildings that its exterior is only visible here and there, and its small, ancient, and neglected cloisters; they sampled the dusty tranquil Place, and finally went and drank coffee outside the Hôtel des Glycines, sitting at a little tin table in the sun. The light filtered through the yellowing leaves of the trellised wistaria onto the shabby little tables, which were without occupants save for themselves—the stalks which in spring had held a wealth of pendent bloom hung down now, wiry, dry and brown, in long narrow spirals; the waiter drowsed against the doorway of the hotel, under the shiny black-and-gilt slabs which announced its name, a rather grubby napkin over his arm. Here there was no wireless, and the place struck both of them as far too remote and old-fashioned to possess such a thing—tucked away in its valley it seemed, James said, to be almost at the end of the world.

"And where is quite the end?" Raquel asked idly, twisting one of the dead spiral stalks round her fingers, amused, contented, and quiet.

He waved his hand on up the valley, where a great ridge, white with the first snow, hung like a curtain across the sky, closing the view.

"Up there, at Prats-de-Mollo." James had the journalist's knack of getting names right at one glance, and remembering them; he gave Prats-de-Mollo no thought; he had just seen the name, and remembered it. The thought that was brushing his mind as they sat there, with the soft fluttering persistence of a moth, was that Arles was a sweet place, lost, forgotten and quiet; and that it would be very sweet to be staying in the Hôtel des Glycines with Raquel; to stroll out, early or late, into those autumn orchards by the river with her, and to climb by peasants' paths up the hills through the golden woods. He pushed these moth-like fancies away, but, moth-like, they returned—he was almost glad of the interruption when Raquel said—"Couldn't we go there?"

"Go where?"

"To Prats—whatever it is."

James looked at his watch. It was after four. He made enquiries of the waiter as to the distance, and the sort of road, and they discussed it. It could just be done, but there would be no time to see anything, since they had to be back by six, and in the end they decided against it, and sat on where they were. Raquel had taken off her hat, and the last of the sunshine fell on her hair; above her black dress the colour of it was startling. It was the true *brun châtain*, the ripe-chestnut bronze which henna tries to imitate and fails—because the gloss on henna-dyed hair is purple, and the gloss on hair like the Condesa's is like the gleam on a polished copper can. She was a startling figure altogether to be sitting outside the Hôtel des Glycines, silhouetted against its pale, rather shabby walls, under the pale withering leaves of the wistaria, by the little table with its faded cloth, in the black dress which she wore with the unconquerable Spanish distinction, with that incredible bronze head, and her long, high-nosed, lovely and archaic face. Sun and air and a real night's rest—however noisy, without bombs or gunfire—had smoothed out some of the strained look that had become habitual with her; her face was relaxed and softened, and tranquil as James had never seen it. Its beauty, and pity for her, beat on James's heart like a series of soft drumming blows, so that presently he said that they had better be starting. They drove back to Perpignan, and at half-past seven, not six, Milcom got his call from Biarritz. Yes, the friend said, the Duquesa de las Illas was at St.-Jean-de-Luz, staying at the Hôtel Grande Bretagne—of which he thoughtfully supplied the number. James thanked him warmly. He told Raquel the news, and they decided that he should take her across to St.-Jean-de-Luz the next day. Then he put a call through to the Grande Bretagne for her, and after the usual immense delays of the French long-distance service—officially called *Inter-urbain*, but familiarly known as "Intaire"—she spoke with the Duquesa herself. Hearing her sister's voice, for the first time in two years, disturbed and moved Raquel; James persuaded her to go at once to bed, against the long tiring cross-country journey, from the Mediterranean to the Atlantic, next day.

But when she had gone upstairs he went out again to the café over the river, ordered a beer, and sat looking down the perspective of lights, thinking about her. Having her on his hands like this, shopping for her and with her, and all the rest of it, was a very odd business—and it was producing a very curious effect on him. To-night, after that gentle afternoon in the country together, he could no longer escape from the realisation that he had pushed aside the evening before. He was in love with Raquel de Verdura. There was no getting away from it. But generally, when one is in love with a woman, one is as it were defended from certain things for a certain length of time; one does not ordinarily at once start travelling tête-à-tête with her, stay with her in hotels, have to see her through hysterical collapses—least of all does one usually have her completely dependent on one financially. These things come later, when one is ready for them, and wills it so—after marriage, or when a liaison has been decided on; not before. But at this point in his relation to the Condesa every stage was being telescoped together, foreshortened, run into one, by the sudden need for her escape from Spain, and by her penniless condition. It was all very peculiar.

James Milcom rubbed his big black head, as he sat before his glass of beer. He was an Irishman even more than he was a Yorkshireman, and therefore reacted to everything after the manner of his race, which is different from that of all other people. Quite apart from his almost shy personal avoidance of love, to his enormous emotional fastidiousness opportunity acted as a deterrent, not as a stimulus; called off his senses, and set his mind perversely and actively to work. In the inn garden at Arles-sur-Tech, idling away the afternoon in unexpected tranquillity, he had loved the thought of staying there with Raquel; being boxed up in a hotel with her sent him out to the café, to sit rubbing his head and thinking how odd and tiresome it was that he, of all people, should have to fall in love with a White. He thought too, more gently, that he had no idea how she felt—that probably she didn't know herself, and no more than he, wished or was ready to be in love at this moment. Or did he wish it? Half awed by the answer which his heart gave to that question, he pushed it vigorously to one side. He *was* in love, anyhow; there was no escape now.

## CHAPTER THREE

### *This Side—St.-Jean-de-Luz*

IT is often quite hot in St.-Jean-de-Luz in October. Mr. Oldhead, sitting in the sun outside the Bar Basque with his wife and daughter, registered the fact gratefully. Among much which he disliked or felt bound to disapprove of, he could cordially approve of the heat—little as he admired the resultant dress worn by most of those about him. During the latter part of the Spanish civil war St.-Jean-de-Luz was crowded with journalists, upper-class Spanish refugees, and diplomats, grafted onto the normal population of French residents, British villa-owners, and the inevitable itinerant Americans—the people sitting all round Mr. Oldhead, at other little tables covered with orange and white checked Basque linen, belonged to one or other of these various categories, and were brightly and incompletely attired in various forms of beach-trousers, sweaters with short sleeves, gaudy sandals, and dark glasses with white rims. Mr. Oldhead shifted his chair a little, to get the sun more fully on his back—he was delicate and rheumatic, and the warmth soothed his painful muscles in a most agreeable way. The light was good too; it shimmered on the neat little saw-edged leaves of the bay-trees which stood in tubs down the edge of the long narrow group of tables, it glittered off the lustrous foliage of the big magnolias bordering the street. One would be able, he reflected, to do some rather interesting photography here. But he did not allow his satisfaction to become apparent; he sat sipping his orangeade with that expression of rather sulky discomfort so common in elderly Englishmen abroad until they know a place well enough to feel—and look— as if they had bought it.

Mr. Oldhead had not yet bought St.-Jean-de-Luz—he had in fact only been there a week. But his wife and daughter, less exacting and less self-conscious, had already decided that they liked it. Mrs. Oldhead was a woman of thirty-eight, and some twenty years younger than her husband; lively and still good-looking, in an unsophisticated way, with her Irish eagerness for fun and interest of any sort undimmed, she sat drinking her vermouth-and-soda and watching the people about her with considerable enjoyment. She liked having people to watch, to speculate over, and if possible to hear gossip about, and the strip of pavement outside the Bar Basque was thoroughly promising in all these respects.

A waiter in a white-jacket, with a glossy black head, blue jaws, and an unusually self-satisfied and impertinent expression, even for a continental waiter, emerged from the restaurant with a tray of glasses, which he carried to a table; the group of men round it greeted him cheerfully, and he remained standing by them, talking and laughing, flashing his white teeth. Rosemary Oldhead gave her mother's arm a little tweak.

"That's Ladislas," she said, indicating the waiter. "He's the spy."

Mrs. Oldhead studied the waiter with interest; Mr. Oldhead looked sceptical.

"Who does he spy for?" he asked.

"At *least* four different governments," Rosemary said, with a small giggle. "It's no good looking down your nose, Daddy— those are journalists he's talking to now; at least one is, that lanky one with the yellow hair. He's Hooters."

"What's his name, darling?" Ethel Oldhead enquired, shifting her attention from the spying waiter to Hooter's local representative.

"Hever—Tom Hever. Oh, and *look*—" Rosemary lowered her voice and leant across the table towards her mother—"there's the Duquesa de las Illas; there, in black."

Mrs. Oldhead looked obediently at the woman who now crossed the pavement and stood, accompanied by a man in white trousers and a blue blazer, looking round for a table. She was in deep mourning; her face was made up in a peculiar tone of orange, and the front rolls of her black hair were bleached by peroxide to a sort of creamy bronze; her lips and nails were a deep carmine. Mr. Oldhead surveyed her with distaste.

"She looks no better than she should be," he observed.

"Yes, she does look a bit tartish," Rosemary agreed.

"You shouldn't say things like that," her Father remonstrated.

"I thought it was what you meant," said Rosemary equably.

"Who is she, anyhow?" Mrs. Oldhead asked, with the double motive of keeping the peace and satisfying her own curiosity.

Rosemary told the story—a common one in the Civil War, but appalling in its completeness. The Duquesa's husband had been murdered by the Republicans more than a year before; she herself had escaped—first to Franco Spain, then to France.

In telling it, Rosemary used the expression "The Reds." This called forth a protest from her Father.

"Why can't you give them their proper name, and call them the Republicans?"

"Sorry—Republicans, then."

Mr. Oldhead, like many Englishmen of his age and class, was secretly an intellectual Red; that is to say his Liberal outlook and traditions, and his hatred of any form of dictatorship or interference with freedom of thought and speech made him feel, rightly or wrongly, much more sympathy for the Barcelona government than for that of General Franco, particularly since the Italian intervention in Spain which had, in his view, aligned the latter with the dictators. Like many other people whose information was derived mainly from their favourite newspaper, he tended to assume that all light and learning in this conflict was on one side. At first he had merely been impatient with a local quarrel in the course of which a large part of the artistic heritage of mankind seemed likely to be destroyed; then, with incredulous irritation, he had seen other European countries gradually becoming involved in a conflict which lacked even the dubious sanction of national or economic interests—to a sensible man, Mr. Oldhead felt, there was something wickedly absurd about a war mainly or solely of idea. Finally, ignoring or forgetting the French and Russian aid to Barcelona, he had watched the veiled but vigorous intervention of the two states whose form of government seemed to him most destructive of human values; and all this had made him, in his secret heart, an active sympathiser with the Republicans.

His wife and daughter did not share these views. Ethel Oldhead was not an intellectual of any description, red or white; she was a good-hearted person, shrewd about people in a rather simple way, inexperienced but intuitive. While Rosemary told the story of the Duquesa, Mrs. Oldhead watched the woman. Her face, under the startling make-up, was a little heavy; impassive except for the fine eyes. But Mrs. Oldhead got an odd impression that the Spanish woman did not somehow match her story; she did not look like a stricken widow—she had the occupied look of a woman with a job, though she was now sitting at a little table in the sun with a flashy-looking man, drinking Cuentra. Of course she hadn't got a job, and her appearance wasn't in the least that of a professional woman—but still she had that busy look. Funny.

For Rosemary, the change from a damp and chilly English autumn, in the damp and chilly class-rooms of her rather dull country school, to hot sunshine and sandal-wearing exciting foreigners of all sorts was one of the purest satisfactions that life had so far brought her. She was nearly seventeen, and her parents had decided that her education would on the whole benefit by a few months spent abroad, improving her already good

French, and learning Spanish. Rosemary's education was not a
thing on which her family built very high hopes, in any case; she
could learn languages, it seemed, but she never got anywhere in
examinations because she could not do algebra, and anyhow would
never work at anything which did not interest her. She was the
complete product of the modern English system of upbringing, in
which the parents count for little and the school, the film and
fiction for much; she already knew more about such things as
perversion, the liaisons of film-stars, the white slave traffic and
drugs than her mother did, and talked more openly about them
than her mother would ever live to do; but fundamentally she had
the curious emotional innocence of this peculiar generation, and
stood possessed of certain secret, strong, individual and on the
whole very just ideas of right and wrong. Nothing surprised her,
little shocked; everything amused and interested her. She was
already taller than her mother, and not bad-looking; there was
an engaging contrast between the exaggerated if becoming
fashionableness of her hair-dressing, rolled immensely high above
the forehead, with foolish curls over the ears, and the eager
amusing face—the long thin nose with a tilt at the tip, the liquid
brown eyes and sharply defined eyebrows, the brownish, very
clear skin, so clear that the very brownness was almost a beauty.
So far she used no rouge or lip-stick—her mother was firm about
this; she had to confine herself to creams and powder, and the
enormous elaboration of her pretty hair, in her attempts at personal adornment. Mrs. Oldhead was amused and resigned at the fuss
Rosemary made about her hair; Mr. Oldhead, on the other hand,
was disgusted and sarcastic. Beauty to him was in architecture and in
Nature, which he photographed with a complicated camera, a
telephoto lens, and infra-red screens to bring out distant detail.
While Mrs. Oldhead was still studying the unstricken appearance of the Duquesa, and Mr. Oldhead was deciding silently that
he would profit by the beautiful light and go out photographing
that afternoon, a stout grey-haired man in a grey flannel suit
appeared among the tables accompanied by a very smart woman
with platinum blonde hair. Rosemary tweaked her mother again.

"Look—there's Mr. Crumpaun. He's Universal Press."

"How on earth do you know who all these people are?" her
father asked, amused.

"Well, he's in our hotel." Catching Mr. Crumpaun's eye, as
he stood looking for a place, she nodded to him.

"Good-morning." The stout grey-haired man moved over
towards them. "Pretty crowded here to-day—that's the sun."

"Why don't you sit here?" Rosemary said, to her father's dismay and to Mrs. Oldhead's secret satisfaction. "My Father, my Mother—Mr. Crumpaun."

"That's very nice—we'd like to." He brought over the platinum lady and introduced her—"Mrs. Jones—Mrs. Walter B. Jones. Her husband's the American consul in Rivas Nuevas; but he pushed her out. Things are pretty hot down there." They sat down; Mr. Crumpaun beckoned to Ladislas, the spy; drinks were brought. Mr. Crumpaun, who had a rather undefined Canadian accent, put through a few genial enquiries as to why the Oldhead family were in St.-Jean, but he did it very nicely—he was a comfortable sort of man. Having satisfied himself that it was for reasons of health, he next enquired if Mr. Oldhead was comfortable at the Grande Bretagne—"it's the best food here, if the pub itself is a bit mothy." And then, as usual, he began to discuss the war in Spain. Both he and the blonde were rather pro-Franco, it appeared; she used the expression "those Reds" more than once. Mr. Oldhead began to get restive, and at last asked her why she thought the Republicans were worse than the Franquistas.

"But they're *Red*!" she protested, opening immense pale eyes, under plucked and darkened eye-brows.

Mr. Oldhead gave a helpless shrug.

"All Spaniards are a lot of killers, anyway," Mr. Crumpaun observed easily—"but I think maybe the Barcelona lot got in a bit ahead of the others and did a bit more. There were some terrible things done. There's a woman in this town who had her husband and son killed before her eyes in a way I couldn't describe to you."

"Do you mean the Duquesa?" Rosemary enquired.

"Yeah—know her?"

"No—do you?"

"No to mention. I know a bit about her, though. I hear she's shifting to our hotel—food's too bad at the Moderne."

"Have all these people got money?—in spite of the Revolution and all that?" asked Mrs. Oldhead, whose first week's bill at the Grande Bretagne had slightly alarmed her.

Mr. Crumpaun cocked a shrewd eye at her.

"You've hit on one of the Great Spanish Mysteries, Mrs. Oldhead—how the refugees live! Her husband *was* one of the very rich men in Spain, but I guess they've lost pretty well everything; all their property was over that side. I hear she's going to take some sort of job, though—going back to run the female Falange, or something."

"She must spend a good bit on her face alone," Rosemary said, glancing again towards the woman in black. Mr. Crumpaun laughed.

Mrs. Jones leant over the table, and lowered her voice confidentially.

"They say she's a spy, and one of the best they've got," she murmured.

"Well, spies get good pay," observed Crumpaun.

"But what does Franco want with spies out here?" Mr. Oldhead asked, a little incredulously.

"Don't know what he *gets*, but it's quite a racket, by all accounts," said Mr. Crumpaun. "They're supposed to have a big organisation this side of the frontier, and I was told the other day that the head of it stays quite close by here—Guéthary or Biarritz."

"Who is the head?" Mrs. Oldhead asked innocently.

"Now you're asking, Mrs. Oldhead! If I knew that, I'd know a lot."

"I wonder if there's any news of the Condesa," Mrs. Jones observed to Mr. Crumpaun. "That's the Duquesa's sister," she explained to the Oldheads—"the Condesa de Verdura. She's the famous beauty, you know; they say she's the most beautiful woman in Europe."

"So far as I know there's been nothing heard of her for months," said Mr. Crumpaun. "She and the child were supposed to have been in Madrid—I've not met anyone who knows whether she's alive or dead." He turned to Mr. Oldhead. "That's one of the *real* horrors of war, this time," he said. "Half these people have no idea whether their nearest and dearest are dead or alive. Of course there are always rumours, but they're worse than nothing."

"The Conde de Verdura *is* alive—he's in prison on the Barcelona side, somewhere," Mrs. Jones volunteered.

"Yes, that's so. Shouldn't think that would break the Condesa's heart, if she's still got a heart to break," said the journalist, lighting a cheroot.

"Why not?" Rosemary asked, her brown eyes immense with interest.

"Well—" Mr. Crumpaun hesitated, and glanced sideways at Rosemary's parents. "He's a bit of a tough guy, the Conde, and runs around rather a lot," he finally said, inconclusively. Mrs. Jones had no such scruples, however.

"Rich as he is, they say he'd pretty well ruined himself over his ladies," she said airily. "Why, he gave that dancer a pearl necklace that they say was worth a hundred thousand pounds."

"It was his wife's, anyway, so that won't have broken him. But we needn't go into all that, Madeleine," said Mr. Crumpaun, with a significant glance at Rosemary. "The best of that family," he went on, briskly changing the subject, "was the Duquesa's brother, Juanito. He was one of the straight Spaniards—went in for politics, and really tried to pull things round. And when the war began they say he made a magnificent soldier."

"You say was—is he dead?" Mr. Oldhead asked.

"Supposed to be—very stickily finished off by the Reds, when they caught him."

"But do they kill prisoners of war?" Mrs. Oldhead looked appalled.

"Some of them, in this war; lots of them, I should say. If they're dangerous people. He was dangerous, because of his politics—and his cleverness."

"Anyway they said he was a spy as well—" Mrs. Jones as usual added her quota.

"I'm surprised that there should be so much spying when there's so little actual fighting, relatively," Mr. Oldhead remarked, addressing himself to Crumpaun. "Do you really believe that there is anything in all these stories?"

"Sure. Do you know that whenever one of the foreign embassies here puts through a long-distance call, the *Inter* at Bayonne Exchange makes a gramophone record of it?"

Mr. Oldhead was amused but incredulous.

"And who gets the records?" he asked.

"Whoever'll pay most for them. You're in France," said Mr. Crumpaun crisply. "There's a reason for the spying, though," he went on. "It's always worse in a civil war, where you have families and relations all mixed up, some on one side and some on the other, and no one can ever really quite trust anyone else. So they all go around trying to keep tabs on one another, just in case. And where you have a complete breakdown of communications, and all these rumours, the suspicions and the spying get worse than ever. This is the most domestic war in history, I should say."

Mr. Oldhead accepted this explanation with approving interest, but when the conversation got back onto gossip and atrocities, he fidgeted off. Mrs. Oldhead and Rosemary however stayed on for a little while—they were both thoroughly enjoying themselves. More Press-men were pointed out to them: Newport of the *Blare*, sandy and small; Hamilton of the *Epoch*, tall and grey-haired, on his way to Burgos, now waiting at St. Jean-de-Luz for his permit to cross the frontier at Irún. Mr. Crum-paun, who seemed to like imparting information quite as much as collecting it, explained that the *Epoch*, like one or two of the other larger papers, had one correspondent in Burgos to cover Franco's activities, one at Madrid with the Republicans, and a third—a dejected-looking red-faced person called Crossman—at St.-Jean. "Crossman picks up the bits, like the rest of us; we don't get much here," he explained with his cheerful chuckle.

It was time for Rosemary and her mother to leave; Mr. Old-head still insisted abroad on lunching at his home hour of 1.15. The two Englishwomen walked down the draughty little street towards their hotel, at each crossing meeting soft, salty puffs com-ing in from the sea—past the abandoned and dilapidated little Casino, with its two absurd and delightful tiled cupolas, and the fragile charm of its broken yellow stucco, past the cinema posters stuck on its aged railings, from which the paint, rotted by the salt-laden air, was powdering rather than peeling off. On the way they talked companionably about the morning's experiences. To Mrs. Oldhead, fresh from an extremely dull suburban existence, life on the Spanish frontier as it had revealed itself that morning struck a note of pure fantasy, crazily improbable—it was so unlike life as she knew it that it seemed to her merely funny; to Rose-mary, on the other hand, whose conception of human existence owed at least as much to the cinema as to anything else it was delightfully thrilling but not in the least improbable.

"The Duquesa does look tartish, whatever Daddy may say," the girl chattered on. Mrs. Oldhead said that she thought Mrs. Walter B. Jones looked like a film-star. "Oh *no*, Mummie—only her hair. Her teeth would be hopeless on a film, and so would her face—it's just a blob." Mrs. Oldhead laughed, but bowed to youth's superior technical knowledge. Coming out on the little circular space above the sea-wall, where cars park in front of the Hôtel Grande Bretagne, they paused as usual to look over the bay. Above the long mole which blocks the centre of the entrance great masses of white spray, like flowers or mushrooms, appeared sud-denly and soundlessly—hung a moment against the blue of sea and sky, and sank again; though it was a fairly still day, there was a swell outside, and a couple of motor sardine-boats shooting across to the exit on the right of the mole began to dip and dance as they approached the opening; they bounced giddily out of sight behind the break-water below the old pharos, which comes out towards the mole to protect the northern curve of the shore. A low steady thundering came from this break-water, where the tide runs strongly. Rosemary narrowed her lids against the glare, snuffed the strong air like a dog, and with a sigh followed her mother in to lunch.

The Hôtel Grande Bretagne was built in the days of Queen Victoria, when the regular winter sojourns in Biarritz of the Prince of Wales brought an annual flow of English visitors to the Basque Coast; and its solid, comfortable, slightly shabby furnishings recalled that epoch, if they did not indeed date from it. The hall was always dark and the dining-room always light, but as no windows were ever opened in either, the same stuffy warmth at all times pervaded both. Crumpaun was fond of cutting a joke about this—"The hotel's air-conditioned," he would say; "The air's in the same condition now as it was when it was built." The competent dapper little Basque manager, Swiss-trained like so many of his countrymen, did not think this at all funny, but he smiled his steely smile all the same; journalists were good clients, they brought custom, and the most lucrative sort of custom at that —drinks. And nothing would induce him to open his windows— most of them wouldn't open anyhow, they were stuck fast by far too many layers of paint: Victorian paint, Edwardian paint, Georgian paint. Rosemary, sitting at lunch, eating the rich un-wonted food in impatient boredom, noticed how these layers of paint had softened all the angles of the woodwork round their window to a mellow, albeit rather shabby smoothness; beyond the window, with its thick lace curtains, she watched a black and white cat, followed by a ginger admirer, going in and out of the railings of the old Casino below the cinema posters, and then romping elegantly on the deserted patch of lawn among the torn and faded fragments of earlier posters, thrown there carelessly when the bills were changed. It was all very like St.-Jean, she thought—an old, haphazard, cheerful little town, the tourist part of it falling untidily into decay, the native part leading its own life with as much zest and indifference as the cats. But she liked it: undoubtedly being here was fun; only the meals were awful, especially lunch, when they and an old parson were the only people eating in that hot bright room. She wished the journalists didn't always lunch out, and so much later; it was much more amusing at dinner, when they were there to be watched.

About the middle of the afternoon, when Mr. Oldhead had rested, Mrs. Oldhead had read the *Epoch* (she read the Burgos article with new interest, having seen Hamilton, the Burgos correspondent, at the Bar Basque that morning) and Rosemary had fidgeted over her Spanish Grammar, they prepared as usual to

set out for a walk. In the hall of the hotel they encountered Mr.
Crumpaun, cigar in hand, bright and jolly after his morning of
drinks and a late lunch.

"Like a drive?" he enquired. "I have to go over to Irún, in
case this Non-Intervention party comes out—they say he may be
along this afternoon. Care to come? Lots of room in the car."

Mr. Oldhead did not care to—he had his elaborate camera
strung round his shoulder, and all his little special gadgets in his
pocket; he was going to do some photography, he explained. But
Rosemary and her mother cared to very much indeed, and Mr.
Oldhead was not really sorry to be relieved of his family for the
afternoon—now he could pause, potter, pace and screw up his
eyes, undisturbed by their patient perchings on banks and walls.
So he walked off along the front alone, and Rosemary and Mrs.
Oldhead squashed into the back of the hired car, one on each side
of Mr. Crumpaun's cheerful bulk, and set out for Irún.

To island-dwellers like the English, frontiers have not the same
significance that they bear for continentals. Mrs. Oldhead's and
Rosemary's personal experience of frontiers had so far been
limited to Swiss customs officials coming into their second-class
carriage at 3.00 in the morning at Vallorbes; they had never *seen*
one in their lives, and when Mr. Crumpaun's car pulled up in
the long straight street that approaches the International Bridge
at Irún, they got out and looked about them with the liveliest
interest. The bridge certainly looked the part perfectly. It was
closed at either end by wire barriers, painted red and white; as
far as the middle, tricolor flags fluttered from little masts on either
parapet, beyond that hung the red and gold of Spain—below
flowed the muddy Bidassoa. A group of journalists already hung
about the passport office on the left of the French barrier, others
were chatting to the functionaries from the police and customs
depot on the right—their cars extended up the street in a long
shiny line. "No sign of him yet," they told Mr. Crumpaun. Mr.
Crumpaun lit another cigar and beguiled the time of waiting by
pointing out various items of interest to the two Oldheads. Above
the bridge the Bidassoa curved between flat damp fields; along
the Spanish bank little sentry-boxes stood at intervals, and between them soldiers in indeterminate uniforms, with rifles, strolled
to and fro. "They look bored," said Rosemary. "Guess they
are," said Mr. Crumpaun. "They're so bored they'll shoot at
anything—in the summer they shot a girl who went swimming
and got farther across than they liked." He took them up the
road a little, and showed them Fuenterrabia standing up, dark,

imposing, a little sinister, across the shining estuary. Then they
went back to the bridge. There was a stir now round the barrier
—a priest had come up in a shabby car; his luggage was taken out
and piled onto a wheelbarrow, and after his papers were examined
the wire barrier was rolled back a little and he went across, followed by his luggage, wheeled behind him by a porter. Mr.
Crumpaun explained that even train passengers were not allowed
to remain in their coaches when the Sud Express crossed the railway bridge, 100 yards downstream; they all had to get out and
cross on foot, with their baggage on wheelbarrows, of which a
dismal little fleet stood outside the Customs office.

A car now drove down the street, and pulled up; the uni-
formed chauffeur got out and showed the passports on one side
of the road, the *triptyque* on the other—the barrier was rolled still
further back, there was a little saluting, and the car passed
through and onto the bridge.

"Who's that?" Rosemary asked.

"The German Ambassador at San Sebastián—didn't you see
the C.D. on the car?"

Rosemary hadn't, and wouldn't have known what it meant if
she had—she had never seen a live diplomatist in her life. She
watched the German car pause before the barrier at the further
end of the bridge, while a group of officials examined the papers
for the second time, and produced a large ledger-like book, turned
the pages slowly, closed it again, and eventually allowed the car
to proceed. The whole business of crossing had taken nearly a
quarter of an hour.

"Some business getting into Spain, even for diplomats," Crumpaun commented.

"Who can go in?" Mrs. Oldhead asked.

"Only people with *salvo conductos*, and only those if their names
are on the list—they keep a list of the people who have *salvos*, but
the chap can't always find their names," said Mr. Crumpaun.
"Not very literate, some of these little Spanish officials."

Rosemary, with the long sight of youth, had been studying the
various uniforms of the group at the far end of the bridge, and
now asked Mr. Crumpaun about them—"Who are the two men
in dark green, with those shiny blacks hats turned up at the back?"

Mr. Crumpaun, always obliging, got out his Zeiss glasses and
explained. The men in dark green were the *Guardia Civil*, the old
police; the youths in red tam-o'-shanters were *Requetes*; the others
were *Falangistas*. Rosemary was thrilled at hearing the Spanish
pronunciation, Guardia Thivil and Falanhistas—she had read

about "Falangists" and recognised the word. "It *is* fun," she sighed. What a day!—journalists, beautiful if tartish duchesses, sentries with rifles, ambassadors, a real frontier, bounded by a river and guarded by armed men. Glorious!

Mr. Crumpaun's preoccupation with the far end of the bridge had prevented him from noticing a fresh stir behind him—another car had driven up, and the journalists, bored with waiting, gathered round it while the papers were examined; he took down his glasses in time to see the Duquesa de las Illas get out of it, and start to cross the bridge on foot, a striking and rather incongruous figure in her fashionable black.

"Hullo! What's she after?" he asked his colleagues.

"She can't be going over for good, because she's left the car, and she's got no luggage," said Hever.

Crumpaun put up his field glasses again and watched the progress of the black figure. At the far side, by the barrier, his glasses and Rosemary's hawklike sight showed a meeting between the Duquesa and a little old woman, also in black; another barrow with luggage on it was let through the Spanish barrier, and the little procession trooped back again towards the French side. This tiny incident let loose a flood of speculation and rumour among the waiting journalists, hungry for news; they fell on it like a swarm of minnows on a piece of bread, pulling it this way and that. The old woman was the Duquesa's mother, her aunt, her father in disguise, a famous spy. The *Blare* man and some of the others put up their cameras and photographed the Duquesa and her companion as they approached—she paid no attention to them, and after a further prolonged examination of the newcomer's papers and effects by the French frontier officials, the party entered the car and drove off.

Mr. Crumpaun now looked at his watch, ejaculated that they had been there over an hour and a half, and after a consultation with his colleagues decided that it was no good waiting any longer for the emissary of Non-Intervention. He suggested having a drink. "We might go up to Biriatou—there's a pretty view." He invited Mr. Hever of Hooters to accompany them, and they drove off.

Biriatou is one of the most amusing of the French Basque villages. It is perched high up on a shelf of hill overhanging the Bidassoa, and is so cramped for space that the tiny square is also the *fronton*, or pelota-ground; deep-eaved Basque houses with chocolate-brown shutters enclose it on two sides; on the third, beyond a low wall on which the spectators lean during matches,

is a flagged space a few feet higher than the *fronton*, set with chairs
and small tables—the fore-court of the inn; beyond that again a
flight of steps between large bay-trees leads up to the white façade
of the village church, which crowns the whole. A stage designer,
bent on producing a *décor* which should represent the Pays Basque
in the smallest possible space, could hardly improve on the lay-out
of Biriatou. The Oldheads were enchanted with it. But Mr.
Crumpaun did not settle down at the tables below the church
steps—he led his party right through the inn, where home-cured
hams hung from blackened beams, and out onto a little terrace
beyond, roofed with a trellis of vines, where he ordered wine, relit
his cigar, and prepared to enjoy himself. The late afternoon sun
poured in onto the rough wooden tables; it was deliciously warm.
Rosemary and Mrs. Oldhead leaned over the vine-clad railings
and looked at the view. Immediately below them flowed the
Bidassoa, winding through the hills, with more sentry-boxes along
the Spanish bank—downstream, where the valley broadened out,
the late sun made a hazy glory of the wooded slopes, and lit
up the white houses and farms on the French side. Rosemary
sighed again with pleasure. The bridge had been thrilling; this
was beautiful.

Mr. Hever of Hooters was a tall emaciated young man with
long yellow hair, a long mediaeval face, and a gloomy expression;
he wore baggy grey flannel trousers and a terrible tweed jacket,
but his voice and manner suggested a long, expensive, and conventional education, probably at Cambridge. When the red
wine was brought, in an unlabelled and uncorked bottle, he
sniffed it, drank, sniffed again, held his glass up to the glowing
light beyond the vine-leaves, and said abruptly—

"What's this?"

Mr. Crumpaun, who had also taken a drink, said—

"Spanish."

"It's very good," said Mrs. Oldhead, who thought Mr. Hever's
question rather unmannerly.

"Much too good to be French *vin du pays*," said Hever. "What
do they charge for it?"

"About five francs a bottle," said Crumpaun, with his jolly
chuckle. "Smuggled, of course."

The wine was indeed good—strong but not rough, a little
heavy, as if burdened with the flowery sweetness and fragrance
that hung about it. Hever sniffed again and drank again.
"Damned good," he said. "And sixpence a bottle! Baptême!"

"I suppose they smuggled it in before the war began," said

Mrs. Oldhead innocently, glancing down at the sentries patrolling the banks of the Bidassoa.

"Not they. Goes on all the time, up in the mountains. The hardy Basques aren't going to go without their good *vino tinto* for a little thing like a war," said Crumpaun heartily; "and the Hispanos want to sell it, too. Suits everyone." He started imparting information again. "They smuggle currency as well, any amount of it."

"How do they get it over?" Rosemary asked, her eyes big with excitement. Smuggling too!—she was drinking smuggled wine!

Crumpaun smiled benevolently at her eager face.

"The wine's run in skins generally, on people's backs, over the high paths. But they say dogs bring the money mostly—dogs and sheep."

"But *how*?" Rosemary was almost beside herself with thrills.

"Little packets strapped round the dogs' necks, and pinned to the sheep's fleeces, under their bellies. Easy enough for a dog to run to and fro, or sheep to be driven from one pasture to another. There's a special convention about frontier grazing-rights up at places like St.-Jean-Pied-de-Port, and all along there beyond La Rhune."

"We're going up La Rhune to-morrow, if it's fine," Rosemary interjected.

"Then catch any sheep you see and look under its tummy— you may get some black pesetas," he teased her.

"What is the black rate now?" Hever asked.

"Hamilton's getting 127."

Mrs. Oldhead had to know what black pesetas were—she was almost as curious as Rosemary about all these strange matters. Mr. Hever took upon himself to explain, in his high Cambridge voice.

"The official exchange rate for pesetas in Spain is about fifty to the pound. . . ."

"Fifty-three," from Crumpaun.

"But there is an unofficial rate, as always in countries with a regulated currency," Hever flowed on, disregarding him—"which is much higher. For some reason it is usually called the Black Rate. It operates inside as well as outside the country."

"But why should people want to get two and a half times as few pounds for their pesetas?" Rosemary put in. Hever regarded her with faint approval.

"Very pertinent. But they either wish to get *some* foreign currency for their pesetas, and will therefore pay almost any price for it, or they have pesetas already, outside Spain, and don't wish to put them back there, so that they will sell at a loss to keep their hands free. You can't do much with pesetas to-day."

"It seems funny that they should want to lose money, all the same," said Mrs. Oldhead, looking a little puzzled.

"They want to so much that they'll risk a good bit to do it," said Crumpaun. "The penalty for smuggling pesetas out of Spain is death."

"When does Hamilton expect to get his *salvo*?" Hever asked. He was not interested in death in Spain.

"Any day now."

"He's an able chap," Hever observed, lighting a large aged pipe and pulling at it—like all other journalists, he could never refrain from discussing his colleagues when the smallest opportunity offered. "Only so deadly melancholy."

"He's nothing like so able *or* so melancholy as Milcom," responded Crumpaun. "Know what they call Milcom in Spain? El Melancolico." Both men laughed. "Milcom's the *Epoch* man in Madrid," Crumpaun explained for the benefit of the two Oldheads. "He's almost the ablest living British journalist, in my opinion."

"He's become so pro-Red," Hever said, in a complaining tone.

"Hamilton's become so pro-Franco," Crumpaun countered. "He got a rap on the knuckles for it the other day—told me so. Good specials almost always do become pro their particular country. Anyhow Milcom gets no end of snuff from being so in with the Reds."

"Crossman got very pro-Bolshevik when he was in Russia, I seem to remember," Hever observed.

"Yeah. Though Crossman's a poor stick," said Crumpaun detachedly, filling his glass—"Drinks too much."

Rosemary's irrepressible giggle escaped her at this point. Her mother gave her a good-natured kick under the table; Crumpaun cocked an eye at her.

"*Yes*, young lady—drinks too much. Spirits, too—not this sensible stuff. Have some more." He held out the bottle.

"She's had quite enough," said Mrs. Oldhead, who was aware that she herself was feeling remarkably warm and cheerful as a result of the Spanish wine.

Hever ignored this family by-play. He was intent on his own ideas.

"It's a very interesting thing, but Spain is producing just the same effect on people now as Russia used to," he said. "Everyone seems incapable of telling the truth about it. Those parties

of M.P.s that go wandering round Spain come back with just
the same diametrically opposed yarns as the Intourist parties
from Moscow used to bring. "I went to Barcelona, Madrid and
Almeria—I saw fifty churches, and they were all either in ruins,
or the doors were boarded up." "I went to Barcelona, Madrid
and Almeria—I saw fifty churches and they were all open and
thronged, and Mass was going on."

Crumpaun laughed.

"I know—I know. You can believe what the ordinary honest
observant guy tells you about Germany or Italy or France or
Turkey, but you can't believe what an Archbishop tells you about
Russia or Spain."

"But why is it?" Ethel Oldhead asked. She had noticed this
phenomenon herself in the English press. "People must be able
to *see* whether a church is open or shut."

"I believe they in fact can't," Hever told her. "Not where
political ideals are involved to the extent that they are in Spain.
There's something about Communism and its antidotes, Fascism
or Nazism, that actually affects the eyesight, I believe; certainly
they always produce this wild partisanship and exaggeration.
Ideology is the death of detachment."

Crumpaun winked at Mrs. Oldhead. "Clever guy, isn't
he?"

"I *wish* I could get into Spain and see for myself," Rosemary
sighed.

At this point the landlord appeared, in his shirt-sleeves, greeted
Mr. Crumpaun warmly, and asked if they had all they wanted.
Crumpaun praised the wine, and enquired after Madame. He
was clearly a regular patron of the Biriatou inn.

"Ask him what he thinks about the war," Hever said, re-filling
his horrible pipe. Crumpaun did so.

"Ah, messieurs, c'est un champ de tir," the inkeeper said. He
spread his broad hairy hands out flat on the end of the table,
leaned his weight on them, and expounded his views. The whole
Spanish struggle, in his opinion, had been engineered by the
Russians, the Germans and the Italians, in order that they might
there try out their latest engines of war. Believe him, that was
the fact. He knew it. Everyone knew it. He took his hands
off the table and stood up. "Nous autres aussi, enfin," he observed, as he moved away with Crumpaun's note.

"Gosh, these peasants are astute," Crumpaun said when he
had gone. "Objectivity, thy name is Frenchman."

"What is a *champ de tir*?" Rosemary asked.

"Oh, a shooting-ground—where you try out guns on clay pigeons and targets, to see if they'll shoot straight."

"But do you think that's true?" she asked him, her eyes very big.

"There's truth in it, if it's not the whole truth," Crumpaun said, shovelling the change which a small girl brought him into his pocket. "That's one reason why Non-Intervention is such a non-starter." He rose—"Well, I suppose we ought to be getting back."

They drove back through the late evening light, down the little winding road into Béhobie, where the yellow-and-white village dogs, with drooping ears and muzzles, are a living memorial to the Duke of Wellington's quiet winter there, and his pack of English foxhounds; along the great Route Nationale, winding up hill and down dale on its way from the bridge at Irún to Bayonne and Bordeaux, where the car flew over the grey-blue tarmac, under the golden foliage of the bordering plane-trees. The speed, the beauty of the road, the red wine and excitement all combined to make Rosemary a little giddy—she sat on the small seat with her face to the window, singing soundlessly to herself, and Mr. Crumpaun opposite watched her with pleasure, and murmured, much too loud, into her mother's ear that she was a sweetheart of a kid.

Mr. Oldhead too had had a good afternoon. He told his family about it when they got home. He had walked to the little pharos at the north end of the bay, had climbed up the chalky knoll on which it stands and photographed the view, and gone down to the breakwater on the far side and photographed the great Atlantic rollers sweeping in across the Bay of Biscay. He had met an elderly Spaniard of academic appearance and, it seemed, tastes, up by the pharos, who also took an interest—and a knowledgeable one at that—in photography; they had strolled back together along the front, and discussed Unamuno and de Madariaga, and had ended up with *cuentras* at the little Café de Paris, and Mr. Oldhead was pleased to have been introduced to it—it was small and quiet, he said, and the olives were good. Mrs. Oldhead asked if he had learned the academic Spaniard's name? No—he hadn't. *Nor* where he was staying? Rosemary enquired, with youth's despairing impatience at the inefficient methods of age. No, nor that either. "Well, what's he *like*?" she burst out at last—"Would you know him again, anyhow?"

Her father laughed a little.

"Yes, certainly. He was like all elderly Spaniards, to look at."

"And what's that like?" she almost snapped.

Mr. Oldhead considered.

"Like a grey marble parrot," he said at length—and Rosemary pounced on him and kissed his bald patch. At last her curiosity was satisfied—she *saw* the academic Spaniard.

That evening went better than usual for Rosemary, because the Duquesa de las Illas had accomplished her transfer from the Moderne to the Grande Bretagne, and sat in the sombre lounge to be watched. "Her mother was English," Mr. Oldhead remarked unexpectedly at one point.

"How on earth do you know that?" his wife asked.

"That old boy told me. Some peer's daughter, I don't remember the name—English or Scotch."

"That's so," put in Crumpaun who was sitting with them—"I remember being told that at the time."

Rex, the grey and bearded hall porter, the one really efficient member of the Grande Bretagne staff, came puffily through the glass doors from the outer hall into the lounge and approached the Duquesa, who sat alone, meditatively examining the lacquer on her finger-nails. "One asks for Madame la Duchesse at the telephone, from Perpignan," he said. The black figure rose swiftly, and followed Rex into the outer hall, where the telephone box was. Mr. Oldhead called ineffectually after him—"Hey, Rex!"

"What do you want?" his wife asked.

"To order breakfast for to-morrow. We shall want it at 7.30 if we're going to catch the early train up the Rhune. Rosemary, go and tell him."

Rosemary went. The outer hall was draughty and chilly after the hot lounge, the front door was jerking and banging with every gust of wind; just inside it Rex stood behind his mahogany desk, reading the advertisements in *La Petite Gironde*; at the far end of the hall, under a brilliant light, the Basque manager and his Swiss wife, behind another mahogany desk, stood listening to the wireless, creaking uncertainly in Spanish from San Sebastián. The telephone box was opposite Rex's desk, and the door had been left ajar; as Rosemary gave her message she could hear the Duquesa's voice screaming a little as people are wont to scream for long-distance calls—she heard cries of joy, caught the name Raquel, and to her great surprise, some sentences in English. "*Si, si,* come here—of course! But yes! Come to-morrow." Her message given, and written down by Rex, Rosemary returned the long-range bows of the manager and his wife and went back into the lounge.

A few moments later the Duquesa reappeared, in tears, but with a radiant face; she swept across the room, oblivious of everything, to the lift, and rang—she was giving little half-sobs as she waited by the brass cage for it to descend—she was dabbing her eyes as, visible to all in the glass box within the brass cage, she was borne aloft to an upper floor. There was something curiously dramatic in this emotional exit—Crumpaun, like everyone else, stared after her.

"I wonder what's up," he said, when the very visible lift had vanished from their sight.

"Someone called Raquel is coming here to-morrow, from Perpignan," said Rosemary obligingly.

The effect of this statement was electrical. Mr. Crumpaun bounced upright in his shabby leather chair.

"*Raquel!* Are you sure?"

"Yes—I heard her at the telephone. But why?"

"But that's the sister—the Condesa! Holy Moses! Then she's alive after all! I must find out about this." He heaved himself up out of his chair, and in his turn hurried out through the glass doors—as they swung to and fro behind him the Oldheads could hear him adjuring Rex to get onto the "Inter" and get him the Hôtel de l'Europe, Perpignan, and pretty damn quick.

## CHAPTER FOUR

### *This Side—St.-Jean-de-Luz*

THE Oldhead family had rather a good day on La Rhune. In the little mountain train, which leaves the square by the main railway station as drably as a tram, and then rambles across the rolling coastal country, they eventually chugged steeply up to the very summit of that handsome irregular cone of grass and rock which is such a striking feature in the view from every part of the French Pays Basque. Though clouds obscured the distance, it was sunny near at hand, and warm enough to make Mr. Oldhead's photographic potterings perfectly agreeable. The Franco-Spanish frontier passes right over the summit of La Rhune, and Rosemary, who was now under the spell of frontiers, was able to marvel at the casualness of this section, as she had marvelled at the elaborate ritual on the International Bridge at Irún the day before. Except for a single wooden notice with the word "Spain," stuck up by some enterprising junior members of the Non-Intervention Commission's observation personnel, there was nothing to show where one country ended and the other began—there were just rough slopes of grass and rock, with jutting crags here and there. Mr. Oldhead was unusually enterprising; the academic Spaniard had told him, it seemed, that if he went eastward along the ridges he would find a charming subject for a picture—a little col or saddle with combes running down from it on both sides, studded with small trees, and some picturesque and prominent rocks. They set out in search of this gem, and eventually found it—and while Mr. Oldhead took his photographs, Rosemary picked late pale-blue gentians, whose calyxes were exquisitely striped with green, and fragile mauve-pink autumn crocuses, and thought about smuggling, and suspected every sheep she saw of having black pesetas tied under its fleece; and Mrs. Oldhead sat on a rock smoking a cigarette, pleased to see her family so happy, and wondering if by taking rooms for herself and Rosemary further along the corridor, away from the view, she could reduce their weekly *en pension* terms at the Grande Bretagne.

They got home about tea-time, and Mr. Oldhead, who was tired and stiff, went early to bed; but Rosemary remained in the hall, in theory learning her Spanish vocabulary, in practice gossiping with Mr. Crumpaun, till he was called away to bridge. So it came about that she was present when, at about 10.30, Rex opened the glass doors to admit the Duquesa, James Milcom, and the Condesa de Verdura. She looked up from her book, as one does automatically in hotel halls at some fresh entrance; noticed the Duquesa, and then, since everything about that lady interested her, gazed at her companions—and saw for the first time those two faces, the long, pale, rather gothic face of Raquel de Verdura, and that other, lined and melancholy, with the deep-set grey eyes. It was only a brief glimpse that she got, before Rex shepherded them into the glass-walled lift and they were borne aloft—but it was sufficient for her. She knew at once who the woman must be, and popped into the lounge where Mr. Crumpaun, in a red plush chair, was paying bridge with the elderly clergyman and two Non-Interveners. Luckily Mr. Crumpaun was dummy at that moment, and she breathed into his ear—"She's come."

"Who's come?"

"The Condesa—the Duquesa's sister."

"Oh, she has, has she?"

"Yes, and a man."

"Spaniard?"

"I don't think so—he looked English and rather dismal."

Crumpaun burst into his loud jolly laugh.

"That'll be old Melancolico! Good for him—I heard a noise to-day about him coming over, but I didn't believe it. They staying here?"

"I suppose so—they went upstairs."

"Well, sweetheart, now you'll meet a really *good* journalist," said Mr. Crumpaun cheerfully. "My deal, is it? Okay."

But actually Rosemary didn't meet Milcom for two days; to her disappointment he didn't stay at the Grande Bretagne after all, he took a room at the Poste. She saw him once in the interval, when her father took her in before lunch to his new discovery, the Café de Paris—Milcom was sitting at one of the little brown tables talking to a man from the British Embassy; but as Mr. Oldhead didn't know either of them, she could only look and speculate. However she was quite content—for Rosemary watching and speculating were becoming, at St.-Jean-de-Luz, a delightful and rewarding occupation. One learned quite a lot merely by doing that. Moreover this turned into a very rewarding morning, for just as they were leaving a short, rather heavily built man came in, wearing a neat urban overcoat of pepper-and-salt tweed with a velvet collar, and a black trilby hat, which he removed with a bow on seeing Mr. Oldhead, revealing a baldish head with the remains of grey hair very neatly brushed above a pale heavy face, with a beaky high-bridged nose and full-lidded grey eyes. His face was so impassive as to be almost sinister, Rosemary thought. When they got outside Mr. Oldhead informed her that that was the academic Spaniard; and Rosemary told her mother at lunch that Daddy was quite right, and that he was *exactly* like a grey marble parrot.

Next morning the yellow-haired Mrs. Jones rang up to invite Rosemary to 12-o'clock coffee with her at the Bar Basque. The Bar Basque was a paradise for observation and speculation, and Rosemary, having obtained the parental permission, gleefully agreed. She fidgeted a little during the end of her Spanish lesson, and when it was over fairly ran down the narrow Rue Louis XIV and out into the Rue Gambetta. This is the main shopping street of St.-Jean-de-Luz, and in it was situated the Photographie La Lune, to which Mr. Oldhead entrusted the development and printing of his precious photographs; Rosemary, acting on instructions, popped in to enquire whether the preliminary prints from the La Rhune expedition were ready—Mr. Oldhead was the sort of photographer who always had a set of medium-sized prints made first, to see the results of his handi-work. But she drew a blank—M. Durand, emerging from an inner room in his long blue alpaca overall, regretted infinitely, but the prints were not yet ready. Rosemary registered an instantaneous dislike of M. Durand, and darted on.

Mrs. Jones was waiting for her already, sitting at one of the tables outside the Bar Basque on the pavement among the bay-trees—and before Rosemary had finished panting and apologising, Mr. Crumpaun strolled up and joined them. "Well, how's the sweetheart?" he hailed Rosemary, having lowered his comfort-able bulk into a chair. Rosemary was becoming rather a pet of Mr. Crumpaun's—he liked her intelligent amusing face and shining elaborate coiffure, and was amused by her eagerness about everything. Now newspaper men love to be amused; they spend such a high proportion of their working life hanging about filling in time—usually with alcohol—and waiting for something to happen, that any distraction is a godsend. And Rosemary Oldhead afforded Mr. Crumpaun a lot of distraction. He had already noted her faculty for watching and observing people, and he suspected her of putting two and two together much more smartly than her sixteen and three-quarter years and her foolish curled head would lead one to expect. This was a thing which the journalist in him admired, and while Rosemary watched people, Mr. Crumpaun watched her watching them, and noted her reactions. Now, seeing James Milcom's tall figure crossing the road towards the restaurant, with his rather slouching walk, he hailed him, summoned him to their table, and introduced him to Rosemary and Mrs. Jones.

Mr. Crumpaun, "sticking around" as he himself described it, "with an ash-can at St.-Jean, waiting for scraps," had plenty of questions to ask the younger man about conditions in Madrid and Republican Spain generally, and the conversation was at first rather specialised; Rosemary listened with all her ears, but Mrs. Jones, attending to her face and poking at her platinum hair, became bored. At last she broke in with an enquiry about the Condesa de Verdura, and their escape. Milcom was not very forthcoming, but presently he turned to Mr. Crumpaun and asked if he knew the Duquesa?

To nod to, Mr. Crumpaun said.

Ah. Milcom's eyes took on that look of desperation which really only meant that he was concentrating on something. "You've no idea how she's situated financially?" he asked at last.

"No. I'm just a guesser," Mr. Crumpaun averred. "She has

all she needs, and lives well, but what her bank-book looks like I haven't a notion. Most of them haven't a bean. But they have ways and means. How's the Condesa's?"

James suddenly smiled, a wry smile which made his gloomy dark face fascinating, Rosemary thought.

"A small competence," he said.

"Well, I daresay she'll find ways and means too," said Crumpaun.

Milcom's smile left his face—his mouth set.

"Fortunately, she won't need to," he said, rather sourly.

At this moment, Crossman of the *Epoch* and Carrow of the *New York Moon* came up together, and with excuses to the others, began to talk to Mr. Crumpaun. Carrow was a thin sandy irritable American, who presently produced an envelope full of photographs, which he showed with a certain pride to Mr. Crumpaun. "Look at these—pretty good detail, eh?"

Mr. Crumpaun put on his glasses and studied them.

"Fine," he said. "You take these?"

"Nope—that photographer at the shop in the Rue Gambetta let me have them. Wish I had the guy's camera that took them."

"Whereabouts were they taken?"

"He swears they're some place up on the frontier—asked me a pretty long price for them, too. Anyway I shall say they're the frontier—this spy racket will make quite a story, especially with pictures."

Mr. Crumpaun shuffled the photographs together, and turning to Rosemary, handed them casually to her.

"Hey, Sweetheart, look at these. Can your old man better that?"

This form of address drew Milcom's attention to the young girl. Up to now he had regarded her merely as an appanage of Mrs. Jones, and as he disliked women of the Jones type, he had barely looked at either of them. Now he noticed the intelligent glance, the big generous mouth and the amusing nose, and found them a pleasant sight—and he watched the girl for a moment as she bent her curled head over the photographs. He saw her start a little, look puzzled, turn back to a picture a second time, compare one with another, examining them with a most unnecessary concentration—and then he saw a quick flush, as of anger or embarrassment, stain the clear transparent brown of her skin. This aroused his curiosity, and when she had finished looking at them, and put the pile together, he stretched out his hand for it, saying "May I see?"

She looked up at him, startled, and the colour again flew into her face.

"Of course," she said, handing the packet to him—and her mouth took a funny little determined set.

"Good, eh?" said Mr. Crumpaun—he had been talking to Crossman, and had not noticed her.

"Very," she said. "Every bit as good as Daddy's."

James meanwhile glanced at the photographs. There was nothing in them to embarrass the most innocent *jeune fille*—they were a series of mountain landscapes, and in particular showed two charming little valleys or combes, dotted with small trees, each with its shadow standing obediently at its side, and a col on a ridge with some spectacular groups of rocks. That was all, so far as the casual observer could see—but James, like most journalists, knew something about photographic processes, and the clearness of distant detail in one or two of the views down the combes told him that they had been taken with an infra-red lens. He glanced at the girl again. Why had she flushed like that? And his mind hit on the truth—those pictures were familiar to her.

He handed them back to Crumpaun. "Does your father photograph much?" he asked her civilly.

"Yes, he's rather fond of it," the girl answered, a little stiffly.

"Does he go in for it thoroughly—infra-red lenses and all that?" he asked, still in a tone of casual politeness.

"Oh yes—he has all sorts of gadgets," said Rosemary, her manner losing something of its stiffness. "He takes some lovely things."

Carrow meanwhile was stuffing the photographs back into an envelope with a big blue moon in one corner—M. Durand's trademark. Rosemary watched him with a baleful gleam in her eye. What business had he to go buying her father's pictures? But for some reason she decided to say nothing.

At that moment the Duquesa de las Illas and the Condesa de Verdura appeared, stepping onto the pavement between the bay-trees, two black and distinguished figures; they paused, looking round for a place—the sunny stretch of tables was now full of people. Milcom sprang up so quickly that he overturned his chair. "Yes, bring them here," said Mr. Crumpaun genially, replying to the action, for he had said no word. James nodded, went over, and piloted the two women to the table—chairs were reshuffled, and they sat down, the Duquesa beside Mr. Crumpaun, the Condesa between Rosemary and Milcom. Carrow had moved off at their advent; Crossman remained, rightly guessing that he would now get a free drink; he sat beside Mrs. Jones. Crumpaun made the introductions, casually and easily; Milcom noticed that the little English girl changed colour as she shook hands with the Spanish women. For Rosemary it was, indeed, another of those improbable and wonderful moments with which her days, now, seemed to be crowded—to meet and shake hands with the two refugees, one of them the most famous of Spanish beauties, both of them the wives of *Grandes de España*. The old phrase, "a Spanish grandee," had at last taken on for her its real and peculiar meaning; she had already heard the Spanish version often enough for that. "A Greatness of Spain"—lovely words, splendidly evocative of the past; miraculous that she, Rosemary Oldhead, should be sitting at a table with two of their female counterparts. While the conversation got jerkily under weigh she watched them; in their deep black dresses, with their elaborate heads, they looked, she thought, like two funeral horses set down in a field of parti-coloured cows, among the rest of the group—the three journalists, Mrs. Jones, and herself. But Rosemary was soon confronted by one of her perpetual miseries at St.-Jean-de-Luz—the "horas españolas." In that little community, so near the frontier, so full of Spanish refugees and journalists who ran in and out of Spain, the Spanish hour ruled—lunch at 2 or 2.30, dinner at any hour from nine till half-past ten. Mr. Oldhead however stuck firmly to his English practices—lunch at 1.15, dinner at 7.30. So the fascinating time of drinks and gossip before meals was always, for Rosemary, cut short almost before it had begun. She glanced at her watch, saw that it was six minutes past one, and resolutely rose. There were protests—"Now, the Sweetheart, don't tell me you're going to leave us?"—"Do you have to go so soon?" from the Condesa—"Why, it's a shame," from Mrs. Jones. But Rosemary stuck to it. "Well, come and have tea with me—at the Moderne. Half after four," Mrs. Jones called after her, as she made her good-byes and went.

Walking back along the narrow street to the Grande Bretagne, meeting the draughty gusts of soft salt air as she neared the little Casino and the sea, Rosemary thought about the photographs, and what she should tell her father. It wasn't Carrow's fault, she decided, with belated justice; it was his job to buy whatever he could get for his paper. But it was brazen of M. Durand to sell them, though all French shop-keepers seemed to be pretty brazen—the lies they told in the *stoppage* about her stockings!— madly cheap as the ladder-mending was here. No, but it was such an odd *sort* of brazenness, to show and sell prints of other

3

customers' pictures; there was something funny about it. She
would like to find out more; she would ask Mr. Crumpaun, or
that fascinating Milcom person, if she met him again. And till
she knew more, she wouldn't say anything to Daddy, or he would
kick up a shindy with Durand, and she would learn nothing at all.
She went in to lunch.

Tea with Mrs. Jones at the Moderne was rather a dull affair,
and brief; Mrs. Jones had an appointment at 5.15 with the coiffeur.

"Oh, *where*?" To Rosemary, as to all the modern female
young, hairdressers were a matter of the utmost importance.

"Well, Jacques, actually—but I shouldn't recommend you to
go there," Mrs. Jones said.

"Why on earth not?"

"Well—he's a terribly good coiffeur, but it's rather a peculiar
place," Mrs. Jones said, gathering up her bag and gloves. "They
say"—she lowered her voice—"that it's a dope den as well as
a shop."

"But what frightful fun!" Rosemary was enchanted. "Oh,
couldn't I come with you, and see it?"

Mrs. Jones was amused at her enthusiasm.

"All right—come along and talk to me; I'm always deathly
bored at the coiffeurs. We'll see who we see. But don't go there
alone, whatever you do. He costs the earth, too," she added
inconsequently.

Rosemary was not surprised, when they reached M. Jacques'
establishment, that a shampoo and set there should "cost the
earth," for it was the most expensive-looking hairdressers she had
ever seen. It was all in pearl-grey, with touches of black; black
tables with flowers on them standing on the deep pearl-grey
carpet, black satin cushions on the grey velvet chairs, black
mouldings round the panels on the pearl-grey walls. Mrs. Jones
was ushered into a small pearl-grey shrine, half-draped by black
curtains, on the ground floor; Rosemary sat just outside, in one
of the grey velvet arm-chairs, and looked about her. The windows
were screened to elbow height by grey ninon curtains, so that
from within, the disembodied heads and shoulders of the passers-
by on the pavement were visible; among these, as she idly watched
them, appeared two that she knew—the Condesa's and James
Milcom's. They paused—she saw Milcom's right hand move to
his breast pocket; then the Condesa came in alone. At the far
end of the shop, where the stairs ascended to the upper floor, was
a counter with cosmetics, perfumes, and toilet appliances, and
conspicuous among them, a pale-pink block of the products of

Elizabeth Arden. The Condesa aroused Rosemary's deep envy by proceeding to select a complete outfit of Arden creams, powders, lipsticks, and toilet-waters—any young girl's dream! Then she went on to the perfumes, causing first one and then another to be sprayed onto squares of tissue—she would not have them on her hands or dress—and sniffing them delicately with her high gothic nose, smiling and discussing them with the girl who served her. At length she chose two of Worth's, Je Reviens and another. All this time Milcom, Rosemary observed, was still hanging about outside the shop. The Condesa paid for her purchases at the discreet cash-desk by the door with two thousand-franc notes, put the change in her purse, and went out and joined him. Through the glass above the grey curtains Rosemary, unable to hear any words, saw their meeting—a brief questioning remark on his side—it might have been "Got all you wanted?" and on hers, as she replied, an expression as of one who thanks, and thanks warmly. Whatever it was, he made a gesture of brushing it off—but with a curious gentleness, unlike his usual dour expression. It all passed in a few seconds, before they disappeared together down the street; but to Rosemary, watching them with her usual acute intentness, the meaning of the little scene was clear—he had *given* her those two *billets de mille*, and she was thanking him for them. How *nice* of him, she thought, warming to him.

By this time, Mrs. Jones's platinum locks had been washed and were being coiled and arranged all over her head by a glossy-haired man—she demanded loudly of Rosemary what was going on, and whether she had seen "anyone amusing." Some odd instinct made the young girl suppress all mention of Milcom and the Condesa; but a few minutes later she was able to report, in an undertone, that the Duquesa had just come downstairs and left the shop.

"Ah—had a set, I suppose," Mrs. Jones commented.

"She didn't look as if she'd had a set—she looked just the same as this morning," Rosemary observed. "And she didn't pay, either," she added after a moment—"she just walked out."

"Perhaps she was seeing someone—people do, here," Mrs. Jones remarked, significantly. But she wouldn't answer any of Rosemary's questions as to why people should see one another at the hairdressers; it occurred to her, belatedly, that it was not her place to explain to a young girl that M. Jacques' establishment also ran to "cabinets particuliers" upstairs. It would not have surprised Mrs. Jones to learn that the Duquesa had been keeping an assignation—she looked just the type, the American thought. Presently Mrs. Jones's head was finished, and she was set under the drum—pearl-grey, like all the rest of the shop—to dry. She asked Rosemary to bring her a *Vogue*, and the girl went over to the black table on which the papers lay. This table was just opposite the foot of the stairs, and as she hunted for a *Vogue*, she saw the academic Spaniard standing on the half-landing in conversation with M. Jacques, the *patron*, whom Mrs. Jones had pointed out to her when they arrived. She was near enough to hear their conversation—they were speaking in French. "Then you will obtain for me four examples of each, in this size," the Parrot said, pointing to a photograph which M. Jacques held in his hand—"the detail in that size will be sufficiently clear." M. Jacques bowed his acquiescence, and the Parrot came slowly downstairs, buttoning his pepper-and-salt overcoat. M. Jacques followed him, and hastened respectfully to open the street door, putting down a small packet of post-card-sized photographs on the table by Rosemary as he did so. But as he bowed the Spaniard out, a gust of sea-wind blew in; caught the little pile of photographs and showered them all over the floor. Rosemary instinctively stooped to gather them up—as she did so, in the bright electric light, she saw for the second time that day her father's pictures of the col, the striking groups of rocks, and the small combes full of those little trees with their attendant shadows.

For a moment she stood looking at them, too stupefied to speak. Then M. Jacques was at her elbow, his hand outstretched. "Merci, Mademoiselle," he said.

In a flash, Rosemary forced a smile for him.

"Comme elles sont jolies," she said, casually shuffling them over; she got a good look at each of them before she handed them back. Yes, they were Daddy's, beyond any doubt. This would take some thinking about. Very slowly, then, she found a *Vogue*, and took it to Mrs. Jones—and soon afterwards she said that she must go home and do her Spanish prep. But it was a very thoughtful Rosemary who walked back in the wave-sounding dusk along the sea-front, through the empty echoing arcades of the closed modern Casino, and on by the narrow path behind the new sea-wall, still a-building. For what could Daddy's old Parrot want with those photos? What did he want them *for*? And just as she reached the little semicircle of tarmac outside the Grande Bretagne she stood stock still, under the arc-light which drowned the last green sunset glow out to sea. But it had been the Parrot who *told* Daddy about the little col, and the two combes and the big rocks!

Then he *meant* him to go there! He *meant* to have his pictures of just that place. And—the Duquesa *hadn't* had a set; she was sure of that; her head wasn't even very tidy. Had she been talking to the Parrot upstairs? He hadn't been shaved, either—his chin was grey-ey-blue. Rosemary went into the hotel more thoughtful than ever.

If the mere fact of staying at Perpignan with her had made James Milcom feel the impact of human society on his relation to Raquel de Verdura, he felt it infinitely more strongly when he got over to St.-Jean-de-Luz. During the few days that he spent there they two seemed to him to be moving all the time in a positive crowd, surrounded by his colleagues, by the Duquesa and her friends, and by all sorts of miscellaneous people like Mrs. Jones and the English couple with the nice little girl—so he mentally characterised the Oldheads. In Olivia de las Illas he confronted the family, he felt; and though she was perfectly civil, and indeed professed the warmest gratitude for all that he had done for her sister—her little sister, she sometimes called her—he was aware of an almost inquisitive scrutiny, occasionally, in her bold restless glance. Among his colleagues he was also aware of a certain interest, aroused by his suddenly turning up with "a beauty in tow," as he overheard Crossman phrase it. But though for the most part they were quite sensible and discreet, the mere fact of their presence, of sitting talking shop with them threw a quite altered light onto him and Raquel, gave him a different yardstick with which to measure himself and her. Here he was not her only friend, her one companion and support—he was forced to see himself as just a journalist among a group of journalists, while she was a distinguished refugee, the wife of a grandee, with a Duchess for a sister. Even her beauty arose now to utter its mute testimony, to set her away from him as her own remoteness had never quite succeeded in doing; the heads that turned after her, as she walked into the Bar Basque, made him feel that the days when he knelt on her palliasse in a cellar and sawed wood for her, while she washed up the supper-things, and her clothes hung from a nail on the wall, were really phantoms of the memory, as un-related to the actual world as the life of dreams. Then, too, when they had moved like ghosts wandering in a world of shadows, their emotions had been gentle, shadowy, frail; now, coming with her into the world of men, the practical factual world of relations and acquaintances and money and arrangements, he found that this gentle undisturbing relationship had taken on flesh and blood, had become a harsh, throbbing, painful reality. And all the time an idea that was half a question pulsed through everything else in him—whether she did not, perhaps, feel the same?

They dined together his last night. He took her to Gaston's, a small restaurant on the Place Louis XIV, down by the harbour, where the cooking is good and the fish superb. They sat outside —it was a warm evening; the wind had fallen after sunset, and only light draughts of air from the water sent the fallen leaves from the plane trees scuffling along the dusty cobbles. Sitting out there they overlooked the whole pretty, rather theatrical scene —the closely-trimmed plane trees yellow in the lamplight above their mottled white trunks, the blue and green sardine-boats bobbing gently on the dark water beyond, the two green lights winking at the narrow harbour entrance, down which, at intervals, a big swell rushed, making the gaily-coloured boats dance afresh under the arc-lights. Now that it had come to the point of actually leaving her, he found that he minded it to a degree that almost surprised him. He had not known that it would be like this, would cause this almost stifling pain, that took away one's breath.

But all this had the effect of making James, that night, very correct. It had taken him some little time to raise the money for her, but he had managed it, and gave it to her now; enough to last for three or four months—he had satisfied himself that whatever the Duquesa's "ways and means" might be, they were not equal to maintaining a second person. He gave it to her in cash, but urged on her strongly the desirability of opening a banking account; and she promised to do so the very next day. He got this business over early, while they took their apéritifs; inevitably it was a little awkward, but she was, as always, quite peculiarly gentle and nice about it—using no emphasis, letting most of her thanks be understood rather than uttered. It was a form of genius with her, he felt, this gentle quiet naturalness which robbed almost any situation of its embarrassment.

When it was settled he sat back in his chair, saying "There— that's over; now we can enjoy ourselves."

She smiled at him a little oddly.

"Can we?" she said. And set that half-question pulsing in him again. But then her long pale face took on another expression.

"I have something to 'get over' too," she said—and blushed, a thing he had never seen her do before.

"What's that?" he asked, wondering about the blush.

"It is something, as usual, for you to do for me," she said, with great earnestness. "Do you ever go to Almadera?"

"I have been there—I might go again, any time," he answered, guessing what was coming.

"If you *should* be there, I would like you to go and see Pascual. As a journalist, I suppose you could get into the prison?"

James supposed so too.

"And then to tell him that I am out here, and safe, and with Olivia. And to let him know about—" her voice wavered for a moment—"Pilar. It will not be nice," she went on, "telling him this; but it would be a relief to me, if you could. He ought to know. And if when you have seen him, you would let me know how he is, I should be grateful."

She always asked for things like that, perfectly directly, with no cajolery and no emphasis, he reflected. Aloud—"Yes, I'll do that," he said, as directly as she, and pulled out his notebook. In it he took down the full name—Major José-Maria Pascual, Conde de Verdura, taken prisoner in hospital at D——, after receiving a slight wound. While he wrote down all the details, in a perfectly business-like way, Milcom's mind was asking itself a string of questions. How much did she really want to know how this man, her unfaithful husband, was? How much did she think he would mind about the child, even? "He ought to know," she had said. Was this request perfectly spontaneous, or did it spring from the Spanish tradition of family life? He found that he wanted quite fiercely to know; he even got the length of trying to frame a sentence in which he could conceivably ask her. This he found difficult—and with a sigh he gave it up. Anyhow, as he was going away, there was no point. He put away his notebook with a gesture of finality, and looked up at her. Something in the still concentration of her face as she watched him hit him so hard that he looked away again.

She said—"Thank you; you do a great deal for me."

And something in the way she said that—said "for me" and not "for us"—made him feel that some time he would be able to ask her that question that he had just stifled, or even that he would not need to ask it. He came back, as he sat opposite to her at the small table, to two constant strands of his thought about her:—how little he knew, really, about the inner lives of Spanish women of her class, well as he knew Spain; and in spite of this, that he always had a feeling of *safety* with her—that however little he might understand her, there was in her a fundamental sincerity and goodness on which any relationship could find safe anchorage.

They continued eating their dinner, but as the meal proceeded

he realised that she had been right—they could not enjoy themselves. They were quiet, and became quieter. He liked the way
in which she praised the excellent food—the grilled fresh sardines,
the 3-year-old *pâté de foie gras* and salad—with real discrimina-
tion, but also that she made no attempt at "conversation," to
divert, to be gay. They just were there, sad and quiet, watching
their long association—so troubled in its surroundings, so peaceful
in itself—drawing to a close; both too adult and too serious to
trouble with any pretences or any effort. Once, looking at the
many-coloured dancing shapes of the sardine-fleet, she said, "I
like the little boats," and he answered—"So do I—I always shall."
But that was all.

After coffee, he suggested going back along the sea-wall. By
an unspoken consent they paused and leaned on the parapet
above the narrow stone-built entrance to the harbour, down
which the dark waves passed at intervals, the black glassy water
faintly lit by the green lights above their heads. The air was
damp and fresh from the wet stone, and full of the clean turbulent
noises of the water, slapping and bouncing; when they turned
from it and leaned their backs against the parapet, there were the
lights of Ciboure burning steadily across the bay, and beyond
them, to the right, the ghostly white spray rising soundlessly above
the outer mole, like huge flowers opening in the silvery blue darkness. He heard her give a tiny sigh.

"It's nice, isn't it?" he said.

"Beautiful." She was silent then for some time, watching the
noiseless blooming and falling of those white flowers. At last she
said, rather hesitantly—"There is something else that perhaps
you could do for me."

"What is that?"

"To find out about Juanito—my brother, you know. I thought
Olivia would have known, but she does not—nothing. Not that
he is dead, or a prisoner—but also no word of him being alive and
serving still. She who is in touch with so many people! It seems
strange."

"When did you last hear anything definite of him?" James asked.

"Seven months ago, Olivia heard. He was fighting then, with
the Navarrese Division—his Division." Her voice caressed the
words with a note of unutterable love and pride. James was
struck by the sudden realisation that he need not wonder what
dictated *this* enquiry—it was most clear that it was an adoring
devotion to her brother. This touched him. It recalled his
mother, who also had loved a brother better than her husband,

perhaps better than anything else on earth—loved him and lost him, he thought, with a sort of pang that was half recollection, half foreboding. Oh, God!—he didn't want her to lose Juanito as well as Pilar—and he had every reason to fear that she had. And little as he liked Whites on the whole, he had heard enough about Juan Torre de Modero to feel that the most exaggerated devotion would hardly be misplaced.

"Right—of course I'll do that," he said; and then because he wanted to hear her talk of someone she loved, and above all because he wanted to postpone the moment when she should suggest going in, he asked—"Is he older or younger than you?"

Again that loving caress was in her voice as she answered—"Oh, just older. He is thirty-one. His birthday is the same day as mine—isn't that funny? We had such fun keeping them together, when we were children."

"When is it—what time of year?"

"March, just when all the flowers begin; the 27th of March. We used to pick flowers the night before, to strew on one another's beds in the morning, so that the other might wake up to find flowers on the quilt—but one was always first, and so someone's flowers were spilt!" She laughed at the absurd recollection. "He used to scold me so gently, if I spilt his flowers. And there was such a fuss if we could not keep our birthdays together!"

"How long did you manage to keep that up?" he asked.

"Oh—but always!" she said, turning to him, as if the question surprised her. "Except twice when I was in the convent, till the war, always. Even when he was doing his military service, as a young man, he came—once in a car and once in a plane! And when I woke there were flowers on my bed, and he was sitting there, all dusty, laughing at me! Oh"—her voice changed from the happy tone of recollection—"I do *wish* I knew where he was! I do wish I could have news of him. It is not *like* him not to find some means to send me word."

"It would have been very difficult while you were in Madrid," James pointed out.

"Difficulty was nothing to him! The word did not exist to him," she said, suddenly very agitated. "No, he must be dead. And yet how could he die, and I not know it? Everything in me would know it, if he was dead! That is what is so strange," she said, turning to him despairingly. "*Do* find out! Please manage to find out! I am sure that you too can do difficult things."

The compliment touched James deeply.

"What is he like?—to look at?" he asked.

3*

"My face, a little—and Olivia's hair; black, that is." She remembered the unnatural gleam of cream-colour on the Duquesa's two winged rolls, and gave a tiny, unsteady laugh. "And he walks as I do—Mamma always used to scold me, that I walked so like Juanito. But I did not do it expressly."

James smiled in the darkness. Raquel had a very individual walk, some trick of the ankle or instep muscles giving it a little lifting spring when she was walking fast—her English blood, he had always supposed, for it was most unlike the gait that is so often seen in Spain. He had been amused at the contrast of her walk with that of the Duquesa, only to-day. Oh, God, when would he see her walking again? It was too dark now, and by daylight he would be going.

"Well, I will do everything I possibly can to find out," he said. "You can rely on me for that."

"Do—oh do! Oh, I know I can rely on you," she said. "Where should I have been, but for you? But do find Juanito for me." Quite suddenly, she began to cry—he could hear the small sounds, she saw the pale gleam of a handkerchief put up to her face. "And now you also gone," she sobbed softly.

James recognised afterwards that it was really her emotion about Juanito that had done it. He came to see, in the weeks that followed, how much their sad sobriety had always depended on her stillness, her gentle fortitude. Once that was broken, he was done. He really had the feeling of having been toppled over a cliff, so immense was the change from the solid ground of their previous behaviour, their tacit convention of pure friendliness, to the cloudy tumultuous depths, shot with raptures as with lightnings, into which he plunged then. He took her in his arms, gently enough, saying "My darling, you know that I have to go," or some such foolish phrase. But she so settled then into his arms, as into her own place, where she belonged; lifted her face, as directly as a child, to his for the expected kiss, and then so clung to him, to his face—all the force that up till then had gone into keeping her still and quiet, now poured out in the expression of her love. They clung together there in the dark, on the windy sea-wall, while the white flowers of the spray bloomed out to sea beyond them in a sort of desperation of love and sorrow and delight and pain, murmuring wild endearments—clung as helplessly, as inevitably, as if each were a drowning man, that had found a rock at last.

With complete mutuality, at last, they drew apart, and both stood staring in the dark at the pale blur that was the other's face with the sort of incredulity that follows the first avowal of love. Raquel sighed—and shivered a little.

"Are you cold?" he asked.

"No—it is warm. But I am tired, a little—and you must travel to-morrow. I think we should go in."

How much more bearable, now, it was to hear those words. James too was tired—exhausted was nearer the mark; and in spite of everything, fulfilled, sunk deep in joy.

"Yes, let's go," he said. They turned back, and walked along the unparapeted sea-wall towards the Grande Bretagne, past the silent houses, where only a faint gleam from the lamps of the little side streets, which all end abruptly against the wall's landward side, now and again broke the peaceful darkness. Before they reached the orbit of the arc-lights outside the hotel, Raquel paused and spoke.

"That could not helped," she said. "Probably it was wrong, but it could not be helped."

"My darling, I love you with all my heart—that can't be helped either," James said.

"No—I know."

"Do you? *Do* you love me?"

"Indeed, yes," she said, almost sadly. "I love you very much." She took his hand. "Please say good-bye now, here—then I will go in."

"Good-bye, my dear love," he said, and kissed her.

"Oh, good-bye. May God take care of you," she said, and slipped from his arms and was gone.

"Find Juanito for me"—her voice came back out of the darkness. It was her last word.

## CHAPTER FIVE

### *The Far Side—Almadera*

MILCOM had no difficulty, when he returned to Spain, in reconciling it with his duty to the *Epoch* to pay a visit to Almadera. With a good harbour and a good railway inland, and even a few factories, it was one of the ports on which the Republicans relied largely for supplies, and it had recently received a lot of attention from the Savoias which plied regularly from the Balearics, in a systematic attempt to block and ruin the ports of Republican

Spain. At Barcelona he went to the Dirección General de Prisiones and obtained an authorisation to visit the Conde de Verdura at Almadera. In the ordinary way, as James already knew, such visits took place either in the Office of the Director of the prison, or in the Sala de Visitas; if the latter, one screamed at the prisoner through a wire grille—in either case, the conversation had to take place in Spanish, with a listening guard standing by. James had little relish for this interview anyhow, and to conduct it under such conditions seemed to him almost intolerable; with the help of the Condesa's Republican cousin he succeeded in obtaining the extraordinary concession that he might visit the Conde in his cell, and a note to that effect was attached to the authorisation. In this way he hoped to secure a reasonable measure of privacy. All this done, he telegraphed briefly to his paper from Barcelona that he was going to visit Almadera, and took a small steamer straight on down the coast—the *Electra*, under Greek charter, in cotton from Alexandria. The captain, a huge Norwegian, prudently hung about in the offing all the afternoon, and crept in after dusk; the pilot, who chugged out in a small motor-boat to meet them, sidled the steamer skilfully in past dismal slanting masts and funnels, sticking up at all angles out of the dirty water, the relics of previous vessels which had neglected to take this precaution. James, by permission, stood on the bridge with the pair of them.

"It gets worse," the captain said.

"Like bloody hell it gets worse," answered the pilot, who came from, of all places, Cardiff. "It's like a flaming bending-race to get in or out now, and what it'll be if they keep this up, Christ knows." They tied up at a pier immediately behind a half-sunk timber boat, from whose decks half-naked dock hands were unloading timber by dimmed blue lights, working with feverish speed; James remained for some time on board the *Electra*, to watch the same process beginning there. The dockers were waiting on the quay, a great crowd of them; the moment the *Electra* was made fast and the stevedore's whistle blew, they crowded aboard her like a swarm of ants, pulling off hatches, burrowing into the holds, working with a desperate busy haste that had something insect-like about its concerted purposefulness. During the hour that he watched them, they made astonishing progress. He commented on this to the captain, who had returned to the bridge after disposing of the ship's papers with the port authorities.

"Yes—they must, now; they have learnt this," the captain said grimly. "Formerly the Spanish were not quick."

"Will they finish during the night?"

The captain stuck out his wrist, on which a luminous dial glowed faintly.

"Perhaps—there is more time now than in summer. Yes, they should empty her before daylight."

"And loading? What are you taking?"

"Lemons—and oil. But I shall go for a little cruise to-morrow," —he grinned—"and come in again after dark to load, if they are not finished in time for me to get out. Since Nyon"—he grinned again—"the open sea is the best place."

"It was the Italians, all those sinkings, was it?" James asked—it was a routine question, but he liked hearing the invariable answer.

"Is a mackerel a fish?" asked the Norwegian simply, and spat over the ship's side. And then let drive about the would-be proprietors of *Mare Nostrum*. "Soldiers, they never were; sailors, they are not—singers and roadmenders, that is all they are. And such will have an Empire, and be great! But to sink unarmed ships from in hiding below the sea, and to throw down bombs from the air on villages and undefended towns—for that they are very good!" He used an unprintable Nordic word, in the plural, and spat again.

James went to his hotel, recommended by the Norwegian skipper. Next morning he presented his various papers and passes to all the relevant municipal and military authorities and set out for the gaol. It stood high up on the slopes behind the town, a large gaunt building; a clerk pointed it out to him from the Plaza. He walked to it, quite glad to see what he could of Almadera. The town was spread fanwise round the harbour, thinning out into villas up on the amphitheatre of hills which surrounded it; factories scattered away down the coast, their chimneys sending dark incongruous streamers of smoke across the sunny air. In one of the main streets he passed an antique shop, and paused to glance in at the window—his eye was caught by a superb bedspread of old lace, laid over heavy green watered silk of the colour of sea below cliffs on a thundery day. A sudden memory of Raquel, lying under a sordid quilt on the bed in the hotel at Perpignan, exhausted after her burst of hysteria, sent him in to ask the price. It was large—too much, he felt, greatly as he wished to think of her as lying under it in the Hôtel Grande Bretagne; it was worthy of her, hard as that was for anything to be; he imagined her in the past as always lying under such a splendour, in bed. He said no. The shopkeeper put on a cunning expression.

"The Señor is English—though he has such admirable Castilian! Has the Señor perhaps some sugar?"

Now Milcom had smuggled in a few pounds of sugar from France, with an eye to his friends in Madrid; he had actually got two half-kilo packets in his pocket at that moment, along with some cigarettes—a small present intended for the Conde. He drew one out now, and let the shopkeeper feel the angular creaking shapes of the flat cubes within. The man's eyes glistened with cupidity.

"For three such, Señor, the coverlet is yours."

James put the packet back.

"Very well—later, I will see." He turned to go.

"Señor, Señor, for two! No, do not go," said the man, catching at his arm. "See, for two—for one and a half!"

"Bueno—bueno," said James soothingly. "This you cannot have—it is a present. But I will return this afternoon with more. Two. Keep the quilt for me—wrap it up." And disregarding the man's anguished protests, he left the shop and went on his way, up the hill to the prison.

From outside it he paused again to look out over the town. There was scattered damage here and there, as he had seen on his way up, but not much; most of the ruined buildings, as at Barcelona, were near the port—he recognised grudgingly that for aiming from the air the Italian pilots, as the captain had said, were good. This morning, with the white walls and pink roofs shining in the bright sun, the place looked pretty and peaceful enough.

Throughout his journey Milcom had looked forward to this visit with a certain nervous distaste. He disliked Whites; he disliked everything he had ever heard—and he had heard plenty—of the Conde; above all he hated seeing anyone in prison—he had always had a morbid horror of the very idea of shutting a human being up, and depriving him of his liberty of movement. And on top of all this there was also the disconcerting consciousness that he, James Milcom, was in love with this man's wife, that he had avowed his love and received her avowal in return. And he had got to tell him that his only child was dead. What a picnic, James said grimly to himself, as he followed the gaoler along the echoing stinking passages, coldly lit from an occasional barred window high in the wall.

But the visit turned out very differently from what he expected. His elaborate and difficult arrangements for seeing the Conde in his cell, which included a final heavy bribery of the gaoler with cigarettes on entering, to persuade him to leave them to themselves, all proved to be useless. The Conde was not in a cell alone—he occupied a largish room with about ten others, obviously drawn from all classes. It was lit by two windows, also set high in the wall—there were some ragged palliasses on the floor, a very small table, and three chairs, one of which was pushed forward for James; five or six of the men, including the Conde, had secured wooden soapboxes, which served them at once for seats and for cupboards, to hold such few belongings as remained to them. James, in a despairing attempt to secure at least a measure of privacy for their conversation, introduced himself and told his errand in French—for the other prisoners, starving for news from the world outside, were clustering eagerly round him. But the Conde, in an unexpectedly soft and gentle voice, asked him if he spoke Spanish—"If you do, it would be kind if you would speak that; they will like to hear about your journey."

"Well, I will part of the time," said James, more glumly than ever—and proceeded to relate to the motley audience the story of his journey from Barcelona to Port-Vendres, to Perpignan, and across France to St.-Jean-de-Luz. They kept interrupting him with questions—one had relations in Barcelona, another a shop in Madrid, while one very merry-faced little man, who wore perpetually a sort of monkey's grin, had been a bus driver in San Sebastián, and was bitterly disappointed that James had not crossed the bridge at Irún and been in to see his beloved town. James could, and good-naturedly did, tell him how conditions were there, for he had heard plenty about the place from Hamilton, Hever, and the British Embassy staff—he even described the extent of the damage in Irún. While he talked, they sat round him in a shabby group, and he noticed that most of them had a bit of glass in their hands, and a small piece of wood, at which they whittled away at intervals. This sight surprised Milcom greatly. Any sort of cutting instruments were most strictly forbidden in the prisons, since they might be used either for escape or for suicide; the only way to account for the presence of all this glass was that the gaoler must be a "radish"—that is, red outside and white inside; in which case, Milcom reflected ruefully, he had given him far more cigarettes than were necessary. Some of the prisoners, with extraordinary ingenuity, were making linked belt buckles of three or four interlocked rings of wood, all carved out of one piece; others, the Conde among them, were carving fascinating little designs on peach stones. It produced a most extraordinary impression on Milcom to see this big, rather fadedly handsome man, about whose wealth and manner of life he had heard such exotic stories, sitting on a soapbox among a group of cab drivers, carving peach stones into a necklace for his wife with a bit of broken glass.

However eventually, having taken the edge off their appetite for news, Milcom told them that he had private business to discuss with his friend, and they all obligingly withdrew with their bits of glass to the far end of the room, while he told the Conde about Pilar's death, and how the Condesa was now established at St.-Jean-de-Luz, with her sister. Pascual de Verdura asked rather awkwardly—almost shyly, James felt—about how Raquel had borne the death of the child; and then went on to enquire about her herself. How was she looking? What had she got in the way of clothes? Had the rough life in Madrid spoilt her hands? "She has such beautiful hands," he said meditatively. "Can she afford now to go to the manicurist?" And by such questions, very simply and directly put, he at last forced James to the admission that for the moment he was paying for her. This was one of the numerous points in the conversation that James had been dreading; he feared that the redoubtable Spanish pride would create a scene about the money. But instead, to his mounting surprise, he met a curious resigned acceptance. The Conde used an odd little phrase—"Things are like this, now. It is a new experience." Milcom was beginning indeed to get a very deep impression that the Conde was altogether undergoing some new and very profound experience, something which went far deeper than the mere fact of being imprisoned, night and day, along with ten scallywags, and in circumstances of the greatest discomfort. James was startled, and almost disconcerted, by the first stirrings of a feeling of sympathy for the man, as distinct from the prisoner. When he asked if there was anything the Conde especially wanted, that he might be able to get for him, to his astonishment Pascual asked for an English-Spanish dictionary.

"Yes, I am trying to learn English in here," he said, smiling at James's startled expression—"I have an English book; the gaoler got it for me." And stooping down, he pulled out of his soapbox a rather tattered bound copy of *Jude the Obscure*, and handed it to Milcom in triumph. James examined it—it was a first edition. This did not surprise him—Spain is full of first editions of the English classics. Pascual read him a sentence or two aloud, with a shocking pronunciation, but quite fluently.

"My wife speaks English well," he said, with a certain pride—"but you will know that. Her grandmother was a Stewart—

Scottish; but you will know that too. Does she speak English with you?"

James said that she did.

"I have never learned it yet," the Conde went on—"I should have done, but I missed the opportunity. Well, I have now this opportunity, so I do not miss it. Do you think you can get me a dictionary?"

"Yes—I certainly will; if not here, in Barcelona or Madrid, and I will send it," James promised. If the gaoler was a "radish," he thought, by the application of some sugar he could almost certainly be induced to smuggle the dictionary in, though such works were as strictly forbidden as glass, since they were invaluable for code communications.

At this point a siren wailed suddenly overhead, intolerably loud and near. James, accustomed to raids in Madrid, automatically began to glance round the room to find the most appropriate corner in which to lie flat, but the prisoners did nothing of the sort—they hastened towards the further of the two windows, which was out of the range of vision of anyone looking through the gaoler's peephole in the door, and silently, with a skill evidently born of frequent practice, scrambled up on one another's shoulders, two deep; then two more of the smallest and lightest, among whom was the bus driver from San Sebastián, were hoisted in turns onto the shoulders of the second man, from which position they could see out. They began a running commentary to those below, in hissing whispers.

"No, nothing yet." "Ah, *si*, there they come." "How many?" "Two." "Pepe, you fool, there are three—don't you see the third?" "Yes, *es verdad*—there he is." "What's in the harbour?" "Only two small ones—one is trying to go out." "Ah, but he's onto him!" "No—missed him." And so on. James found himself caught in the infection of their excitement; like the Conde and the rest he stood gaping up at the windows, as if in this way he could the better see through the eyes of the two men looking out, while a series of shattering explosions filled the air. In between them they could hear the high faint drone of the planes. The two observers presently hissed joyfully that a ship had been hit, and was sinking, and that smoke was going up from some buildings near the port. This announcement was greeted with murmurs of "*Arriba España!*" by the others; even the two men at the bottom of the living ladders, who were breathing painfully with the weight on their shoulders, managed to emit strangled grunts of triumph. James could not but admire their spirit, even while he was sickened at their delight, Spaniards as they were, over the destruction of Spanish life and Spanish property. He thought, for the thousandth time, that of all evils that can befall a nation, civil war is the worst and the most disruptive.

At length the explosions ceased, the nasty whining hum of the planes died away, and the observers and their living supports were carefully lowered to the floor again, where they gave more full and graphic details of the raid to their delighted audience. That a ship had been sunk was considered highly satisfactory, but the real interest, Milcom learned, was whether the ship was British-built or not; everyone hoped that it was, not out of any particularly anti-British feeling, but because shattered British-built ships provided more fragments of teak, the ideal wood for whittling into belt buckles, necklaces, and their other artistic products. The chances of persuading their gaoler to go and bring them up some more teak and a fresh supply of broken glass, of which their stock was running low, were eagerly discussed. Milcom at this point tactfully produced the cigarettes which he had brought for the Conde de Verdura, and the half-kilo packets of sugar. The other prisoners looked on with glowing eyes. It was clear that they had now become a roomful of millionaires—the Conde could buy anything he chose from the gaoler. James could not help liking the way in which Pascual de Verdura at once handed out five cigarettes to each man, with the exception of a huge gruff old fellow, one of the weight carriers at the window, who did not smoke. They smoked immediately, beaming.

Time was getting on—the gaoler poked his head in once to hurry Milcom up, was bought off with a lump of sugar, and retired, promising to come back in half an hour. But James too had things to do—people to interview, the town to inspect, visits to pay. The Conde asked in a barely audible murmur if he could possibly write a few lines to his wife? This was a risky proceeding, for both parties, but James took the risk; he produced his reporter's notebook and indicated to the Spaniard that he should write on the back of some used sheets—then, as the Conde retired with his soapbox to a corner to write, James occupied the attention of the other prisoners by asking them how long they had been there, and hearing the details of their various captures. At last the letter was done, and Pascual handed the book back to James unobtrusively.

"When you see her, tell her that I am well," he said. "When shall you see her?"

James, embarrassed, said that he did not know.

"I hope you will see her soon," the Conde said. "You have been so good to her, I am sure that she must like you. And she will be lonely now, without the child. Please try to see her whenever you can." And again with that hint of shyness, he said—"And give her my love, and bid her to take care of herself. Tell her too that I am"—he gave a funny little smile, of a peculiar secret sweetness—"very happy."

James, in spite of himself, was moved by this man. Nothing he had heard previously had prepared him for a person like this. But at this point he suddenly recollected that the Conde might conceivably know something about Juanito and he asked him—"Do you know at all what has become of Juan Torre de Modero, the Condesa's brother? She is in such anxiety about him."

He had the oddest impression, then, that the question was an unwelcome one. Pascual de Verdura seemed to shut up, all at once. He made some formal remark about how charming his brother-in-law was—"but I have no idea what has become of him." The contrast between this chilly and obvious insincerity of manner and his expansiveness of only a few moments before was most marked.

"I am sorry for that," Milcom said very gravely—he was sure that de Verdura was lying. "This silence about him is causing your wife acute distress."

The Conde fiddled his fingers.

"Yes—it is distressing, this lack of news, but alas, it is one of the features of this war," he said, with the same airy falsity as before.

Pepe, the San Sebastián bus driver, looked up from where he sat carving away, cross-legged on his palliasse.

"The little Paquita should know," he said. "Why does not the Señor ask the little Paquita?"

The Conde smiled at Milcom. "Pay no attention to him," he said; "he is——" He touched his forehead significantly. Milcom was not so sure about this—Pepe had shown no special signs of lunacy, apart from his silly monkey's grin; indeed, his account of the raid had been quite as good as the other man's. But before he could do or say anything more the gaoler reappeared, this time with an air of decision, and said that he must now go. The prisoners scrabbled round the man, telling him to come back when he had taken the Señor out—"*Cigarrillos!*" "*Azúcar!*" they said importantly. The gaoler ignored them with a completeness of which only Spaniards are capable. James meanwhile was taking his leave of the Conde, all of whose former sincerity and warmth reappeared at the moment of farewell.

"*Adiós*, my dear friend." He took Milcom's hand in both of his. "Thank you—no, you must believe in my thanks; I cannot find words for what you have done for my wife. *Adiós*." And as James made to go—"Do come back soon, if it is not too far," he said, almost wistfully. "And do not forget the book." He was careful not to use the word "dictionary" in the gaoler's hearing.

The prisoners all insisted on shaking hands with James also, but at last the door clanged to behind him, the gaoler turned the key, and they tramped back along the corridors and down flights of stone stairs. The man chatted a little about the prisoners they had left. As they walked on—"Is it possible for me to see La Paquita?" James asked, as casually as possible. He was drawing a bow at a venture—from Pepe's one remark he was not even sure whether she was in the prison or not. He soon learned. The gaoler started, and glanced nervously round.

"Certainly not. *She* is not allowed any visitors," he said. He looked timidly, sourly, and suspiciously on James, and in spite of the earlier bribe showed a distinct tendency to hustle him out. Clearly she *was* in the prison—and from the gaoler's sudden change of manner, James could make a pretty shrewd guess at what she was in for. There was only one thing which aroused such strong feelings in this war—spying. He walked away thoughtfully, barely giving a glance of the clouds of smoke which still hung over the port after the raid. This business of La Paquita was worth going into. He did not for a moment believe that Pepe was potty—on the contrary, he believed that the man had given him a very useful tip; and the Conde's denial and change of manner only confirmed him in this belief. If he could get hold of La Paquita—whoever she was—he felt convinced that he would learn something about Juan Torre de Modero. But if his guess at what La Paquita's crime consisted in was right, the implication was that Juanito was also mixed up in the spying racket. God, what a piece of news to send to Raquel! For there was only one end to spies in Spain, sooner or later, and not always a short one. James had seen too many dead and dying men, horribly muti-lated and contemptuously labelled, in the outskirts of Madrid to have any illusions about the fate of spies. He thought too, as he walked on, about the roomful of men that he had just left, with their glass and their soapboxes, and their bribable radish of a gaoler. He had seen enough of the reforms in Republican prison administration carried out during the last year by the brilliant young Basque Director-General of Prisons to be surprised to find here, in Almadera, the old sloppy muddle and casualness.

Remote, or a stubborn Governor, he supposed, and wondered if this state of affairs would make his next move easier.

But while he walked back down the hill through the hot clear sunshine towards the centre of the town, on his way to visit the Consul, revolving in his head schemes for getting in touch with La Paquita, something happened which for the time being put her and Juanito and everything else out of his head. In the smaller Republican cities, and even in Barcelona itself, the system of air-raid warnings did not always work very well—incompetence about machinery, vagueness about duty and discipline, fairly frequently caused a hitch in the arrangements. It was so in Almadera that afternoon. Without the smallest warning, the sunny air suddenly contained a faint high drone, almost as faint as a bee's hum—and before James had even clearly recognised it for what it was, there came the long whining moan of a falling projectile. James looked up—he could see the planes, and glanced round for a doorway in which to lie down, head inwards. But he was still in the suburban part of the town, where the villas stood widely spaced—he decided on the next one downhill, and started to run. He was too late. There was that mixture of the moan rising to a crescendo, somehow combined with the roar and the blow, which hit him simultaneously and indistinguishably, knocking him clean out of consciousness.

When he came to he was lying against the railings of a garden across the road, and a good deal further up than where he had been when the bomb fell—his hat, as he presently noticed, had fallen off, and marked the spot where he had stood; the cigarette which he had been smoking lay beside it, the smoke still rising from it in the sunshine. The villa in whose doorway he had intended to shelter was gone—mortar dust was rising like smoke above the heap of rubble on the spot where it had been. James knew vaguely that he ought to do somthing—go and pull people out of the ruins, perhaps. Sitting up, he felt himself rather gingerly all over—he seemed to be sound, except for a wound in his forehead, from which the blood was beginning to trickle down into his right eye. He took out his handkerchief, folded it into a pad, and tied it over the place with his necktie. Then he raised himself cautiously to his feet. H'm—no; he wouldn't be able to help anyone else very much—he could barely walk himself. It must have been a big one, for the blast to knock him so completely silly—and it had been very near. He began to make his way downhill, holding on by the railings; his strength would come back presently—he was familiar with the effects of blast, and the curious paralysis of all the faculties that it often produces. When he came level with the ruined villa he stopped and looked at it, and listened. He could hear no sound. A woman's head and shoulders lay in the white dust of the roadway, with a string of cheap beads still round her neck—one arm and the trunk had gone. James, holding onto the railings, was violently sick. Meanwhile the raid was still going on—the air shook with the booming of explosions, vibrated with that moan and hum; evidently it was a bad one. From where he now stood he could see people, in ones and twos, scurrying across the road, a phenomenon which he recognised—it meant that there must be a shelter somewhere down there. He made for it as fast as he could, damning the blood which in spite of the pad kept running down into his eyes, wiping it off angrily with his right hand, while he held onto the railings with his left. There was the shelter, not one hundred yards ahead—he reached it somehow, a long slope going down into the ground. It was full to overflowing; people were standing elbow to elbow from the point where the roof began. But James, with his blood-smeared face, must have been a ghastly enough spectacle to inspire sympathy; he was drawn a few paces inside, and made to sit down with his back against the wall. Here he was promptly sick again, and then fainted for the second time.

When he came to the raid was over, and all had left the shelter to resume their normal tasks except one old man, who offered to conduct him to a dressing-station in the town to have his head seen to. Thither they went, James leaning on the old man's arm, glad of his support to an extent which astonished him. The dressing-station was in the cellar of a wine merchant's establishment, and was the dirtiest thing of its kind that James had ever seen: the wounded lay on the unscrubbed bricks or propped against dusty barrels; mould-laden greenish cobwebs hung from the vaulted ceiling. However, a young Scottish doctor, assisted by a middle-aged Spanish lady and two girls, one Irish and one French, was doing a very efficient job of work; and when James's turn came the hole in his forehead was promptly plugged with gauze, and bound up with strips of what James recognised as a torn-up bedspread—the same sort of honeycombed material as that quilt he had so hated when he spread it over Raquel in the bedroom of the hotel at Perpignan. The doctor then briefly examined him all over for further injuries, found none, announced that he was suffering from shock and loss of blood, gave him a shot if something in the arm with a hypodermic, and told him to go home and lie down. "Do you live here?" he asked.

"No—I'm here on a trip."

"Sight-seeing?" asked the doctor grimly.

"Journalist," said James.

"Ah—well, I suppose you can't help yourself. What paper?"

"*Epoch*."

To James's amusement, at that mighty name the grimness of the young doctor's expression relaxed a little

"Ah—well, tell them all about it," he said washing his hands in a tin basin held for him by the young French girl. "You do, though, I know."

"Tell me," said James, an idea striking him, "who looks after the sick in the gaol, if there are any—do you?"

"No—a Spanish doctor. Quite good, too. Why, do you know someone up there?"

"Yes—I was there this morning. Do you know anything of a girl called Paquita?"

"I know a lot about her," the doctor replied, his grimness returning, while he began to dry his hands on a rough towel. "She was a spy, and one of the really good ones. It was a very smart piece of work catching her. They've got some sort of relation of hers in there, too—a Count something or other."

James was startled. "Not the Conde de Verdura?"

"Yes, that is the name," put in the French girl, who had emptied the basin into a bucket and was now standing waiting for the towel.

"But he's not a spy, surely?" James asked.

"Not that I know of—but the girl's a cousin or something," the doctor said, carelessly. "Why, do you know her?"

"No, but I rather want to see her," James said.

"Only the Military Governor could give you permission for that," said the doctor, going over as he spoke to a rough table, over which hung an unshielded electric light, and beginning to examine a man who was laid on it. "And don't go visiting any Governors to-day or to-morrow—go home and lie quiet. You've had a fair bump. Come back and see me in two days' time."

James followed him over to the table.

"One more question—forgive me," he said.

"Yes?" said the doctor without looking up, his hands busy.

"Juan Torre de Modero—you haven't heard anything of him down here?"

The doctor straightened up and stared at James through his glasses.

"Upon me soul, for the *Epoch* correspondent in Republican

Spain, you are in with the Whites!" he said. "What on earth do you want with Torre de Modero?"

"Only to find out where he is, for a refugee relation who worships him," said James—he was stung by the Scotchman's tone, and shock had taken away some of his self-control.

"No—I have no news of him whatever. I'd tell you if I had," the doctor said, less abruptly. "By all accounts, he's a good man. Pity he's on the wrong side. Now, get you home."

James went. He found himself wishing that he could take a cab, but cabs are at no time abundant in Almadera, except in the Plaza and down by the docks, and they had all been requisitioned by the army long since. So he set off on foot. His head was painful, and involuntarily he put up his hand to it, and met the unwonted roughness of the improvised bandage—this reminded him of the quilt for Raquel, and he decided to go back that way and take a second look at it. The streets were already full of people, going about their business again as usual: breakdown gangs were at work on the ruined and damaged houses, lorries were carting away rubble, and between them country carts were bringing in supplies, or hawking them from door to door; housewives trotted to and fro on errands, or swept up broken glass from their doorsteps with the most normal air in the world. God, they were a tough people, the Spaniards, James reflected.

But when he got to the antiquary's shop, it was gone. Just disappeared, like the villa up in the suburbs, outside which he had been blown down; crumpled up into a heap of rubble. The breakdown gang was already at work, setting such bits of the stock as were not smashed aside on the pavement—a woman with greying hair stood by, wringing her hands and weeping silently. James paused to look on for a moment—somehow this sudden ruin affected him much more than that of the house in which he had never stood. While he watched, two of the salvage men came out from under the ruins of a half-crushed doorway carrying a body between them, and set it down by the woman—she knelt beside it, drawing her shawl over her mouth, while her tears rained down on the dusty face. It was the shopkeeper, quite dead; his right arm had been broken, and lay bent in a horrible angle at his side—but the fingers were still passed through the string of a parcel done up in paper. A painful curiosity drew James across the street to the woman's side. Yes—the paper was torn at one end, and within was the rich green gleam of watered silk, like the green of water under rocks on a thundery day. Poor wretch—how badly he had wanted that sugar! James did nothing, except to push a few notes into the woman's shabby little bag, which lay on the ground at her side. Probably she too would have been glad of the sugar, but his head ached intolerably, he felt sick and giddy, and he had a sudden revulsion from the whole thing. Since seeing the Conde, he somehow felt less sure of his right to give Raquel bedspreads—and anyhow he could not give her one taken from the hand of a corpse. With difficulty, he struggled on towards his hotel, wondering it if too would be a heap of ruins.

It wasn't, strangely enough, since it was not far from the harbour; it was still standing, its shabby and rather ugly self. But just before he reached it he had one more encounter, the last of that peculiar and exhausting day. Out of a side street leading down to the docks a man emerged, heavily burdened with some uncouth load, a man whose face was vaguely familiar to James. He looked again to see who it was, wondering to meet a familiar face in Almadera, and recognised the gaoler. A huge bundle of damp teak under one arm, slivers of broken glass wrapped in rag in his other hand, he was hastening towards the prison. Exhausted as he was, the sight brought a sour grin to Milcom's face. Evidently the Conde had used some of his sugar to good purpose. He turned into his hotel and went to bed.

## CHAPTER SIX

### *This Side—St.-Jean-de-Luz*

On a fine morning early in November, about a month after that day when Mr. Crumpaun had first driven her over to the Bridge at Irún, Rosemary Oldhead went down to the flower-market early, to get some blooms wherewith to fill those big pale-grey earthen-ware jars which she and her mother had bought together, standing among piles of rope and sacks of dried peas, in various small shops round the market square—shops with a clean, sour, malty smell which they both liked. It had become a habit with Rosemary to slip into the flower-market two or three mornings a week, to potter round, choose what was cheapest, and dart back to the hotel with it before her Spanish lesson at ten—it was part of the easy pleasant routine into which the Oldhead family had by now slipped, of Spanish lessons in the mornings for Rosemary, while Mrs. Oldhead did minor shoppings, washed her own and Rosemary's jumpers and Mr. Oldhead's socks, and generally

speaking kept her family mended and tidy, and of walks or an
expedition in the afternoons. They felt quite at home now in
St.-Jean-de-Luz—at the English Church, and in one way and
another they had got to know quite a number of the very considerable English population, who for reasons of health, finance,
or education were settled in villas in and around the town, and
mixed to some extent with the friendlier French residents—mostly
people who came regularly to spend the winter in that soft and
gentle climate. There were modest tea-parties and cocktail
parties, little lunches in this hotel or in that. Mrs. Oldhead,
running out to buy jam or Lux, found people to nod to now in
the street, which always produces such a domesticated feeling;
Mr. Oldhead could exchange views with acquaintances at the
Bank and the lending library. Rosemary and her mother had
theories now as to which were the most reliable of the various
cleaners and *stoppages*, and which the cheapest shops for hairpins
and toilet soap.

Rosemary, darting out of the hotel door at 8.30 a.m., ran
across as usual to the railings to look for a moment at the sea.
The beach stretched away on each side of her in a long pale curve
of sand; the dogs of the town were out on it, also as usual, taking
their morning constitutional together—running along the water's
edge, examining bits of wood and other flotsam, and fighting
amicably for any especially interesting piece; one large white
sheepdog creature was digging at a huge hole in the sand, and
presently the rest joined him and began barking and scuffling as
to which should get into it—a sort of game of King-of-the-Castle
upside down. They did this every morning, and it always made
Rosemary laugh to see them; she called the absurd assemblage
"the Dogs' Club." She laughed now, standing there with the
wind whipping her cheeks to a fresh colour; then turned and
headed for the market. By now she knew pretty well every
street, alley, *place* and turning in the cramped confusing little
town, where you come suddenly on squares, complete with close-
clipped plane trees, no larger than a small drawing-room; and
where almost all the houses still preserve their Basque characters
of deep projecting eaves and chocolate-coloured shutters. She
scurried down the Rue Garat, crossed the Rue Gambetta, and
zigzagged through passages too narrow for a cart to pass and
along quiet lanes flanked by high walls, whose overhanging trees
charm the passer-by with the thought of the gardens within. In
one of these she came on the *bouvier*, the town scavenger, standing
outside a back door emptying garbage-buckets into the long cart,

drawn by two oxen, from which he derived his name; he knew her by sight, smiled and wished her good-day.

Arrived at the market, Rosemary proceeded as usual to a careful inspection of all the flower stalls; she always did this, noting the prices and the freshness of the flowers; she never bought in a hurry. The more expensive stalls were in the big glass-roofed building, and she examined these first, though she seldom bought at them; she liked the clean country smell in the market-hall, the green and whitish piles of vegetables, the baskets of eggs and neat stacks of butter and cheese, and then the blaze of colour and sudden perfume of the high banks of flowers on the wooden stands. Oh dear, they were getting expensive; carnations seventy-five centimes each! But marigolds were still there in masses, and cheap—orange and pale lemon yellow; and there were huge sheaves of cosmias, shaded from deep carmine to almost white, at a franc the *botte*; and red, yellow, bronze and white chrysanthemums, in *bottes* and in pots. She went out, and pottered among the outside stalls; here she found those little brick-red carnations, carelessly grown, all bushy and full of buds—they were quite cheap. She bought some of these to smell nice in a small vase, and masses of marigolds and cosmias to go in the larger ones. Fumbling in her purse for her money, the flowers tucked into the crook of both elbows, she heard herself addressed in English— "Good morning, Miss Oldhead."

She looked up from her purse and saw the Condesa.

"Oh, good morning. I can't shake hands!" she said, smiling.

The Condesa smiled back at the young girl, standing there in the sunshine, her arms full of flowers; she herself had a few of the big carnations which Rosemary had thought too expensive in her hand.

"Do you often come here?" she asked, when Rosemary had finished paying, as they moved away.

"Yes—I like the market," said Rosemary.

"So do I—I like the people; they are so simple, and busy, and yet have time to laugh and make jokes," said the Condesa, a little wistfully. "And I like flowers—I see you do, too."

"I adore them," said Rosemary. "I waste *hours* here, just looking at them."

"Which way do you go back?" the Condesa asked, as they waited for the Biarritz bus to pass before crossing the broad street.

"A different way each time! I love pottering in these funny little places," said Rosemary. "I thought of going round by the port this morning, it's so nice."

The Condesa, who seemed to have nothing much to do, came

with her; they crossed the Place, and went over to the water-side. The port was almost empty—the sardine boats were out, and they looked clear across the sparkling green water to the line of houses along the waterfront of Ciboure just opposite, with Ravel's house, grey and imposing, among them. Across the Place, the little tables, only one row now, were set out in front of Gaston's; a waiter in a green baize apron was sweeping out the restaurant; the dust puffed up into the sunlight. Raquel de Verdura's thoughts went back to the night when she had dined there with James, and on an impulse she said—"That is such an excellent little restaurant"—indicating the waiter and his broom.

"Gaston's? Yes—I've never been there, but they say the food is lovely," Rosemary answered. "Daddy and Mummie aren't very keen on restaurants. Do you often go?"

"I was there once with Mr. Meelcomm."

"Oh yes—I wonder how he is. He was so nice," Rosemary said. The Condesa warmed to her.

"He got hurt in an air-raid in Almadera—he very kindly went there to see my husband, to bring him news of us—of me," she corrected herself, "and he wrote to me."

"Oh dear," Rosemary said. "I'm sorry. Was he badly hurt?"

"His head was hit. He was ill there for some days—then he went back to Barcelona; he wrote from there."

"I'm sorry," Rosemary said again. She wanted to ask about the Conde, but was shy of doing so—like every one else in St.-Jean de-Luz, she knew that he was in prison at Almadera. "Did Mr. Milcom send you good news—apart from being ill?" she asked at last.

"Oh yes—he saw my husband, and he was well, quite well."

"Oh, I *am* glad of that," said Rosemary warmly.

"Yes—he was well. And do you know," the Condesa went on, expanding under Rosemary's friendly interest, "he sent me a message that he was very happy, also. Is that not odd?—happy in prison! And Mr. Meelcomm wrote that he believed it true—he seemed so content, he said."

"Is he comfortable? Are they well treated?" Rosemary asked, deeply interested.

"Treated not badly, I think. But comfortable—oh no! He is in a room with a lot of very odd men, and straw to sleep on, and no chairs! Poor Pascual, who always liked so much comfort."

"It is wonderful of him not to mind," said Rosemary, remembering some of the things that even she had heard about the Conde's manner of life in the past.

"Is it not? Formerly, everything had to be just as he wished. —his clothes laid out so, his shaving-water at such a temperature! His food—so much exactitude! But it is for Spain," said the Condesa piously.

Rosemary was sufficiently acquainted with her Father's views to have at least a doubt as to whether the White revolution and the Conde's consequent sufferings really were wholly to Spain's advantage; and as they strolled along past the House of the Infanta, where the bride of Louis XIV stayed before her marriage, standing up high, pale, elegant and formal among the genial countrified little Basque buildings, she turned the conversation by asking the Condesa if she had news of any of her other relations in Spain. This brought out the Condesa's anxieties about Juanito. She had asked "Meelcomm" to find out, and there was nothing. "He is so clever, Meelcomm—he can do anything and learn anything. And yet there is no news at all. And in Burgos and Salamanca, also no news! No one knows. It is as if he had vanished. Because when people are dead, in time one hears it," said the Condesa simply. And because her heart was full, and it is often easier to speak one's secret thoughts to an acquaintance than to one's own people, and because this little English girl was so sympathetic and friendly and safe, as they walked back to the Hotel along the Rue Gambetta, past the great church where Louis XIV and his Spanish bride were married, she spoke of her brother, his goodness and his intelligence and his force of character, his daring and his charm, all the things that had made him the delight of those who loved him, and the hope of a whole party in Spain. Rosemary, like Milcom, asked what he was like, and got much the same answer: that he was like the Condesa, only dark, and had the same walk—"his eyes too, are grey; is that not odd, when he is black?" The girl carried away a very vivid impression of the noble splendid creature, a sort of Spanish Sir Philip Sidney, when at last they parted in the hotel, and she went to put her flowers in water before darting away to her Spanish lesson. To her delight, the Condesa invited her to coffee at the Bar Basque at twelve. It had been fascinating, having her all to oneself like that. She was charming, even with that funny remoteness of hers, as if she was talking to you from a mile away—and this morning she had not been remote, when she spoke of her brother; she had been warm and living and near. It would be wonderful if one could really make friends with her; perhaps at coffee she would go on talking about Juanito. He must be a wonderful person.

But when, punctually at twelve o'clock, Rosemary turned up

at the Bar Basque, there was no sign of the Condesa—neither inside, among the brown leather chairs and sofas, nor outside at the orange-coloured little tables. Crumpaun was sitting there in the sun—he hailed Rosemary: "Looking for someone, the Sweetheart?"

"The Condesa, Mr. Crumpet," said Rosemary, coming over and sitting down by him. She and Mr. Crumpaun had made great friends—Hever and Crossman and Carrow had all become familiars by now, but Crumpaun was really a confidant—she was fearless and easy with him. It was to "Mr. Crumpet" that she intended, one of these days, to tell that odd story about the photographs, and Daddy's old Parrot. For some reason she had never done so yet; she had waited to see if anything more would happen, whether something else would turn up. Rosemary was a great one for hoarding up bits of information, arranging them in her mind and puzzling away at them—and if you mentioned them to people, so often something was done or said that made it impossible to find out anything more. She had already learned at school, observant little magpie that she was, to go about with her eyes open and her mouth shut—and when a major scandal (on the school scale) exploded at the end of term, she hugged herself silently to think how much of it she had either known or guessed by the middle. So she had kept silence, and hoped to keep an eye on the Parrot. But the Parrot seemed to have gone to ground lately—she had only seen him once, at the Bar Basque, since that windy evening at Jacques'.

"Ah—pretty creature. But all Spanishes are unpunctual," said Mr. Crumpaun. "You better have one with me while you wait. What's to-day's?"

"The usual, Mr. Crumpet," said Rosemary, smiling at him saucily—it was always a source of remonstrance on his part that she would only drink orangeade.

"You're an addict!" said Crumpaun, and shouted for Ladislas.

"Well, what are you going to see this week?" he asked her, when she sat sipping the yellow drink. Mrs. Oldhead's conscientious passion for sight-seeing had become a joke between Rosemary and Crumpaun.

"The Grotte de Sare, I *think*," said Rosemary, with a small giggle. "It isn't very educational, but Pierre Loti had tea there, or something."

"Oh—and what do you know about Pierre Loti?" Crumpaun enquired.

"He was a French writer who wrote a book called *Pêcheur d'Islande*, which all schoolgirls read, and a book about Basquery which nobody reads, called 'Gigolo' or something," said Rosemary carelessly. "And he wrote one about Japan and one about Turkey, which I've forgotten the names of, but I know we weren't supposed to read then at school. Not that I want to—he's so fearfully old-fashioned. I like my dirt modern, if at all. Hullo, there she is!" she exclaimed, springing up, as a car drew up at the pavement behind the bay-trees.

But though the Condesa got out of it, Rosemary was destined to disappointment in the matter of a further talk with her. The Condesa was dreadfully sorry, but she had unexpectedly to go into Biarritz; she was on her way there now. "For business," she said. She was charmingly contrite and distressed, and said they must meet next day; but she was obviously in a hurry, and sprang back into the car, where the Duquesa also sat, and drove rapidly off. Rosemary, crestfallen, returned to Mr. Crumpaun and her orangeade.

"Let you down?" said that gentleman.

"She said she had to go into Biarritz on business," said Rosemary.

"Ah—see a woman about a hat, I expect."

"I don't think that, quite—I was wondering what she was going for," said Rosemary thoughtfully. "I don't think she's the sort to let people down for nothing."

"If it's business, it's probably funny-business," said Mr. Crumpaun darkly.

"What do you mean?"

"Oh, buy a black peseta with ten centimes and a hairpin," said Mr. Crumpaun easily. Rosemary laughed in spite of herself.

Crossman slouched up and joined them.

"Was that the Duquesa I saw buzzing off?" he asked, holding up a thumb to Ladislas to indicate his usual drink, rye-whiskey and ginger-beer. "Wonder where she's going?"

"Biarritz," said Crumpaun.

"Ah—there you are. Wish I knew who's running that show," said Crossman, lighting a cigarette.

The words "What show?" were on the tip of Rosemary's tongue, but she bit them back, and took a pull at her orangeade through a straw, with an air of great detachment. You heard much more by keeping quiet.

"Any news?" Crumpaun asked.

"I think there's no doubt about the new offensive coming off pretty soon—but I don't know where, or when."

"Ask Ladislas," Crumpaun suggested.

Crossman ignored this sally. "Carrow has a story about getting hold of a dirty little tyke who was tight last night in a dive in Biarritz," he pursued, "and let out that he was in the pay of the boss there. Full of money, he was. And he talked about 'the lady.' I don't think there's much doubt but that she's in it, and that Biarritz is the place."

"None at all, I should say," said Crumpaun, losing a little of his genial air of laziness. "Biarritz is the obvious place. It's in neutral territory, anyone there can pick up the threads from both halves of Spain *and* the outside world, and it's handy for frontier-hopping." He took a pull at his drink. "And there's all this story that Hever's so full of, about Number 17."

"Think there's anything in that?" Crossman asked.

"He swears it's copper-bottomed, though he won't give his source, naturally. Just says there *is* a White Agent in Red Spain, who gets his stuff out somehow, and he declares he knows his number. It looks like it; there was that leak about the counter-offensive last month."

"I wonder how they get their information across—most of the frontier's pretty tightly *bouchée*," Crossman said, "though of course there's wine-smuggling going on all the time."

"Yes, but that sort of thing *must* come verbally, as a rule," Crumpaun objected—"and peasants would be too stupid to carry much in their thick heads—especially Aragonese." He too lit a cigarette. "It isn't so easy. And it isn't going to get any easier. The French aren't so keen on having their territory used as a stamping-ground for spies. I hear the Perpignan authorities closed one passage last week."

"Yes, I heard that. And I'm told the lovely Olivia isn't going to find it so simple in future to get her permits to pop in and out across the Bridge at Irún," said Crossman, smiling rather sourly. "The Bayonne authorities are getting rather fed up with her—and indeed with the whole refugee racket. How *can* you control spying when an entire district is flooded with strangers, and murky-looking types at that?"

Crumpaun laughed. The two men had forgotten Rosemary by now, as she had hoped they would, and talked on rather technically about whether and how much they could "use" any of the information, or hypotheses, which they were discussing.

"Hullo, here's Hever," Crossman said presently. "Morning, Tom."

Hooter's representative, followed by the hovering Ladislas, came and sat down by them. Crumpaun ordered fresh drinks all round.

"And make it snappy," Hever said menacingly to the waiter—

"Telephoning in this country makes me thirsty." Ladislas grinned and hastened away, with his titupping waiter's step.

"You had something to telephone about? You're lucky," said Crumpaun, his geniality returning.

"Yes—and as I've got it safely off, I don't mind telling you, you slothful old seal," said Hever, giving him an affectionate prod in the ribs.

"Well, what is it?" Crossman said, with nervous impatience.

"Wait till I've got my drink—I'm rather sick of screaming news," said Hever coolly. He was obviously in tremendous spirits. But when Ladislas had brought the drinks, and been shooed away again by Hever—"None of your eavesdropping, you shady pot-washer!"—he leaned over towards Crumpaun.

"Three Bolo planes were burnt out on the ground the night before last near Bourg Madame, about four hours before they were due to start on to Barcelona. And, the same thing happened to two others the week before, in another place; only those were French. Quite close to the border each time, and each time just before the final hop."

"Sabotage," said Crumpaun.

"Yes—and *informed* sabotage," Hever rejoined. "Somebody knows precisely when the stuff arrives and *where* the stuff arrives, each time."

"How did they come, packed or flown?" Crumpaun asked.

"Flown. And that's one of the things the French manage to keep pretty quiet, that I *do* know," Hever said. "We all know that the French and Russians have been sending in nearly as much stuff as the Boches and the Itis, only they don't send in technicians as well, and the Reds are too miserably incompetent to fly it, or shoot it off, or assemble it even, as the case may be." He drank again. "No," he went on, "the information must come, in my opinion, from the other side, when they're expected. There have been a lot of accidents lately to material destined for Barcelona, and always near the frontier, and always at the last minute."

"You mean that someone—your Number 17, or whoever it is —gets the information, and sends the *saboteurs* across to cope?" Crossman asked, much interested.

"No, I don't. I think the *saboteurs* are out here in France, sticking around with suitcases full of dynamite in the back of their Peugeots, and when they get the word to go they buzz off and do their stuff. And I think they get that word from this side, too. You can't telephone across the frontier, you see; but you can telephone from anywhere in France to anywhere in France."

4

"In fact, our old friend the Hidden Hand in Biarritz runs the sabotage as well as the rest—that the idea?" Crumpaun enquired.

"Got it in one!"

Crumpaun turned this over in silence for a moment or two.

"Wonder where the devil they get across," he then said, thoughtfully.

"A smart man *might* get across anywhere. But my own idea is that someone very smart indeed comes right out each time, with the news in a false tooth, and gets it to the organisation here at Biarritz. And for that reason, I fancy he crosses towards this end."

"Why?" Crossman asked.

"Because it's obviously much easier to 'circulate' in Spain than in France," Hever said, banging his glass on the table as a signal to Ladislas. "The line between Red and White Spain is pretty vague and fluid, and they're all Spaniards anyhow—it would be far simpler to get the information across from South to North *inside* Spain."

"And then let the frontier-hopper hop, straight to Biarritz—yes, I get the idea," Crumpaun said.

"Exactly. And the instructions go out by telephone, and the thugs start up the Peugeots," said Hever, with his wide Cambridge grin.

"All this is hypothesis, though," Crossman objected—"I don't see how you can use it."

"Four-fifths of all your stuff is hypothesis anyway, with an occasional fact, like the currant in a school bun," said Hever cheerfully. "I've got my currant, and the rest is intelligent anticipation. Anyhow one can never do more with spies and *saboteurs* than deduce them from their results—they don't go about in a special-coloured shirt, like a bloody S.S. man, singing their own theme-tune. Don't be foolish, Crossey."

The others laughed. Poor Rosemary glanced at her watch, conscientiously. Oh *damn*—ten past one already. Really Daddy was a menace! Fancy having to leave *now*. To avoid any temptation to linger, she sprang up out of her chair with her usual suddenness.

"Mr. Crumpet dear, I must fly. Thank you for my wholesome beverage."

"Hey, nonsense—what's the time?" Crumpaun said, tugging away at the gold and platinum chain of the slim watch which in spite of its slimness, would not readily leave his pocket while he was sitting down.

"High time I was gone!" said Rosemary, blowing him a kiss, and fled.

She was very quiet at lunch, and Ethel Oldhead, always afraid that the child would be bored alone with her parents, suggested that they should go to the cinema that evening. "I see there's a new film on to-day," she said, indicating the poster stuck on the railings of the old Casino, just opposite the window—"The Goldwyn Follies. But I don't know what it's like."

"Oh, there's that dancer in it—she's lovely, only she's gone all plastic since she went to Hollywood, and she's forgetting how to dance," said Rosemary, producing her usual wealth of inside knowledge about all cinema productions. "But there's the blue-and-white ballet, which is lovely. Yes, let's go after dinner—or to-morrow."

"I thought we might have gone to the early house," said Mrs. Oldhead, who had none of her little parties that afternoon, and was at a loose end.

"No, Mummie—not early."

"Why not?" asked Mr. Oldhead.

"I think I ought to work—and I hate doing it at night," said Rosemary, wishing that parents weren't so tactless, and didn't force one into the sort of fibs that would shut them up. Her silence was not in the least due to boredom, but to intense thought. She had practically decided already, as a result of the journalists' conversation that morning, that the time had come to tell Mr. Crumpaun about the photos and the Old Parrot; but there were one or two things that she had to think out first, and she had got to work up some plan by which she could get the Crumpet to herself. She would anyhow want the afternoon and early evening free for that, if she finally decided to do it. But one couldn't think properly in that boiling-hot dining-room, with the Archdeacon gnashing his false teeth, and the Spaniard whom she and her mother called The Executioner smiling his sadistic smile at the fat head-waiter and talking about the food, and the exhausted-looking underwaiter trundling the *hors d'œuvres* trolley about and bumping the back of one's chair, and above all with the Non-Interveners yelling heartily at one another at their huge table in the middle of the room. She fidgeted restlessly through the end of the meal, and the moment her parents rose, refusing coffee in the hot and stuffy lounge, she hurried away to her own room.

Here it was cool enough—the management of the Grande Bretagne economised on bedroom *chauffage* in the day-time, and the French windows giving onto the narrow balcony stood wide open; the sea wind blew in, fluttering one of her jumpers and some stockings which her mother had washed for her, which hung from two chairs just inside the window. She pushed them impatiently aside, shoved the one arm-chair, a high-backed Victorian affair, padded within a carved mahogany frame, up into the window, and sat looking out. She saw, without seeing, the delicate steel-blue tracery of the tiny slates, so cunningly arranged on the small hexagonal dome of the old Casino just across the street, its graceful bulk cutting into the further view of the sea and the villa-strewn shores of the bay out towards the little pharos. When she remembered her decision afterwards, she remembered these things, which her eyes had etched on her brain while she thought —at the time she was unaware of them.

The only thing was the Condesa. She would not for the world do anything which would hurt the Condesa. And if the Duquesa was in the racket, as they all seemed to think, was it not possible that the Condesa was in it too? No one had suggested it, and it didn't seem like her; but it was possible that she might be in some way involved. But even if she were, would the fact that Mr. Crumpet knew about the photo business do her any particular harm? Even if it led his suspicions, as it had led hers, Rosemary's, to the Parrot? The French couldn't do much even to proved spies, she supposed, since they weren't spying against France—and she was sure the Condesa *wasn't* a spy. They might try to put a stop to it, she imagined, if they really found anything out—but would they? All she proposed to do at present was to tell the Crumpet what she had seen, and to see if he agreed with her conclusions. And anyhow, she didn't care how many spokes were put in the Duquesa's wheel, the stout busybody! (Rosemary had taken a hearty dislike to the Duquesa.) Yes, she *would* tell him. Then when, and where?

Since they were staying in the same hotel, this might seem an easy matter to arrange; but in fact it is not so easy to manage a tête-à-tête in a hotel with only two sitting-rooms, one of which is commanded by the front door—nor is it perfectly easy for young ladies of under seventeen, staying with two watchful parents abroad, to make assignations unobserved, even with someone of Mr. Crumpaun's highly respectable age. In the Hôtel Grande Bretagne there was the further difficulty of getting a message conveyed to anyone. The servants were all Basques, and their knowledge of the French language correspondingly limited. They put up a façade of "Bonjour Madame"s and phrases connected with "*petits déjeuners*" and baths; but it was a fake façade, behind which lay an almost total incapacity to understand, remember or reproduce anything said to them in French, let alone a foreign name.

Jean-Louis, the lanky *valet-de-chambre* on Rosemary's floor was worse than any of them in this respect. (It need hardly be said that the Grande Bretagne had not yet risen to room telephones.) The only person who could be relied on to give or take a message was Rex, the concierge—and Rex always had two hours off in the afternoon. .

But fortune was on Rosemary's side to-day. Flying downstairs to try and catch Rex before he went off duty, in the glass-walled outer lobby she caught sight, through the front door, of Mr. Crumpaun's broad grey back disappearing into the Rue Garat. Out she darted after him. "Mr. Crumpet! Mr. Crumpet!"

"Now what do *you* want, the Sweetheart? You'll catch cold, rushing out without a coat like that," Crumpaun said.

"Crumpet dear, I want to talk to you some time," the girl panted. "Oh, not now"—as she saw him beginning to tug at his watch-chain. "Go and get you *hora español* lunch! But will you come for a tiny tiny walk later on?"

"Where to? I'm not a great walker, you know," said Crumpaun warily.

"Could you totter as far as the end of the Front, do you think?" she asked, tilting her chin at him. "There are lots of nice seats!"

"Now I wonder *what* you're up to, you little baggage," the journalist said, looking at her attentively.

"Got a tiny tiny *scoop* for you!" she said, making her hands into a trumpet, and hissing the words into his ear.

"More likely making a fool of me! O.K.—what time?"

"Quarter to five—if you'll have slept it off by then?" she said impertinently.

He made a gesture as if to box her ear, but she danced out of reach.

"Yes?"

"Yes."

On which she ran back into the hotel, and he lumbered off to the Grill Basque, to eat fresh sardines, fried in batter, with Tom Hever.

Rosemary had fixed the hour of a quarter to five because with any luck her parents would then either be out walking, or having tea. Luck was still on her side, and she and Mr. Crumpaun got out of the hotel and clear away along the front without any hindrance. At the far end, sitting on a seat under some tamarisks, Crumpaun turned to her and said "Now what *is* all this?"

"Mr. Crumpet dear, probably nothing. I expect you'll think

it too trivial, only I thought I'd tell you. Do you remember those photographs that Carrow showed us one morning at the Bar Basque, ages ago, that he bought at the photographer's?"

"And wanted to pass off as illustrations of the frontier? Yes, I remember it happening. Good pictures, too," said Crumpaun. "What about them?"

"They were Daddy's pictures."

"What do you mean?"

"Just that. They were some Daddy took up on La Rhune, two days before. That lousy Durand at the Lune told me they weren't ready, that very morning—and when I got to the Bar Basque, there was that unutterable Carrow with a whole set!"

"Didn't you recognise them?"

"Yes, of course I recognised them. But, Mr. Crumpet, the point is——"

"Hold on," Crumpaun said. "Do you mean to say you knew they were your father's photographs all the time, and never said a word?"

"Yes. I—well, I thought I'd wait and see. You see, it seemed a bit funny, to me."

"Funny enough. You're a cool customer, though," Crumpaun observed, looking at her with a sort of amused respect. "Well, go on."

"Well, did you ever meet Daddy's Old Parrot?"

"Daddy's *what*?"

Rosemary giggled.

"No, I daresay you didn't. Well, there was an old Spaniard that Daddy met up at the Phare one day, when he was photo-graphing, who looked like a parrot—'ence the word 'orse-'air,'" pursued Rosemary obliquely. "And they got talking, and Daddy happened to mention that he was going up La Rhune, and this old beano told him that if he went down in a particular direction, he'd find some lovely rocks and things to photograph—and we went, and he did. And those were the pictures."

"Go on," Crumpaun said choosing a cigar. "I don't see light yet, but I daresay I shall."

"P'raps it's nothing. Anyhow I'll tell you. Well, Daddy'd told us about the Parrot, and one day—*before* that day that Carrow had the photos—he pointed him out to me at the Café de Paris, so I knew him by sight. And later that same day, I went to Jacques —you known, the dope-den coiffeur—with the Jones; just to talk to her. And while I was there, the Duquesa came out."

"That needn't mean anything—I should think coiffeurs with

dope-dens were right up her street," Crumpaun said judge-matically.

"I know—it may have been just chance. But she went out without paying. Anyhow, a little while after that I went over to get a book for the Jones, where I could see up the stairs, and there half-way up was the Parrot talking to old Jacques, and I heard what they said. Old Jacques had some photographs in his hand, and the Parrot said—'Then you'll get me four copies of each, in this size'—and he tapped them. In French, of course."

"But you couldn't see them?" Crumpaun asked.

"No, Crumpet, no—of course not—not then. But—I don't even know if the *affaire* Carrow had made me suspicious or some-thing, but anyhow I stayed at that end of the shop, and the Parrot came down and went out—without paying anything either, come to think of it! And old Jacques went to open the door for him, and put down the photos on the table, by me—and when he opened the door, the wind puffed in and blew them all over the floor. So I picked them up, naturally—and there they were, Daddy's photos again!"

"Holy Moses! You don't say so!" Crumpaun was really startled this time. "Are you sure of that?" he asked, turning to stare at her from under his bushy grey brows.

"But of course! I had them in my hand and looked at them. There were the rocks, and the little col, and the trees in the two glens going down——"

"Hold on," Crumpaun interrupted her—"Where exactly is this place? Could you find it again?"

"Of course," Rosemary repeated. "You go up La Rhune, and then you go down, sort of away from the Bidassoa—oh well, I can't explain, but I could go there."

"And you say the place was a col, with valleys going down on two sides? Could it have been part of the frontier?"

"Well that's what we *thought* it was, when we were there. And after this business at Jacques', it struck me as a bit funny that the Old Parrot should have put Daddy up to going there, and then be buying up his pictures, unless he had some rather good reason for wanting to make it easy for someone else to identify that par-ticular place. But if it was somewhere for someone to cross, who didn't know the place, the photos would be quite useful."

"Useful! I'll say they would! Here, what did your Father say to all this?"

"Oh, Daddy doesn't know," said Rosemary blithely. "I didn't tell him."

"Who did you tell then?"

"No one—no one till you now, Mr. Crumpet."

Crumpaun fairly gaped at her.

"Do you tell me you've kept all this under your hat for the better part of a month?" And suddenly he broke into a great roar of laughter. "You little card!" he cried, slapping his knee and shouting with mirth—"you doggoned little card!"

"Hush up, Mr. Crumpet—people are staring at you," Rosemary said repressively. (They were, indeed.) "I didn't see that there was any need to tell Daddy," she went on, a little defensively —"I thought I'd wait and see if anything else funny happened. But nothing did. And then this morning, when Hever and Crossman and you were all talking, it struck me that this might be one of the places where they come over, Number 17 or whoever it is."

"It may be *the* place," Crumpaun said, serious again now. "Look here, Sweetheart, I want to see these photographs. Think I can get a set, like all these other guys?"

"You could see Daddy's, anyhow—they're all in his album."

"Oke. Now tell me something else. Who is this bird you call the Parrot?"

"That's just what I *don't* know. It's just like Daddy's sort of pottiness that he never asked, or found out, or anything."

"Would you know him again?"

"Oh, of course."

"And where do you say you saw him? Besides Jacques'?"

"At the Café de Paris. But *ages* ago. In fact he hasn't seemed to be about for ages," said Rosemary, rather gloomily.

"Ar-rum. Well, it's no good asking about him at Jacques', obviously. But we might try George at the Paris—he's pretty smart," said Crumpaun hopefully. "Come along, Sweetheart— we might as well breeze in there on the way home. I could do with a drink after all this—and you can get your nauseous fluid there, I don't doubt."

But George, the urbane and skilful barman at the Café de Paris, disclaimed all knowledge of an elderly Spaniard of distinguished appearance, who resembled a grey parrot. He pointed out, as Mr. Oldhead had done before him, that many elderly Spanish men "ressemblent plutôt à des perroquets gris." And that was that. "Oh well, we'll find him somehow," Crumpaun said, as they walked through the echoing Casino arcades towards the hotel.

"Mr. Crumpet, do you think this is—well, at all important?" Rosemary asked, with a note almost of anxiety in her voice.

"It might be—very important. Or not. Can't tell yet," Crumpaun answered.

"Do we have to tell Daddy? I'd rather not. I'd rather keep it to ourselves, for a bit anyhow," the girl said.

"You *would*!" he laughed at her. "All right, Sweetheart. We'll keep it to ourselves for the present," he promised, wondering why she wished just that. "But you get me those pictures, there's a good girl—as soon as you can."

Later that evening—"Daddy, can I have your photo-book?" Rosemary asked her parent.

"What for?"

"To show Mr. Crumpet."

"All right—but take care of it."

Rosemary bore away the book to show to Crumpaun in the lounge—it was dressing-time, and there was hardly anyone about. Crumpaun examined the photos carefully, along with a large-scale map which he had brought, asking Rosemary question all the time. "It took you an hour to go down, you say, and over an hour and a half to go up? Ar-rum." At last he put his stubby finger on the map at a certain point.

"That looks like the place," he said. "Well, we'll go and see it."

"But there are no trains up La Rhune any more," Rosemary objected. "The La Rhune railway's closed for the winter."

"I know. We'll have to find it from below—I can't go prancing up mountains at my age," said Crumpaun cheerfully. "But if we take that little road"—he indicated a thread on the map—"And then go up that little hill—see, where the contours go round in a circle—we ought to be able to look across at it."

"When shall we go?" Rosemary asked, her eyes shining.

"To-morrow—if I can get what I want in time. Did you see any soldiers, or gendarmes, when you were there?" he asked her finally.

"Only the two gendarmes up at the top of the railway. We thought it funny that they were so vague, when the frontier goes right over La Rhune."

"Ah—no roads go near it there. The roads'll be stopped all right. Never mind—I daresay I can fix it. Now, Sweetheart, can you keep hold of that book and bring it along when we go?"

"I'll try," the girl said.

What Crumpaun wanted was a special *permis de circulation* near the frontier, over and above his usual Press passes—and thanks to his good relations with the French authorities he got it within twenty-four hours. So not the following day, but the day after he and Rosemary set off in the hired car, Crumpaun armed with

4*

his map, Rosemary with her Father's album, which she had pur-
loined afresh for the purpose, wrapped in brown paper. They
drove for some distance along the Sare road, but presently turned
off to the right, and plunged into the network of little lanes and
by-roads which covers the rolling country round the foot of La
Rhune. At length, after many wrong turnings, checks, and re-
treats in reverse down lanes too narrow for the car to pass further,
between the autumn hedges gay with rose-hips, yellow and purple
leaves, and scarlet festoons of briony-berries, they did in fact find
themselves near the foot of a small round hill. Short of this they
had met a couple of *gardes mobiles*, in their belted black overcoats
and neat gaiters, but Crumpaun's permit enabled the car to pass
their stop-point on the minute road.

Rosemary was enjoying herself. The sleuthing instinct, strong
in the Anglo-Saxon section of humanity, had got the upper hand
in her, and she thought it all the greatest fun. It was a nice day,
too—a regular Atlantic coastal day, damp, blue and soft, with
rain so near that the air was moist on the cheek, and the distances
were clear and blue; yet the rain never quite fell, and there were
even watery gleams of sun here and there on the blue landscape.
Their hill, after the manner of the Basque countryside in autumn,
was soaking wet—the ditches and brooks were running full, and
they splashed and squelched upwards over the sodden turf, Rosemary prancing ahead, Mr. Crumpaun puffing and blowing behind her. At last they reached the top. From here they looked
out across the tangled uneven green country towards the blue
tangle of the hills, rising to La Rhune, whose top was swathed in
white cloud. Into this tangle Rosemary peered, screwing up her
eyes, while Mr. Crumpaun got his breath, pulled his binoculars
out of their leather case and adjusted them. It was difficult at
first for the girl, unaccustomed to map-reading or to recognising
from below places seen from above, to make out where to look for
her valley with little trees; Mr. Crumpaun muttered and
grumbled, and wished he had got a prismatic compass. But at
last, with the help of one of those travelling watery patches of
sunshine, Rosemary squeaked that there it was, there it was!—
Mr. Crumpaun focussed his Zeiss glasses on the spot, and then
bade her take them and study it to make sure, while he took the
album and looked again at the photographs. There was no doubt
about it—away across the interfolding slopes of a long winding
valley lay the little combe, trees and all; even the oddly-shaped
projecting rocks were visible through the powerful lenses. Mr.
Crumpaun then studied the valley. It appeared to be quite

empty; there was not a house to be seen, and only a faint path or woodcutters' track wound up the bottom of it, where that was visible. He made some notes in his pocket-book, replaced his binoculars, and they started down the hill again in triumph.

And then, when they were nearly back at the car, the disaster happened. Rosemary, bounding ahead, made to leap the brimming ditch beside the road; landing, she caught her foot in a root, stumbled, and fell forward—the album flew out of her hand and landed in one of those small cuttings which led surface-water from the road to the ditch; the ditch being bank-high, the cutting was several inches deep in muddy water. With a cry, she snatched the book out as soon as she had picked herself up; but in those few seconds the water had penetrated the wrapping, and the back of it and the two front pages were stained and soaking wet. They wiped them with handkerchiefs, and did all they could, but there was no disguising the fact that the album was spoilt.

"Gosh! What *will* Daddy say?" Rosemary exclaimed, examining the wrinkling cover with doleful eyes.

"I'll tell him," Crumpaun volunteered.

"No—I'll tell him myself," said Rosemary. "But I can't *think* what he'll say."

Mr. Oldhead had in fact a great deal to say when the injured photograph album was shown to him. "I took it out with Mr. Crumpet, to look at something, and like an utter owl I dropped it in a puddle," was all that Rosemary would say. "I'm *terribly* sorry, Daddy. I'm quite willing to buy you another—and you've got all your negatives, so you can have more copies made." But Mr. Oldhead, parent-like, was determined to know *why* she had taken it, and at length applied to Mr. Crumpaun. Crumpaun, who did not in the least realise the strength of Mr. Oldhead's pro-Republican feelings, and was of course entirely ignorant of Rosemary's secret wish to avoid any publicity for fear of getting her beloved Condesa into trouble, came out with the whole story of the photographs, the Old Parrot, and the episode at the coiffeur's —a story which he felt was amusing in itself, and rather creditable to Rosemary. But Mr. Oldhead did not see it in that light at all. Parents dislike nothing more than that children should keep their own counsel, and in this case Rosemary had kept hers in a way that seemed to her Father positively disloyal. She had known that the photographer was selling prints from his negatives; she had found out that he had been tricked into taking pictures by a stranger, for a purpose almost certainly nefarious—and she had said nothing! Worse, when she had spoken, it had been to another stranger, and not to him. He was hurt and indignant. His wife tried to soothe him. "She loves keeping things to herself—she always did, from a tiny thing," she said; "it isn't any lack of affection for you. No, it *isn't* disloyal, and you ought not to say that it is—that's being silly."

But Mr. Oldhead was not to be soothed. Like Crumpaun, he was practically convinced that the academic Spaniard had wanted the photographs for spying purposes, and that he must be in some way connected with the Biarritz organisation; and he bitterly regretted that he had never troubled to learn his name, or more about him. He made all the enquiries he could, without result—that Parrot had, as Rosemary said, gone to ground. But what maddened Henry Oldhead was that he should have been made the unconscious instrument of Franquistas; the sabotage stories had become public property by this time, and the thought that the Republicans might owe the loss of planes they so desperately needed to an agent armed with *his* photographs really tortured him. He took counsel with Crossman, who shared his Republican sympathies, and a couple of days later they went off together to the *Préfecture* at Bayonne and put the whole case before the French authorities. Crossman's prestige as *Epoch* correspondent made access to the *Préfet* easy, and Mr. Oldhead had been astute enough to charter for the drive that same chauffeur who had driven Crumpaun and Rosemary on their expedition to the little hill; the photographs, and his evidence, made it possible to establish precisely where the col was. Mr. Oldhead was warmly thanked, the photographs were sent to Bordeaux; the authorities acted promptly, and three days after a little English girl had dropped a photograph album into a puddle on a Basque by-road, a whole posse of extra police were guarding the stretch of frontier on which the small col lay. For whatever purpose that route might have been used, it would be used no more.

# CHAPTER SEVEN

## *Under—the Grotte de Sare*

JAMES MILCOM had taken back with him to Spain the stimulating burden of a love avowed and returned; and during the long hot days and nights when he lay in his uncomfortable little hotel at Almadera, attended at intervals by the young Scottish doctor from the dressing-station in the wine merchant's cellar, he had plenty of opportunity to brood over it. Now the difference between an unavowed love and a love confessed and reciprocated is that the first as it were exists by itself, moving invisible and unassailable in its own shadowy world of dream and longing, where no material hand can pluck at it, and no voice decry; but from the moment of mutual avowal it comes out into the glaring dusty arena of actualities and facts, to be stung with the brightly-coloured barbs of possibilities, to be menaced by the implacable sword of morality, and to face the red lure with the whole of society for audience. So at least the situation presented itself to James, to whom the imagery of the *corrida* now came quite naturally, as he lay in pain and fever, thinking about his love for Raquel and hers for him, and what the future might hold for them; thinking also all the time of that middle-aged man in the big yellow prison on the hill above the town, one corner of which he could even see, blurred and distorted, through the cheaply-glazed window of his small hot room—the man whose treatment of his wife had been a shameful legend, but who had seemed to him, James, to be in some indefinable way *good*. He saw no certain outlet for his love, no clear future; and yet it stood in him savage and strong, challenging attack, vital and untamed. He was relieved when the young doctor, worried by the state of his wound, packed him off to Barcelona, where he might hope for cooler quarters and more adequate remedies. The supply of medicines and dressings in Almadera was neither large nor varied.

In Barcelona he improved, but even there there was a shortage of everything, it was noisy, and he was not fit to do much work; and when the doctor there remarked one day that it would be a good thing if he could go away for ten days or so to France, to rest and have better treatment and make a real recovery, James's heart, with a great bound, urged him to seize on his excuse and go back to St.-Jean-de-Luz. And back he went.

He did not announce his coming—for some reason he wanted simply to walk in on Raquel, unexpected; he felt that her face, so, might tell him something, give him some answer to the problems that had tormented him. The trains were awkward, and he slept at Pau; next day he got a lift from a member of the Prisoners Exchange Commission there, and, with him, walked into the hall of the Hôtel Grande Bretagne at half-past four in the afternoon, a few days after Mr. Oldhead's excursion to the *Préfecture* at Bayonne.

The first person he saw was Mrs. Oldhead, sitting reading

*Life*; from her he learned that the Condesa and Rosemary were out walking, gone to the Phare to see the waves—it was a rough day, and the white mushrooms were appearing continuously above the mole in the centre of the bay. He took a quick cup of tea with her, booked a room, and went out after the two of them—driven, now that he was so near, was in the same town, by an over-mastering hunger for Raquel's face and quiet grey eyes, and the low sound of her voice.

They were not on the top of the small grassy hill, where he went first, nor in the square walled enclosure by the little chapel—a fierce wind tore at everything, up there, as if it would pluck the very masonry from the turf; the waves below, huge and green, flung themselves at the breakwater, worrying it, retreating and returning like a pack of rollicking wolves, and a continuous bellowing thunder, as from the throats of a hundred giant wolves filled the air, deafeningly. Sight and sound alike were splendid, immense, inspiring. He went down one of the little chalky paths on the further side of the hill, bent against the wind, carrying his hat, till he struck the narrow track that curves round it, leading down to the break-water—and there, between the cliff and the sea, suddenly he met them, coming up laughing, their faces bright with spray and excitement, their damp hair streaming out from under the coloured handkerchiefs that they had tied round their heads.

Rosemary saw him first. And his expression, and still more the Condesa's, when a second later she turned from speaking to the young girl, and caught sight of him also, told her the truth. The sheer beauty of the look that passed between them then caught the girl up on a sudden wave of exaltation—to let her drop, presently, with a vague sense of having struck something and been bruised, as a body is bruised that is flung by a wave far up on some harsh shore. It was not till some time afterwards that she recognised the absured and impossible origin of this feeling—that that look, on James Milcom's face, could have meant for her something of what it visibly meant to Raquel de Verdura.

They cut across behind the Phare, dropped down the hill and strolled back along the front, all three together; near the Casino, Rosemary made her Spanish preparation an excuse to slip away, and the other two walked on towards the Bar Basque together, and turned in there for tea—at tea-time the Bar Basque is practically deserted. Sitting there, he told her in detail about his visit to the prison, and Pascual, and his fellow-prisoners—

she listened, now grave, now amused, but always kind and
interested. At last, rather cautiously, he asked her who La
Paquita would be—saying that he had heard of her as being in
the prison, but without mentioning the peculiarity of the Conde's
manner when she was spoken of. The Condesa knew at once
who he meant. "That will be Francisca de Verdura—she is a
cousin of Pascual's. I heard that she was 'working' "—James
was familiar with this euphemism for the trade of a spy—"but
I did not know that they had taken her. She is a most dear
child—she was often with me. She is young and very brave.
You saw her?" she asked eagerly.

No, James had not seen her.

"Poor child—I wish you had. I would so have liked to know
how she is; how they treat her. I expect they will soon kill her,"
said the Condesa flatly. "But of course to get to her would have
been most difficult—I realise that." She spoke proudly and
sadly about this girl, and others like her who risked their lives
"for Spain"—it struck James that La Paquita's imprisonment
really caused her much more concern than her husband's.

Then, with a change of face and voice to an almost faltering
nervousness, which moved him very much, of course she asked
about Juanito. "You heard no more, after you wrote? Nothing
in Barcelona, from anyone?"

No, he told her gravely, nothing. He had decided before his
arrival to make no mention of the possible connection between
La Paquita and Juanito; that one remark thrown out by Pepe
the bus driver, and the Conde's change of manner at his brother-
in-law's name, were too tenuous to be considered as real information—and since the very suggestion that Juanito might be
"working" too would add to her anxiety, it would be foolish and
cruel, he felt, to worry her with such rumours till he knew more.
Actually, here he was wrong; but he was not to know that till
much later.

They hardly spoke at all, that first day, of themselves, though
both were intensely conscious of the growth and strengthening of
their feeling for one another which avowal, followed by absence,
had brought about—when, over the cheap garish tea-table, he
looked at her with deeper eyes, their mutual avoidance of speech
was like an open communication. But the first effect on James
of seeing her again was to sweep away, for the moment, all
thoughts of the Conde. He was still weak after his wound, and
the physical weakness made him tender and unguarded. The
sheer lovely comfort of looking at her again, after weeks of

absence, would have sufficed him then. And the simplicity and eagerness of her questions about the air-raid, and the Doctor, and his fever and his treatment brought back to him, with a funny sense almost of regret, the way they used to talk about wood and eggs and tinned milk in the days in Madrid, days that had now taken on the spurious preciousness of the period before awareness came—days like the dawn of time, when in the cool clear early light one held a jewel in one's hand, and knew it only for a pebble, to be cast away at will. Precious partly because of the wonder of that unconsciousness, partly because then one was still safe, was still one's own man; one reached out fearlessly to the other, not recognising the godhead that can blast— Psyche confident in the sheltering dark, before she lifted the terrible lamp of revelation. In James Milcom, with his conditioned fear of love and the tyranny of love, this feeling, common in some degree to everyone, was particularly strong; but in the days that they spent together then it was gradually overborne by the full tide of a complete human emotion, a fully conscious love, of body as of spirit. The whole of him loved her—and came to rejoice in the completeness of his love, and its mastery of his mind and heart; he came to exult, after his years of insulation, even in the deep pangs, the strange pains and fears which love inflicts, in knowing the fulness of human experience at last. Sometimes the Irishman in him derided himself for his subjection, but the derision was of the mind alone; his manhood rose up in him, the soul and the blood triumphing over the chill reason, and brought him again to an accepting, a splendid joy.

He was less afflicted, this time, by the sense of moving in a crowd. The Duquesa seemed to be busy, going over often to Biarritz, and left them to themselves; the patch and plaster on his forehead afforded him an excellent excuse for avoiding alcohol and noise, which let him out of much frequenting of the society of his fellow-journalists at the Bar Basque. He walked with Raquel a good deal; she was a surprisingly good walker for a continental, as he had begun to find in Madrid, and under his supervision bought a pair of strong low-heeled shoes for their expeditions. One day he remembered especially, because it was the first time he actually saw her confronted with flowers growing wild, often as he had heard her speak of them. Though it was now November, on the Basque Coast the days were still mild and sunny; they walked up to S. Joseph's Chapel, on a low ridge behind the town. The poor little building, reached by a turf track, stands practically in the farmyard of one of those substantial, deep-eaved, chocolate-shuttered Basque farms; inside, bouquets of artificial and withered natural flowers, and other cheap offerings, surrounded the gaudy simple image and shrine. They looked around. "These are from the girls who have prayed here, and got sweethearts in a year," Raquel said, indicating the votive offerings.

"Really? Why should they pray to S. Joseph for sweethearts?" James asked.

"I suppose because he was Our Lady's fiancé, and in the end married her," Raquel said, with that little sophisticated smile of hers. "Anyhow once a year the girls who are without a fiancé come here, from all the country round, and pray for one—and if they get one in a year, they bring an *ex-voto* afterwards."

"How do you know all this?" he asked, as they emerged again into the mild sunshine.

"Rosemary told me. I think she came here and saw them."

"I shouldn't think she would ever need to pray for a fiancé!" he said—"Nor you either, my darling."

She put on her enigmatic look, that was yet so sweet.

"I *might* have to," she said. At which of course he put his arm round her and kissed her, out in the grassy lane. Then they wandered on, following the lane till it wound out onto the Ascain road. Close to the junction, by the roadside, there was a little flat-topped grassy knoll, with a group of young oak trees on it; they walked up to get the view, and found the deep greyish grass under the trees full of the slender weak-stemmed autumn crocus, that is so much more pink than mauve, and has an unearthly fragility, appearing as it does among withering grass and fallen leaves. Raquel gave a soft exclamation of delight, when she saw them first, and moved gently about, holding her hands out in a sort of tender wonder over each fresh group, in the loveliest gesture James had ever seen—then she stooped and gathered a few, and then more.

"But they will fade if I carry them in my hand," she said. So James had to produce his handkerchief, and in that, most carefully, they carried them home down the road.

But at the back of James's mind, during these exquisite first days, the picture that he had of Pascual recurred over and over again, and the strange contradictory impression of his goodness —and wrestled in him with that strong human tide. More than once, holding her hand, playing with it, as they sat somewhere in the sun, studying its strength and beauty with the most direct naturalness, he surprised her by laying it back gently in her lap, and saying—"Let's go on—shall we?"

But it was some time before he could bring himself to speak of this to her. Raquel surprised him, she whom he had known always as so contained, so quiet, by a sort of direct recklessness, a passionate simplicity in her declarations, when they spoke of their love—and this was so wonderful to him, so unimaginably strange and precious, that he could not for some time bear to do anything to imperil its continuance. Indeed it was she who first touched on it, on a day when he had in fact decided that at length he must speak. They were sitting out in the big glen up beyond S. Joseph's chapel—a wild place, empty, with steep tawny slopes of dead bracken shouldering up against the sky behind them, and in front a long view down to the sea. With her head on his shoulder, his arm about her, she picked up his other hand and held it against her cheek—then she drew it to her lips, kissed his fingers, lightly as a moth, and still holding it there, spoke actually through his fingers.

"Even if it is very wrong to love you, as the priests would certainly say, it is not unkind or cruel, as it would be if Pascual loved me. It is a sin, but of another sort."

He could have laughed at her calm casuistry. But he did not.

"My darling, are you sure that he really doesn't love you?" he said, taking his arm from round her, to lean forward and look earnestly in her face. "You know, I got the impression that he cared for you very much indeed. He talked about you a great deal. It—it upset me, rather."

"Oh no," she said, with soft decision. "You are quite mistaken. Since years, he has not cared for me at all. It does not matter," she said gently, as if disclaiming any hint of reproach, "and he has always been most courteous; but he has not cared at all. He is not that sort of man, you know," she said with easy finality—"he is of quite another sort."

"That may have been so in the past," James objected, "but I think you are mistaken now. I must tell you this, my darling —it wouldn't be fair not to. I think he must have changed. He almost said as much; he said it was all quite a new experience for him. I think something is happening to him, in there—and that it won't be at all the same thing when he comes out."

She stared at him, puzzled and incredulous.

"Just what do you mean? How changed?"

"I think—it's hard to explain—but—well, he surprised me very much. I expected him, however bravely he might be put-

ting up with everything, to be the complete man of the world,"
James said, incompetently.

"But so he is."

"No—not now. He wasn't just stoical, he was *accepting* what
happened. I tell you, I felt that he was *good*—and that was the
last thing I expected to find," said James bluntly. "And he was
carving away and carving away at those peachstones to make
you a necklace."

"Yes, that was sweet of him—and it would pass the time,"
Raquel said, still with that soft tolerant matter-of-factness. "But
for the rest"—she looked at James—"it is not so. Gentle and
polite and brave, of course he is; but serious, no."

"God, how I wish I could be sure of that," he said.

"But you can. I know it. Who should know him if not I?"

"Oh, my darling, I suppose so! I'd give my soul for you to
be right, you know that." He took her in his arms again, with
a sudden boundless sense of relief, and kissed her as if he could
never stop.

But the relief did not last. They discussed the subject several
times; she was so much surprised at James's impression of Pascual,
and still more—he realised this, though she never said so—at the
fact of his having imparted it to her that she recurred to it more
than once. "It is so *strange* that you should have thought this,"
she kept saying. She stuck to her own point of view, of course;
quite without rancour, smoothly accepting a familiar situation,
she held to her knowledge of Pascual for what he was—not
serious, and not good; least of all in any sense devoted to her.
Her incredulity was quite gentle, but complete. She ended by
almost convincing James that he really had been mistaken.
After all, he had only seen the man once, for a short time, and
without knowing him before; he had only the contrast between
his preconceptions and that one interview to set against her
years of experience and the known facts. And after brushing
aside James's scruples, she came back, then and always, during
the whole time that he was at St.-Jean, to the joy of being, at
last, loved, and to how much she loved James. Blindly in love
himself, it was not human, James felt, to expect him to go on
setting up an impression formed at one interview with a stranger
as a barrier between himself and his heart's delight. So they
dined together, and lunched together—in the little trellised inn
garden at Ainhoa, at the Etcheola at Ascain, on the terrace of
the inn at Biriatou, where Rosemary had drunk red wine weeks
before, and at Gaston's, down by the port; and walked together

—through the brown oakwoods above the Nivelle, along the cliffs between St.-Jean and Hendaye, where to Raquel's delight, the striped gentians still bloomed in the yellowing grass, and *lithospermum prostratum*, its first flowers blue as jewels, sprawled over the earthy banks; or else among the dunes and pinewoods along the shore beyond Biarritz, where thyme and small strong-smelling plants made an aromatic scent when they sat and crushed them in the sun. It was a time of wonder, of tender delight, such as James had never known.

One thing surprised him a good deal about Raquel. Though she was not in the least efficient, in the busy British sense of the word, he had always found her perfectly practical, in a quiet unobtrusive way, in her judgement, whether on people or situations; without stressing it, she had a good head on her shoulders. But in their present situation, which was full enough of difficulties even if she was right and he was wrong, and her husband was really fundamentally indifferent to her, she never seemed to think of the future, or to wish to make any sort of plan—whereas James, the Irishman, to whom love meant marriage, was constantly concerned with the next step, and many steps beyond. But not Raquel—she seemed perfectly content to rest in the exquisite present, or at most to look forward to a very near future, when they would become lovers. She never actually said this in so many words, but James realised almost at once that it was so—that he had only to put out his hand, as it were, to take that final bliss. He guessed that the strain and horror of those months in Madrid, coming on top of the long loveless years, had combined with the collapse of the whole society in which she had been brought up to induce this happy indifference, this obliviousness, almost, to all practical considerations. As to her apparent obliviousness to moral ones, that he felt he understood better. Years of marriage to a man who gave away his wife's inherited jewels to his mistress of the moment might well, in spite of anything the Church might say, make a woman of spirit feel that she had regained her freedom in respect to love. And he was sure that she was perfectly genuine in her disbelief in a change of heart on Pascual's part. But most of all, on that side, lay Spain, and the attitude of the Spanish people to love after marriage. James had once escorted a sober British delegation, visiting Madrid on some financial mission, on a round of sight-seeing which included one of the great historic country mansions outside the capital. He could see now their faces of horror when a grave major-domo, speaking French, showed them a magnificent four-poster bed in one room with the calm announcement—"Here His Excellency the Duke of D—— slept with the Duchess of P——" referring to living persons. Spain was like that.

But it was his obstinate inner conviction about Pascual which nevertheless enabled him, at the end, to go away without taking that for which everything in him craved. A cobweb film with a nightmare strength, linked somehow to that Irish fastidiousness and to his abnormal sensitiveness to others' pain, impalpably blocked his way. Did she understand? He didn't know. She had almost convinced him that he was wrong, and yet he could not move forward. Whether she understood or not, he also realised that she loved him so much—to James, it was a frightening realisation—that she would accept his wish, his impulse, even if it conflicted with her own ultimate need; and further that she was too schooled, too clever, too skilful to seek to impose her own needs and wishes on any man. There, he always felt a hint of inferiority with her—that terrifying disciplined technique of a great lady who came of a long line of great lovers was altogether beyond him. For she was potentially a great lover; his intelligence, as well as his blood and his nerves, proclaimed, fairly shouted that at him. Oh, God—why did he have to have these scruples? Why had she ever sent him to see Pascual? If he had not seen him—well, it would all have been different, he said to himself doggedly, setting his big ugly jaw.

This time, when he left, she got up to see him off; so far they had advanced, that both felt it quite natural that she should do this, and either assumed that the Duquesa and anyone else who was aware of the proceeding should take it for granted too, or else just didn't care whether they did or not. In fact the little group of James's colleagues had come to take him and the Condesa rather for granted as a unit—to that extent they had imposed themselves on normal human society, which will, in the end, stand quite a lot from the beautiful, the able and the determined, especially if they are perfectly fearless and unconcerned, as Raquel at least certainly was. The idea that she should for one moment consider what a group of foreign newspapermen might think of her actions would certainly never have occurred to her—James realised that, and envied this aristocratic freedom.

He sent his luggage down to the station by the hotel cab— they walked, round by the sea-wall and the Place Louis XIV. It was a lovely morning; the Dogs' Club was in session on the beach, and Raquel, laughing, pointed it out to James—"Rosemary calls that one The President," she said, indicating a grave brindled object of uncertain breed, with a grizzled muzzle. This pleased James; he had seen a good deal of Rosemary on this visit, she had been with them sometimes for lunch or tea, or in the evenings, and the lively objective amused quality of her mind had won his approval. "What a nice child that is," he said as they walked on.

"Is not she? Oh, she will help me when you are gone," Raquel said, turning to him with one of her quick movements. "She has so much heart."

"Oh, God, my darling, I wish I didn't have to go," he said, drawing her arm through his and pressing it against his side.

"I know—so do I also wish it," she said. "But you must, I know. But you will return as soon as you can"—and she turned her face to him.

"Yes. But it won't be very soon," he said. "This offensive —no one knows when it will come off, but there's bound to be one soon, and then I shall be stuck."

"It won't last long once it begins," she said, proudly, confidently—"and then you will return." Then, seeing his expression change—"Oh, forgive me!" she said. "But I cannot be other than what I am—I must feel as I do."

"I know—never mind," he said gloomily.

"And James——" she paused. "I do not wish to be tiresome to you, but you will do all, *all* you can this time to get some news of Juanito, will you not?" Her lovely face, suddenly, changed to an expression of deep distress. "I do so very much wish to know what is become of him. I *need* to know it," she said, with a moving simplicity.

"Dear love, I know you do. And I will do the possible and the impossible to find out," he said. "You know that."

She dabbed at her eyes.

"Yes, yes. You are so good."

"I'm not good!" James said, pausing and taking her by the elbows. "I adore you, and you know it, and I don't care what I do for you. Besides, I understand," he said in another tone. He was thinking of his mother.

"Let's say good-bye here," he said suddenly. "Don't come on." They were standing just where the sea-wall abuts against the harbour entrance, beyond the last houses; the whole curve of the bay, green slopes, gay villas, the etched block of the town lay sparklingly distinct in the early light; the white mushrooms of spray put forth, silently, out beyond the mole, golden in the morning sunshine; the blue and green sardine boats, emerging like bullets from the narrow mouth of the port, bounded over the blue water towards it. He looked round at it all; he looked back at her.

"Oh, how lovely it is! And how lovely you are!" he said, and put his arms around her and kissed her.

"Good-bye, my dearest love," he said. "Take care of yourself, for pity's sake. Write me to Barcelona. Sure you've got enough money?"

Even at that moment, the amused enigmatic look came on her face, at those last words.

"Yes, my darling Englishman!" she said. "Plenty of money!" Then her face changed.

"Oh, good-bye!" she said, and put her face up to his, and kissed his mouth violently. "Come soon! I shall be half dead till you do," she said, and slipped from his arms and walked rapidly away, with her light individual step, along the narrow sea-wall, back towards the hotel. Slowly, heavily, James turned in the other direction and went on to the station.

He sat in the train on the long cross-country journey back to Toulouse and Perpignan, his luggage crammed with little gifts from Raquel to Pascual—cigarettes, sugar, pocket-handkerchiefs; she had no difficulty, it seemed, in reconciling a lover with such correct and even kindly attentions to her imprisoned husband. He sat heavily, exhausted with the pain of parting, and thought about Raquel. Much as he loved her, safe as he felt with her, he never quite understood her; never really knew what her mind within said to her. Because she was Spanish; the Scottish grandmother had never overcome the Spaniard in her. And thinking about the differences between the Spaniards and the English, easy as the two races found it to like and respect one another—because both were proud, silent, and combative, perhaps?—he remembered his first sight of Spain, and the illumination that that rapid impression had thrown on the whole race for him, over years.

He had been on a motor tour, and had gone in at Irún, after ten days spent in France—and after an early lunch at San Sebastián had driven straight on to Burgos. And he remembered still, clearly, the peculiar shock that that first aspect of Spain had given him, when the car had climbed by the great looped road up to the pass that leads out of the coastal country, and dropped, less far, to the high plain which stretches away to Vitoria and Miranda. It was most beautiful, this high bare land between low mountains, where the eye travelled for miles over the brownish uplands, set with the villages which crowned each small eminence like islands in a lake—though they were far apart, he had counted fourteen in sight at once. Beautiful independently of any graces of rich vegetation, grass or tree—a beauty of the very bones of the land, of shape and structure and line, grave and austere. But it was the villages themselves that had caused the surprise, the shock. James Milcom had long held a theory that nothing so gives away the inherent character of a nation as its architecture, and especially the architecture of its villages and little towns, built by simple people for daily use, unpretentious and unfaked. And he had come straight from France, where even in the smallest village the houses were built in rows, facing neatly on the tree-bordered street—orderly parts of a common whole, arranged in a disciplined unity. How different were these villages of northern Spain! Strongly, even splendidly built of creamy or golden stone, the houses were set in no order at all —they faced all ways at once, to the back, to the corner of the next house, as irregular and haphazard as yellow bricks poured out of a sack—without any attempt at paths or gardens, surrounded by a sea of mud, through which men and cattle alike ploughed their way. And the churches! Each village had its church, set high in the midst; splendid buildings, these too, immensely lofty, reinforced with high narrow buttresses—but except for the east and west ends, without windows. Milcom had gone on his way marvelling, wondering what could be the inner character of this people. And he had found, as time went on and he came again and again to Spain, loving it each time more, that the village architecture had spoken no more than the truth—that in the Spanish character there was a haughty and ferocious individualism which did not readily brook any aims but private ones, or at least insisted on carrying out public aims in its own way, and had accepted for centuries a religious organisation which, while it had produced such a superb flowering of religious thought and mystical experience as was represented by S. Ignatius Loyola and Santa Teresa, had somehow failed to shed much illumination on the Spanish peasantry. And always there was also present that indestructible and defiant beauty in the very shape of the land, matching the dignified hauteur of the race. Grunting, James Milcom travelled on towards Spain.

For one reason and another the Oldhead family postponed their expedition to the Grotte de Sare till a day or so after Milcom left. Though Ethel Oldhead was firm and energetic about visit-

ing (and causing her family to visit) places of historic interest, her
two main passions were really shopping and the cinema and in
Biarritz and Bayonne she could gratify both—but especially in
Bayonne. Oldhead and Rosemary hated Biarritz, with good
reason, and could seldom be dragged there. Built flaringly and
largely for a fashionable and expensive class of winter visitor, it
was a dreary place now that winter-sports had deflected its international clientèle to the mountains, leaving it moribund—the
closed Casino, the huge shuttered hotels, the almost empty streets
produced a dismal effect of desolation; and the few shops that
were open sought by exorbitant prices to recoup themselves for
a scarcity of customers. But Bayonne, busy, shabby and unpretentious, its river crowded with tramp shipping, its narrow streets
with provincial housewives, contained innumerable cheap and
excellent shops, and was always alive with a cheerful, bustling,
middle-class activity. There was that little shop in the Rue des
Arcades where they made up both scent and powder to suit the
individual purchaser's complexion and taste, miraculously cheaply
—catching the two o'clock bus from St.-Jean, you could nip in and
buy your little paper screw of powder before the early house at
the cinema, and afterwards go and drink frothing rich chocolate
at Cazenave's, before catching the seven o'clock bus back.
Further up the same street, if you had courage to a degree lacked
by the parent Oldheads, you could buy oysters for 3d. a dozen!

A succession of good French films: *Retour à l'Aube, Entrée des
Artistes, La Maison du Maltais*, above all *Prison sans Barreaux* (which
Ethel Oldhead insisted on seeing twice), caused a number of these
expeditions to Bayonne during Milcom's visit, but the day after
he left Mr. Oldhead announced that they might as well do the
Grotte de Sare and get it over, while the weather was still tolerable; and the following day they chartered a car and went,
Crossman accompanying them, as his Press pass might assist in
getting past the Gardes Mobiles—a wise precaution, since the
entrance to the great cave is within a hundred yards or so of the
frontier. But the French authorities were not minded to let
military considerations interfere too much with financial ones;
and though the party came on a police post about a kilometre
short of the frontier, the chauffeur's curt statement "Foreigners—
for the grotto!" sufficed to get them past.

The Grotte de Sare is rather an imposing specimen of those
caves which abound both to the East and West of the Pyrenees.
It has not the archaeological interest of the Mas d'Azil, nor the
superb prehistoric drawings and paintings of the Altamira and

other Spanish caves—a few rather doubtful scratchings are all it can boast in that line. But it had the distinction of sheltering Don Carlos and, it is said, seven hundred of his followers, for weeks on end, during the Carlist wars of the last century. Certainly, there would be room for them! From the great mouth, ninety feet across and perhaps forty feet high, whose stony upper lip is fringed with pendent ivy, to the furthest limit of the electric lighting provided for the benefit of tourists must be the better part of half a kilometre; and there are other unlit portions beyond. Rough steps and paths cut in the rock, rough wooden gangways and ladders lead the visitor in and out, up and down—now through long high galleries, now through shallow tunnel-like passages, now into huge caverns like vast rooms, or strange places of stalactites and stalagmites, where even the walls are as it were upholstered in the glittering whitish deposits of lime. Water drips, or gurgles or rushes at intervals, mostly out of sight—the Carlists must have got very damp. In two or three places colonies of bats hang from the stony roof, head-down and close enough to touch—a sinister sight, a dirty smell.

To this odd place the three Oldheads and Crossman arrived on a soft misty November afternoon. An old peasant with a stubbly chin and very bad breath emerged from a cottage close by and sold them their tickets; he muttered something about sending "le jeune homme" and motioned them towards the entrance. Most of this was filled with a sort of shallow pool, in which an old punt lay half-submerged; a small stream chattered away from it over a stony bed—but by a path along the right-hand wall they picked their way into the cave. Even here by the entrance it seemed very dark at first, after the autumn sunshine outside, but presently their eyes grew accustomed to the gloom, and Rosemary and Crossman ranged about, trying to see where the pool ended and the stream which obviously fed it began, and being re-called by anguished and angry protests from Mrs. and Mr. Oldhead respectively. In the course of these explorations they came on a câche of candle-ends and small bits of board with a nail driven through each, clearly intended for use as candlesticks; they both took a candle and a board, heated the nails with matches and affixed their candles, and then began to explore further. But at this point a tall, rather handsome youth in shirtsleeves, with a very sulky expression, appeared with the old man—scowling at the strangers, he switched on the electric lights and motioning the visitors to follow, set off into the cave. They tailed after him, Rosemary and Crossman last, still sticking to their candles, in spite of his frowns and head-shakings. Perfunctorily, and always with the same appearance of resentment, he pointed out the various sights—the chamber attributed to Don Carlos; a horrid set of models of primitive man, clad in imitation skins; the stalactites, a waterfall, and so on; the only time his expression relaxed was when Mrs. Oldhead, walking along a wooden gallery, suddenly came on a colony of bats close in front of her, and screamed—this seemed to amuse him, and he laughed loudly and harshly.

"What a surly brute," Mr. Oldhead said, disgustedly.

"Lousy," Rosemary agreed from the end of the line.

At length the guide announced that they were now under Spain—which was easy to believe, for they seemed to have been walking for at least twenty-five minutes—and presently he led them to the most curious sight of all, the "Arbre de Noël" as he called it. This was certainly a most singular object. In the centre of a vertical circular hollow in the rock, like the inside of a factory chimney, and perhaps as much as eighty feet high rose a tall slender rock column, plastered all over with limy deposit, and grooved with flat rings or ridges, a foot or more wide, for the whole of its height, which was the same as that of the enclosing chimney; it did indeed strikingly resemble those toy wooden trees which used sometimes to be sold with Noah's Arks. The space between the stone tree and its enclosing chimney was so narrow that the visitors could only just edge past in single file; the guide pointed out that by craning their necks and looking up, they could see the sky overhead. While Crossman and Mr. Oldhead began to discuss exactly how this geological phenomenon had been formed, presumably by stones and water cutting down through the softer rock round a hard core, Rosemary, who still carried her candle, began to climb the stone tree; standing on the ledges and pressing with her free hand against the corresponding bulges and grooves of the chimney wall, she found it quite easy to get up, and reached a height of several feet. Here she paused, and as usual began to look about her; she was on the opposite side of the pillar to the guide, who did not see what she was doing till she suddenly called out—"Daddy! Mummie! This is most extraordinary! People go up and down here—there are nail-marks on the stone."

They all crowded round then, as well as they could, to see what she was up to—the guide with them; when he saw her on her perch, he called furiously to her to come down, come down at once.

"But it is very interesting," she called back to him in French—

"One goes up and one comes down by here—one sees the traces on the rock."

Rudely, he shouted back that it was ridiculous, what she said—no one passed that way. She must descend instantly—to climb about in the Grotte was forbidden. And he made as if to climb up after her and pull her down.

Mr. Oldhead, at last exasperated, intervened.

"Here, here, here!" he said, pushing the young man aside with surprising vigour, "we've had about enough of your temper, my friend. Assez, assez!" he went on, recollecting his French; "leave Mademoiselle alone; she will come down. She has done no harm. Keep *still*!"—as the Basque, after the first astonished recoil, made a step forward again; he said this so threateningly that for the second time the guide stood back. "Come on down, Rosemary," he said—and then turned and examined the ledges on a level with his face. "You see well that there are here the marks of feet," he said to the guide, pointing to unmistakable scratches on the slippery calcareous surface.

"Mademoiselle has made them herself," said the boy sulkily.

"Mademoiselle, as you can very well see, is wearing shoes with soles of rubber," Crossman put in. "Such make no marks. Why all this fuss?"

Scowling, the guide shrugged and gave it up; when Rosemary had got down he led the way out of the chimney, and took them back through the cavern, by a much shorter route than the one by which they had come.

"Funny, that," Crossman remarked to Mr. Oldhead as they went along—"Someone certainly has been going up and down that thing, but I don't see why this guide chap should get into such a stew about it."

"Don't you?" replied Oldhead, laconically.

"Smuggling, I suppose," put in Mrs. Oldhead.

"By Jove, yes—and this young fellow or the old boy outside are the *receleurs*," said Crossman, delighted.

"What's a *receleur*?" asked Mrs. Oldhead.

"*Mummie!* surely you know that! It's a receiver of stolen goods."

"He looked rather a nice old man—much nicer than this horrible sour creature," said Mrs. Oldhead, who always passed these little judgements on people to whom she had spoken twice.

"His breath wasn't nice," said her husband, who was invariably irritated by the said judgements.

"Shall we tip him, think?" Crossman asked, as a faint glimmer of light ahead showed that they were nearing the mouth of the cave.

"I shall, yes—after all, he did take us round, if he made a fool of himself," said Mr. Oldhead, whose Liberal ideas had given him a passion for justice even in small things. And when they reached the spacious chamber inside the entrance, which now seemed bright to them, he offered some coins to the guide. Surly to the last—"Give it to the *vieillard*; he needs it most," the young man said, switched off the lights, and shepherded them out past the pool and the half-sunken punt, onto the open space where their car waited for them.

To the old man, accordingly, they gave the tip; he was still hanging about outside, and the young one said something curtly to him in Basque before he disappeared. The old man led them to Pierre Loti's tea-garden, a peculiar spot just beyond the entrance to the grotto; little tables of stone in curious shapes, and rustic seats of stone or wood, were set among young fruit trees—it was very "Ye Olde" as Rosemary said, and actually rather ugly, with the ugly fantasy of a gnomes' paradise in a Teutonic fairy-tale; but at that hour it had a certain charm. The sun had gone down behind the line of hill which stood close above them, and mist was rising from the stream—a diffused golden light filtered through the mist and between the late yellow leaves of the young fruit trees, a thin moon hung in the sky above the tawny ridge. The old man, who was as friendly as the young one was unamiable, chattered freely; he told Mrs. Oldhead all about his cancer of the stomach, and gave Mr. Oldhead and Crossman his views on the Spanish War—eventually he pointed out where the frontier ran, not two hundred metres from where they stood, and volunteered to take the party "a few steps" to where they could see the sentries guarding it. Crossman and the two Oldheads, still talking, went with him, but Rosemary remained behind, unnoticed. She was suddenly invaded by an overwhelming longing for Milcom; she had just been under Spain, and he was in Spain! And in that misty orchard, in the tender uncertain light, she felt that for a moment or two she simply must allow herself to think about him, to recall his face, with the deep-set eyes and the corrugated forehead, the grim mouth that was yet so amazingly sweet when he smiled—and to remember his voice, uttering his brief appropriate sentences and penetrating, illuminating comments.

Since that meeting with him on the path below the little Phare, when she first realised that Milcom and the Condesa loved one another, the young girl had travelled a long way. The sudden discovery that she herself cared for him had taken her completely by surprise, as much so as if an earthquake or some other natural disaster had overtaken her. Indeed it was rather as a disaster that she regarded it. She loved him, of course, and must always love him; but he could never compete with the Condesa, beautiful and gifted with every charm—it was a life sentence that she was contemplating. And in this knowledge—none the less desolating because time might at length prove it false—she had passed one of the hardest weeks of her life. The Condesa, her other idol, was by this time very fond of her, and liked to have her about—all unwitting, she treated her as a small and convenient third, an innocent gooseberry, to chaperone a number of minor meetings. And Rosemary, unable to refuse anything that her adored Condesa asked of her, and drawn irresistibly by the enchantment of seeing and hearing Milcom, had sat with the pair at the Bar Basque, at Gaston's, at the little restaurant at Guéthary, in such a mixture of rapture and pain as left her quite exhausted. Now that Milcom had gone, that pain had taken on a different shape—less of a spear, more of a burden, a heavy treasure that she carried about through the long hours of each day, feeling its weight without, usually, pausing to examine it. Now, in that misty golden orchard, she did as it were undo the parcel—sitting on one of the rustic seats, half-hidden by a low bushy tree, she gave herself up to dreaming of him; without hope, but in a stillness that was like music.

She was sitting so, gazing idly before her in the direction of the grotto, when she saw a man emerge from the depths of the cave and appear in the entrance. He started to walk along the small path beside the pool, till he came within sight of the car, standing waiting on the parking-place; she saw him check, hesitate, and then turn and go back into the cave. The oddity of this behaviour roused her attention, and brought her thoughts back to earth. It was not the sulky young guide—she had seen that much; but if there was another man in the cave, why had they not seen him? Before she had done more than ask herself this question, the man appeared again, this time to the left of the pool; he must have waded across, for the legs of his rough trousers were dripping. Glancing cautiously round, he nipped out of the cave, and slipped in among the trees of the little orchard.

All Rosemary's faculties sprang to attention at once. He didn't want to be seen, that was clear. Perhaps he was a smuggler, and had come in by the chimney! Then was that why the guide had been so cross when she had found the nail-marks? Her mind leapt from point to point. The guide must be in league with him—perhaps had been expecting him to-day; that would explain his evident reluctance to show them round the cave. But if he was a smuggler, it must be currency, for he carried no bundle. While her thoughts raced, her eyes were watching the man as he moved through the trees. He sat down on one of Loti's fungoid seats, and wrung the water out of his trousers; he had not seen her. Then he walked a few steps forward again, stood, looked and listened. He must be wondering where the people from the car had got to, she thought. He was still not near enough for her to see his face clearly, but in spite of his rough clothes he did not walk like a peasant. Now he moved forward again, in her direction—sitting quite still, half-hidden by the tree, in that faint light she was practically invisible, till in a moment he stood before her.

Even then he did not actually start—it was more that every muscle in his body became almost visibly tense, and his right hand half-moved towards his left arm in a gesture that American films have made familiar to the whole world; then dropped again. He was tall, slight, rather graceful, with black hair and grey eyes; the skin much tanned, but with an athlete's clear brown rather than the weathered roughened mahogany of the peasant; his hands were long and fine, she noticed, with beautiful though grimed nails, narrow as filberts. This was no peasant. His face was long too, with a long high-bridged nose and a shapely sensitive mouth; the forehead magnificent, and about the whole face an appearance of vigour, intelligence and resolution, with just that touch of reserve, of withdrawnness, that sculpture gives to a face—a look that Rosemary was coming to think of as typically Spanish. Beyond all doubt, as he stood there in his shabby jacket, rough shirt, and torn wet trousers, he was one of the most splendid human beings she had ever seen.

For a moment or two they remained, staring at one another. Then Rosemary spoke—she had the advantage of him, she felt; he could not know how much she had seen.

"Bonjour, Monsieur," she said civilly.

He bowed, but did not return her salutation; then suddenly he smiled at her.

"Where do you come from, Mademoiselle?" he asked in French.

"From the grotto—my friends have just gone up to look at the frontier," she answered—she felt a curious wish to put him at his ease. Her heart was beating rather violently—this was no common smuggler, anyhow.

"And you remained here?" he asked.

"I remained here. Je rêvais," she said.

She saw him give a half-glance over his shoulder, and knew

that he was trying to see how much she could have seen of his movements. Then he turned back and studied her face.

"It is beautiful here," she said casually, still under that curious impulse to put him at ease, to make him relax that tenseness that she felt, rather than saw. "Do you live here?"

That did it. His voice was quite different as he answered— "Near here—a little way down the road."

She didn't believe it for a moment, though she was glad that he accepted her pretence. For what should such a glorious creature do, living in this out-of-the-way valley?

"And you, Mademoiselle?" he asked her then; "where do you live?"

"Oh, we are staying at St.-Jean-de-Luz," she said.

"Tiens, St.-Jean. In a hotel?"

"Yes—the Grande Bretagne."

He looked at her curiously.

"You find it comfortable?" he asked.

"Oh yes—perfectly. It's a little old-fashioned, but very nice."

"The nourishment good?"

"Oh yes—the best food in St.-Jean, as hotels go. Why, do you know it?"

"It is well spoken of," he said. He put a foot up on one of the seats, leaned his elbow on it, and spoke now with a sort of casual ease. "It is very full?" he asked.

"Fairly."

"There are any Spanish people there? Refugees?"

"One or two—ladies mostly," Rosemary said, a little surprised at these questions.

"And you know them?"

"One I do, quite well," she replied, her thoughts flying back to Milcom and the Condesa.

"And they seem cheerful, well? One wonders if they are in good spirits, leaving the beloved hearts behind," he said thoughtfully.

"*She* is," the girl said, recalling the Condesa's brilliant face of joy all the past week.

"It is well, that. The poor ones!" he said. Then he took his foot down off the seat, straightened up, and looked her full in the face.

"You are English, I expect, Mademoiselle. Ah, what good fortune you have in England, rich and at peace, compared with poor Spain!"

"But France is all right," the girl said, looking as straight at him.

"Ah, France!" the young man said with a shrug. "No one ever

knows how it is with France, well or ill. Au revoir, Mademoiselle."

"Au revoir," she said.

He walked out through the trees, crossed behind the cottage, and disappeared. A moment later she saw him come out onto the road and walk down it, till a bend hid his figure from view. There was something odd, something almost vaguely familiar about his walk, but she could not think of what it reminded her.

She was unusually silent on the drive home, her Mother noticed. She was thinking intently about the man from the cave, going over all the facts, again and again, piecing them together, as her habit was. He might of course have been in there all the time, lurking in some side gallery beyond the lights, and have come out when he expected them to be gone; or he might have come in down the stone ladder formed by the Arbre de Noël after they had left it. In either case, when he did come out, he had been checked by the sight of the car; that was certain; and he was sufficiently anxious to avoid being seen to wade across the pool, wetting himself to the knees. That closed all possibility of his being just a peasant, living close by, idling about the cave, for such would have no objection to meeting people. Then there was his brief gesture when he saw her. She was sure she was not mistaken about that. She did not imagine that he had meant to shoot her, at any point—but it was the instinctive movement of a man who goes armed, and is accustomed to use his weapon. Peasants in the Pays Basque did not do either of these things. It threw a rather lurid light on him. Smugglers, even currency smugglers, seldom shot, Crumpaun had told her; that movement was the gesture of the spy, who carried his life and more than his life in his hand. And everything about him, bar his clothes, pointed to his being a man of education and of birth. Argue it as she would, minimise as she would, her mind could not resist the fantastic conclusion that she had probably seen and spoken to a real spy. Perhaps even the famous Number 17 himself! She remembered the journalists' talk of him that morning at the Bar Basque, after she had met the Condesa in the flower market. "One of their best men," someone pretty smart, who crossed the frontier at the Irún end and made direct for Biarritz. Well, if that glorious young man was not one of their best men, she would like to meet the ones who were, Rosemary thought. He was heavenly!

While Rosemary thus meditated, on the drive home, her elders discussed the nail marks on the Arbre de Noël and the behaviour of the guide. It was all very peculiar, Crossman said.

"Very suspicious, if you ask me," Mr. Oldhead observed. Rosemary, catching the drift of these remarks, put in her oar.

"Silly bat-wit of a guide!" she said breezily. "Of course the smugglers use it. But if he had kept his stupid mouth shut, we should never have paid any particular attention to it." She had already decided to keep her own mouth shut about the man from the cave for the present.

But Mr. Oldhead was not so easily satisfied. He was worried and anxious about the Republican cause at this time, and angry with the British Government for closing its eyes to the frequent and flagrant German and Italian breaches of the Non-Intervention agreement; the sabotage stories were still upsetting him, and he was not blind to the other use to which that stone staircase could be put. Later that evening Rosemary heard him discussing the whole thing with Crumpaun, and found that he was meditating a second trip to Bayonne. This she determined to prevent, if she could. She said nothing to her Father, but she sought out Crossman on her own account, and begged him not to encourage the idea. "They'll really think him utterly potty if he goes *on* reporting every rabbit-run he sees near the frontier! There's *no* evidence this time, bar the nail marks—and those were probably smugglers, or even just 'boy meets girl.' "

Crossman laughed.

"No, but do get him to lay off it, Crossey dear. We don't want him shut up in a *maison de santé* for spy mania."

Crossman laughed again, and agreed; he succeeded in persuading Mr. Oldhead to let well alone this time. Rosemary heard this with considerable relief. Spy or no spy, she felt that the world was a better place with that young man whom she had seen in Pierre Loti's orchard in it than out of it.

## CHAPTER EIGHT

### *The Far Side—Almadera and Barcelona*

ON the man or woman who really loves profoundly, over whom love has fully extended its terrible sway, a parting from the beloved always produces certain effects. There is a curious dislocated feeling, as if the will had broken its neck; it is hard for some time to relate present impressions to either thought or action—people, sights, news in newspapers float past like fish in an aquarium, a world close as touch to the lover, but not his own; and with this dislocation goes an appalling moral lassitude. The only reality is the immediate past; into that one slides back, remembering, re-feeling; handling the lovely vanished moments like jewels or cameos, and weighing, assessing, conning over every look and tone and aspect of the heart's delight.

So did James Milcom occupy himself on his journey back to Spain. Oblivious to his surroundings, his eyes fixed, desperate but unseeing, on whatever happened to be before them, he thought about Raquel, considering her as this last visit had revealed her to him. The strength of her passion was the great miracle, the supremely revealing surprise. But one question posed itself constantly. Why, seeing the effect that even one visit to Pascual had had on him, did she now send him again? She must know that he hated it—and did she not, must she not feel it a risk?—putting their great love in hazard, and for what? To send him some cigarettes and sugar, and to conform to an almost automatic standard of behaviour? He puzzled over this, worriedly; it wasn't like her, it was almost tactless. He came to the conclusion at last that she had done it because she had never really taken what he had felt and said about Pascual seriously—in the fullness of her own happy love, the ardent expansion of that side of her nature, though she had listened and argued, her *heart* wasn't paying attention. He was too modest to realise how reckless the very depth of her own passion might make her; and in spite of his dread of beauty as such, he failed to allow for another thing—the quite unconscious belief of the very beautiful woman in her own power, so that she did not even see the menace for what it was. James however did feel menaced; an undefined foreboding, lurking at the back of his mind, subconsciously disquieted him as he went on his way.

On his return to Spain this time he pushed straight on to Almadera, only pausing in Barcelona long enough to get two authorisations from the Direccion General de Prisiones. He wanted to get his more than ever distasteful mission to the Conde over as quickly as possible; besides, the rumours of an imminent Nationalist offensive were becoming daily more persistent, and once that began he would have to be, if not at the front, at least close behind it. He had also made up his mind that this time he would make a determined effort to see La Paquita and find out, once for all, what had become of Juanito. James felt that Raquel might really worry herself ill, left alone, unless he could do something to set her mind at rest.

He arrived in Almadera on November the twenty-seventh, and at once sought out the Scottish doctor who had attended him before. The young man accepted with gratitude two bottle of whiskey which James had brought; he examined the freshly formed scar on his forehead, tapped his skull here and there, and asked for headaches.

"Ye'll do," he finally pronounced. "You've done well. But do not press yourself too hard for a month or two yet. I'm glad to have seen ye." His eye rested on the bottles. "And those will be a godsend." Then he grinned sourly at James. "Going to see you White friends again?"

"Yes," said James, grinning back just as sourly. "I want badly to see La Paquita."

The doctor gave a dismal whistle.

"Man, ye'll have to hurry," he said—"they're executing her on the twenty-ninth."

"Good God!" James exclaimed, horrified.

"Ah well, she asked for it," said the doctor grimly. "A pity—they say she was brave *and* pretty. But actually, as far as seeing her goes, you've struck it lucky. This fantastic nation," he said, with a sort of sardonic admiration, "allows prisoners to see their friends on the day of their execution. It's usually quite a party, I'm told. If you get your name put down on the Governor's list, I should say you'll have no trouble. Have you an authorisation?"

James nodded.

"Not much of a moment for a stranger to go barging in on her, asking questions," said he gloomily.

"Ah, she won't care. They get quite exalted then," the doctor said. "Astonishing, they are."

James spent the whole of the next day getting his local permits to visit the Conde and to be present at the execution. He disliked the idea extremely, but it was his last hope of finding anything out. And he had seen enough of death in Spain to know that the doctor's last words were perfectly true. La Paquita would almost certainly not mind seeing him, or being asked questions—whether she would answer them was another matter.

The execution was fixed for 10 a.m., and visitors were allowed in to see the prisoner from 8.30 onwards. Milcom was to visit the Conde when it was over. The whole arrangement was as gruesome a one as could well have been devised, but there was no help for it—he did not wish to stay over an extra day, and he had to see Pascual and deliver Raquel's presents and messages. He slept wretchedly, fell into a heavy doze about six, was not called according to promise at seven, and only woke, heavy and unrefreshed, soon after eight. He shaved and dressed in a frantic hurry, gulped down some scalding coffee, and arrived hungry, sweating, and perturbed at the prison gates as the great clock overhead was striking nine. There were still further delays while the doorkeeper was fetched from his breakfast to examine his special pass, and his internal state of nervousness, irritation, and embarrassment by the time he was finally ushered into the prisoner's presence was extreme.

It was, as the doctor had foretold, quite a party. Some twenty men and women, mostly dressed in black, made a funereal group in the large dirty room, coldly lit by high northern windows; by the door were several warders and hangers-on. The priest had been with her, and still knelt, praying, a little apart—his face and attitude reminded Milcom of a Zurbarán apostle. Embarrassed, Milcom stood for a moment or two, taking stock of the situation. There was no mistaking Francisca de Verdura. She was a girl of perhaps twenty-three, small, and slighter than is usual with Spanish women, dressed in some sort of uniform; her black hair was cropped short, which gave her a boyish air; her face had the chiselled finished look of so many Spanish faces, but with an appearance of extreme delicacy and fragility. Someone had brought her a great bouquet of red carnations, and she was holding these while she talked, in a low voice but with great animation, to two or three of her friends; the others stood round in a still patience, a sort of frozen emotional quiet like that of the crowd in an El Greco martyrdom—it was extraordinary, James thought in passing, how true to type the Spaniards run, century after century. She herself showed no sign of nervousness or fear at all.

James stood for some time watching them—but he had a job to do, and he presently nerved himself to do it. He moved over and touched the arm of an elderly man standing on the fringe of the group. "Por favor," he said—"I have need to speak with the Condesa. Is it possible? My name is Milcom."

"Inglés?" the other asked.

"Inglés."

The elderly man, without further question, in his turn went forward and spoke to the girl; she turned at once, and came to Milcom, with a quick light step.

"You wished to see me?"

"With many apologies, yes," said James. "I come from Raquel de Verdura."

Her face lit up.

"Raquel? Oh, how I love her! How is she? Is is true that she is in France? Are you her friend?"

In spite of himself and of the occasion, James found that he was smiling; her pleasure, her eagerness, were so infectious.

"Yes, we are friends," he said. "She is at St. Jean-de-Luz, with the Duquesa; and when I left her there, just a week ago, she was very well."

"And you come to see Pascual? You are the English who came before?"

James assented. "But this time I wished also to see you. There is a question I wish to ask—otherwise I should not have disturbed you. And I beg you to pardon my intrusion."

She waved that idea away with another of her brilliant smiles, and a light gesture with the bunch of carnations.

"Ask," she said.

He bent nearer to her, and lowered his voice.

"Raquel is well, as I said," he murmured, "but she is almost in despair because she has had no news of Juanito for many months. She does not know if he is alive or dead. She is fretting herself to death on his account. And I wondered—" he paused—"I wondered if you could perhaps put me in the way of getting news of him."

She narrowed her eyes at him.

"Will you tell me why you thought that?"

"A chance word, the last time I was here, from a fellow prisoner of your cousin. I ask it only for her sake," he said earnestly.

She still studied his face.

"You are our friend?" she asked at length.

"No," said James bluntly. "I am not, in politics. But I am her friend."

She laughed at that.

"Oh, I like you! For that, I trust you. Do you ever go to Barcelona?"

"Yes—I go back there to-morrow," he said, a little puzzled.

"Then go to a barber's shop in the Calle de las Floras, with over it the name 'Pablo'; go in and demand that Pablo himself shaves you, and while he does, and his face is close to your mouth, ask him for news of Manuel Jereda. I have no recent news, but Pablo will know."

"Will he tell me?"

"Say that I sent you. And if he still will not, say that you will ask him the same question seventeen times. I think then that he will answer."

"Thank you," James said, gravely. "I am beyond measure grateful to you."

"No hay de que," she said, smiling.

"Indeed yes"—and once more he begged her pardon for troubling her then.

"For a friend of Raquel's I have time, even now," she said, still smiling. "Give her my love, and tell her that I was happy," she went on; "but whatever Pablo tells you, tell *no one* but her." Quite casually, then, she glanced at her wrist watch. James bowed—really he could not speak—and moved away, while she returned to her friends.

His job was done, and he could have left then, but some obscure impulse of loyalty to this gallant creature made him decide to stay. If she could go through with it, he could, he thought stubbornly. Also it occurred to him that Raquel would wish it, would be glad to hear how Francisca died. So he remained, leaning against the wall at the side of the room, till a group of officials came and led her away to the prison courtyard, followed by the priest and the little group of friends, James among them. The courtyard was a big yellow rectangle; the sun streamed onto the upper wall at one side, so that the square was warmly lit with a golden reflected glow, a curiously theatrical light. The other inmates of the prison stood in close ranks along two sides of the square, guarded by warders—James noticed the Conde's tall figure among them; on the third side stood the firing squad, some sixteen men and an officer; the fourth wall was empty. La Paquita, still carrying her bouquet, walked quietly towards it with the priest, the Governor, and a couple of warders; the rest of the little party ranged themselves at one side. One of the warders came up to her with a scarf in his hands—she waved it aside with the flowers, with the same gesture of negation that she had used to James. She turned, kissed the woman who stood nearest her, kissed the crucifix which the priest held out. Then, stepping up to the Governor, she broke one of the red carnations off her bouquet, and put it in his buttonhole. He bowed gravely. Still quite quietly, but quickly, she walked across to the firing squad, and breaking off the carnations one by one, she put a flower in each man's buttonhole. One of the warders made a movement as if to stop her, but the Governor raised his hand, and the man stood back. When she came to the last, she said in a ringing voice—"It is for Spain," and walked back to the fourth wall and waited, standing there alone, the broken stalks of her bouquet, with two or three flowers remaining, still in her hand—very small, very slight, very fragile. "I am quite ready," she said in a small voice to the Governor—and then, very clearly, "*Arriba España!*" As she spoke the volley rang out, and she crumpled up and fell sideways. The priest dropped to his knees, holding out the crucifix towards the small body; the warders closed ranks round it, quickly. The group of friends also knelt, while the firing squad, obeying a word of command, turned about and tramped out; the prisoners followed; last of all the little group of friends, James again with them.

He left the prison with the rest, and waited in the sun outside till the prisoners should have got back to their cells—all over the building there was a tramp of feet, and the clang of doors being slammed and locked. He felt a strong desire to have a whiskey and soda, or to go into a church and pray—or even both; as he could do neither he sat on the parapet, glad of the sun—he was one of the people whom emotion makes physically cold—and watched the little party of La Paquita's friends trailing away down the hill. Even outside, walking, in their rather shabby black clothes, they somehow kept their look of people out of a religious mural painting; so might the disciples have looked, he thought, trailing away downhill from Gologotha. Francisca's death had hit James rather a full blow. Her courage and gallantry, combined with her grace and air of fragility, had made her death in his sight a thing of beauty and terror. He remembered how in the *corrida* the Spaniards call the second when the matador stands poised at the final stroke "the moment of truth"—which really means almost the moment of understanding. In his brief exchange of sentences with that graceful creature he felt that he had somehow partaken of that moment with her. And it left him at once exalted and shattered. Yes, damn it, it was a religious war, this; that brave pretty creature inside had died for her faith in Fascism, and the courteous marble-faced Governor had had her shot, firm in his faith in Communism or something like it—anyhow an opposed political faith. And unless this terrifying infection could be checked, presently all Europe, all the world, would be fighting with religious zeal for or against some creed or other. Why the hell couldn't all the extremists let the thing alone, and allow sensible people, who didn't want to be either Fascists or Communists, to get on with the job?—the job being to live the good life, attend to education, improve living conditions and so on. But that, he realised, was the Englishman in him speaking, or rather the normanised Anglo-Saxon—outside the British Empire and the United States, where normanised Anglo-Saxon humanity ruled, and compromise was in the blood, everyone was to some extent infected with these new faiths, new dogmas. They were believed to be a short cut to the Good Life, as religion was once thought to be— only a few nations, indeed only a few individuals, relatively speaking, realised that there is no short cut to the Good Life; only long years, long centuries of painful complicated ding-dong struggle and effort.

The little procession was out of sight now. He got up, yawning with hunger, and went back into the prison to see the Conde.

Pascual greeted him with a warmth which rather touched James.

"Ah, my friend, I have waited for you!" He held Milcom's hands in both his, and if Milcom had thought that Francisca's friends, ten minutes before, looked like the disciples, he himself at that moment felt like Judas.

"I saw you *there*," the Conde went on. "That was good of you— to go with her. Raquel loved her much. Did you speak with her?"

James said he had.

"She was firm? As outside?"

"Perfectly. She sent Raquel her love."

He reddened as he spoke. In the simplicity of his emotion he had used her Christian name to the Conde, a thing he had not done before. But Pascual took it with an equal simplicity. He asked in great detail for his wife, as before, and read the note she had sent, and heard her messages; and smiled with the direct matter-of-fact pleasure of a nice child over her presents, the sugar, the cigarettes, the handkerchiefs—his fellow prisoners, Pepe among them, as before crowding round and getting their share. Then they went over and sat in a corner, the Conde on his own soapbox, Milcom on one which Pepe brought him, and the Conde spoke again of Francisca.

"She was brave, very brave," he said. "It moved me, the flowers. That is how one should die! Ah, friend, we have much to learn from women, concerning courage and concerning love. With their slight bodies and their delicate spirits, they have yet immense courage, and they turn all to beauty, as she did. I have thought much lately about women," said the Conde, still with that simplicity which seemed to be his keynote that morning. He stooped, and once again pulled the worn first edition of *Jude the Obscure* out of his soapbox, along with the dictionary which James had sent from Barcelona.

E*

"So glad I was, to have that," he said, tapping it. "I have learned so many words. And with it, I have understood this much better." Now he tapped the Hardy. "I have learned much from it," he said. "Never have I read a book like this before. It is wonderful. He knew a great deal about women, no?"

"He knew much about all humanity," James said. "He was one of the great understanders."

The Conde sighed.

"*Si*. You are right. Understanding is what one needs. One does not think, and so ones does not understand, or know; one is not careful enough. Women, now—one is accustomed to think that external things, and a little love, suffice for them. I see now that this is not so. External things are most unimportant. These poor simple creatures"—again he tapped the novel—"had great souls, a great love—in effect, a great life. One may truly say that of them. And yet they were altogether of the people." He sighed again. "And at last I see also that those with great possessions, with a high position, may all the time be leading a small mean life, within."

"All that is most true, what you say," said James; he felt that it was time for him to say something. The Conde's self-revelation at once touched and disconcerted him.

"Ah, I knew you would understand," Pascual said. "I can speak to you as a friend. What a friend you have been to us! Both! And since you came before, I have wearied for your return. When the soul is full of some idea, one wishes to speak of it, to one at least—and I have now no one but you. See," he said, settling himself squarely on his soapbox and looking earnestly at Milcom—"much is now clear to me that before I was blind to, about Raquel. You forgive me, *amigo*, that I speak to you of our own concerns? But indeed we have never had such a friend as you."

"De nada," said James. "Please do not speak of the little I have done. It was a happiness."

But nothing would stop the Conde.

"That is your good heart. Before, I had no such idea of the English—I though them haughty and cold, and lacking in heart. Now I know better. But concerning Raquel—if I get out from here, I shall try to make things otherwise for her. It will not be as in the past. I understand so much more, both what she is and, being what she is, what she needs." He looked ahead of him, past Milcom, as if gazing at Raquel standing in the future as in a landscape. "She is not too old to have another child, or even several," he said with great naturalness. "I shall make all otherwise for her," he repeated. "At least, I shall try," he added humbly.

"I am so glad," he said presently, "that I have spent these two years here, and been given this opportunity to learn something of the truth about life. This book, too—and those." He waved at his fellow prisoners. "Outside, in my life as I lived it, I should never have come to know such as they, and learned what they have to teach. I have been fortunate."

James listened to all this with mounting feelings of distress, of horror, that were yet most strangely mixed with compassion and even an unwilling admiration for the man before him. So he wanted Raquel to go back to him and be his? Everything in James cried out in protest at the bare idea. And yet—oh God!— he had been right about the Conde the first time, and Raquel wrong. If there had never been that most sacred thing, a change of heart, in the world before, there was one now, and there it was, sitting in front of him, on a soapbox in a prison.

But besides telling James his hopes for the future the Conde had, it appeared, a request to make. He did it with great humility—"You who have done so much for us should not be asked to do more." Of course James told him to ask away, little guessing what was coming.

There was, it seemed, a chance that the Conde might be got out, and that quite soon—exchanged for a well-known Republican prisoner. And for this he wished to invoke James's good offices. A word to the British Embassy at Barcelona might help —they were concerned in the exchanges; so was the Madrid Embassy, now at St.-Jean-de-Luz. There were one or two Spaniards in Barcelona who would certainly be of use—he gave their names and addresses; one was that of Raquel's Red cousin, who had assisted in their escape and whom she had shuddered to meet.

James was appalled by this request. His first sensation was one of wild revolt, of an absolute refusal to contemplate doing this thing, to which, if he did contemplate it, decency would ultimately compel him. He actually got up from his stool and took a step down the room, his very body seeking escape in movement from the pressure of this intolerable situation; then he realised that this would attract the attention of the other prisoners, and disconcert Pascual, and he sat down again. It was no good. Of course he would have to do it. But that his must be the hand to undo the door and let the fellow out was one of those turns of events which he privately called "needless." He had listened to the Conde's humble outpouring of his hopes and happy resolutions with an almost passionate wish that they could remain unspoken, or at least that it need not be he who heard; but he had been profoundly moved by them all the same. And now, as he sat on the soapbox scribbling down names and addresses, the Conde watching him with trustful happy eyes, the other prisoners chipping and whittling away at their bits of teak at the far end of the room, he had one of those moments of desperate lucidity which come to us, unsought and undesired. He too saw the future as a landscape, through which he must walk, with the figure of Raquel in it, bidding him farewell; he even had a momentary irrelevant wonder as to where and how they would say good-bye. During that brief flash of illumination the end was as clear as that, whatever desperate turns and twists his mind and heart might make, vague and dim as the intervening passages might be. It was one of the bitterest moments of Milcom's life.

The first step, however, was to finish the interview with decency. He could not hurry away. They sat and talked for some time, discussing when the offensive would begin, and where. James gave news of the outside world, such as there was. The Conde, again stooping to his soapbox, fished out a finished necklace of the carved peach stones threaded on a piece of thin string, for James to take to Raquel; it was an extraordinarily delicate and beautiful piece of work to have come from those big hands.

"It should be on a silken cord," the Conde said wistfully— "and a snap I could not make. I thought that perhaps you could get that done in Barcelona." James promised to do so. Then the Conde pulled out of his breast pocket his *magnum opus*—a belt buckle, made of four rings of teak, each one interlocking with the next. It was not quite finished.

"That, if God is good, and with your help, I shall give to her myself," he said, with such an enraptured face of simple happiness that it was more than James could stand. He spoke of his hunger —which existed—and took his departure. This time the Conde embraced him at parting; James left the prison asking himself, with a sour smile, which of them was really the Judas.

He set out for Barcelona next day with a profound distaste for both the errands which he had undertaken there. To have to go and bother the Embassy was the least of his worries, though it meant getting all the way out to Caldetas, and was almost certainly a work of supererogation—if the Embassy thought that any useful purpose would be served by getting the Conde released,

they would be trying to get him released anyhow. James had the
healthy respect of most better-class and experienced journalists for
H.M. Diplomatic Service abroad—quiet sensible helpful people,
he thought them, and uncommonly well-informed as a rule. He
knew something of the back-breaking work that these particular
members of that service had been putting in over the exchanges of
prisoners. It was a most thankless task, which in each case could
only be carried through with any hope of success if someone sufficiently influential at Salamanca were sufficiently interested in
some White prisoner on the Republican side to be willing to persuade the authorities to "trade" him for some Red prisoner on the
Franco side, in whom someone sufficiently influential at Barcelona
was sufficiently interested to be helpful. There then inevitably
ensued a long wrangle over the respective value of the two
prisoners, in which the Franquistas were undoubtedly the harder
bargainers. Both sides were tiresome, the Republicans offering to
trade unimportant Dukes or Marquises for "key" Red leaders,
while the austere Nationalists would frequently not stoop to consider the wishes of their own families, and in any case seemed to
care little whether any prisoners were released or not. Unless
they had some religious significance—Milcom, like most journalists in Spain, had heard of the famous Franco attempt to exchange
a quite valuable Republican prisoner for the famous statue of
Nuestra Señora de Covadonga, "*Esta muy sagrada y muy venerada
Imagen*," which had been carried off into captivity by the Republican troops. No, apart from his own private feelings, which were
wretched and conflicting enough, what James disliked in this
business was all this getting himself mixed up with Whites and the
relations of Whites. With the offensive pending, everyone in
Barcelona would be as nervous as a sackful of witches, and touchy
and suspicious in proportion—and it was the last moment when
he wished to do anything to queer his own pitch.

He reached Barcelona on the second of December, and got in
touch with Raquel's cousin at once. The cousin was not particularly pro-Conde, but he was most anxious to hear about La
Paquita, and when he found that James had actually been present
at the execution, and had heard his story, he was so much im-
pressed that he undertook to do all he could, as much for James's
sake as anything, the latter gathered. This produced a grimace
from James—there you were! Just what he didn't want. From the
cousin he made his way out to Caldetas. The Embassy, he found,
was already on the job—that is to say the Conde's name was high
up on a list of exchangees submitted by the British Agency at

Burgos. James contributed Raquel's Scottish grandmother, which the smooth-faced courteous young man whom he saw promptly noted in red on the list; he would put it up to the Minister, he said. These people were personally known to James? Friends of his? Ah yes. That went down too—James guessed at the note: "Personal friends of the *Epoch* correspondent."

"But of course—you got her out, didn't you?" said the smooth-faced young man, smiting his well-brushed brow. "Stupid of me! This bombing makes one so stupid, don't you find?"

James did find that the bombing made him both tired and stupid. Barcelona was getting a pretty good plastering early in December of '38, though mostly by daylight; the nights were pretty quiet, thank goodness. But all this popping into shelters and running for doorways, and the noise and dust and general strain, were both fatiguing and stupefying.

His own misery would have been sufficient to exhaust him anyhow. It increased from hour to hour. A flash of illumination, a foreseeing of the future, was one thing,—but walking through that future, step by step, was quite another, he found. The struggle between his love and his sense of right never ceased for an instant; even as he sat in the Embassy at Caldetas, talking to the smooth-faced young man, his heart was asking wildly how he could ever give Raquel up, even if the Conde were freed ten times over? He might be a changed man now, but in the past he had ill-used her cruelly, neglected and humiliated her; he had had his chance and he had thrown it away—why should he be given a second one now at his, James's, expense? And at hers? Was this man's newly-found goodness to be as much the enemy of Raquel's happiness as his scoundrelism had been in the past? That would be the supreme irony.

But his conscience would not let him accept any other solution. Back and back he came to the impossibility of knocking a man's soul on the head at the very moment that it had come to birth. He, James, had no rights except what his love gave him—and Pascual, if he was any judge of a man's heart, now had that right too. Night and day the conflict went on, his own inner stress and struggle mingling with the urgent stress around him. Barcelona was in a state of strain and tension; more and older men were being called up, women were more and more in evidence doing the work of men. God, how tough they all were!

He went on the second day to Pablo the barber, in the Calle de las Floras, a small dirty street on the fringe of the harbour district. He went early in the morning, partly to avoid notice, partly be-

cause the bombing generally began later in the day; the shutters
had only just been opened—there was no glass left in the windows
—and a small boy in shirt-sleeves was sweeping out the shop.
James asked for the *dueño*, and sat down with a cigarette to wait
for him. The shop was fairly large, with five or six shabby leather
chairs facing a row of fly-blown mirrors—at least it had been a
row, but three had vanished altogether, and of those that remained, one was in two halves and one was splintered. After a
leisurely interval the barber appeared, in his shirt-sleeves, carrying a copper can of hot water—a small thick-set fellow with
grizzled curly hair and a magnificent moustache, like that of a
Victorian dandy, who responded rather glumly to James's greeting, and set about shaving him. James asked if he was the Señor
Pablo, and received an affirmative nod. Early as it was, there
was no one in the shop besides themselves and the small boy, who
shuffled about in broken shoes much too big for him, rather in-
efficiently dusting and polishing; but James waited till his face was
well enveloped in white lather and then, as the man bent over him
with the razor, asked—"Where is Manuel Jereda?"

The man either did not hear or pretended not to; he began to
run the razor down James's cheek. James put up his hand on the
other side, wiped his lips free of foam, and said again—"I want
news of Manuel Jereda."

"Never heard the name," the barber muttered grumpily, and
went on shaving James. It was a ridiculous situation; to talk
through the lather was next to impossible—for a moment he wondered if Francisca had been pulling his leg. No—not then. He
tried again; putting up his hand warningly, he muttered—"Nevertheless, La Paquita told me that you could tell me of him."

The barber laid aside the razor, took up another, felt the blade
with his thumb, and muttered, as he bent over James's whitened
face again—"What do you know of La Paquita?"

"I saw her die, four days ago," James said. "She sent me to
you half an hour before she died."

The barber turned and shouted to the small boy—"Diego! Go
and fetch the newspaper!" Then he turned back to James again
and went on shaving him. When the child had left the shop he
said very low—"Why should I believe you? Who are you?"

"I am English," James muttered back. "And I shall ask you
the same question till I get an answer, if it is seventeen times."

"So," Pablo said thoughtfully. "So." He glanced round—
the shop was still empty; with a dingy cloth he wiped James's
face, and asked—"What is it you want to know?"

"Where he is; what he is doing; whether he is well?"

"And why do you, an *Inglés*, want to know these things, already knowing so much? You are a *partizan*?"

"His sister, who is in France, desires to know these things," James said, evading the question.

In the splintered mirror in front of him he saw the barber's face take on a faintly astonished expression.

"His sister? She should know more than I, that one."

"On the contrary, she knows nothing. For months she hears no word. Therefore La Paquita sent me to you."

The barber shrugged his broad shoulders.

"Well, as you know, he is 'working'," he said; "he is an officer with *los rojos*. He gets information, and he gets it out." A grin, a mere movement of his beard, gave Pablo's face a sudden frighteningly cynical and wicked expression. "He gets special leave for that, because *they* think he is working for *them*. And indeed he is always given something to tell them—small, and not important, but always true. He has to work fast, and he has done well. But it gets more and more difficult to do it fast enough," he said, with a sort of thoughtful discontent.

"Why?"

"Ah, those pigs of French!" He used an excessively bad word. "Tighter and tighter they draw the net. One passage after another stopped. But he is a quick worker."

"And he is well? She will wish to know that—she is anxious."

"Blood of martyrs, a sick man could not do what he does! But you can tell her this—there is one more big job to be done, perhaps two; and after that, if all goes well, it will be over, and he will return to his own place."

"How soon?"

"Depending on how all goes, within two weeks or three."

Diego, the boy, came shuffling back, bringing the newspaper. Pablo handed it to James, who opened it and made a pretence of reading while Pablo wiped his razors. "See," Milcom said presently, pointing to the page; and as the barber leant over his shoulder—"I thank you," he said. "I go soon to France, and I will give Manuel's sister this news—and to no other."

He put down the paper, got up, and paid. Diego the boy was sent out to fetch change. While he was gone:—

"That is right," Pablo said. "But that she should not know this—that is the mystery! I thought she was seeing him regularly. After all, she is working herself."

"She is in France," James said.

"*Verdad*—I know she is."

A sick spasm of suspicion ran over Milcom like cold water down the spine. Could it be that Raquel, for some reason, had been fooling him all this time? Then, for the first time since he entered the shop, he remembered that Juanito had *two* sisters. But Diego at that moment returning with his change, he gave no explanation, but said "Adiós" and went.

He continued to think hard about what he had learned, all that day, with a sort of sickness at his heart. So Raquel's brother was definitely a White spy, and Raquel's sister another! A nice kettle of fish for him, Milcom, to be mixed up in. And if the Duquesa was in the Biarritz racket, as Pablo's last words implied, could it really be that Raquel knew nothing of it? He went carefully over all Pablo's words. "I thought she was seeing him regularly . . . I know she is in France . . . He gets information and he gets it out—he gets special leave to do that." This could easily mean that Juanito himself was crossing the frontier—indeed it could hardly mean anything else. But if that were so, could the Duquesa really be so brutal as to keep all knowledge of it from her sister? Yes, he finally decided, easily—she was a tough-minded woman, and a fanatical White; and spies must have no feelings, and no loyalties but one.

James had not been at St.-Jean-de-Luz when Hever's sabotage story first broke and gossip about Number 17 was so particularly rife, and on this last visit he had been too taken up with Raquel to have much time to spare for his fellow journalists; but he had, as in duty bound, compared notes with Crumpaun and Crossman —he had heard Number 17 mentioned, and some talk of sabotage in connection with him. And of course he had heard of the various acts of sabotage at the time, in Barcelona itself, where they naturally caused enormous indignation and concern. Latterly they seemed to have slackened somewhat. But his own position was a horrible one. With the White offensive pending, it was vital to the cause he cared for that there should be no more leakages and no more sabotage—and a word from him could have one of the main causes of leakage removed forthwith. Yes, and have Juanito, the being Raquel loved most in the world, stood up against a wall and shot, as he had seen Francisca de Verdura shot a couple of days ago—that would be nice, too. God, what a mess it was! Suddenly angry, almost breaking under the dual strain of these two internal conflicts, he thought how right he had been in Perpignan, two months before, when he told himself what a silly business it was for him, James Milcom, to have fallen in love with a White. It *was* a silly business. His job, his life was with politics, mankind, the world—not with love and spies and Spanish grandees' souls and what-have-you! He ought to have left her then, cut the thing off and finished with it. He was in love with her then, already—but not as now—not as now! And he had never imagined at the time that it could lead to anything like this, that that gentle helpless creature, his fellow ghost from the city of ghosts would end by involving him in a situation where he must betray the cause he believed in and held just, out of a complex of loyalties, and for her sake. For his silence, his complicity in Juanito's activities amounted in his own eyes to active betrayal.

Ah, and he had never dreamed then, either, of how far his love would lead him, though he had hesitated, jibbed, and feared. He remembered, with a sort of wonder, his doubts then as to whether she did or ever would love him too, recalling her passionate tenderness of his last visit to St.-Jean. It had still been in the shadows, that time at Perpignan—and then the sun had come, breaking out and illuminating his whole life with an undreamed-of radiance and glory. And now that had got to go, too.

He couldn't give Juanito away, of course. He owed his present knowledge to the trust of a woman about to die, and to that same woman he had given his word to tell no one but Raquel. But the mere possession of that knowledge made him unutterably wretched during those days in Barcelona, days of tense forboding, feverish and despairing preparations, and fierce resolution.

He learned on December the tenth from the Embassy that the Conde's transfer had been arranged, and that he was to go to Burgos almost immediately, through Spain itself—so the smooth-faced young secretary at Caldetas assured him. How amusing they were—and yet how efficient—these young men, with their baby faces and their pontifical manners, James thought, thanking him. He went and left a little money for the Conde's expenses with the cousin, and then sent Raquel a telegram—GOOD NEWS OF BOTH COMING ST.-JEAN ABOUT SIXTEENTH. He had decided to go at once, and get it over, and to hurry back before the offensive broke, if it could be done. Anyhow he must go, and give her his two pieces of news as soon as possible. But he had an interview with del Vayo fixed for the twelfth, so he could not leave till after that. He filled in the interval by working on one of those long dispatches, reasoned and yet somehow glowing with restrained passion, which the *Epoch* valued so highly from him—giving a picture of the mental tone in Barcelona on the eve of the offensive, and assessing, as well as he could, the chances of the Republicans.

He would air-mail it from Perpignan. It was delaying to post dispatches from Spain. He had his interview, and on the thirteenth, heavy-hearted, he set out for St.-Jean-de-Luz.

## CHAPTER NINE

### *This Side—St.-Jean-de-Luz*

DURING Milcom's absence the Condesa and Rosemary had seen a great deal of one another. Adolescent girls in love are rarely jealous, and the instinctive sympathy and liking which had grown up between them was if anything nourished by the fact of their both loving the same man. It may be doubted whether Raquel de Verdura in fact realised that Rosemary was in love with Milcom, though she was certainly sensitive enough to have taken such a feeling seriously if she had realised it. But they liked being together, they liked talking about him—and did, a great deal; and Rosemary had a boundless appetite for hearing about the Condesa's own life: her girlhood in Spain, her parents, her married life, Pilar's childhood, her experiences in Madrid, and above all and woven through it all, Juanito, Juantio, Juanito. The girl prompted these confidences, partly out of a perfectly spontaneous interest in other people's lives, which made her an ideally sympathetic listener, partly out of a self-protective instinct, half unconscious, to build a sort of ring-fence of other interests with which to defend herself against too many thoughts of Milcom.

This self-protectiveness led her in other directions beside the Condesa—made her in fact snatch at any occupation which would rescue her, if only for a time, from her own pain; and one of the things at which she so snatched was the Count de Barrial and his boats.

The Count de Barrial was one of those French residents at St.-Jean-de-Luz whose social circle overlapped with that of the permanent British colony, into which Mrs. Oldhead had penetrated; she met him and his pretty intelligent literary wife at a number of those little lunches, little cocktail parties—and she introduced him to Rosemary one day at the cinema. Talking afterwards, her Mother—with a slight envy of the child's extraordinary ease and skill in personal contacts—heard Rosemary eliciting from him the fact that he was a passionate amateur yachtsman; that he had a thirty-ton cutter with an auxiliary engine in which he sailed to England, to Portugal, and to Morocco, as well as a speed-boat and a tiny sailing-boat. And the next thing was that Rosemary and the Count—for all that the official sailing season was over—were scooting about the bay in the speed-boat, and sailing down to Hendaye in the small sailing-boat. The de Barrials had a pretty old villa with thick walls and vaulted ceilings out at Socoa, quite near the yacht-club, and after an afternoon's sailing the girl often went in for a meal, before being driven back to the Grande Bretagne in the Count's Chevrolet. Those days at sea were the best alleviation for a sick heart that could have been devised; and between the Count's boats and the Condesa's past life, Rosemary did herself pretty well in the way of a ring-fence against grief.

It was of course natural that she should have been almost the first person to whom the Condesa showed Milcom's telegram.

"See—he says 'Good news of both'; that must mean that he has news of Juanito too. At *last*!" she said, her lovely face alight. "And he is coming to tell me. It might not be wise to telegraph it. I wonder if he got it from Pascual."

"What do you suppose the good news of the Conde is?" Rosemary asked.

"That he is well, I hope—I expect it is that," Raquel said. "Think—in five days I shall hear."

Rosemary rejoiced with her, sincerely—but what her own heart said was "in five days I shall see him." The idea brought an absurd gladness that nothing could repress. Sitting in her bedroom, looking out past the small tiled cupola of the old Casino at the bright picture of the bay, she argued vigorously with herself. "You're nuts to be so braced, you silly owl; you'll only have to stick around and watch him worshipping her—naturally. And then you'll be wretched. And serve you right." But it was no good. As an addict craves for his drug, and the more after being deprived of it, so Rosemary craved for the mere sight of Milcom; just his presence, his face and hands and tall figure, the sound of his voice, fed her secret hunger. And this she would have—in five days.

Milcom wired again from Toulouse giving the time of his train, and at nine in the evening the Condesa went down to the station to meet him. She had wound about her head a little black lace scarf, such as women in the Pays Basque, in this hatless age, carry in their handbag to put on when they go into Church; she stood on the windy platform, watching the polished lines of rails shining under the arc-lights, up towards Bayonne, down towards Irún. Then the train came roaring in; Milcom, from the coach door, saw her standing there, her copper-coloured hair gleaming through the black lace, and his heart seemed to turn over. Was it really possible that there was a place in the landscape of his future in which she would stand and bid him farewell?

"Have you dined?" she asked him at once, when they had greeted one another.

"No—and you?"

"Not yet—I thought we might go somewhere quiet, and talk."

"Excellent idea," James said. He gave his bag to a porter to be taken up to the hotel, and they walked across the windy Place under the cropped leafless plane-trees, towards the harbour. In a dark angle between houses he stopped and drew her to him. "Oh, my darling!" Holding her in his arms again, after so long, with hands and lips and breath declaring their oneness, he felt afresh a sick surge of revolt at the thought of what he had come to do, and must do.

They dined at Gaston's. It was too cold for sitting outside, but they had a corner table, and the place was nearly empty, so that they could talk in peace.

"Yes, I have found out about him," James said in a low voice, in answer to her question. "He is safe enough, so far. He is 'working'—as a Republican officer, it seems, and sending his information back. He is being very valuable, I was told. So that is why you didn't hear."

"Yes," she said. "I wondered sometimes if it was that. And yet it seems odd that we should not have heard a word, Olivia and I. After all, others have worked, and one has known it."

His work was particularly important, James reminded her. He was not going to tell her of his private suspicions that the precious Olivia *had* known, all along; nor of the probability that Juanito had actually been crossing the frontier—it would only disturb her. "I gathered that it will soon be over, this job," he went on. "They told me he had one or two more particularly big things to do, and that then he would go back."

"How soon?" she asked.

His heart warmed to her for never once referring to the danger of the task on which Juanito was engaged.

"Two or three weeks," he said.

"That was when?"

"On the second."

She counted. "Then in a week he should be out of it. Thank

God! How did you manage to learn all this?" she asked. "Not from Pascual?"

"No," he said, "not from him. It was La Paquita who put me in the way of hearing it."

"Ah, the dear child! So you saw her. How delightful! How is she? Didn't you find her charming?"

"I thought she was the most gallant creature I have ever seen," James answered gravely. "But, my darling, I see you haven't heard."

"Heard what?" she said, very agitated. "Heard what, James? What have they done to her?"

"They shot her," he said. "On the twenty-ninth. I was just in time to see her."

"Please tell me," she said, in a small voice.

"I will. I was there," James said—and he told her the story, and how the girl had sent her love to Raquel and bid him tell her that she was happy. "And she was," he said. "She was absolutely calm. And so courteous and gay to me." He went on to the end. When she heard about the carnations Raquel sat up very straight.

"Valiente! That is just like her. I am glad." She dabbed at her eyes with one of James's handkerchiefs. "So then you went and saw this barber person in Barcelona?" she went on, turning away from a subject that she could see distressed him.

Yes, James told her. He made rather a funny story of his conversation with Pablo, blowing his questions through clouds of lather at the suspicious grumpy old man—Raquel laughed.

"I wish I had seen you—I wonder he did not cut your throat! And I wonder that he would tell you," she said thoughtfully, "not knowing you."

La Paquita had given him a pass-word, James said. (He was not going to mention the figure seventeen either—she must certainly have heard about that.) "And also she had told me under what name to ask for him. Oh by the way, yes—you ought to know that. It is Manuel Jereda."

She repeated the name, softly and carefully.

"They do that," she said. "Turn the names round, family name and baptismal name, using the same initials." She sighed, lightly. "Ah, how I thank you for finding out all this. And for staying with that darling Francisca. Now tell me about Pascual. Does he know about her?"

"Oh yes. He was there. They had them all out to watch," said James rather bitterly.

She looked at him thoughtfully. "Spaniards are a cruel people," she said slowly—"that is a fact. I believe it is partly their courage that makes them so."

"I have sometimes thought that myself," said James. But he wanted now, wretchedly, to tell her Pascual's news and get that at least over. He used the beads as an introduction. He felt in his overcoat pocket and pulled out a small package, which he handed to her. "A present from Pascual," he said.

"From Pascual?" she looked at him in surprise. Then she undid the package, and took out the necklace of carved peach stones. James had duly had them strung on a silken cord with a proper snap. It was, by any standards, a pretty thing.

"*Pascual* made this?" She looked astonished. "But it is lovely. How did he do it? He could not carve at all, that I know of."

"I told you before that he was doing it. They all sit for hours, chipping away with bits of glass."

"It is lovely," she said again, and he saw the tears come into her eyes. "Poor Pascual," she said. "He is well?" she asked then.

Now for it! James thought. Aloud——

"Yes," he said. "And Raquel, he is going to be released almost at once."

There—it was out. His hands were cold, he found, and yet he was sweating.

"Released?" she said. "But how?" She spoke incredulously, as if it were impossible, her eyes fixed on his face. The news made her cold too, he could see; after she had spoken she shivered, though it was warm in the stuffy low-lighted little restaurant.

"Exchanged," he answered her question. "It was all settled when I wired you from Barcelona. He will be back in Burgos any day now—he may be there already. He promised to send word as soon as he could."

She sat very still—she was always rather a still person, but this was a sort of concentrated immobility.

"This, too, you did for him?" she asked at last.

"Not much," James answered. "I think it was pretty well settled already. I saw your cousin Rodrigo about it in Barcelona, and our Embassy, and just gave the thing a push—that was all."

Does she blame me for doing that? he thought—does she think I wouldn't have done it if I had loved her enough? Oh, God, if she only knew how I love her! He watched her face; she was looking at him with an expression that he could not fathom, except that there was certainly love in it—and for some time was silent.

"I am glad for him," she said at last. James said nothing. "He goes back to Burgos, you say?" James said yes. She stirred her coffee, but did not drink it.

"He will rejoin his regiment, I suppose," she said. James agreed that Pascual had in fact hoped to do this. Then they were both silent again. By now they were the only people left in the small restaurant, and a waiter was hovering round them uneasily—some of the lights had already been put out.

"Let's go, shall we?" James said. He called for the bill, paid it, put her into her coat, and put on his own. They went out in silence.

They walked across to the edge of the quay, where the blue and green sardine boats danced gently on the heaving water under the high arc-lights, as they had seen them dance the first time that they dined at Gaston's, more than two months before. Both were thinking of that other night, but neither spoke of it. That had been the beginning—this, James at least knew, was near the end. Did that knowledge brush her, too, with its wing? Her face, under the high lights, didn't tell him; it had that strange, almost alarming remoteness, partly Spanish, partly hers. Still without speaking, they turned and walked along past the House of the Infanta to the harbour entrance, and stood as they had stood on that other night, watching the waves surging high, one after another, down the narrow stone channel. It was a very dark night, and overcast—the white mushrooms out on the mole were invisible, but the noise of the waves on the breakwater under the Phare travelled across the bay to them, like muffled thunder. For a long time neither spoke. At last Raquel gave a little shiver.

"Cold?" he asked, putting his arm round her. It was in fact very cold. He thought—does she realise, too? Is that why she is shivering?

"No," she answered—"not really." Then—"This makes it all rather difficult for us, dear love," she said.

"Oh, my darling, don't I know it!" he groaned. He realised as she spoke that she was going to put up a fight for her love, for her happiness, and that he would have to oppose not only his heart, but her.

She put up her hand and took his. "I think," she said, speaking in a very soft level voice, "that we have wasted a good deal of time. Do you not think that we should waste no more?"

"Oh, my dearest"—He gripped her hand tightly, crushing the fingers together. "How can we?" he jerked out—the words were propelled out of him by some inner force, by that terrible Irish sense of right and righteousness out of which such countless fanatics and martyrs have been made.

Her voice was soft and level as ever. "Very easily, we can. We have the right—our love gives us the right," she said.

Those softly-spoken words shook James to his foundations, Suddenly he saw them together, that night, that very night, in her room—and everything that he had learned to be and learned no longer to fear to be rose in him to grasp that vision, craved for it, clamoured for it. He put his other hand out, trembling, and touched her hair; he couldn't see her face in the thick muffling darkness, but he was intensely aware of it, *watching* his silence. That silence was prolonged. What could he say? At last, out of a convulsion such as he had not known that a person could endure and yet live, he heard his own voice, wavering and small, temporising.

"My darling, I am so tired. I'm all in. To-morrow—we shall be together to-morrow."

Then he had to change that—it could mean something he didn't intend to mean. "We can talk then," he said. And again he felt her trying to see him, in the dark, trying to understand why he spoke of talking, when she had made her meaning so plain. But he couldn't help that; really he could do no more now. He took his hand away from her hair, and leaned back against the harbour wall; actually he could hardly stand any more. He made a last effort to meet the thing that was so manifest in her, the surprise, the painful question which came beating on him like aerial waves through the enveloping dark : in that same exhausted toneless voice, he said : "You will never know how much I love you—but now I simply must get to bed. I'm half dead." And then he wished he hadn't said 'To bed.' Nothing he could say was right, everything was discordant, because the whole situation was so utterly impossible and false.

But whatever else of bewilderment or pain his incompetent words had brought to her, she understood at least the fact of his exhaustion. "Of course, you poor darling," she said. "Come." And most tenderly, as he had often seen her leading Pilar, holding his hand, she led him back along the sea-wall to the hotel.

Rosemary, sitting with Crumpaun, saw them come in when they stepped out of the cold dark into the lights and warm stuffiness of the hall at the Grande Bretagne. Milcom's face appalled her. There was some awful tragedy there. She glanced quickly from him to the Condesa. That other face, lovely, a little

drawn with the cold, told her much less—whatever was wrong,
Raquel had not yet fully grasped it. Oh goodness, is it Juanito? the
girl wondered, and he hasn't dared to tell her? Still wondering
what it was, disturbed, anxious, soon after the glass cage had
borne them upstairs she too said good night to Crumpaun, and
went up to bed.

Milcom slept heavily. He had the sensible habit of ensuring
sleep when sleep was essential, and took a big dose of something.
He woke refreshed; the morning was fine and full of sun; and
while he drank his coffee and shaved he came to a decision. He
just couldn't kill the thing at once; he would take one more day.
Once more, just once, he would walk with her in quiet country,
watching the grace of her movements; once more he would hold
her hands—her beautiful hands!—and take her in his arms, and
kiss her. He would give himself that; he could trust himself for
that. And to-night—well, to-night he would just have to be good,
he thought. The instinctive phrase brought a smile round his
mouth; it took him back to his childhood, and his mother. Her
eyes were so like Raquel's eyes! "My son, I wish you to be good"
—so often she had said that; he could hear now the lovely fall of
her voice on the last words. He went on thinking about her, and,
irrelevantly, there came into his mind the tale he had heard so
often on so many war-fronts—that men dying on the battlefield
call not for their wives, but for their mothers. Or was it so
irrelevant? Was he not on a battlefield, and death near?—the
death of this new thing in him that could have grown to such
beauty. Sighing a little, he went downstairs to order a car for the
day.

In the morning they drove through the soft Basque countryside, the wooded hills plum-coloured with winter, the valley
floors still a brilliant green; they lunched at Ainhoa—no longer
in the garden, but in the darkly-timbered dining-room—off trout
and stewed wood-pigeons. In the early afternoon they went up
again to the glen behind S. Joseph's Chapel, hoping there to be
out of a teasing little wind that had a bite in it. They left the
car in a lane's mouth, and on the way they went up onto the
little flat-topped knoll with the oak-trees. But there were no
crocuses any more; the bright fragile beautiful things were all
dead and gone; the withered grass held only the pale rough-
surfaced shapes of the dead oak leaves. "As grass and as the
flower of grass, it is cut down, dried up and withered," James
muttered to himself. Solomon or David or whoever it was knew
all about it, he thought.

Up in the glen they found a strange happiness—the strangest he had ever known, James thought afterwards. Raquel did a wonderful thing. All day, he had known that she knew, now, that there was a catch in all this; that something was wrong, and that this day—to him, this stolen day—was a kind of make-believe. It was an inevitable knowledge, to a person of her sensitiveness. But she had asked no questions, let no hint of concern or anxiety escape her, and up there, as they sat among the soft browns of the withered bracken, she made of the make-believe a thing of unbelievable beauty. Relaxed, soft, tender, she slid into his arms, slid into passion, with a completely un-exacting ease; let her mouth rest on his mouth, or her cheek on his cheek, like a blissful lover who has not a care in the world, for whom Fate is smiling and the future secure. Something about the way she did that melted and subjugated James to depths of devotion that made his earlier love for her seem as nothing. It exalted him, too—the contemplation of her selfless-ness, so expressed, and his own love carried him away into realms beyond music or the utmost beauty of earth. He actually turned white under the pressure of this experience.

She saw it. She said—"You are cold, my dearest love—you are pale."

He didn't answer. She said then—"Where are you?"

Those words roused him. She knew everything. She knew how far he had travelled, beyond the bourne of common exper-ience. Slowly he raised himself, looked at her, and laid his hand over her eyes. She knew why he did that, and wept then. But he, after a moment, laid his head on her breast, like a child on the breast of his mother, with a deep sigh. She stroked his head and his cheek with infinite tenderness; at that moment the rare and wonderful fusion of the lover with the mother was completed in her. He moved a little, shifting his position into deeper com-fort, and almost at once actually fell asleep.

He slept for perhaps twenty minutes. He woke with a start, rubbed his eyes boyishly, and looked about him. There was her face, her breast, her supporting arms. He apologised abjectly. "Darling, how could I? I am sorry."

She smiled at him, with a wonderful look of contentment and peace.

"You have slept and waked again in my arms. I have wanted that for so long."

He turned and stared at her then, in startled enquiry.

"So long? Not before we came here?"

She nodded. "Before."

"Even in Madrid?"

"Yes, in Madrid."

He turned his head away thinking—"If only I had known!" Oh yes, if he had known then, if he had understood then, before he had ever seen the Conde, all would have been so simple. He would have had none of these scruples. Ghosts in a city of ghosts could have loved quite irresponsibly. She roused him from those bitter thoughts by saying very simply—"Was it not so with you?"

He turned and looked at her again—the long long neck, the gothic face, the eyes, and said, with a sigh—

"Probably."

She laughed, at that, and her laughter brought him back to the present.

"It's getting cold—let's go," he said.

It was getting cold. The mild winter afternoon was drawing in; the late light warmed but faintly the tawny slopes behind them, the green villa-studded coastal stretch away in front, and faded even as it deepened. He rose, pulled her to her feet, and stood for a moment looking at it all. He wanted to be able to see this place, for ever, just as it was. Then they walked off, slowly, to the car.

The day had been good so far, he thought—but there was the evening to be got through yet. How, he wondered, almost wishing that days need not have evenings. As they drove home he suggested taking her to dine in Bayonne, and she assented, as she did to everything. They went back however to the Grande Bretagne to have tea and change. As they came down, an hour or so later, Rosemary Oldhead was standing in the hall; they spoke to her, and James had a momentary panic-stricken impulse to invite her to come too. But he checked it—that wouldn't do. He must manage to fight the thing through alone.

They drove in to Bayonne, spinning along the great winding highway through a night that was full of wind, and parked the car on the space outside the Cinema, near the bridge. They dined slowly, in a small simple place with admirable food and good claret—they lingered over their dinner, over their coffee, over their brandy; but even so, it was early when they finished, and James began to wonder wretchedly what to do next. The cinema? That, too, was so obvious as to be almost insulting.

"Have you ever been to the Barre?" he asked her suddenly.

"What bar? The Basque, yes," she said, puzzled.

He laughed. "No, sweetheart, the bar at the mouth of the Adour, where the ships come in to come up the river. It ought to be rather splendid to-night, with this wind."

"But what is it? What does one see?" she asked.

"Big waves," he said, signalling to the waiter for his bill. She was right, of course—it was ridiculous to go at night; there was no moon, and they would see nothing. But he had set his heart on the Barre, suddenly. And presently they drove down beside the river, and out through the pine trees near the coast road, and parked the car on the flat sandy space close to the sort of tower where the signal is run up to inform ships that the water is high enough for them to ride in across the bar on the incoming tide, or out on the outgoing one, between the two great stone-built walls that control the river's mouth. Down here the wind was strong; in the faint glimmer from the tower light they could just see the great waves surging in and battling with the river's current, where they met it coming down. They walked out along the embankment, slippery with spray and rough with flung shingle; beyond, in the starlight, the white crests of the breakers were dimly visible as they foamed shoreward, and broke on the sandy shoals. That great wind, salty and clean in the night, the roaring noise of water all about, and the splendid shock when a huge wave struck the solid stone beneath their feet were inspiring to James—he breathed deeply, for a moment forgot his pre-occupations. But a burst of spray slapping up close in front wetted them, and he drew her back. They wandered off along the shore, in the direction of Biarritz, feeling a sandy track with their feet, the roar of sound and those great white shapes in motion keeping them company on their right.

James had chosen the Barre to visit, partly because he loved it, partly because he felt that out there it would be windy enough, open-air enough, cold enough to discount passion. But it was not. On the rough track, in the dark, Raquel stumbled over something and nearly fell. He put out his arms to catch her, and then was suddenly overcome. There on the open shore, with the roar of the Atlantic in his ears, and the wind sending scuds of spume flying overhead, he stood still and pulled her roughly, violently to him; kissed her with unwonted violence, violently used his hands. Sighing, relaxed, utterly surrendered, he felt the completeness of her response. It was too much. He threw in his hand. It was no good; he couldn't and wouldn't go on with his ridiculous struggle. Love had its rights, as she had said—and by Heaven, it should have them!

"Come along," he said, in a tone she didn't know—and led her back to the car.

If James had driven back by the shore road and through Biarritz, everything might have turned out differently. But he didn't know Biarritz very well, and the exit onto the main road is muddling; he was, now at last, in a hurry, and went back into Bayonne and out onto the Route Nationale. Just short of where the Biarritz road debouches onto the highway there is a bad bend—and there, driving fast, James nearly ran into the débris of an accident. A Peugeot car had hit a peasant's cart—lightless, no doubt—and had shot half off the road and turned over on the grass verge; hay from the cart was strewn all over the tarmac, mixed with broken glass; the horse was plunging about between the shafts of what was left of the cart, while the frightened and angry peasant tried to soothe it. James, as his headlights revealed all this, pulled in to the edge of the road, stopped his engine and sprang out. The Peugeot's engine was still running, as the exhaust showed; the air was full of the smell of petrol. He ran over, forced open the upper door—the car was on its side—and managed to switch it off. He could feel a man's body inside, and hear breathing; but, alone, he could not get him out. He went back to the car where Raquel sat.

"Have you got a torch?"

She had, a little midget of a thing, in her bag.

"Good. Hop out," he said. "Do you think you could hold that horse?" he asked her, as she stood in the road.

"Of course."

They went over to the peasant. "Madame will hold the horse," James said briefly—"we must get that man out."

The peasant was sulky and reluctant; the car had broken his cart and spilt his hay; it was not for him to pull people out of cars; let the gendarmes come and do it. James, furious at his brutish inhumanity, cuffed him sharply over the head; as the man staggered back he gave the reins to Raquel, took the peasant by the collar, and urged him towards the car, cursing him in fluent French the while. "We will see if you will help or not, mon ami! Had you a lantern lit, for example, on the back of you cart? I see none in the road." The peasant, cowed, admitted that he had, in fact, had no lantern—he was only making a small piece of road on the great road. Jame's threats of what would happen to him brought him to help, quite efficiently, in dragging out the occupants of the Peugeot. There proved to be two of them; both were considerably cut about; one was unconscious, and remained so, the other revived in the night air, and soon spoke. They were two of the Non-Intervention Commission's couriers from St.-Jean, who had already made the double journey to Burgos and back, four hours each way, that day; on their return they had been sent on into Bayonne to collect some document. They had dined there, and on the way home rammed the cart. "No light, the wretched bastard, as usual," the young man growled.

This adventure, and the ensuing fuss and activity which it involved did for James what wind and waves and cold night air had failed to do. He laid out the unconscious man on the grass, covered him with his coat, and drove in to Bidart to notify the police, leaving Raquel in charge; then he rang up a doctor in Biarritz and the head of the Non-Intervention Commission at the Grande Bretagne, summoning them both. He could not leave till they came, and besides the police required a full deposition from him—since the peasant, peasant-wise, had walked off into the night, horse, cart and all. By the time he had attended to all these things, and the ambulance had been fetched, the emotional spell was completely broken. It was nearly midnight before he and Raquel got back to the Grande Bretagne, and when they did he ordered a whiskey for her, told her to be sure to take a good hot bath, and sent her to bed—after which he sat in the hall with Crumpaun, drinking whiskey himself, and discussing the accident and the methods of the Non-Interveners with their couriers, perfectly comfortable and manlike, in the curious emotional release that a sudden violent event brings to highly civilised people.

Rosemary was there too. She had been bitterly disappointed to see so little of Milcom so far; only just those two glimpses. She was going sailing with Count de Barrial to-morrow morning, and couldn't be sure of being back in time for lunch, even if Raquel asked her to lunch with them, as she half hoped she would. Restless and unhappy, she had hung about downstairs all the evening, hoping to see Milcom on his return; when the telephone call interrupted the Non-Intervention bridge, she heard about the accident. This was of course an excellent excuse for staying downstairs longer still—she had rushed up to tell her Mother: "I'm with Mr. Crumpet—I'm perfectly all right. But I *must* hear about it"—and got permission to stay up. So, shortly before the ambulance arrived, she saw Milcom and the Condesa come in, and to-night it was the woman's face which struck her. She was white, and had a curious drained look, as if something had somehow been emptied out of her. That might just be the effect of seeing a bad accident—or it might not. She couldn't be sure. She puzzled about it vaguely while she sat on the fat leather arm of Crumpaun's chair, sipping an unwonted whiskey and soda, listening to the two men's talk, and watching Milcom's face. He looked quite different to-night. He looked—funny, that—he looked as if he had achieved something. In that case it couldn't be Juanito. And she had looked awful. Then what on earth was it? Still speculating, Rosemary at last went to bed.

The next morning was again fine and sunny, though not warm; there was a keen wind. Rosemary went off for her sail, and about eleven Milcom and the Condesa, in the car, drove out on the coast road to Hendaye; when they had gone about a third of the way they left the car and walked along the cliffs, where they had picked striped gentians on James's last visit. There are combes, some deep, some shallow, breaking the line of the cliffs here, and in one of these, as James had expected, they found a sunny hollow facing seaward, in the sun and out of the wind, where they could sit; there they settled themselves down on James's coat, spread on the thick tufted grass. The day of make-believe was over; he had got to do the thing now. Between the green banks of the combe spread a segment of the sea, intensely blue, with the sardine boats rocking about, looking for all the world like tiny cigars, on the swell—their abrupt disappearances and reappearances, and an occasional burst of white spray appearing over the green lip of the combe when an unusually large wave broke on the slabby rocks below were the only visible evidences that that blue expanse was not perfectly calm. They sat looking at it for some time without speaking. At last James pulled himself together. Taking her hand, he looked searchingly into her face.

"Raquel, you believe that I love you, don't you?"

"Yes—that I do believe," she said, her eyes on his.

"Well, go on believing it," he said, almost roughly—"but listen to what I say, and you must believe that too." She nodded in assent.

"How long is it since you last saw Pascual?" he asked abruptly.

She reckoned. "It was in that hospital, in August—no, September of thirty-six; he was wounded near the end of August and we went to see him when we heard, at the beginning of September."

"So you haven't seen or spoken to him for over two years?"

"No—it is so."

"Nor had letters from him?"

"Except the notes you brought me, no."

He paused, thinking how to make her understand what she had got to understand, if she was to accept the situation as he saw it.

"Did you ever read the Confessions of Saint Augustine?" he asked her.

She stared at him. "No—at least I don't remember it. Why?"

"Or the Life of Saint Francis of Assisi, then?"

"Yes—we had all the lives of the Saints read to us at the Convent, of course, but I forget them rather."

"Perhaps they didn't tell you their early lives in great detail, in the Convent," said James, with his grim smile. "But surely you must remember that both Saint Augustine and Saint Francis were frightfully wild as young men, drinking and sleeping around and all the rest—they say Saint Francis was put in prison at least once. Did they tell you that?"

"That they began as rather wicked, yes—at least Saint Augustine."

"And then you know what happened—in each case, something came along that changed their direction, as it were, and opened their eyes to a reality that they had never seen, and they turned and followed that reality, and became Saints."

"Yes. And so?"

"That is what has happened to Pascual, that's all."

"To *Pascual*? But you are being funny, no?" she said, staring at him.

"Indeed I am not. I wish, God forgive me, it weren't true. But it is. Pascual has changed his direction, while he's been in prison, as completely as Saint Francis and Saint Augustine changed theirs. If he isn't a Saint yet, he's well on the road to it."

"It seems impossible," she said slowly, staring out to sea.

"You promised to believe me, remember," he said.

"I do—I try. But I simply cannot understand it. Could you explain a little more?—why you think this, I mean? *Pascual*," she said again, with that note of utter incredulity in her voice.

"Now look here, Raquel darling," James said, "we have never discussed your husband, and I've loved you for not telling me anything about him. But I want you to understand that I haven't lived in Spain for so long without getting a very fair idea of what he used to be like. I know that he was constantly unfaithful to you, that he spent your money as well as his own, that he entertained his mistresses in your houses, and gave them your family jewels, and that altogether after the first he treated you about as badly as a man could. That he was ever actively cruel to you I doubt; but that he caused you all the pain possible by the moral cruelty of neglect and humiliation, I am sure. Is that about right?"

"Yes. It was so. I did not know that you knew all this."

6

"Everybody knew it—that was what I couldn't forgive him," James said savagely. "You can't have any conception of how I hated having to go and see him the first time, feeling as I did about you."

"I did not know," she murmured—"dear one, I did not know."

"I know—it didn't matter. But now you understand what a shock it was when I did see him, and found him all set for turning into a saint."

"But *how* can this have happened?—that I cannot comprehend," she said.

"Well, to begin with, I believe that for the first time in his life, he began to *think*. He'd never given himself time to do that before; he just rushed around with women, and fished and raced and shot. But in prison, with nothing on earth to do but chip away at fruit-stones, you have a hell of a lot of time for thinking. I don't fancy that Pascual is particularly intelligent"—James observed candidly; and even in her distress and deepening anxiety, Raquel laughed—"but such mind as he had, he used, for the first time in his life, on something beyond how to gratify his next desire."

"But you might have known him!" she exclaimed.

"I *do* know him. And the next thing," James went on, "was that he was boxed up day and night with a lot of poor toads from the bottom of society, not the top—the sort of people he'd never noticed before, except to kick them out of his way or give them a peseta for holding his horse. And they taught him a lot, too—and he was humble enough to learn from them and to like them."

"It is extraordinary," she murmured.

"That's what I tell you. It is, most extraordinary. And then there was the book. He decided to try to learn English, or go on with it, in prison, and he got the gaoler to bring him an English book. And of all things, the gaoler fetched him *Jude the Obscure*. Do you know it?"

"No. What sort of book is it?"

"It's a novel by Thomas Hardy, one of our greatest writers."

"Who wrote a book called Tessa Something?"

"That's the man. If you've read Tess, you know a bit of his really frightening penetration, of his remorselessness about human life, and his power. It's amazing," James said, leaning back against the bank and tilting his hat over his eyes, "that it should have been that one novel, of the hundreds that must have been

kicking about in Almadera, that he got hold of. Think!—it
might have been a Ouida or a W. J. Locke! Much effect *that*
would have had!"

"And what is it about, this book?"

"It's the story of a poor boy, quite *du peuple*, who had a passion
for books and learning, and for Oxford, the heart and centre of
English learning. He gets there, after great struggles, and begins
to learn—and then he falls in love with a girl called Sue, a school-
teacher, poor like himself, and they live together and have children; and that destroys his chances of studying, and it all ends
in tragedy. Oh, it's no good trying to tell you about it in a few
words," said James impatiently, "but the main point for Pascual,
I think, was Sue's character; and Jude's. The whole thing is
described with a sort of terrible faithfulness—the combination of
reality and tragic poetic sense that was Hardy's strong suit. Anyhow Pascual has been reading this book over and over again,
studying it, line by line and word by word, and—plus his bus-
driver fellow prisoners, of course—it has opened his eyes to the
reality of life in classes other than his own, and to the beauty
and terror of love."

"It is extraordinary," Raquel said again. She sat very still.
"Go on, please, James."

"Naturally, as he had begun to think at last, Pascual started
comparing his own life with the lives of Jude and Sue—and his
own love, too. And he saw then what a poor wretched thing,
judged by any ultimate standards, his life was compared with
theirs."

"He didn't *tell* you this?" Raquel interjected, staring at him
wide-eyed.

"Most certainly he did. He used the words, 'a poor, mean
life' about himself."

She sat back. "I can't understand it."

"Yes, but darling, you've got to take it. It is so. He has seen
a lot more, too," James went on, his voice becoming strained.
"He sees quite clearly at last how atrociously he has behaved to
you, and he wants to—to repair that injury."

"How?" Her voice was very small indeed.

"By living with you again and treating you decently; loving
you, actually, now that he has learned what love means. His
whole soul—the soul he has just found—is set on that. He
knows nothing about us, remember. He's extraordinarily
humble about it, but he wants to try."

"You mean"—her voice was hardly more than a whisper—

"that possibly I should go back to him again, and live with him as his wife, and give up—you?"

"Just exactly that," he said doggedly, his face set. He did not look at her as he spoke; he looked away at the sea, where a small white sail had crept into the blue triangle between the green walls of the combe. "He ought to have his chance," he said.

Suddenly, she did a thing that in all those months of danger, strain and distress he had never seen her do. She burst into loud and violent sobbing.

"Oh no no no!" she cried out, in a voice terribly loud; the syllables were cut by the sobs into a series of horrible staccatos— "oh no no no!" She sprang to her feet and ran away down the slope towards the edge of the cliff, still sobbing and calling out "No"; she stumbled as she ran, a pitiful black figure, in flight from the unendurable.

James leapt up and rushed after her. He caught her just at the edge, where the cliff fell away, and held her close. "My darling, my darling!" he said in agony. "Don't. Stop crying. Don't"—he hardly knew what he was saying.

She turned her face up to his; it was quite wild.

"You can't ask that of me!" she said, speaking very fast, and in Spanish. "He can't ask that of me! No one can ask that of me!"

"Come back, my darling," he said, drawing her away from the edge of the cliff. He began to lead her up the hill again, speaking all the while. "Come and sit down and talk about it quietly." They went a few steps. "Oh, God!" he groaned; the sweat was pouring down his face—"Oh my dear love."

The absolute agony in his voice seemed to rouse her. She stopped, and put her hand up to his cheek with a gesture like a child's. "My love," she said, and went quietly on with him. They sat down again on his coat; James was quite exhausted. He took out his handkerchief and wiped his face.

"I am sorry," she said then, in English. "Dearest heart, I am sorry. Forgive me." She took his hand.

"We've got to," he said, stupidly.

"Why?" she asked quickly, in a low voice. "Why should it not be he who makes the sacrifice, if he is become so saintly? Why should he not divorce, and we be together?"

James pondered this. That solution, with its Latin common sense, had never occurred to him. Why not? He sat silent for a long time, watching the white sail of the little boat moving slowly across the blue triangle of sea at their feet. Oh why not? Why on earth not? But this battle, he found now, when he came to it, had been fought out before. It had first been joined when he had had that vision of the landscape of the future, sitting with Pascual on a soapbox in the prison at Almadera; it had gone on through those exhausting days in Barcelona, when he had moved, however reluctantly, step by step towards this end and no other; it had been continued even yesterday, on his day of make-believe, when spiritual and physical conflict had actually brought him to fall asleep, by daylight, in Raquel's arms. The battle was now won, in him—at least so far, that he could no longer surrender. Last night—well, that had been simply a gust of physical passion, a thing he knew about. And that accident had dealt with that. But his soul, through a thousand small motions, long-continued, had taken its position. (Which is how the soul does in fact move, more often than not.)

He had to say this, somehow.

"If he could, I couldn't," he said at last, very low.

"Could not what?"

"Couldn't accept the sacrifice, if he made it." He turned and took her in his arms, holding her and turning her face up to his with the other hand. "Oh, my dearest love, you *must* understand this," he said, "or take it from me if you can't. I've seen him and you haven't. You don't know what he is now. He has died and been born again. Are we going to knock him on the head *now*?" He stared almost fiercely into her eyes, at once forcing and beseeching her to understand, to agree.

She dropped her eyelids—she couldn't drop her head, because of his hand—and two tears slowly slid out from under them. She knew then that she was beaten—beaten in her fight, her fight for her love and her happiness. In her heart she had known it before—known it two nights ago, out by the harbour, when he had said he was too tired to be her lover; known it all yesterday —only the heart is so unwilling to accept defeat. And this was more than losing James—much more, and much worse. But after that one involuntary act of almost physical revolt, when she ran away down the hill, she would do no more. Schooled all her life to graceful acceptance, this also behind her dropped lids, she accepted; those two slow tears were her only protest. Her face still held in his hand, she steadied her lips and said at last, very low—"Very well."

She put up her hand, then, and gently freed her chin; turned her head away and wiped her eyes.

"Then what do I do?" she asked after a moment.

"You ought to go back to Spain, I think," he said slowly, as if each word were being drawn out of him on a rope. "He can't see you out here. To San Sebastián, I suppose—there's so little room in Burgos."

"You have thought it all out!" she murmured almost bitterly.

"Naturally I have—what do you suppose I've been thinking of, night and day, since I heard that he was coming out, since I understood what has happened to him?" he asked almost angrily. "Do you suppose I could think of anything else?"

"When shall I go, then?" she asked.

"I should say the sooner the better," he said flatly. "I must go back myself, and Pascual may get there at any time. And if he rejoins, he won't have long before he goes to the front. You'll have to see about a *salvo conducto*, of course."

"Olivia will be able to arrange that," she said dully.

"No doubt." (He thought—like Hell she will!) "But you will have to get an exit permit."

"What is that?"

"A permit from the French authorities to return to Spain—you get them in Bayonne as a rule. It takes some time, too. We'd better go in and see about that this afternoon."

"But since I am Spanish, what have the French to do with it?"

"They control their own frontier. You can't expect anything else, with war just over the border—a war in which their deadliest enemies are taking an active part," he answered. "France is only just not at war with White Spain, remember."

She sighed. "I see. Yes. We had better go." She got up, and he rose too. Then suddenly she flung herself on him, in a passion of weeping.

"Oh, my love," she murmured in Spanish; "my soul, my treasure! Oh, I love you so!" She clung to him, murmuring wild endearments; the soft syllables beat round James's heart and head like a cloud of tender moths.

"Must I?" she asked at last, turning up her white tear-stained face to his. "Must we? Can't we?"

"Oh, my heart's love, no!" he groaned. "We can't. I should feel like a thief. You must—O God, why does it have to be so much worse for you?" He stared out to sea again for a moment. The little white sail had nearly crossed the blue wedge of sea now, he noticed. He turned back to her. "You can—and you will, I know. Come on!" he said, and dragged her up the hill towards the road.

Rosemary, as she had expected, got back very late for lunch—she refused to stay and take a meal with the de Barrials, on the

score of having work to do. A car was standing in front of the
Grande Bretagne, and as she went in, Milcom and the Condesa
came out. The Condesa's face was pale, with remote eyes—
Milcom looked exhausted, and more like his Spanish nick-name
than ever.

"Oh," the girl said. "How do you do?" she said to Milcom,
with a certain embarrassment. "Are you going out to lunch?"
she asked the Condesa, talking at random.

"No, we have lunched—we are going to Bayonne," the Condesa said. They got into the car and drove off, leaving the girl
staring after them.

"So it *was*," she said under her breath, and turned and went
indoors.

Sailing along below the cliffs between Hendaye and St.-Jean
that morning with the Count, Rosemary had frequently glanced
shorewards, admiring the beige, creamy, and pinkish cliffs and
rocks, and trying to identify from the sea the places that she
knew on land. She had seen a car, shiny in the sun, drawn up
on the road; and some distance off, on the side of one of the
combes, she had observed a spot of black and bluish-green which
her long-sighted eyes presently recognised as being composed of
two people sitting on the ground. Even then, she wondered if
it could be Milcom's well-known suit of Lovat tweed and the
Condesa's invariable black. Naturally, she kept on glancing that
way, and at one point she saw the black figure running downhill
towards the cliffs, a tiny speck of motion on the immobility of the
slopes, followed by the blue-green one; just at the cliff's edge the
two specks merged again, and then, very slowly, returned up the
hill. Even at that distance, there had been something agitated and
unusual, to her eyes, about these movements; she felt certain
that it must be Milcom and the Condesa, then, and wondered
what was wrong. That something was badly wrong she felt sure,
and that was her real reason for refusing to stay and lunch with
the de Barrials—she wanted, vaguely, to get back and find out.

Now, eating her own belated meal in the stuffy dining-room
of the Grande Bretagne, she reflected on their expressions at the
hotel door—her unseeing eyes, his air of exhaustion and misery.
And why Bayonne? She was completely foxed this time, she
said to herself.

Except for the Executioner, who was eating his lunch with his
usual expression of sadistic pleasure—"as if he was eating Reds"
she privately phrased it—she was the only person in the dining-
room; but presently the door opened and two of the Non-Inter-

vention Commission couriers came in. These young men, mostly
Scandinavians, drove their Peugeot cars almost daily between
St.-Jean and Burgos, keeping up a regular service of mails between the two places; sleeping now at one, now at the other, and
sometimes doing the double trip in the day. Rosemary knew
them slightly; they were the opposite numbers of the two who
had been involved in the accident the night before. While one
sat down at the big Non-Interveners' table in the middle of the
room, the other came over to her.

"Do you know where the Condesa is?" he asked.

"She's gone to Bayonne," Rosemary said.

"How long ago?"

"Just now—about ten minutes ago."

"How awkward—bother!"

"Why?"

"I had a letter for her—and I must start back in an hour;
there's another bag to go."

"Give it to Rex," said Rosemary.

"Rex is off—and anyhow, I was to give it into her hands,"
the young man said. "Could you give it to her?" he asked.

"Of course, if you like."

He handed her a fattish envelope, with the Hôtel Condes-
table's name stamped on the flap, and smiled his rather ingenu-
ous Nordic smile.

"It's from the husband," he said—"he's back."

"Back? The Conde? But he's in prison—he can't be back."

"No, he's been exchanged—he is in Burgos. I spoke to him.
'Meelcomm,' their good angel, got him out, it seems," said the
young man, still smiling.

"Cripes!" said Rosemary succinctly.

"Pardon?" said the young man.

"Nothing," the girl said hastily. "O.K.—I'll give it her."

"Thanks—and I'll eat. Have you ordered, Nils?" he asked
his companion, returning to the big table.

"So *that's* it," the girl said to herself, staring out of the window
at the white mushrooms of spray, expanding and disappearing,
noiselessly, above the mole. "He knew, and he's told her. Oh
dear!" She went gloomily upstairs.

Milcom and the Condesa got back from Bayonne about tea-
time. The Duquesa, thanks to her position, had been able to
arrange for a *salvo conducto* to be ready within two days, but the
exit permit presented difficulties; since the closing of the frontier
the French authorities had tightened up their regulations, and it

was only by going to Paris in person and having the application made by the Spanish representative there that the Condesa stood any chance of getting it. James, now anxious to put an end to a situation which was merely torturing both of them, urged her to start that very night on the Sud Express, and get it over. He had bought her some suitcases in Bayonne—she had arrived at St.-Jean with no luggage but one suitcase got in Perpignan, and the shabby little despatch-case—and while she packed he went and got her sleeper and tickets. It was the last time, he supposed wretchedly, as he pulled out his pocket-book, that he would be buying anything for her—oh, for this darling woman who was not his wife, but whom he had nevertheless had the sweet privilege of clothing and supporting for more than three months. It had been something of a strain on his resources—James was not a rich man; it had meant a number of minor economies which he had made, how joyfully! It had been the most blissful happiness to order a bad bottle of wine instead of a good, or take a cheap noisy room in an hotel instead of a more comfortable one, because it was for Raquel. Handing over the notes, James felt as if the meaning, the motive power of his life were, with her, being taken from him.

Rosemary had seen the pair come in on their return from Bayonne, but a delicate instinct prompted her not to hand over the Conde's letter in the hall, under the eyes of the Archdeacon, the Executioner, and an assortment of Non-Interveners. She waited till she saw Milcom come down in the glass lift and go out again, and then went up and tapped on Raquel's door. When she went in she found her friend putting her clothes into the new suitcases, with deft movements, but still with those remote eyes. Rosemary was startled—she had not expected any development as sudden as this.

"You're not going?" she said, distress in her voice.

"Yes—to-night."

"But where to?"

"To Paris."

"*Paris?* But why?—I mean, I don't understand."

"Pascual is to be exchanged, and I am going to him; but first I must go to Paris"—and she explained about the exit permit.

Rosemary was so upset by this announcement that for the moment she forgot all about the letter, which she still held in her hand. She sat down on the edge of the bed and stared distressfully at the Condesa.

"But you'll come back again?"

6*

"Just for a day or two, to pick up my *salvo*—then I go."

"Oh dear!" the young girl said sadly—"I wish you weren't going."

Raquel's eyes filled with tears; she dropped an armful of clothes on a chair and came and sat down beside Rosemary, putting her arms round her.

"Oh you dear child, so do I!" she said simply. "I shall miss you very much," she added, as if to explain her regret, and kissed her.

Rosemary kissed her in return, warmly.

"Oh goodness!" she said after a moment, recollecting herself —"I was to give you this. One of the couriers brought it while you were out." And she handed her the Conde's letter.

The Condesa held it in her hand for a little while, staring at it, as if it were some strange and possibly venomous object.

"Brought it?" she said, stupidly.

"Yes—from Burgos. What did you hear about Juanito?" the young girl asked, hurriedly changing the subject.

"Oh—Juanito. Yes. He is well—he is in Spain. I shall see him soon—when I go back," the Condesa said disjointedly.

"Oh good—I am glad," Rosemary said. She jumped up. "I must go," she said briefly—"Mummie will be wondering where I've got to. When do you go?"

"To-night."

"Oh well—I'll be seeing you," she said lightly, and scurried away with her usual schoolgirl haste. That was about all she could stand, she muttered to herself savagely as she ran along to her room, of seeing Raquel being put through the hoops like that. And *him*! God, how bloody life was—and bloodiest, always, for the most darling people. She dashed unwonted tears angrily from her eyes.

James and Raquel dined that last night at Gaston's. They felt vaguely that it was more theirs, their place, than anywhere else in the town. James remembered how quietly and sadly they had dined there together the first time, before another farewell, that then had seemed so final and so sad. This was much worse. But one sits through those meals somehow—one even eats some of them.

On their way to the station, walking side by side, she said, touching her bag—"I had a letter from him to-day."

"Pascual?"

"Yes. And—I think you are right."

She spoke quietly enough, but then suddenly she burst into a terrible storm of weeping, as she walked along. James stopped

and took her in his arms—her sobs were shaking her body as if
they must end by shattering it. It was more than he could stand.

"Oh my darling, we can't," he said. "We really can't go
through with this. It's altogether too much." He clung to her,
kissing the tears on her wet face, as he had wanted to kiss those
two slow tears that morning when he held her undefended face
in his hand—and had not.

"Come back," he whispered. "Say you missed the train.
Why should we throw all this away?"

For a moment or two she was silent, just resting in his arms,
still shaken with gradually lessening sobs. At last she freed her
hand and wiped her eyes.

"No," she said very slowly—a long soft negative. "It would
be no good—I know now how you are. For a little, we should
be happy—oh, we should be so happy!—but these ideas that you
have would return, and then you would be miserable, and on my
account. And that would *really* kill me. I shall go."

She took out her little case and powdered her tear-stained face,
there on the windy square under the arc-lights—for some reason
that small conventional action was to James the most moving
thing he had ever seen.

But he knew she was right; that was the desolating thing.
He *would* be wretched. There was a thing in him which, combined with her circumstances, made happy love between them
impossible. What a hideous trick for Fate to play—that he, who
had steered clear of love for so long must at last love, irrevocably,
in a quarter where it must all be frustrated, and end in agony
and loss. He kissed her for the last time, long and slowly, and
led her across the square towards the railway-station.

So it was after all the station at St.-Jean-de-Luz that was the
place in James Milcom's future where he took his farewell from
Raquel de Verdura. Less than forty-eight hours after he had
stood at the coach door as the train steamed in, watching her red-
gold head under the black lace, and wondering if such a spot
could really exist, he stood there again, on the platform this time,
looking his last on her lovely archaic face, framed in the window
of her sleeper. They were very quiet now—the whole thing seemed
to him completely unreal. This couldn't really be happening to
two people who loved one another as he and Raquel did; it
wasn't possible that he would never see her again, never take her
in his arms, never again hear her soft syllables of endearment and
rapture. It was just something that they had got to go through
with, quietly, formally, like a part in a play. And just so they

did go through with it—she at her window, he on the track. Slowly the train steamed out, and long after it had gone he still stood, watching the four sets of rails gleaming under the arc-lights, up towards Paris, where his heart had gone.

## CHAPTER TEN

### *This Side—St.-Jean-de-Luz*

ROSEMARY had certainly not got much of her anticipated bitter-sweet happiness out of this visit of Milcom's. Except for that session with Crumpaun, she had hardly seen him—and it was from Crumpaun that she learned, on the night of Raquel's departure, that he was going back to Spain next morning on the ten-thirty train. So neither of us will ever see him again! was the desperate thought on which she went to sleep.

She slept little and restlessly; then towards morning fell into a heavy slumber, and woke late, as the bells in the great church were chiming for eight o'clock Mass. As her habit was, she sprang out of bed, threw on a dressing-gown, and still knotting its girdle, went over to her window and stepped onto the balcony. The great frost which was to afflict Western Europe that Christmas had not yet reached St.-Jean-de-Luz, but it was on its way South—the morning was a cold one, grey and harsh, with an ugly light from a dark sky onto a bitter sea. What a morning for him to wake up to his grief on, she thought, as from habit she craned from the end of her balcony to watch the antics of the Dogs' Club, whose members, undeterred by the weather, were assiduously playing "This is My Hole." As she watched, a man's figure appeared among them on the beach, walking close to the water's edge in the direction of the new Casino—she knew that long loose stride; it was Milcom. Even at that distance there was something indescribably desolate about his aspect—the set of his shoulders, his very walk, at once rapid and purposeless, beside that leaden uncomforting sea. Suddenly she felt that it was more than she could bear, to have him walking there alone in his misery—and obeying the most preposterous impulse that she had ever known, she ran back into her room, slammed the window, and began flinging on her clothes. She had no definite idea as to what she was going to do, beyond the fact that she was going after him, so that he should not be alone; but she was aware of something new and unknown boiling up in her, a power, an understanding, a resolve. There was none of the usual thirty-five minutes fidgeting with her hair this morning—a scrape with the comb, a coloured handkerchief tied over, and she was gone.

Quickly as she had dressed, he was already out of sight when she got out of doors. She set off round the bay, keeping to the esplanade above the sea-wall, where she could travel faster and yet watch the beach. Passing through the arcades of the new Casino she ran, rousing echoes; emerging at the other end she saw him far ahead, crossing the sand to the last flight of steps leading up to the end of the sea-wall. She guessed where he must be going—up to the Phare, where they had all three met on the day of his first return to St.-Jean. She began to run again, fast and lightly; whatever happened, she mustn't lose him. Rosemary was a good runner—she kept it up, swiftly and easily, for a quarter of a mile, till she reached the stone steps under a group of tamarisks, leading up to the Phare. By this time Milcom was out of sight again, vanished over the top of the hill, but she felt certain of where she would find him, and went straight on, pounding up the steep path, over the summit behind the little chapel, and down the narrow track beyond towards the breakwater. And there, sure enough, he was.

At the sight of him she stopped. He was standing on the path some distance above the breakwater, absently watching the thunderous assault, recoil, return of the great waves; but he seemed hardly to see them, to be aware of anything but his own disastrous thoughts, for when a burst of spray shot up within a few feet of him, spattering his coat with the fringe of its heavy drops, he never stepped back, but remained perfectly still, staring at the tumultuous waters—and again about his whole figure there was a desolation that dealt the young girl an almost physical blow. Breathing heavily from her run, but still borne on by that strange new sense of power, she went up to him and put her hand on his arm.

He turned and looked at her, without surprise—she was shocked at his ravaged face.

"Oh—hullo," he said dully.

"Good morning," she said, panting.

He seemed to rouse himself then sufficiently to notice her odd appearance—out of breath, her clear brown cheeks scarlet with running, the handkerchief fallen back off her undressed curls.

"What's up?" he asked. "What have you been running for?"

"I had to," she panted out—"I had to catch you."

"Why, is something wrong?"

"Only you," she said, on a great gulp that was almost a sob. "I saw you on the beach, and I couldn't bear it—so I came after you." She gabbled the words out pell-mell; out of breath as she was, they were hardly intelligible.

Milcom's attention was fully aroused now. He took her arm, and gave it a little shake.

"My dear child, what *is* all this? Talk sensibly, and tell me what's the matter." Very pardonably, he did not in the least understand what she was driving at; all he knew was that his last sad meditations were being interrupted by a girl who seemed to be almost hysterical.

But Rosemary was not hysterical in the least. This was difficult, but she had never expected that it would be easy; she knew now what she had come out to do, and she would do it. She took a couple of deep breaths.

"Sorry," she said. "I was so puffed." She dabbed at her scarlet face with a handkerchief. "There's nothing whatever the matter," she went on, "with anyone. Only I know that she is going back to him—she told me last night—so I knew what that must be for you. And just now I saw you from my window, walking on the beach, and you looked so—so frightfully *alone*, that I simply couldn't bear it. So I dressed and ran out after you. I knew you would come here."

Still holding her arm, the man stood stock still, staring at her. When he spoke, it was her last words that he took up.

"How did you know that I should come here?"

"Because you met us—her—here that day, when you came back last time; when you were both so happy."

He let go of her arm and sat down on a rock, without taking his eyes from her face.

"How do you know all this? Did she tell you?" he asked.

"Oh *no*—she never said anything. I just saw," the girl said simply. "And when I took her his letter, she told me that she was going back. So then of course I knew."

"Knew what?" Milcom asked. In spite of himself, he was at once astonished and as if fascinated by this recital—these revelations from a person whom he had thought of only as a particularly nice honest-faced child.

"Oh, just how utterly *desperate* it was, for both of you," she said, in an indescribable tone of purest pity. "And I do love her so, I minded most terribly. But I minded more for you—that's why I ran after you."

Incredulous, quite out of his depth in this improbable scene, Milcom found himself, almost without his own volition, asking the most obvious question—"Why did you mind more for me?"

He never forgot the expression that came on her face then—the pure poised concentrated look of the swimmer braced for a plunge, or of some primitive Archangel about to stoop in flight to announce a wonder to men.

"Because I love you, too," she said, swiftly, with a seraphic swoop of words that matched her face. She held up a hand of authority, enjoining his uninterrupting silence. "Oh, I know you'll think I'm nuts, that I'm only a schoolgirl with an idiotic crush on someone. But it isn't like that. I love you, and I always shall, whatever happens. I know that isn't any good to you now," she went on—"you're full of her, and you can't even *see* anyone else. I don't expect you to. Perhaps you won't ever—she's so lovely and so darling. But before you go off alone, I just wanted to say that if you ever *do* want anyone, either to marry and look after you, or just to be about with, I shall always be there."

James heard this declaration with an amazement which, as he listened, turned more and more to a tender and quite unamused respect. Wretched, emotionally exhausted as he was, and incapable of making any sort of response, nevertheless her action had a beauty which moved him very much. While he listened he had remained sitting on his rock, looking up at her as she stood in front of him, the wind blowing out her hair, the spray damping it —now he stood up, and took her hand.

"Rosemary, I'll never call you a child again. I see that you understand—well, everything. I'd no idea——" he stopped.

"Yes?" she said quietly.

"No idea that you were like that—or that you cared so much about her. She was very fond of you—now I see why. It's amazing!" he said, passing a hand over his forehead; he seemed almost to have forgotten her. "Quite amazing," he repeated. She said nothing—she knew that he was thinking now about Raquel and her, trying to get that relation into focus, and she waited quietly. Was not her hand in his?

He seemed to come to himself again after a moment.

"It was very good of you to do this," he said, a little awkwardly. "Thank you. I shan't forget that you did it." And now he studied her face, almost curiously.

"That's all right," she said briefly. "I only wanted you to know. You don't have to worry about me, either. Good-bye." She bent over the hand that was holding hers, kissed it, and was gone, scudding off up the path like something blown by the wind.

"Rosemary!" he called after her—"Rosemary!" Suddenly he felt that there were things he ought, wanted to say. But either the thunder of the waves drowned his voice, or she would not hear—she ran on, rounded the bend at the top of the path, and disappeared.

Milcom stood for a moment looking after her; then he pulled out his watch. Just on nine—he would have to hurry. Ramming his hat down on his head he too went up the path. But all the way back to the hotel, and on his long following journey, he was aware of a curious sense of having been in some way soothed, if not comforted. At least she had afforded him a genuine distraction, giving him something besides his own wretchedness to think about. What an extraordinary child! And often, during the next few days of tension and suspense before the offensive began, and the following weeks of confusion, fatigue and danger, he found himself, at the most unexpected moments, recalling Rosemary Oldhead, and her extraordinary gesture of fearless pity and love.

Rosemary herself contrived to conceal all knowledge of her escapade from both her parents. It was more than ever desirable just then to conceal things from Mr. Oldhead. His rheumatism, in the increasing cold, was beginning to bother him again, and he was getting discontented with St.-Jean-de-Luz. This town, though visitors do not always realise it at first, is not a good place for rheumatic subjects; its very name, if one knew Basque (which nobody does) would tell one so. For St.-Jean-de-Luz means, not Saint John of Light, as most people very naturally suppose, but Saint John of the Marshes; the streets down by the harbour are built on the swampy flats at the mouth of the Nivelle, and the suburbs which are steadily spreading inland behind the railway-station have their foundations on the town's rubbish, tipped out onto the marshy water-meadows along the river to afford holding for bricks and mortar. This, carping persons say, accounts for the condition which gives the place its other, mocking nick-name of St.-Jean-des-Puces,—Saint John of the Fleas. Certainly there are a great many fleas—and what with them, and his rheumatic twinges, and the cold, and his worry about the Civil War—the futile desperate worrying of the inactive over a cause dear to their heart—Mr. Oldhead, in those last days of December nineteen hundred and thirty-eight, was getting very grumpy indeed.

The chilly winds out of doors had latterly driven him more and more into frequenting the Bar Basque; it was warm there, and the gossip of the journalists did something to allay his nervous irritable thirst for news. Suspense about the Franco offensive was now at fever-pitch in St.-Jean, and on the morning of Milcom's departure Mr. Oldhead, about noon, betook him to the Bar for his usual glass of sherry and spot of gossip.

He ran into quite a mouthful of news, as it happened. Crumpaun, Carrow, Crossman and Hever were all there, discussing with great animation an item collected by the indefatigable representative of Hooters. A very large number of planes from Russia, long awaited and long delayed, were at last said to be about to arrive in France—possibly had already arrived. Crossman was jubilant; fifty or sixty extra planes might make all the difference to the Republicans in the coming offensive—it was the German-Italian command of the sky, he said (as everyone already knew) which weighted the scales so heavily in Franco's favour.

This news delighted Mr. Oldhead too; he sipped his sherry with relish, while he registered agreement with Crossman.

Provided there wasn't any more sabotage, Crumpaun said, throwing his usual philosophical lump of caution into the conversation; those damned wreckers were everywhere.

"Here, listen, Crumpaun, don't start dismal-jimmying like that," Carrow said, irritably. "I guess there isn't going to be any more sabotage. No one this side knows *where* those planes are, and there aren't any runways left for the *espions* to cross the frontier any more—thanks to you and that smart little girl of yours, sir," he added, turning to Mr. Oldhead. "There's been no wrecking worth mentioning since that col was blocked."

The episode of the photographs, the Old Parrot, and Rosemary's and Crumpaun's expedition had become common property among the journalists, and had brought Rosemary a certain fame; so much so that Mr. Oldhead had quite got over his resentment, and secretly nourished a modest pride in his intelligent and tight-lipped child. But on this occasion he did not accept Carrow's tribute with his usual demure satisfaction. Instead he set down his glass of sherry on the table so sharply that it spilt, and sat bolt upright in his chair, staring straight ahead of him, without making any reply at all. At Carrow's words, like a thunderclap, had come to him the recollection of the Arbre de Noël in the Grotte de Sare. No, by Jove—all the frontier runways were *not* closed; whether spies used it or not, that stone ladder was still open to them—the safest, the most secret route of all. And it must be closed at once. He rose, beckoning to Crossman, and led him down to the far end of the room, where they stood whispering together for some moments. Then Crossman, nodding, returned to the group of journalists, and Mr. Oldhead went out, leaving his sherry unfinished. (Crossman, needless to say, finished it for him.) Mr. Oldhead tramped back to the hotel, told Rex to order a car, and sat down, early as it was, to lunch ; he was just finishing when his wife and daughter came in, at the usual hour.

"Got to go out—back for tea," was all he would vouchsafe in answer to their questions; Rosemary needn't think she was the only one who could keep her own counsel !

"Daddy's really getting *impossible*," Rosemary said resentfully, looking after his departing back. "Really, if we've got to have lunch at *twelve-thirty* it'll be the end !"

But Mr. Oldhead, that usually quiet and liberal-minded man, drove off to Bayonne in a state of savage satisfaction. At last he could do something that might help the Republican cause; he ought to have done it long ago, and not let Crossman talk him out of it. Pray God he was in time. "Faster," he kept telling the driver, who was anyhow shooting along the winding blue-grey ribbon of road at the usual reckless pace of the hireling French chauffeur. In his hurry he had omitted to go up and get his thick overcoat, and in his thin one he was cold—but what of that? At the Préfecture he told his tale with such convincing detail that he was readily believed—all the more because suspense about the offensive was as prevalent in Bayonne as elsewhere. There was telephoning—orders were given; Mr. Oldhead was effusively thanked. Driving back under a leaden sky which threatened snow he was colder than ever ; he shivered, his leg began to hurt. But a Republican fervour, burning in his heart, warmed him within.

Once back, his errand safely accomplished, Mr. Oldhead could not refrain from telling his family what he had done. Rosemary listened with knitted brows, and as usual betook herself to her own room to think it over. Oh well, she thought, sitting at her small writing-table, on which her Spanish copy-books were spread out, it didn't so much matter. It couldn't affect Raquel now anyhow, as she was going away. She sighed—oh dear ! How much she would miss her dear Condesa. On the open copy-book before her was a page of Spanish written in Raquel's bold pointed hand—one of the exercises that she had occasionally set to help her little friend ; it was one of those small kindnesses that were intensely characteristic of her. She would never set her another ! No more exercises ; no more walks, and morning coffee together, and laughter and fun. And no more Milcom either, suddenly appearing to make life, for both of them, flame up into wonder. Lousy —everything *was* lousy in the end; but one knew that in advance —one expected it. But this morning—he had been *nice*; he had neither snubbed her nor laughed at her. And he had said that he wouldn't forget that she had done it. She was glad that she had. Rosemary had no qualms, no regrets. Tilting the table-lamp, putting on her reading spectacles, she settled down to translate the Condesa's last exercise.

Mr. Oldhead meanwhile, warmed with tea and achievement, got his wife to rub his leg, rested and read *The Times*; shortly before seven, saying that he might be a bit late for dinner, he put on his thickest overcoat and a scarf, and stumped off to the Bar Basque. "I've got to see Crossman," he said.

Crossman was not there when he arrived, but Crumpaun, Hever, Carrow and the rest were already in session, still discussing the Russian planes and the possibilities of sabotage. To journalists short of material, to have thrashed out a subject exhaustively before lunch is no reason at all for not repeating the process before dinner. Mr. Oldhead sat rather silent, watching the door; he made no reference to his dash to Bayonne. When Ladislas the waiter brought fresh drinks, Oldhead made the others stop talking; when he attempted to linger in their vicinity, Hever shooed him off, menacingly—whereat Ladislas grinned his Central European grin, showing his splendid mouthful of white teeth. At about seven-thirty the door opened, bringing a gust of cold air, and Crossman walked in; his red face was redder than ever, he stamped his feet and beat his arms about his body before taking off his hat, coat and muffler—he yelled to Ladislas for a double whiskey and soda. "Hell, it's cold," he said. And nodded reassuringly to Mr. Oldhead.

"Here, where've you been at this time of night, you old rip?" Crumpaun asked him.

"Doing some reporting, old thing—covering a break," Crossman retorted, burying his purple face in his whiskey-glass.

"Take your nose out of this, laddie," Hever said threateningly to Ladislas, who retired laughing. "Now then, spill it, Crossey."

"Is it all right?" Mr. Oldhead asked in a low voice, leaning over to Crossman.

"Right as rain. Ten of 'em there, and more up the road—motor-cycle combinations, guns, and the whole outfit," Crossman replied. "Anyone got a stinker?"

"Here, what is all this?" Carrow asked. "You and Crossey in

on some racket together?" he asked Mr. Oldhead. "Poaching, eh?"

"Oldhead, Oldhead & Oldhead, Inc.—Supersleuths," chanted Crossman, on whom the whiskey was taking its usual immediate effect.

Hever quietly impounded his glass.

"Not another drop till the beans come pouring out, Crossey my boy," he said amiably.

"All right—all right; give a fellow a chance. It's only that we —or rather the child—spotted another sneak-way t'other day, over at the Grotte de Sare; and when this plane racket came up, Mr. O. here thought the matter better have attention. So he pranced into Bayonne this afternoon to tip off the cops. And I just breezed over to the bally old grotto to check up, and found results satisfactory—Gardes Mobiles all over the place. So that job's done. And now, Tom, I'll trouble you for my glass." He raised it. "Here's to Miss Rosemary Oldhead, the Queen of Counter-Espionage."

"I never knew a man get so tight, so quickly, on so little liquor," Hever observed in an undertone to Crumpaun, while they drank.

"Did you get any photographs?" Carrow asked Mr. Oldhead.

"No—he's put wise to that, Carrow; no more free photos to the Press! He stands over the boy-friend while they're being developed now," Crossman answered irrepressibly.

"No, I didn't," Mr. Oldhead replied for himself. He rose stiffly, and stiffly struggled into his overcoat—having not the good news that he had come for, he wanted to go home. "Thank you, Crossman. Good night."

"Good night."

"Good night."

He stumped back through the bitter streets to the Grande Bretagne, ignoring the cold, and thoroughly pleased with himself.

His satisfaction over this *coup* not only raised Mr. Oldhead's spirits, it seemed actually to improve his physical health as well; when, two days later, the Archdeacon invited him to a round of golf on the Chiberta course, just beyond Biarritz, to Ethel Oldhead's surprise and pleasure he accepted, though the weather was colder than ever—quite Christmassy, as she said. She and Rosemary were taken along for the drive. Mrs. Oldhead was to be dropped in Biarritz—with Christmas only four days off, she wanted to do some shopping; Rosemary, who—as has been said—loathed Biarritz, took her ever-present Spanish exercise-books

along—if they would put her out on the Chambre d'Amour, she
said, she would find a sheltered corner to work in, and would
walk to the Club House for tea at four-thirty.

The Chambre d'Amour is the name given, Heaven knows why,
to part of the sandy stretch of dunes, pine trees and windswept
shore which begins at the bathing-place just beyond Biarritz, and
continues to the mouth of the Adour at Bayonne. In summer it is
thronged with sea-bathers, sun-bathers, and picnickers—but in
winter it is practically deserted. Rosemary, decanted from the
Archdeacon's car, strolling along, observed that there seemed to
be no one about except herself.

No wonder, she thought, as she sought a sheltered spot. A
bitter northeaster was blowing offshore, raising little flurries of
sand between the dark trunks of the pines, and sending smoking
ribbons off the exposed tops of the dunes; great rollers were coming in from the Bay of Biscay, their white crests blown off backwards by the wind. Eventually she went right down to the
beach, and tucked herself under the low unfinished sea-wall
which here protects the coast from the winter storms; there, in an
angle of the wall, she was comparatively warm—and quite hidden,
as it happened, from anyone walking along the path above. As she
settled herself down, in full sight of the waves, she noticed with
surprise that she heard them very little—the wind carried their
thundering out to sea; on the other hand it brought clearly to
her ears every sound from the landward side: the bray of a
donkey tethered under the pines, the honking and engine-roar of
cars that passed along the road. She began to work, and was soon
absorbed in her task.

Rosemary liked Spanish, and had made a good deal of progress
with it in the past three months—apart from her lessons, she had
spent a lot of time talking it with the Condesa, and she could now
follow pretty accurately the conversations of the Executioner with
his friends in the hall of the hotel. So when, after a time, she
heard voices, men's voices, speaking Spanish close by, it was
natural enough that she should prick up her ears and listen.

". . . Exasperating that you should be delayed like this," were
the first words she caught—"And possibly dangerous. But to-
morrow night all should be arranged at the far end. I will let you
know, in any case. Those damned French!—I wish I knew what
had possessed them to do this just now."

"Then, since I must in any case wait another day, can I not see
her? It is the last chance, and she is so near. There is no risk, I
assure"—the voice faded, as the speakers passed out of hearing.

This fragment intrigued Rosemary enormously. 'Delayed like this'—'damned French'—and Spaniards talking! And out here on the Chambre d'Amour, on this intolerably inclement day! She must go into this. Very cautiously, she poked up her head till she could look over the top of the low sea-wall. The two men had come to a halt some thirty yards away from her, on the Biarritz side; they were still talking, though now the wind carried their words out to sea—but their attitudes and gestures were the very diagram of an argument; beyond them, some distance along the shore, a big car was standing solitary on one of the parking-places to which sandy tracks lead down from the road. Straining her eyes, Rosemary studied the pair. One was tall and slight, and there was something vaguely familiar about his head and profile; the other shorter, stouter, and older—as he turned fully in her direction, gesturing negatives with his hands at his companion, she recognised the Old Parrot.

This discovery flung Rosemary into transports of excitement. It was!—it was!—it must be the closing of the Grotte de Sare that they were talking about, and the Old Parrot *was* the super-spy! But who was the other? She could not see, for now—how maddening!—they had both turned their backs towards her. But there was something curiously familiar and distinctive about the young man's walk—either she had seen him before, or he walked like someone she knew. Who was it? Who was it? But before she could catch the elusive memory, they stopped again, turned and came back towards her—and now she knew where she had seen the younger man. He was the splendid peasant who had talked to her outside the Grotte de Sare, on the day when she discovered the Arbre de Noël route, though now he was dressed in an ordinary town suit and light overcoat.

Her heart beating with excitement, Rosemary cautiously withdrew her head out of sight, and sat listening, while her thoughts raced. So he *was* the spy! And her Father's intervention had prevented him from getting back that way—"at the far end" must mean somewhere near Perpignan, at the other end of the frontier. But who was the "her" he wished so much to see? She checked her speculations as the voices came within earshot again, and strained to catch the words.

". . . you can let me know the date and place exactly," the first voice said—the Parrot's. "Whatever the risk, you must remain until you have secured those details. As to *how* you will let us know, probably this time you must" . . . Again the voice faded out, as their walk took them out of hearing—and again Rosemary's thoughts darted this way and that over the words. Thank God he wasn't caught, anyhow! was her first instinctive reaction. After a moment or two she poked her head up once more, but quickly withdrew it again. They had parted; the Old Parrot was coming back towards her, alone; the young man was strolling on in the opposite direction, towards Bayonne. Huddled down, hardly daring to breathe, she listened to the Spaniard's heavy steps go creaking and scrunching past her on the sandy track. When the sounds had quite ceased, she poked her head up once more. Hunched in his overcoat—the pepper-and-salt overcoat that he had worn that day at Jacques'—the Parrot was trudging along towards the car; the young man was still strolling in the Bayonne direction, but slowly, pausing now and then to throw a stone out to sea. Alternately crouching and peeping, Rosemary waited till she saw the older man enter the car and drive off. By this time the young man was some three hundred yards away; when the car had gone, he turned and began to walk back in her direction; but still slowly, as if purposelessly—and still pausing to send stones spinning seawards.

Instantly, without a thought of the risk she might be running, she decided to intercept him. Seizing a moment when he was watching one of his flung stones fall short of the incoming breakers, she popped up over the wall, copy-book and all, and sat down under the lee of one of the loose concrete blocks with which the wall was, one day, to be finished, but which now lay scattered by the shore track. The block, though large, afforded little shelter —goodness, it was cold!—but Rosemary did not care; opening her copy-book on her knee, pencil in hand, she pretended to be absorbed in her work. If only he would come as far as where she sat!

He did. Slowly, moodily, dawdling along with many pauses, as if anxious to kill time, he was presently within about fifty yards of her. Crouched under her block, Rosemary's small figure was not very conspicuous—it was only then that he appeared to see her. When he did, once more that curious tenseness seemed to make all his body taut; he walked rapidly up to her. When he was quite close, he evidently recognised her, for his rather stern expression broke into a swift smile. But his eyes remained watchful.

"Bonjour, Mademoiselle! We meet again!" he said.

"Mais oui, Monsieur," Rosemary said, smiling too.

"May one ask from where you come?" he asked, and now his eyes were not only watchful, they were suspicious.

Readily, the girl slipped out her white lie.

"I came down from the road," she said. "My Father has gone to play golf at Chiberta—I shall join him for tea."

"Tiens," he said. "And you sit out in the cold, on such a day? For what?"

"I'm doing my Spanish," she said, still easily, though by now his expression was beginning to frighten her a little—and she held out her copy-book.

"Alors, you learn Spanish?" he said, taking it from her, with an air of casualness, and a faint smile—and as if in idle curiosity, he began to turn the leaves. As he did so, a remarkable change came over his face.

"Who wrote this?" he asked sharply, holding the cheap copy-book out to her.

She glanced at the page. It was one of the Condesa's exercises.

"My friend, the Condesa de Verdura. She often sets me things; she makes them better, more colloquial than my teacher," she answered.

"Tiens," he said again, and sat down beside her under the block of concrete. "And since when is she your friend?" he asked.

"Since she came to St.-Jean from Madrid; she is staying in our hotel. Why, do you know her?" the girl asked curiously.

An oddly wistful expression came over the man's fine face—he paused for a moment before replying.

"She is—a very old friend," he said slowly. He smiled, a sudden brilliant smile. "I am glad that she has found a friend in her exile. You like her?"

"I love her," the girl said eagerly. "I think everybody must—she is so beautiful and so sweet. I wish she were not going away."

"Is she going away?" he asked, casually—but his eyes were suddenly intent. The girl studied his face curiously—an idea, a suspicion, was beginning to form in her mind. This man had a delicate high-bridged nose, and those surprising blue-grey eyes under his black hair and brows. What was it Raquel had said about Juanito?—"Like me, and with blue eyes; but black."

But she remembered to go on playing her part.

"But yes—she is returning to Spain, to Burgos or to San Sebastiàn. He is released, you know—the Conde, I mean."

"It is true? No, I did not know. Since when?"

"Since a few days. It is Mr. Milcom who has arranged all that—her friend—the one who brought her out from Madrid." (She could not resist the sweet pleasure of mentioning Milcom.)

"Ah yes. And you know him also, this Milcom? What is he like?"

"He's a fascinating person," Rosemary said, thoughtfully. "Very clever; and good—and very sad, somehow. He's a journalist, of course." She smiled suddenly. "In Madrid they call him 'El Melancolico'."

"Vraiment? And why?"

"His face—because he looks so gloomy. But he isn't gloomy in himself; not always. I think it's that he sees the—the dreadfulness of things so clearly. He's—" she hesitated. "He's a *pitying* person," she finally brought out.

He bent dark brows upon her.

"You are a close observer, I remark," he said. "Is this Milcom also a friend of yours?"

A curious expression, brilliantly triumphant, came over the young girl's face.

"Yes," she said ringingly. "Not so much as hers, of course—who would be? But we are friends."

He looked at her clear face, her immense eager eyes, with their wonderfully candid expression, and smiled his sudden smile again.

"*I* should like to be your friend," he said. "Perhaps one day, after the War, I shall be. Meanwhile"—he stretched out his hand for her copy-book, "may I begin by writing you a *devoir* in Spanish? If you cannot translate it, I am sure that your friend the Condesa de Verdura will help you. Perhaps you will show it to her?"

"Of course I will," the girl said, a little breathlessly. Her heart was beginning to thump again. Was it? It must be. Incredible as it seemed, it must be. "Will it be very difficult?" she asked.

He looked up—he was already scribbling away on his knee.

"Fairly difficult," he smiled. "It is a story. Now let me write."

They sat for some minutes in silence, the man writing, the girl examining his face, bent over the book. In profile, the likeness to Raquel was really marked. No, there was no doubt at all in her mind. But, as usual, she decided to say nothing to him of her knowledge. Probably he guessed that she must guess, she thought, but considered that she was too young and insignificant to matter. Being young and insignificant was very convenient, and made life very amusing, Rosemary had long ago decided.

"Tenez," he said at last, handing back the book—"There you are. You must try and do it yourself first, and only when it is finished, show it to her. When will that be? To-morrow?"

"I don't expect she'll be back by to-morrow," Rosemary said.

"Comment? Is she not at St.-Jean?"

"Not at this moment—she is gone to Paris, to see about getting her exit permit for Spain. She only went three days ago, and Mr. Milcom thought it might take some time."

His face clouded at her words.

"So—so," he muttered to himself—"and of course I do not hear! Inhumanity!" Then, recollecting himself, he turned to her with a little smile.

"The French are very *difficiles*, these days," he said—"so many restrictions!"

Rosemary agreed—but she did not think it was the inhumanity of the French that he had been muttering about; she thought his vexation was much more probably—and more reasonably—directed at the Duquesa and the Old Parrot. The one certainly, the other probably, must have known both about Raquel's immediate journey, and her impending departure—and evidently had not told him.

"Alors," he said, getting up—"I must go. Au revoir, Mademoiselle. Give Raquel my love, and tell her that I shall see her soon, in Spain."

Rosemary decided to risk it.

"Whose love?" she asked.

He tapped the copy-book in her hand.

"That will tell her," he said. "Au revoir, Mademoiselle!" And he walked off.

When he had gone, in the direction of Biarritz, Rosemary glanced at her watch. Gracious—ten past four already! She must hurry. She hastened inland through the pine trees, hit the road and plugged along it towards the Chiberta Golf Club.

It was another three days before the Condesa returned from Paris, armed with her exit permit. Rosemary had in the meantime, as may be supposed, made as complete a translation of the *devoir* as she could, and with the help of a dictionary it was pretty accurate. It was really in the form of a story, and began simply: "Once upon a time there was a man called Manuel Jereda who dearly loved a woman called Raquel, but for reasons of duty he could not always see her when he wished to." It was couched in terms which might just as well have referred to a lover as to a brother, except for certain references to their childhood; he hoped always—"perhaps even on her next birthday, to strew flowers over her where she lay sleeping, as in the old dear days." The references to his "work" and his "duty" were such as he might well have supposed would convey nothing to a third party—but to Rosemary, knowing what she did, they were significantly clear. When he had accomplished "one last and most important task" he hoped to return to his own people. The little tale was elegantly, even brilliantly done—but at the last his love and longing had broken through. "Oh, my dearest, my little darling one," he wrote in a final paragraph, "all this has been so hard, for you and for me—but soon, soon, we shall be together again."

Rosemary chose her moment rather carefully to show this document to Raquel. Even when the Condesa was in her room, the Duquesa had a way of popping in and out all the time—so much so that Rosemary wondered if she herself had fallen under the suspicion of the alert Spanish woman. It was quite possible, she argued—after three months spent in France, in the company of that disillusioned breed of men, journalists, Rosemary had few illusions left about the French; she did not suppose for a moment that the Bayonne authorities were any more reliable than the rest of their compatriots—there might easily have been a leak about who was responsible for the closing of the Grotte de Sare. Anyhow, late at night on the day of the Condesa's return she went, already in a dressing-gown, and tapped on her door. She found her in bed, and alone, and asked her to come along to her, Rosemary's room. "I have something important to show you—please, you must come," she said urgently.

A little reluctantly, the Condesa got up and went with her—and curled herself up on the foot of the bed. "Well, what is it, this important thing?" she asked, with a smiling hint of mockery.

But smile and mockery alike left her exquisite face when Rosemary handed her the shabby copy-book, folded open at the pencilled *devoir*. She glanced at it, stared at it with astonished eyes, and then with a lovely gesture clasped it to her breast, and over it faced the girl in violent agitation, with a stream of questions whose urgency made them sound actually angry.

"What is this? Where did you get this? Why is it in your book? What does it mean? How can you have come by it? You can't have *seen* him?"

"Yes, I did see him," the young girl said steadily. "Quite by accident. I——"

"Where? When? It's impossible!"

"Oh, please be quieter. Listen, and I will tell you. Don't raise your voice—we don't want people to hear."

"Go on then—go on!"

"It was three days ago—I was on the Chambre d'Amour, doing my Spanish, and he came by . . ."

"Juanito? There in Biarritz? Oh my God! And I was away."

"Raquel darling, *do* be quiet! I can't tell you if you keep on interrupting. Yes, he came by, and we talked."

"Why should he talk with you?" Raquel asked.

"Because we'd met before, outside the Grotte de Sare some time ago; I was sitting there alone—the others had gone off—and he came out of the Grotto. And I guessed then that he was a spy."

"You too know this? How?"

Poor sweet, you wouldn't make much of a conspirator, Rosemary thought. Aloud—"I didn't *know* it then—I just guessed," she said. "And of course then I didn't know who he was."

"And whom did you tell? Your father? This Crump person?"

"No—I didn't tell anyone, of course," the girl said, almost scornfully. "He was so splendid, I didn't want him to be caught, if he was ten times a spy! We just talked, and he didn't worry about me, because I'm so young—and I went away and thought about him, and that was all. But when we met on the Chambre d'Amour the other day, of course he recognised me, and so we talked again."

"Well, and then? How did you know it was Juanito?"

"I wasn't sure, at first. He was rather suspicious, and he asked me what I was doing, and I said learning Spanish, and showed him my book. And then, naturally, he saw your writing in it, and got very excited, and asked whose the writing was? So I told him it was yours, and that we were friends, and that you are in the hotel."

"And he did not ask to see me?" Raquel asked with hurt eyes.

"I told him you were in Paris, of course," Rosemary replied—she was not going to embark on the story of the Old Parrot if she could help it, to Raquel. "And I told him about the Conde being in Burgos, and that you were going back to Spain. He didn't know any of that. And he told me to give you his love, and to tell you that he should see you soon, in Spain."

"And he said then who he was?"

"No. He never said. Only that you would know who had written the story. But he is so like you that I guessed—that, and the way he talked about you, and his knowing your writing. I'm not sure that he realised that I should guess—I think perhaps he hoped I should think he was your boy-friend," said Rosemary with great naturalness.

Raquel smiled faintly at that.

"Did he say when he was going back himself?" she asked then, eagerly.

"The next day or the day after—that would have been yesterday."

"Ah yes. Then he is gone now." She sighed a little. "How did he look—well?" she asked, with a renewal of eagerness.

"Very well—tired about the eyes, a little," Rosemary said.

"And dressed how? In uniform?"

"Goodness no! In plain civvies, and an overcoat. The time before he was in peasant's dress."

"And you liked him? Isn't he nice?"

"He's an enchanting person," the girl said sincerely. "He said he hoped to be friends with me one day."

The Condesa asked a few more questions, the foolish simple questions of hungry love, and then Rosemary tore the two precious sheets out of her exercise-book, and the Condesa took them away to her room. Next day she left for San Sebastián. But before she went she sought Rosemary out again, questioned her further about the encounter at the Grotte de Sare, and thanked her for her silence and discretion. At the last she flung her arms round the English girl's neck, and burst into tears.

"I shall miss you," she sobbed out. "I have been so happy here—and you were part of it. And they both liked you," she added inconsequently.

She was going by car with the Duquesa as far as Irún, and on from there by train. Rosemary obtained her mother's permission to go in to Hendaye on the bus to see the Condesa off at the Bridge. Ethel Oldhead herself was not able to come—Mr. Oldhead had got a touch of influenza, and his rheumatism had flared up after that cold afternoon of golf at Chiberta; the Doctor was talking of getting him away to some place with a warmer climate, like Vernet or Amélie-les-Bains, where the sulphur waters would help his complaint. The cold had fairly reached St.-Jean by now; on that Christmas Eve frost gripped the ground, and sparse flakes of snow were whirled by a bitter wind out of a harsh and leaden sky as Rosemary sat in the bus, bowling along the grey road between the blotched creamy trunks of the leafless plane trees towards Hendaye. She sat looking out of the window, her two little farewell gifts for Raquel—a bottle of Lenthéric Eau-de-Cologne and a big bunch of violets—on her lap, thinking of her first drive along that road with Mr. Crumpaun, not quite three months ago. How much had happened in that short time: her friendship with the Condesa, the Condesa's love affair with Milcom, and their separation; the sudden growth of her own love for the sad-faced journalist, the curious series of accidents which had brought her into contact with Juanito, and to some knowledge of his activities. Well, it was all over now, she supposed, as she climbed out of the bus and walked down to the Bridge—when she had first stood here by the barrier, she had never even seen any of them, and now she would never see any of them any more. She would be dragged off to Vernet or Amélie or some lousy unknown watering-place, she thought, shivering in the cold wind, and would never see or hear anything again, ever, of these people who had filled her life— her dear Crumpet, Raquel, Juanito, and Milcom.

But there she was wrong.

## CHAPTER ELEVEN

### On the Crest

THE long-awaited Franco offensive broke round about the New Year. The world has heard—but has probably since forgotten— of that bitterly-fought campaign, and the gradual tightening of the net round the doomed triangle, hemmed in between the French frontier, the advancing enemy, and the sea; the gradual falling back—back to Tarragona, back to Barcelona, back to Figueras.

It was not really part of James Milcom's assignment to cover the actual fighting in the field, but he did this for the first two or three weeks. Then he went back to Barcelona to keep in touch with the government, and when the evacuation of that city too was decided on, he realised that the time had come to get out to France, and meet the retreating cabinet and armies there. But he did not go by road—he got on board a dirty old orange-boat, crammed with refugees, which made a risky but successful get-away and arrived at Port Vendres, the first harbour beyond the frontier, at the end of January 1939.

It was at Port Vendres that he had landed with Raquel four months before, and from the sea, as the orange-boat steamed in, the aspect of the charming little place was unaltered; the pale multi-coloured houses still clustered thickly round the port, and straggled sparsely up the steep green-grey slopes behind— autumn, winter, spring and summer bring only the slightest of changes to a Mediterranean landscape. But in James's heart it was midwinter. In spite of activity, excitement and danger, the days had crept past with leaden slowness since he parted from

Raquel, and his misery over the defeat of the cause he cared for with such intensity joined hands with his private misery. But activity, excitement and danger had at least kept his thoughts at bay to some extent—now, leaning on the rail of the boat, for the moment with nothing to do, the sight of the little town brought back such a flood of memories of the last time he steamed in there, with her at his side, that his wretchedness was almost unbearable. He had heard no word of her—he hadn't expected to; but whenever other preoccupation left him off guard for a moment, his mind jabbed at him with pictures of her and the Conde together, with a desperate speculations as to how she was solving her end of the problem—however much he fought them off, they returned again and again, stinging like angry bees; they did so now. To get some relief in action he went below, making his way through the stinking crowded passageways, collected his bag, and brought it up on deck.

But for James, public affairs could still transcend private ones —the habit of a lifetime is not easily broken; and the aspect which Port Vendres presented when he finally stepped ashore there that day drove all thoughts of anything else out of his head. The quay was piled high with crates of Spanish oranges, waiting for the ships which never came to carry them away to Northern Europe; much of the fruit had rotted, and the sinister velvety blue-grey of mildew showed through the slats. Among the crates, and all over the street along the water-front sat heaps—the word is really. accurate—of refugees, desolate little groups piled on their miserable belongings; one or two cheap suitcases, bundles of bedding, two-handled metal cooking-pots slung over their shoulders, wretched paper parcels of clothing. They sat on the pavement, in the entries of shops and houses, at the edge of the roadway. They had broken into some of the orange-crates and pulled out the fruit that was not yet rotten and were eating it; orange-peel, strewn all over the place, added to the general effect of desolation, dirtiness and distress. Port Vendres is normally one of the most beautiful coastal towns in Europe, with its mediaeval moles and harbour-buildings silhouetted against the lovely blue of the Mediterranean in front; but on that January day James Milcom lost all sense of its beauty, it so epitomised human misery. The refugees were not going anywhere or doing anything—there was nothing for them to do and nowhere in particular for them to go; there never is, for refugees—they were just sitting where they were put, eating oranges.

James, his suitcase in one hand and his typewriter in the

other, walked round the harbour, looking for a car. The harbour-master was distractedly supervising the unloading of yet more refugees and crates of oranges from James's and another ship, and could give no help. At a quay on the further side a French destroyer, having decanted the French Minister to Barcelona and his staff, was preparing to put to sea again to pick up another cargo of human jetsam. On the wharf behind her a big empty warehouse was receiving a fresh type of goods—derelict human beings; fresh straw had been laid down on the floors of all three storeys, and the refugees were being put in there. James, showing his Press pass, was allowed to enter. All over the ground floor men, women and children were sitting on the straw; they too were eating oranges. In a small glass-walled office one nurse and three young girls were heating tinned milk on spirit-stoves and doling it out to the younger children—in another officials were going through the wretched luggage of the Spaniards, looking for arms or compromising documents; in a third their papers were being examined to establish their identity. Every few minutes a lorry, laden with yet more of this dismal cargo, rolled in from Cerbère, dropped its load on the wharf, and roared off again. The scene on the two upper floors was a repetition of that to be witnessed downstairs. Outside, two field kitchens were theoretically producing coffee and hot soup for the people, who waited in queues, tin mugs in their hands—but the soup machine had just struck work for lack of coal. James handed the boy in charge a hundred-franc note to buy some more, and went on. There was no sanitation but to go outside, he observed; but this the refugees were not troubling to do. He fell in with one of the junior officers from the French destroyer, returning from a hurried trip by car to Cerbère. "Si nous n'en avons pas pour dix ans de typhus, cela m'étonnera," observed this young man.

It was through this young officer that James eventually found the car which drove him to Perpignan. He took two refugee passengers with him, an American representative of a telephone concern, and an elderly and discouraged Spanish lady, who had managed to salvage a surprising and most inconvenient amount of her personal luggage, including two typewriters, but had no French money. She offered Milcom one of the typewriters to pay for her share of the car. In the next few days he was to learn how often typewriters were proffered as currency along the French frontier.

He went straight to the Hôtel de l'Europe where, being known to the management, he succeeded in getting a room. The hotel was already crowded out with refugees, Spanish as well as foreign, and with journalists from every part of Europe; the parrot-cage re-echoed with voices; little Spanish children ran about, yelling; women without luggage sat drooping in the chairs along the gangway, making James's heart contract as he remembered Raquel sitting there, four months before. The one telephone by the bureau was besieged by journalists, and this feature prompted James to an astute move—he went straight into the garage next door, from which he had hired a car on his previous visits, interviewed the manager, and booked up the garage telephone from five-thirty to six-thirty p.m. every evening for the next week, paying a large sum down for the privilege. He also hired the best car available, with a tough-looking chauffeur. James had learned something about refugeeing by this time, and knew that an unattended car would stand small chance of remaining in the possession of its owner anywhere near Perpignan during the next few days. Then, having made these dispositions, he went back to the hotel to get some dinner.

Almost the first person he met in the parrot-cage was Crumpaun, consuming a whiskey-and-soda.

"Hullo! So you got out," was the worthy's salutation.

"Yes. Where did you get that whiskey?" James asked. He knew by bitter experience that the Hôtel de l'Europe did not provide whiskey.

"Here." Crumpaun tapped his ample chest. "More upstairs too. Have one?"

"*And* how!" said James, pulling a chair away from one of the small tables, and dropping into it beside Crumpaun, who called for another glass, and mixed him a drink from a capacious flask. "How did you get here?" James asked.

"Drove—with Tom Hever. There's nothing doing any more at St.-Jean. It's a splendid drive," said Crumpaun meditatively. "Did you drive out?"

"God, no—boat."

"Her-rum. Well, I daresay we shan't need a car. Probably pick up all we want right here."

"I've got a car," said James. "You and Tom can come round with me if you want to."

"That'll suit Tom," said Crumpaun comfortably. "He always wants to get about. Any news of the Condesa?"

"No," said James bleakly.

Next day, however, Crumpaun decided to join Hever and Milcom when they drove out to see what there was to be seen.

7

Just as they were leaving the hotel a clerk came out with some
mail for Crumpaun; he glanced at the envelopes, muttered
"Time enough for that later," and stuffed them into his pocket.
It was beginning to rain as they bowled along the road which
Milcom and Raquel had taken on their drive to Arles in the
autumn—the start of that seventy-two-hours downpour which
added so much to the misery of the refugees.

"Where are we going?" Hever asked.

"Le Boulou and Le Perthus," said James, who had a map on
his knee.

A group of Gardes Mobiles stopped the car at the cross-roads
outside Le Boulou, but allowed it to proceed after seeing the Press
passes. They drove to the railway-station, and on the way
encountered the first refugees which Hever and Crumpaun had
seen: they leaned out to stare at the women carrying children,
with others tagging at their heels; at wounded Republican
soldiers, with grey blankets rolled round their ragged grey uniforms. Two quite young girls staggered along, carrying an immense trunk between them. The big yard in front of the station
was full of refugees, and in the station itself stood a long train,
already packed with humanity, into which yet more damp
creatures were very slowly being stowed, to be sent off to the
interior of France. Crumpaun remained in the car, but Milcom
and Hever went in. Everything was in hopeless confusion: people
were being put into coaches and pulled out again, families were
getting separated, children howled. The train had been in the
station for six hours, they learned, and would not leave for
"several hours" yet. Milcom asked the harassed station-master
why not, since it was already full?

"It will not, *voilà tout*, Monsieur," the man snapped.

"What a mess," said Hever as they left. "I didn't realise that
the French were so infernally inefficient."

"They're always inefficient where any money has to be spent,"
James replied gloomily. "They simply can't spend money."

"God help them in a war, then," said Hever.

"He won't," James replied with conviction.

They drove on towards Le Perthus, past an improvised internment camp full of soldiers in the vineyards at the edge of the town.
The road soon left the plain, and climbed gently up a long valley
with a stream in the bottom of it, whose rocky slopes were thick
with cork-oaks and wild olives—here and there almonds were
springing into a faint flush of chill pink bloom. It rained harder
than ever—Milcom and Hever, already wet, shivered; and still

down the road came the refugees—old men, women with suit-cases, other women carrying and dragging babies, more girls swinging trunks. "God, how their arms must ache!" Hever exclaimed.

At Le Perthus even Crumpaun was moved to leave the car, so fantastic was the scene. The one long narrow street was crowded from end to end with refugees, between whom Gardes Mobiles, officials, sightseers and journalists pushed their way; they were sitting all over the pavements or perched on the steps of the houses, vainly seeking some shelter from the beating rain—all were wet through, and had been for many hours; some had thrown their blankets over their shoulders, others their bed-spreads (most had brought some form of bedding)—the exhausted faces of women, the drawn ones of infants, looked peculiarly wretched peering from under the gay flounces of a peasant quilt. Girls who two or three days before had still had the spirit to paint their faces now had streaks of rouge running down their necks; the white hair of the old men and women was plastered by the pitiless rain on their yellow skins. In the middle of the village the journalists came on three trucks, each mounting a field kitchen, from which several harassed and unshaven young Englishmen were doling out soup, noodles and coffee to the people who stood waiting in long queues—they received the food for the most part in two-handled copper or iron stew-pans, which almost all the refugees, as Milcom had already noticed in Port Vendres, carried slung at their backs; they then took the filled vessel over to the pavement, and the children and elders fell to, each with his own iron spoon. The stew-pans and spoons, Hever observed, seemed to be a regular part of refugee technique. But what horrified Hever and Crumpaun was the use to which the soaked wretches put the muddy yellow water of the roaring gutters, which carried a filthy burden of orange-peel, bits of paper, cigarette-ends and cess; having eaten, they rinsed out spoons and vessels alike in them, and some—thirsty, it seemed, even in the rain—actually dipped their mugs into the nauseous stream, and drank. To Milcom the whole scene had the nightmarish quality of a prophetic dream. This was whither ideologies led; to this, if ideologies spread and gripped the nations more firmly, mankind would come—to sit homeless in pouring rain, fed on charity if fed at all, and drink the contaminated waters of the gutter. God, what a spectacle for the twentieth century to produce!

He asked an old fellow with a rather clever face who the young *Ingleses* were who were feeding the people.

"Los Quaqueros," (The Quakers) he replied.

Being journalists, they soon managed to rout out the Captain of the Gardes Mobiles and the Mayor of the village, and questioned them. About ten thousand here now, the Mayor said, and more coming in all the time. No, no more *miliciens*; on an order from the Préfecture at Perpignan that had been stopped—only old men, women and children might now cross the frontier. "Ask him what's happening to the *miliciens*," Hever said. James did so. "*Mais*, they are up there, at the barrier—go and see them," the Mayor said. They did so—but first James asked him also who the young Englishmen were who were feeding the multitude, and why?

"The Quakers—they do that. It is their *métier*," said the Mayor with a shrug, and turned away to answer a policeman who arrived with some question.

They walked on up towards the pass itself. On either side the hills, sparsely covered with green and dripping cork-oaks, rose into the clouds; over them smoke puffed up here and there, mingling with the wreaths of fog and cloud—from the camp-fires of the troops and Gardes Mobiles who were posted there to prevent the passage of the Spanish soldiers, so a weary Lieutenant told Milcom. "But further along, they are coming in all the time, arms and all, by the mule-tracks," he said. "Que voulez-vous? La frontière est un peu vaste par ici."

The scene at the barrier, when at last they reached it, was horrible beyond description. A stout wire rope was drawn across the road and beyond it on both sides, in all for some four hundred yards; on the French side of this stood a company of Senegalese troops with fixed bayonets, their black-coffee-coloured faces seamed with tribal initiatory scars, grinning with cheerful African idiocy. On the Spanish side stood a solid block of human beings, four hundred yards square, packed vertically like sardines in a tin, forced by steady pressure from behind towards the barrier, France, and safety; from them rose a ceaseless roar of appeal, fury and despair, like the howling of a million wolves. It was the most horrible sight, the most horrible sound, that the three Englishmen had ever seen or heard.

"Christ!" said Hever, appalled. "Blast the French!"

"They can't help it; they can't very well let them all in," said Crumpaun reasonably.

"They could if they chose," said Hever. He was right; a few days later they did—for a reason.

Hever and Milcom climbed the slope towards the old fortress, where several hundred *miliciens* were already interned, till they could look down over the mountain road leading into Spain. The first nine kilometres were a solid block of motor-cars, waiting in the hope of being allowed to pass into France. Wet through, the two men returned to the village. In their absence Crumpaun had effected a scoop—he had met and interviewed Del Vayo, the Republican Minister, who had got out on foot.

"Where's he gone?" Hever asked.

"Down to Perp.," Crumpaun replied.

"Let's go after him," Hever said urgently to Milcom.

"All right—go on and get the car turned. I want to talk to these fellows for a moment," said Milcom—by this time they had pushed their way back as far as the food kitchens.

Acting on the assumption that they were in fact Quakers, as the Mayor had said, Milcom merely asked the young men with the trucks how they were getting on.

"Oh, it's enough to break your heart," one of them said, handing his tin soup-dipper to a girl with a weary—"Here, Suzanne, get to it. You been up to the rope?" he asked Milcom. "They've been like that for twenty-four hours. Out behind it there are women and children dying of hunger and exposure, and we can't do a thing for them, though we've got five tons of chocolate and tinned milk and sardines over there"—he waved his hand at two more trucks, parked by the roadside and guarded by Senegalese. "We tried yesterday and again this morning—yelled at them through megaphones in Spanish to make way and let us through and we'd feed them. But it wasn't any good—they're raving mad. As soon as we walked in with the cases on our shoulders they nearly murdered us—tore them down and broke them open, and fought, so everything was trampled to pulp in the mud in five minutes. No one got a bite."

"Couldn't you have gone in with an escort?—the Gardes Mobiles are pretty efficient," Milcom asked.

"So *you'd* think! No, the French mustn't cross the frontier—unneutral act! Even in an emergency like this," said the young man bitterly. "But we're doing a job, all the same. Seen our hospital?" He led James across the street to the village school, where two elderly and three young women, under the direction of another exhausted young man, were dressing the wounds of *miliciens* and administering first aid to women and children. As they walked back—"By the way, you haven't got a gasper, have you? We're out," said the young man.

Milcom gave him two packets of Players, which he accepted

gratefully. "We don't get much time to get down to Perp.," he said—it amused Milcom to notice how widespread this hideous abbreviation had become in a few hours.

"Is your head-quarters down there?" he asked.

"Head-quarters? No—we're here. We sleep in the trucks," the young man replied, puffing with intense satisfaction at his cigarette.

"But where's the Quaker Relief? Haven't the rest of them got out?"

"*I* don't know," said the young man.

"But aren't you part of it? You are the Quakers?"

The young man gaped at him.

"Quakers nothing!" he then said, with emphasis. "We're the Amalgamated Society of Printers! Sent out six trucks and all this food, and we haven't even had time to get in! And we can none of us talk French—on'y Spanish. Quakers!—I'll be blowed!"

James left him almost incoherent in his repudiation. But as he shoved his way down to the car he thought a good deal about this small incident. No, they weren't Quakers—they were the emissaries of a Trades Union in London. But they were, regardless of personal danger and discomfort, feeding the hungry and tending the sick, the things that Quakers do—from Bilbao to Vladivostok, he thought, this was the distinguishing mark of the Quakers, so that anyone who did those things must, to Spanish and French alike, be Quakers too. Some testimonial! "By their fruits ye shall know them," muttered James, who was unfashionably familiar with his Bible, as he reached the car.

It was after three o'clock when they got back to Perpignan, and they had all been wet through for several hours; over a whiskey with Crumpaun, James decided to call it a day as far as the frontier was concerned. But, leaving the pursuit of Del Vayo to Hever, he managed to get an interview with the Prefect, and learned that the order to keep the *miliciens* out had been cancelled —they were to be let in again.

"Every two hours, they change their minds in Paris," the Prefect said gloomily. "It brings complications—which, for the rest, are already sufficient." James, in elegant French, said that he betted they were, and listened sympathetically to the hastily improvised plans for distributing the non-combatant refugees, and the wounded, in various parts of France, and for interning the *miliciens*. "There are one hundred thousand of them!" the Prefect said despairingly. "Where are they to go? We have no camps, but they cannot roam at will. We must create camps—

and you cannot do that quickly with men working a four-day week. They say they will send us fifty thousand troops to guard the frontier—but that is fifty thousand more to feed! Believe me, Monsieur, sympathy is all very well—but on the spot it is not so simple."

When he got back to the hotel and went to his room to change James found an envelope with a scrawled note from Crumpaun on the outside: "Sorry—this was enclosed in one for me." He opened it. Inside was a letter from Raquel. Still in his wet clothes, James sat heavily down on the one chair with the letter in his hand; his heart was pounding. Why was she writing to him? They had agreed not to write. It wasn't like her to break an agreement. The thing was over—why open it all up again? Then an idea struck him—had something happened to the Conde? The Navarrese Division had been in heavy fighting. He tore open the letter.

But it was not about the Conde.

"I beg you to forgive me that I write to you," Raquel wrote from Santander—"but I am in great distress about Juanito. He has not come back, as you said he would; he has not been heard of at Burgos, and Pascual writes that he has not rejoined the regiment. I greatly fear that by some accident he was prevented from returning before all this began, and that he is still where he was, you understand. Or that something has happened to him. And as you will be in a better position than we to find out, since you will certainly be on the spot, I beg you to make every enquiry and try to find him for me. I send this by the good Crumpaun, as I have the opportunity to send it by a safe hand, and he will see that you get it, I know. Oh my dear friend, do find him and let me hear. But for this, I should not have written. I pray that you are well and safe. I am quite well. Raquel.

"P.S. Here is a photograph of him. It is not very good, but it is the only one I have."

James read this through twice, and then groaned. Oh Lord, this would have to happen, he thought. During all these weeks of separation and misery he had stayed himself on the thought of her being with Juanito again, and of their joy at recovering one another, brief as it must probably have been; he had held at bay the insistent and intruding pictures of her reunion with the Conde, which his mind thrust ceaselessly before him, with willed pictures of her and Juanito together, laughing, talking, teasing and understanding, as she had so often described their intercourse to him. And now all that was gone—his defence against his own tormented curiosity, her defence against an intolerable situation and her own loss.

And what the devil had happened to Juanito? Had he been discovered and shot, as La Paquita was shot? Probably not—if he had been, the chances were that he, James, would have heard some mention of it. No, Raquel's guess was much the most likely thing: that something had delayed his return so long that the offensive had caught him still on the Red side. If that had happened, he would almost certainly have found it impossible to get back. The passage across country from Red into White Spain had been difficult and dangerous enough across a fluid and shifting internal frontier; across a roaring battle-line it would be hopeless. So what? James lit a cigarette and thought. So he would just have to stay with the Red armies and stick it out, trusting to luck to get into France and then somehow manage his return. Or he might be wounded—he might be one of those *miliciens* they had seen that morning, limping along the street at Le Boulou towards the improvised internment camp beyond the station, or one of the men the pseudo-Quakers had been tending up at Le Perthus. And with that name a horror that made him sweat broke over James—he, Raquel's Juanito, might have been one of the thousands that stood packed in that roaring mob up behind the wire rope there. God, why hadn't that lazy old ass Crumpaun opened his mail that morning? Then he could at least have set enquiries on foot, asked. Anyhow, it was a hopeless job; the Prefect had said that there were a hundred thousand of them, and they were pouring in all along the frontier, according to the Lieutenant of the Gardes Mobiles. Of course if Juanito were on the staff, as his job rather suggested, he might come out later—if they came out, the Brass Hats—but even so he might be hard to find; and he would more probably try to separate himself from them, lose himself, if necessary, before crossing the frontier. Yes, he would be sure, *if he could*, to try to cross the frontier alone, and work his way back either to Biarritz, through France, or else to recross the frontier into White Spain further along. If he could—but could he? He might not succeed, in which case he might be among any of the *miliciens* in this region.

It all came back to that—a hopeless hunt; but he would have to do his best. It was at least something to do for her again, after these terrible, detached weeks. That would be an infinite comfort. He took up the letter and read it over slowly, three or four times, studying each word, trying to extract every shade of meaning from the simple phrases, that futile task to which lovers, inevitably, find themselves compelled. "I am well"—how little that told him! Well in body, yes, and even that was something; but what of her mind and her heart; Nothing—except that she prayed for his health and his safety, loving him then still. And turned to him in her need, still sure of him, of his instant help. Her apology, twice made, touched him deeply; the tears sprang into his eyes as he read it the third time. "Oh, my darling, as if I *minded* your writing! As if I minded being asked," he said aloud. Presently he took the photograph out of the envelope and studied it. Raquel was right; it was not much good—for identification purposes it was almost useless. It was an old snap, rather faded, of a girl and a young man on horseback—the horses, superb creatures, came out magnificently, of course, but the two human beings were just two graceful figures with good seats and grins. James would hardly have recognised Raquel, with her hair done in that funny way—he supposed that she was about eighteen when it was taken, her face had so much less form and character; as for the young man, even with a magnifying glass there was little to make out but the youthfulness and the grin. No, that gave nothing to go on—but there was Raquel's description of him. James went over that in his mind, carefully. Like her—well, that was something; with the same grey eyes, but dark hair. Not an unknown combination in Spain by any means, but with Raquel's nose it was still something. And Juanito had her very individual walk, she had said. Alone in his nasty little room, James laughed out loud, a harsh grim sort of laugh, at the thought of going round camps and fortresses and warehouses, saying to interned *miliciens*—"Please get up and walk a few steps." What a hope!

He didn't attempt to answer Raquel's letter that night; he was tired and chilled, and churned up emotionally by the spectacle of mass flight and human misery in bulk that he had been witnessing. If he were to start writing, he thought as he changed, words would flow; too fast, and the wrong things, tenderness or bitterness—forbidden tenderness for Raquel, useless bitterness about man's inhumanity to man, and Spaniard's inhumanity to Spaniard. He must take his time and write a proper letter, that wouldn't upset her. Though how he, James, could write a proper letter to her, God knew! "Don't make me laugh," grumbled James to the fly-spotted walls of his noisy unventilated room, and went down to dinner.

Next day they went to look at Cerbère, the frontier post on the coast road beyond Port Vendres and Banyuls. Crumpaun had caught a bad cold from his wetting of the previous day, but insisted on coming too. It was still pouring with rain. They splashed at speed across the flat plain through Elne, and then slowed down to negotiate the dangerous twists and bends of the section beyond, where the narrow highway crawls across the steep face of the seaward end of the Pyrenees. They passed through Port Vendres, which presented just the same aspect as forty-eight hours before; the oranges still rotting in crates on the quay, the sodden refugees still sitting in the rain on pavements, eating them— only the destroyer had gone. James insisted on going round to the warehouse on the wharf to make enquiries about Juanito; no, they had no *miliciens* there, they said, only *civils*—the *miliciens* were being dealt with at Cerbère. They went on again. For James the brick of excitement, of wondering what was coming next, of being a participator in unwonted and stirring events which even newspaper men feel was now weightened to a painful tension by his quest.

Beyond Banyuls they had a curious encounter. As the car wound round the slope of a ravine to cross the narrow stone bridge at its head they saw, stumbling down a stony path between the vineyards and dripping shrubs on the opposite slope, five men in grey uniforms.

"Hullo, there are some of them," Hever said.

"Let's stop and talk to them," said Crumpaun. James needed no urging—he wanted to scan the face of every Spaniard he saw, now. The car accordingly slowed down on the far side of the bridge; seeing this, the *miliciens* began to wave and shout, and increased their stumbling pace to an unsteady run. Milcom stuck his head out of the car window and called to them in Spanish not to hurry—"We wait for you."

When they reached the car, they crowded round the windows, asking questions, "Was this France?" was the first.

Yes, Milcom told them, they were in France, and safe.

"We shall not be sent back?"

"No—interned here."

The white, drawn, unshaven faces relaxed into an expression of glorious relief.

"Where are we?" the one who seemed to be the leader asked.

"Between Banyuls and Cerbère."

"And how far?"

"Banyuls is four kilometres, Cerbère about two."

They nodded at the mention of the distances.

"Where have you come from?" Milcom asked in his turn. He

had been studying their faces during this interchange. No—
every one of them had brown eyes.

"From Figueras—but possibly we took the wrong way; we have
been walking for thirty-seven hours."

"Food?"

"No food, no."

James asked them if they had heard anything of the Teniente
Manuel Jereda?—but they had not. Crumpaun and Hever,
whose Spanish was limited, were beginning to ask impatiently
what this conversation was all about. James turned to them.

"They've been walking for thirty-seven hours without food,
and as the crow flies they've come about sixty kilometres—over
the mountains. God knows how far they've actually walked."
While Crumpaun muttered "Good God!" he turned to the
Spaniards again.

"I recommend you to go to Cerbère," he said—"in this direction—as we are going. There you will be fed, and put into a train
and sent somewhere in France." They moved him to an immense pity—they looked so white and frail; and their relief at
being out of the hell of retreat and pursuit was so evident and so
profound. As he spoke, they thanked him, all shaking his hand.
One of the men felt inside his soaked and tattered tunic and pulled
out a packet of cigarettes, which he proffered to Milcom. "For
you," he said. "You have given us good news."

Milcom tried to refuse the gift—he knew what cigarettes meant
to the Republican soldiers; foodless, their one support and
comfort.

"Keep them," he said; "I thank you, but we have plenty"—
and he signalled to the chauffeur to drive on. As the car started—
"Hombre!" the Spaniard cried in a great voice, and tossed the
packet in through the window of the car. Milcom stooped, as
they drove away, his throat contracting, and picked it up off the
floor. It was a cheap make of near-Virginia cigarette—on the
packet was the picture of a ship in full sail, and the name "Home-
ward Bound." He put it in his pocket.

They drove on into Cerbère, through the steep narrow streets,
and pulled up at a railway station. Here the usual immense
confusion reigned. The first thing that caught their eyes was two
ambulances, into which Spanish wounded were being loaded out
of lorries by French hospital orderlies and nurses, under the
supervision of a French Lieutenant. Hever spoke to this officer.
He was almost blind with fury. "Do you know where we got
these?"—he indicated the ambulances. "They are, as you see,

Spanish. That unutterable—" he used an unprintable French word, and named a well-known member of the Republican Cabinet—"was bringing them out, filled with his own effects! Up there on the pass."

"Was he really?" Hever asked—this was a story.

"But assuredly. I threw them out, his effects, and told him we had other uses for ambulances, we."

They went into the station. One corner of the entrance hall was occupied by a pile of loaves of bread, at least seven feet high, which a corporal and a railway porter were cutting in halves and doling out to the swarming refugees, who were being packed into trains and shipped off, much more efficiently than at Le Boulou the day before. Milcom sought out an official, showed his pass, gave his name and address, and caused the name of Lieutenant Manuel Jereda to be written down, with a request for information if he should turn up. It was all he could do. In return he listened to an account of the problems which reigned at Cerbère. Chief among these was "the sacred tunnel," as the official bitterly called it, which carries the railway through under the pass from France into Spain. This tunel was now, it appeared, blocked with *miliciens* who, to escape bombing by the Savoias at Port Bou, at the Spanish end, had swarmed into it, thus stopping all rail traffic through, and forcing the refugees to go over the pass. "They say there are ten thousand of them in there," he said; "but it is being *déblayé*—the Senegalese have gone in to push them out at the other end."

"Why not bring them out at this end?" Milcom asked.

"Ah, but they may not enter—not the *miliciens*. All who cross the frontier are to be sent back," the official said.

Milcom was horror-struck, remembering those five cold frail figures on the road to Banyuls, to whom he had just given the assurance of food and safety in France.

"But how?" he said. "Only last night the Préfet at Perpignan told me that now they are to be let in."

"Ah, but that was yesterday," said the official with a shrug— "this morning we had fresh orders. Now they are all to go back. The government sends us fifty thousand troops to hold the frontier against them. We have enough to do with ces autres" —he indicated the teeming refugees. "To feed them is going to cost milliards."

Heartsick at this fresh change of policy, Milcom collected his two companions, and they drove on up to the pass. The road climbed over high open slopes, grassy like downs; an icy wind drove the rain savagely across the bleak country, and whipped up the leaden sea below—it was bitterly cold even in the car. All down the loops of road came a straggling procession of refugees, with quilts and blankets over their heads and shoulders, laden with the dismal burdens of cooking-pots, bundles, and bits of luggage, which were becoming so familiar; slithering along in the mud, beaten by the driving rain. Some distance below the pass a Garde Mobile stopped the car, and they got out and squelched up on foot towards the frontier; walking in the deep clayey mud, lashed by wind and rain, was difficult and tiring even for a few paces—Milcom thought of the exhaustion of those who were even now passing him, who had been doing it for hours. Here and there open suitcases lay on the ground, their contents trodden into the mud—cheap flimsy cardboard things, they had disintegrated in the rain and come to bits, after being dragged God knew how far, and the cherished possessions, chosen in haste before a desperate flight—imagine that choice!—were lost after all. James turned the contents of several over with his stick—clothes, children's shoes, a little frock, some shirts; the very poverty of the things added to the pathos of their final abandoning.

There was a small wooden hut beside the wire rope which here, as at Le Perthus, marked the frontier, in which French officials were examining papers; there was a small crowd of journalists, sightseers, and Spaniards waiting to cross, but nothing to compare with the roaring mob at Le Perthus the day before. There were hardly any *miliciens*—they had mostly taken to the hills, an officer said, or chosen the tunnel route, whence they were even now being pushed out by the black troops. James made the usual enquiries of the frontier officials, and left Manuel Jereda's name and his own address. Then they passed the rope and walked down the road on the further side till they reached a projecting point which commanded a view down the valley for several miles. The road stretched away into Spain like a long shiny serpent, glistening with the wet roofs of the automobiles which stood jammed nose to tail as far as the eye could reach. Most of the owners were sitting inside the cars, but a few were walking restlessly up to the pass to enquire about their chances of proceeding; one such man, who spoke to Milcom, said that they had been there for forty-eight hours. Past the cars, in a thin but never-ending stream, plodded the carless refugees, on foot.

Several other people hailed Milcom out of the windows of their motors, asking him how soon they would be allowed to go on; nearly all of them tried to sell him a typewriter for francs. One or two women even offered him jewels. They all wanted, at any sacrifice, a few French francs—enough to buy a cup of coffee and a piece of bread, at least, after fasting in the rain for two days. If they ever got on to Port Vendres, he reflected grimly, they would be able to eat oranges. On his way back to the rope, soaked through, he came on Hever and Crumpaun in conversation with a smartly-dressed chauffeur—Hever called him over to translate. The chauffeur was trying to sell them a new seven-seater Packard car; the price he asked was two thousand francs—about £25, or one hundred dollars. James actually had papers which would have enabled him to bring the car in—his own was left in Spain. But he wanted something smaller in any case, and the idea of profiting by distress on this scale was repugnant to him. He gave the chauffeur a hundred francs for himself, and turned down the offer.

They got back in good time that afternoon, and after he had changed his wet clothes James went out to the café over the river, ordered a brandy with his coffee, and sat down to compose his letter to Raquel. He began as she had done, with no opening—because there wasn't any opening that he dared now set down that could meet the needs of either his heart or hers.

"I got your letter," he wrote, "here, which was the best place I could have had it in, because I am right on the frontier, and am therefore in a position to make a certain number of enquiries. You don't need to be told that I shall do every single thing that I can to get you the news you want. But don't be surprised or anxious if you don't hear for some time; at this moment there is naturally a certain amount of confusion, and it will take quite a time before one can find out where anyone is." Then he crossed out the last two words and wrote instead—"people are." There was no telling into whose hands this letter would fall on its way from Perpignan to Santander—you couldn't be too careful. "People are" was better—more general.

He tilted himself back in his chair, balancing his fountain pen between his second and third fingers, and flipped it to and fro, thoughtfully, for some time. What next?

"I am very well," he wrote down, like a child penning an exercise, "and hard at work. I am very glad that you are well."

There—that covered that. He leaned back again. He couldn't ask any questions—none of the questions to which he so desperately wanted the answers; still less could he say all the things he wanted to say—how miserable and bleak his existence was without her, how glad he was to have something to do for her at last. He took out her letter and read it again—by now for about the twentieth time. "I pray that you are safe and well." He couldn't say he prayed for her because he didn't pray. He could perhaps write a chatty account of what he was doing, but even that was beyond the terms of the bond—that they should not write. She had only written because of Juanito—he was sending only the needful answer. So that was about all. Never had his sense of despairing frustration been more acute than as he sat by the window staring out over the river, the two letters on the little table in front of him beside the coffee-cup. At last he slid his pen down into position again and wrote—

"I shall write again as soon as I have any news for you. You know that you can count on me to do everything I can. God bless you."

And signed it with both his names. There. He sighed gustily, folded the thing up, put it in an envelope and addressed it. "What a godless mess," he said to himself. It was his epitaph on his love.

Later that evening—"Is Crossman still at St.-Jean?" he asked Crumpaun.

"Yes—he was when I left," the older man replied.

"He was going to stay on a bit, I gathered," Hever put in.

So James enclosed his letter to Raquel in one to Crossman, bespeaking his good offices to get it forwarded to Santander by the best means available. And that, again, was that.

The next few days were more or less a repetition of those first two; the three journalists drove about, visiting camps and frontier-posts, and watching one of the most desolating and menacing spectacles of modern times. Along a hundred miles of frontier an entire army and the population of three provinces was in motion, pouring down like water—here a trickle, there a flood—into France. To James the whole thing became a nightmare. As he saw it, French and Spaniards alike were locked in a sort of deathly wrestling-match with one another and with forces outside their ken or control—the ideological forces which were beginning to menace Europe. Horrible as the spectacle was, the menace behind it was even more alarming. French sympathies were with the Republicans, undoubtedly; but to admit them would create enormous local problems and cost enormous sums—on the other hand there was some first-rate modern war material, guns, planes and motor machine-guns, supplied by the Russians and by the French themselves, which could be acquired for the army if the troops were let in. But Franco had won—and there was his supporter Italy to be reckoned with, let alone Germany. No wonder that French policy swung to and fro, like a demented pendulum. However, in the end sympathy and the *matériel* had it; and the *miliciens* were let in.

It was with this background to his thoughts that James drove up and down the south Pyrenean frontier—this, and his haunted and despairing search for Juanito. They went up to Prats-de-Mollo, where they saw the Spanish mules and ponies tethered in a long row under the sunny wall of the square outside the main gate—Prats is a walled town; they saw the little parties coming in down the mule-tracks off the snow-covered frontier ridge: Grandmamma riding the cow, Grandfather the mule, bedding strapped to the backs of sheep and goats, Mother carrying a child, while others trailed at her skirts. A foot-and-a-half of snow up there, they told him—it was hard. Their faces showed how hard it had been. Again a phrase from the Bible sprang into James's mind—"Pray that your flight be not in the winter." Theirs had been. Goodness, how apposite all those words of Christ about the end of the world were! "Then shall they say to the mountains and rocks, Fall on us, and save us from the wrath to come." The *miliciens* in the tunnel at Cerbère—they had invoked the aid of the mountains. On another day, starting early, the three went over to Bourg Madame and visited the internment camp there—if one could call a barbed wire enclosure where men crouched in the open, in winter, at twelve hundred feet, a camp; on the way home they saw, with sour amusement, the devastation caused at Vernet-les-Bains. Here the municipality, too frugal to allow the empty hotels to be occupied by the Spanish soldiers, had shut them all up in the public gardens, which contained a famous collection of rare trees and shrubs; these the famished *miliciens*, during the very first night, tore up and cut down to make bonfires to warm themselves—so a doleful official informed the party. Hever laughed out loud.

"Good for them!" he said heartily. "Monsieur, what else could you expect?"

Both Milcom and Crumpaun had felt a good deal of sympathy for the French predicament to begin with; but as the days passed, and they saw more and more of the suffering entailed on the helpless internees by the French combination of inefficiency and parsimony, this turned slowly to a dull anger. And this anger, in

Milcom's case, was finally fanned to a flame by the state of affairs at Argelés.

It is not possible to pretend that the camp at Argelés was anything but highly discreditable to the French. Argelés lies on the sea, on a stretch of sandy beach; here the authorities massed thousands of men behind barbed wire, exposed to the bitter east wind which in February and March rasps the whole Mediterranean coast like a steel file. There was no wood, no vegetation; when the wretched soldiers tried to dig in the loose sand for shelter, they came in three feet to water, so that their dug-outs were colder than the bare ground above. The water was brackish, and did nothing to solve the drinking problem, which was acute. Food was short. There was dysentery and pneumonia; there were cases of gangrene. As more and more men were brought in the conditions became so bad that the authorities eventually refused to allow any foreign observers into the place, and extended this ban to the International Red Cross, the Quaker Hospital Unit, and the Swedish Red Cross, which last had four motor hospital vans, fully equipped for operations, parked outside the gate. Meanwhile, as a Garde Mobile informed Milcom, there was not so much as a tube of aspirin in the whole camp.

James had gone down to Argelés for the second or third time to pursue his enquiries for Juanito, and found himself locked out. Standing there in the tearing wind, seeing the shivering huddled limping figures behind the barbed wire and the idle hospital lorries outside, a true cold Irish fury seized on him. He drove straight back to the hotel, packed his bags, drove on to Toulouse, and took the afternoon train to Paris. There he first saw one of Tom Hever's colleagues at Hooters, and told him about Argelés; then he went and worried the Embassy; finally he wrote a despatch for the *Epoch* which was so blistering that that demure journal would not print it. Nevertheless something happened. A special correspondent flew from London to Perpignan, and a week later a terrible article on the camp appeared in one of the English Sunday papers; soon afterwards a reasonable amount of medical help, at least, was given to the interned Spanish.

Milcom stayed in Paris for a few days to watch the results of his efforts, and while there something happened which added to his anger. Up till then he had tried to believe that it was mainly inefficiency and parsimony, rather than deliberate policy, which was at the bottom of the French ill-treatment of the interned army. The political position was more difficult than ever—the French naturally wished to open relations with the victorious

Franco government, but they wanted to retain the surrendered war material which had induced them to allow the *miliciens* to enter; the Franco government, for its part, was making the return of this material a condition of opening diplomatic relations. Meanwhile the refugees were costing France three million francs a week, a figure to give any Frenchman the shivers. Loud-speakers were promptly installed in all the camps, blaring out recommendations to the *miliciens* to return to Spain, where they would receive "just treatment." The *miliciens* did not respond very well. Deputies scurried in and out of Spain, desperately trying to bargain. In the middle of all this, at a luncheon, James happened to overhear one of the aforesaid deputies discussing this burning problem with a rather well-known Franquista who was "watching" affairs in Paris.

"Ah, mon cher," said the deputy, "je pense que le faim et le froid feront peu à peu notre affaire."

For a moment James thought that he would not be able to refrain from knocking the man down. He succeeded in controlling himself; but then he went over and made an excuse of illness to his host, and left—sit at table with that deputy he would not. He went round to Hooters and told the story to Hever's colleague. The colleague drummed his fingers on the table.

"Yes—that's the line," he said. " 'Qu'est-ce-que j'y touche, moi?' That's the only question a Frenchman asks himself to-day. They're done for, you know, Jim; they're rotted through and through with avarice."

"But it's murder—murder in cold blood," James raged. "God damn them!"

"He will, don't you worry," said the colleague. "This country's going down the drain—you mark my words." And he gave James some facts about the French Air Force. James groaned, and wired to the *Epoch* to ask for a month's leave; he was angry about his article. Then he went back to Perpignan to go on looking for Juanito.

# CHAPTER TWELVE

*This Side—Amélie-les-Bains*

NOTHING remains "news" for long in the modern world, and the Spanish retreat was no exception. By the time Milcom got back to Perpignan from Paris practically all the journalists had left,

including Crumpaun and Hever. Numbers of refugees and a
few business men remained in the Hôtel de l'Europe, waiting for
an opportunity to return to Spain, or for news of their relatives
or their concerns; they sat listlessly about in the parrot-cage,
adding to the dismal effect of that always dismal place. James
began to find it intolerable. He was lonely, he was miserable;
his aching need of Raquel seemed to get worse, not better, as the
days and weeks went by. And he was increasingly discouraged
by his total failure to get any news of Juanito. This search had
become to him a sort of symbol of his love, the one thing left of
it that had any actuality; his eyes more desperate than ever, day
after day he trudged round offices and camps, questioning
officials and searching the faces of prisoners, but to no purpose.
And at night he came back to the hotel to sit, now quite alone,
dining in the parrot-cage, hearing again the sobs and laughter of
Raquel's hysteria echoing up to its glass roof, or seeing her sitting
lax with fatigue in the gangway. It tormented him that he could
not be absolutely sure which chair she had sat in that day. It
was on the right, and the fourth or fifth—near that horrible palm
—but he could not be certain which. Sometimes he walked
round to the various shops where they had purchased her stockings and things, and made some excuse to enter, bought some
trivial object, just to stand there again and try to re-see her as
she had stood, to recall the words in which she had made her
choice. But what made these memories insupportable was what
she had said that last time that they sat up in the glen behind
S. Joseph's Chapel, that she had loved him already in Madrid.
Oh, if he had known! If he had known when they were here!
Blind and a fool—that was what he had been.

After about a week of this, James found it quite unendurable,
and decided to look for other quarters. He consulted the garage
proprietor. The garage proprietor recommended the Hôtel des
Thermes Jadis at Amélie-les-Bains, and thither the following day,
after telephoning for rooms, Milcom removed himself, alone in
his hired car; with order restored, the chauffeur was no longer
necessary.

The Hôtel des Thermes Jadis is a peculiar place, in many
ways. It is one of those second-class French provincial hotels
to which foreign visitors almost never find their way, except as
the result of a motoring accident, though it thrives (or did thrive)
on an ample French middle-class clientèle of rheumatic patients.
(To find the real France it is much more rewarding to go to such
a place than to Paris—let alone Biarritz or Cannes.) Other

things besides the inmates, however, make it peculiar. To begin with it consists of three quite separate buildings. One, containing the dining-room and other public rooms, and the hot sulphur baths—reached by a lift to the basement—is built almost over the hot springs themselves; a second section, separated from the first by a broad gravelled drive, contains bedrooms and the bureau; the third is on the far side of a small tip-tilted public square, in which stand two or three magnificent plane trees and a fountain with an ever-flowing spout of hot sulphur-water, as well as plain cold, from which the housewives in the tall buildings round the square fill their *brocs* of a morning. Finally, and oddest feature of all, the hot water in the bathrooms and the central heating owes nothing to furnaces or the hand of man; it is heated by God, in the bowels of the earth. Like all places of its sort the Thermes Jadis is shabby, sparsely furnished and fairly clean; and unlike many others of its kind it has also a quite excellent cuisine, in which fresh trout from the River Tech and Pyrenean mutton figure largely.

James arrived there late one evening at the beginning of March. He had spent another exhausting and fruitless day checking names and interviewing Republican officers at the camp at Le Boulou, and it was already dark as he drove into the town over the bridge, where the smell of sulphur, coming up from the steaming waters below, first assailed his nostrils. It reminded him sharply of Raquel; he remembered how she had sniffed and put up her handkerchief the first time he crossed that bridge, with her beside him. But in spring another smell contends with that of rotten eggs for mastery in the streets of Amélie—the sharp spicy fragrance of mimosa, growing all about the town gardens, growing wild on the rocky slopes above; in the windy darkness he was aware of this also, as he pulled up in the little square, to which a passer-by had directed him for the Thermes Jadis. The slope was so steep that his brakes would not hold; he left the car in gear, locked it, and set out to look for the hotel. Painted letters over an archway at one side of the square led him into the central section, where a notice above a bell said "Bureau." James rang the bell and waited. No one came. He proceeded to explore. There up a few steps was the Bureau, sure enough, behind glass doors; but it was empty, and the doors locked. He rang again, called; there was no answer—no one seemed to be about. James began to get impatient; he was tired, hungry, and discouraged after his day of fruitless search—he wanted his dinner. He went on through

the archway, which pierced the whole depth of the building, and
came out onto the drive beyond, which crossed a hidden river
by a stone bridge; he could hear rushing water in the darkness,
and smelt the twin odours of sulphur and mimosa again—a lighted
window or two gleamed in a building ahead. The whole business began to take on the quality of a dream, almost a nightmare,
to James in his fatigue—could this be right? He went on up the
drive, noticing on his right what appeared to be a long conserva-
tory of coloured glass, also dimly lit; goodness, what an extraordinary place! Rounding a curve, he emerged onto a wide
gravel sweep, glimmering palely in the darkness, and saw below
him to his left, through plate-glass windows, the welcome vision
of a large dining-room, brightly lit, and full of people eating.
But how to reach it? It was at least two stories below the spot
where he stood. Again he went on, crossing the sweep towards
the lighted windows—ah good, here was a door, and another
bell. He rang vigorously, and stood looking through the glass
doors into a rather dismal hall set with a few wicker chairs and
tables, and most economically lit. At length a boy in rather
dirty chef's clothes appeared, and ushered James into the hall,
which smelt stuffy and airless; James's heart sank in the familiar
irrational despair of the traveller who arrives late and weary in
a strange place, and finds the auspices unfavourable. However
he firmly demanded dinner, and followed the boy down two
flights of concrete stairs to the dining-room. Please God there
would be something edible at least, he thought, as he sat down
at a table and ran his eye over the room, which was full of the
most extraordinary collection of people he had ever seen; elderly
men with grey or black tufted side-whiskers, and women with
what appeared to be antimacassars of purple or bright blue wool
drawn over ample alpaca shoulders—because really it was
a nightmare otherwise, inside *and* out! He bent and studied the
menu which an elderly waiter put down in front of him, when to
his immense surprise he heard himself hailed in English—"Mr.
Milcom! It *is* you." He looked up into the shining face of
Rosemary Oldhead.

"Good heavens!" said James, rising—"What on earth are you
doing here?"

"Just what I was going to ask you," she answered, her eyes
dancing. "*You* haven't got rheumatism, have you? Because
why anyone who hasn't should come to this God-awful place—"

"Monsieur desires?" the waiter interrupted.

"Yes, go on—order," Rosemary said resignedly, sitting down

opposite to him. "They're mad about meal-hours here, and we're all eating pudding already. I should have the soup—it's quite good; and the trout—they're always lovely."

James found himself smiling, in spite of his fatigue.

"All right—I'll leave it to you. What else?" he asked.

"Well, the pudding's horrible, as usual, and the beef's tough —also as usual; I should have twice of the trout and then cheese, if it was me. They've got some very good Brie. And the red wine is perfectly *potable*," she added.

James ordered in accordance with her suggestions, demanding an immediate apéritif as well. Then he turned to her again. This was just what he needed, to-night, a friendly face and some-one to take charge of him; he was aware of a genuine and grateful sense of comfort. "Now tell me, why are you here?" he asked.

"Oh, for Daddy. It's supposed to be *the* place for rheumatism —'un climat plutôt africain,' Dr. Gilliard called it. We came about the middle of January."

"Oh, so you were here for all the doings," said James.

"Yes—but I didn't see anything of it really," said Rosemary. "You see I had no one to go about with. I just saw the tables set up in the street, and the townspeople feeding the refugees that came down from Prats by lorry, but that was about all. And of course we had the Embassy here—from Barcelona. That *was* fun; it stirred up Amelia-the-Baths, no end. Telephone exchange open till midnight instead of closing at eight p.m.— sensation! Poor M. Dupont said to Daddy—'Monsieur, nous ne sommes pas de mauvaises gens, mais ici nous avons l'habitude de beaucoup de calme.' But then they went away again. Of course Daddy's baths make him too feeble to go about much, and Mother can't leave him. It was sickening," she went on reminiscently, "to have a really *big* thing like that happening right on top of you, and not be in it at all. I wanted to go down to Perp. and help nurse with the Quaker Relief, but I wasn't even allowed to do that."

"Can you nurse?" asked James, eating his soup contentedly. She was right—it was quite good.

"Well, I've done the advanced First Aid Course at school, and got all my chits—and anyhow anyone can scrub floors and empty slops," said Rosemary. She gave a little groan, then visibly pulled herself up and smiled at him again. "Now tell me about you. Have you just got out?"

"Oh Lord no—I got out at the end of January."

"Where to?"

"To Perp., as you call it."

"Oh NO!" Rosemary's voice was raised in something like indignation. "Oh, you're not going to tell me that you've been at Perp. for a whole month, and I—we—didn't know it?"

"No no—not the whole time. I was in Paris for nearly a fortnight—I've just come back from there," James said soothingly.

"But you were here at the beginning, going round and seeing things?" Rosemary almost groaned.

James nearly grinned at her.

"I'm sorry—yes, I was. Your friend Crumpaun was here too, and Tom Hever."

"Oh damn, damn, damn! My darling Crumpet! Is he still here?" the girl asked eagerly. "And Crossey?"

"No, Crossey never came. They've all gone home now," said James.

"Then why are you here?"

"Oh well—I've nothing else on at the moment, and I've got a piece of work to do here on my own, more or less," he said, choosing his words rather carefully. He did not want to tell the girl about his search for Juanito.

"Writing work?"

"Research, more," said James. "This trout is frightfully good —you were quite right," he went on, indicating the fish on his plate.

She took the hint at once. "Yes, aren't they?" She rose with her usual abruptness. "Well, I must go back. The parents will be wondering what on earth I'm up to."

"No, don't go—stay and talk to me. I haven't had a soul to speak to for a week," said James. He suddenly realised what a relief it was to be soothed and amused, to have the pressure of his own wretched thoughts lifted off him for a little while. "Tell me about this place," he went on. "What's it like?"

"The Jadis, or Amelia?" She sat down again.

"Both."

"Well the hotel, as you see, is a sort of silent film of Tchekov," the girl said. "Golly, they are incredible. Do you see that old man over there sitting with his feet on the hot brick? Oh, he's gone—but you can see the brick if you lean this way. Half of them have bricks at meals." James laughed. "And of course there's never anyone in the bureau, and the chambermaids wear shawls round their shoulders all day long, and the bedside lamps only have five-watt bulbs in them, and the water in your basin makes you smell of sulphur the whole time. But it's madly cheap and the food is quite good—much better than at that lousy Grande Bretagne, where they smothered everything in sauce to disguise the taste of stale fish. Which building are you in, by the way?"

"I've no idea," said James, still laughing. "I followed my nose to the restaurant."

"Oh—well. There's not much to choose, any way. We've tried all three. In the one across the square you have a bath-room and about three hours sun, and the radio from that restaurant place drives you mad; in this one you have no bath unless you go down to the *établissement*, and only about two hours sun—and in the middle one you get four and a half hours sun and no bath at all without walking a mile. It's a matter of choice really. We're in this one."

"Why so little sun?" James asked.

"Oh, because the whole place is jammed into the mouth of the gorge where the waters come from, and hulking great cliffs keep it off," Rosemary said. "So much for the African climate! 'Tisn't so frightfully African anyway—there's been a tearing East wind the whole time we've been here. M. Dupont says there always is, in spring—'cela balaye toute la côte,' he says."

"And what's the place like?" James asked, beginning on his cheese.

"Oh, delicious, *I* think—I love this rocky shrubby country. If we had a car, or I had anyone to walk with, it would be Heaven. Mummie and I did go in the bus once to Arles-sur-Tech, and once we walked to Palalda—but that's about all."

"I've got a car," said James on an impulse. "We might do some drives together. There are some very good little churches to see—Romanesque. Quite a lot of early ones, too—eleventh century."

Her eyes shone at him across the table. Really, she was quite pretty, James thought—he had never noticed before how pretty she was.

"*Would* you?" she said. "Oh goodness, that would be mar-vellous. You can't think what a difference that would make. There's not been a *soul* here. I have so missed"—she checked herself—"Crumpet and everybody." He knew she had been going to say the Condesa, and warmed to her, in spite of a stab of pain.

"Well, we'll do that," he said. He rose. "Now I'll come over and pay my respects to your parents, and then I must find my room. I wonder which disadvantage I shall get?"

The Oldheads greeted him with the warmth that was to be expected from people who have been badly bored for over a month. He took coffee with them in that funereal lounge under the dim lights that made the place, as Mr. Oldhead rightly remarked, look like a morgue. The people would be at home in a morgue, too, he added. Mrs. Oldhead, with wifely inconsequence, inserted the remark that the place was doing him good, all the same. "Agreed, my dear, thank God—but that doesn't affect its appearance," said Mr. Oldhead.

Then James went and found M. Dupont, the proprietor, a courteous old man whose stomach and beard were equally remarkable—for a wonder, he was in the bureau. And by him the weary man was at last escorted to his room. It was in the building across the square—what was wrong with that, according to Rosemary? James tried to remember. Ah yes—the radio. Well, it was silent now. "This was the room of his Excellency the English Ambassador," M. Dupont said complacently. James glanced round it; it was very bare, with a lot of white mats on such furniture as there was—he wondered a good deal what the Minister (he wasn't an Ambassador) had made of it, as he soaked thankfully in a hot if odorous sulphur bath. Afterwards, lying in the hardish but still tolerable bed, he reflected, first, that it was much nicer than the Europe, and next, what a blessing it was to find the Oldheads here. They would keep his thoughts quiet in the evenings. And Rosemary would sometimes be company by day. For the first time that night he remembered, then, when he had last seen her, up by the old Phare at St.-Jean-de-Luz, and what had passed between them there. And he was suddenly struck by the fact that she had not shown the smallest embarrassment this evening, as might well have been expected —she had come straight over to him, taken him and his dinner in hand, and soothed and amused him all through it. What an extraordinary child! An encounter with a self-conscious drooping girl would have been the last straw, to-night. "She's a first-class little thing," he thought gratefully, and fell asleep.

Milcom had an immediate objective in the Tech valley itself —to search in the two *miliciens*' camps outside Arles-sur-Tech and Prats-de-Mollo for Juanito, or at least for news of him. Accordingly the next morning he set off to see the Sous-Préfet at Arles, to get the necessary permits. While in Paris James had heard from his friend in Hooters of the committee set up in London to arrange for the emigration of suitable Spanish refugees to Mexico and Latin America; he had been at pains to get in touch with the committee by letter, and intended, while enquiring for Juanito, to keep an eye open for possible emigrants at the same time.

He found the Sous-Préfet in a big villa a little way up the road from the Hôtel des Glycines. He waited for some time in a large dreary hall—a typist was clattering away at a table under the stairs, and gossiping with the clerks who passed through, and the two or three Gardes Mobiles who hung about—on a bench inside the door four Spaniards sat waiting, two in officers' uniform. When he was at last shown in James found the Sous-Préfet a charming person, loaned to the overworked Préfecture in Perpignan from one of the Paris ministries; he was most sympathetic to the journalist's search for Jereda, and as for the emigration scheme, he was enthusiastic about it. He opened a drawer in his desk and pulled out a large caricature of himself, wittily conceived and admirably drawn.

"Look at that," he said. "Is it not good?"

"But excellent," said James. "Who has made it?"

"A poor devil here from the camp. He was political cartoonist to one of the Barcelona papers. But he can never go back to Spain. He should certainly try the New World. And here," he went on, pulling out another sheet, on which a pair of dancers was brilliantly depicted—"Look at that."

"Is he here too?" James asked, examining it.

"But certainly. If you want any drawings like that, I can put you in touch with him. I like to put them in the way of earning a few francs when I can, poor devils."

"I'll buy the dancers, if it's for sale," said James.

The Sous-Préfet was delighted. He showed James his wrist-watch, on the glass of which was painted a fascinating scene of a bull-fight, microscopically clear and vivid. "Would you like such a decoration?"

"Another of your protégés?" James asked.

"Assuredly."

"Well, I have some English friends down at Amélie," said James. "We might arrange something. How can I get hold of these fellows?"

"Very easily." He rang a bell on his desk, and gave an order to the clerk who answered it. "They will come, at once. These three and some others I have got here in the town, in lodgings;

the artist is with his wife, who expects her child. Meanwhile, I will arrange your permits. You want to go where?"

To visit both camps, at will, James said—and as far as possible, to move about freely in his car—up towards St.-Laurent-de-Cerdans, for example.

"Vous voulez parcourir la frontière?" the Frenchman said smiling. "Very well." He wrote. "When you gentlemen of the Press were here in hundreds a few weeks back, we could not do this; but for one—" he smiled and wrote again; then handed James three small slips.

"If, when these men come, you find them agreeable," he said, then, "I could always arrange to send them down in a car to Amélie to see you. It distracts them, you understand, to meet people and have a little conversation. Of course you speak Spanish?"

James said that he did.

At this moment the clerk popped in again to say that two of the Messieurs Espagnols were there, and ushered in the two officers whom James had already seen waiting in the hall—they proved to be the cartoonist and the man who painted dancers. After the introductions, James expressed a polite desire not to derange the Sous-Préfet further, and took them off with him to have a cup of coffee. The Hôtel des Glycines was the nearest place, and in the sun and out of the wind, it was warm enough to sit in the open; they sat under the wistaria trellis, bare now save for the small fat silvery tassels which promised bloom to come, and over coffee each told James his story. They were nice intelligent fellows—intellectual Liberals, not Communists, and one a devout Catholic; but both agreed that there would never again be any safety for them in Spain. They would like nothing better than to go to Mexico, they said. James listened with attention and sympathy, and jotted down their names; but half his mind was going back five months, to the day when he had sat under that trellis with another Spanish refugee—a White. Behind their dark Spanish faces and shabby olive-green uniforms he saw a slender, slender figure in a shabby black dress—how shabby war made everyone! both sides alike—with a gothic face and red-gold hair, who twirled a spiral twig in her long fingers, and smiled, and looked contented and at rest. The Spanish men saw his eyes darken and his face twist, and wondered what they had said amiss. They hastened into praise for the kindness of the Sous-Préfet; if there were more like him! they said.

Of course James asked them about the Teniente Manuel

Jereda. The artist looked blank; the cartoonist, whose name was de Novelles, after a pause said—"But yes—surely; wasn't he wounded up on the Segre, right at the beginning?"

"No, I didn't really know him, Señor," he went on, in response to James's question; "he was on the divisional staff, I fancy. But I heard him spoken of, I seem to remember, and that he was wounded in the leg, or lost a leg. Something like that."

James became interested, eager, at this. The Spaniards noticed how his face changed again. He leaned forward and asked if there was anyone else who had been up on the Segre, who was likely to know, in the camp. The cartoonist was not hopeful—most of the Segre people had got out "further along" he believed—i.e. they would be at Bourg Madame, where James had already drawn a blank. But the possibility of Juanito being wounded had given James a new idea—somehow he had never thought of him as wounded. The hospitals—he would have to try that. And when they had drunk their coffee and an Amer Picon, he went back to the Préfecture, and asked the Sous-Préfet if it would be possible to let him have a list of hospitals where there were Spanish wounded, so that he might circularise them with the name? The préfet said assuredly, and promised to send a list of hospitals later in the day.

It was by now so late that it was hardly worth going all the way back to Amélie for lunch, James thought, since he wanted to go to the camp at Arles in the afternoon. But then he remembered Rosemary. Poor kid, boxed up there with her parents, and nothing to do—he might as well go back and eat something and bring her up to Arles for the drive.

Rosemary was delighted. She had been rather dashed to learn that he had gone off alone that morning—though it's no good expecting that he'll take you *often*, owl!—she adjured herself. As they drove up the road, out of the cold shadow and into the sun, he turned to her.

"I'm afraid it'll be rather dull for you—I shall have to spend quite a bit of time at the camp; I've got a job to do there." He mentioned the Refugees Committee—it was a good camouflage for his main object. Rosemary was quite unperturbed. "I shall be in the sun, anyhow," she said.

The camp at Arles-sur-Tech was a very different proposition from Argèles. It was quite small, containing only about twelve thousand men, for one thing; and its situation was rather agreeable, a large barbed wire enclosure on sloping pastures beyond the town, looking south. The *miliciens* had contrived with great ingenuity to makes themselves a species of wigwams by cutting down the young chestnut growth on the slopes behind, lashing the slender poles together and then either thatching them with wild box, or turfing them over with turves cut from the pasture. It was not very good for the pasture, the officer in charge admitted; but *que voulez-vous*?—at least they could sleep in shelter. The river was only a couple of hundred yards below the camp, and cold as the water was, it was bright with the naked bodies of men, splashing and sluicing themselves in the shallows, while others were washing their clothes along the bank. Yes, one hundred and fifty at a time, for an hour, all day long, the officer said—it made them more contented to be clean. "They are, after all, human beings." The peasants complained, he said, about the turf and the chestnut-poles—"and indeed, they are like locusts if you leave them to themselves, these others! Monsieur has seen what they have done near Prats? Whole hillsides stripped! But here we control them. They go in parties, under guard, to get fire-wood, as they go to bathe—and so they do but little harm."

Rosemary listened so far with deep interest; then as Milcom showed signs of getting down to business she took herself off, sauntering along the wire, looking at the wigwams, the cooking going on over camp-fires, and exchanging a few phrases of Spanish with those who came up to the fence to talk to her. They all asked for cigarettes, and she made a mental note to get some on her way home, in case they came this way again. She wandered on, and sat down on a boulder beyond the camp, in the late afternoon sunshine, and thought about Milcom. It was wonderful for her, an incredible piece of luck, that he should have turned up like this, and he didn't seem to be going to hurry away again—this Mexican business might keep him quite a time. Of course she wouldn't see much of him, but even a little was something. (Rosemary was at the age, and of the unexacting disposition, which will accept love on any terms.) And he hadn't seemed fussed to meet her last night, as he might well have been, after those things she had said to him the last time! Perhaps he had forgotten, with all that had happened in between. No, she thought, more likely he just hadn't thought it very important— as indeed it wasn't, of course, to *him*. The fatigue and wretchedness of his face the previous evening as he sat in the *salle-à-manger*, before she spoke to him, had told her a lot—he was no better in his heart, he hadn't got over Raquel a bit. Well of course not, she thought; who would?—and least of all a person of his type.

But she had distracted him; she had made him smile, laugh, eat his dinner; and that she could go on doing as much as he would let her, and as long as he stayed.

Her thoughts turned to the woman. Poor Raquel! If only Juanito had got back to her, to distract her too. Perhaps he had, by now; she did hope so. Sitting on the boulder, Rosemary opened her bag, pulled out a letter, and read it over. It was from Raquel, sent via the Duquesa, and was about four weeks old. It was almost all about Juanito, and Raquel's distress that he had not returned: that there was no word of him at Burgos, in the regiment, anywhere. She sounded almost distracted with worry—and as the girl read it, her fine dark brows drew together in a frown of concern. "You well remember, I know, how important it is not to speak of J. to *anyone*," the Condesa had written; "till he returns, we do not know *where* he is, and it might be unsafe." Sez you!—Rosemary grunted to herself. What the dickens could have happened to Juanito, anyway? Had he been too late to return to White Spain through the lines, because of that beastly Arbre de Noël being blocked? He must have cut it pretty fine, anyhow. Oh dear—she wished she knew. And she wondered if she dared talk to Milcom about him. How much did he know? Raquel must have talked about Juanito to him endlessly—she couldn't help herself!—but did he know about the spying? Here he was, buzzing round all these camps like a blue-bottle, on this Mexico-refugee racket; he would have endless chances to make enquiries. Hadn't she better tell him? Oh no, she thought, with an impatient sigh—better not. Raquel had said not, and anyhow it was always better not to talk. And it might sort of churn him up about Raquel even to hear of a letter from her. Were they writing to one another? She had no idea. What *did* one do when one parted from the great love of one's life-time, who was married to somebody else? (Rosemary had no doubts but that these two were each the great love of the other's life-time.) And had he sent her back to that miserable Conde, who was by all accounts a prize louse, or had she just gone? No idea, again. Oh dear, oh dear—what a miserable business. She sighed again, more impatiently than ever, stuffed the letter back into her bag, and got up off her boulder; the sun had gone down behind the hills on the far side of the valley, where Spain lay, and it was getting chilly. Anyhow, she thought, strolling back along the barbed wire, he's here!—and a tiny smile played for a second about her mouth.

When Milcom at last reappeared they drove back to Amélie,

calling round by the Sous-Préfecture, where Milcom arranged
for the Spanish artists to come down for drinks that evening,
bringing specimens of their work. They came, and sat awkwardly
under the lights in one of the horrible sitting-rooms, looking
curiously alive, with a sort of savage life, among the old whiskered
men and the antimacassared old women; their sculptured faces
had that tragic touch which always lies just below the surface of
the Spanish expression. Their works were spead out on the
table, and Mr. Oldhead was persuaded to commission one or
two. Milcom observed with amused admiration Rosemary's skill
in handling her parents, and her delightful ease with the
Spaniards; she didn't speak Spanish very well but she did speak
it without hesitation, stumbling out her faulty phrases rather fast,
laughing at herself, helping the guests to drinks very nicely, putting everyone at their ease. Ease!—what a precious quality it
was, and how rare. Milcom was painfully aware of not having
it himself—he could never do anything with an awkward situation
but make it more awkward. Raquel had it, though, to a supreme
degree—and so had this child. Odd that the two best examples
of this delightful quality that he had ever known should be two
such diverse types as the wife of a Spanish grandee and a little
English schoolgirl.

Next day he drove up to visit the camp at Prats-de-Mollo,
taking Rosemary with him. The road, splendidly engineered,
winds up the valley of the Tech through gorges increasingly high
and steep, clothed with woods of beech and chestnut, till the
mountains fall back to leave the high wide cup in which Prats
stands, a little walled town perched on a sloping site above the
river, dominated by the fierce outline of its great fortified church,
frowned down upon by the Fort de le Garde just above, to which
Vauban's genius has given his peculiar touch of heavy severity.
But they did not visit the town itself, that first time. The camp
lay just short of it, on a flattish shelf of pasture down by the river
—another collection of wigwams roofed with turf or thatched
with box and wild broom, and smoky with camp-fires. This
camp was not wired; Gardes Mobiles, patrolling it with rifles on
all sides, apparently kept the occupants in sufficient order. While
Milcom pursued his business within the camp, Rosemary wandered about the nearer slopes, or gossiped with the Gardes
Mobiles who, terribly bored, seized thankfully on the opportunity
of a little conversation with a stranger, who was moreover a
pretty young lady. Oh, the Spaniards were not so bad, once
you had them in a camp; but, out in the open—my God, how

they terrorised the farmers! Coming at night, armed; demanding food, menacing the women. And dirty! Ask the people of Preste, up there—they waved on up the valley beyond the walls of Prats—in what state the village school was, after the refugees had been housed in it! A disinfection was necessary. But, *les pauvres bougres*, they had fought well, that was certain. In the hospital there, by the main gate, many had died, of the wounded brought down from the Col d'Ares.

When Milcom returned they took a side road on the north side of the main valley, very steep and narrow, which led up through woods and open pastures till it ended abruptly at the very lip of a cliff which dropped to the next valley of Corsavy. Here they ate their lunch of ham rolls and fruit, sitting on the grass in the sun, and talked with a shepherd who, having beaten his savage dog into silence, told them his experiences with the *miliciens* in atrocious French, half Catalan. To his house too they had come, but he had his son and his gun; he had locked up his women and loosed his dogs, fed the men, let them sleep, and next day escorted them down to Prats, son, gun, dogs and all. In effect, they were not so much trouble, he said. Milcom and Rosemary laughed, as they drove home, at the peasant's rough-and-ready methods of defending his *mas*, while observing the mountain traditions of hospitality.

Spring in the Pyrénées Occidentales has a certain charm, in spite of the prevailing East wind. In the valley-floors a pink mist of almond and peach blossom spreads over the bare earth; through the evergreen shrubs along the rocky slopes the wild mimosa seems to run like a yellow flame; up on the shoulders of the Canigou the greenish-white of the tall heaths in flower is set against the silvery-white of the rocks, while westward, in the deeper valleys, the running sap in the beech and chestnut woods clothes the slopes in a purplish bloom. Over all is the extraordinary light of that region, at once silvery and fierce, and the tonic exciting dryness of the air, with sudden contrasts of hot sunshine and cold wind. This was the setting for three of the happiest weeks of Rosemary's life. Mrs. Oldhead liked Milcom, and was delighted that Rosemary had found such a nice trustworthy person to take her about; Milcom, heart-broken, lonely and at a loose end, gladly and rather thoughtlessly accepted this pleasant easy companionship. They spent almost the whole of every day together. They would leave the Thermes Jadis at about eight, and driving to some village, breakfast at the inn, usually with the posse of Gardes Mobiles quartered there; then they would drive further, or walk for hours, returning between two and three to coax a late lunch out of the *maître d'hotel*, after which Rosemary slept, or amused her parents, while Milcom wrote about Manuel Jereda to the various hospitals of which the amiable Sous-Préfet had furnished him with a list. In the evenings he talked politics with Mr. Oldhead, or entertained the Spanish officers from Arles. He and Rosemary examined the local churches, going down sometimes into the plain; but mostly they explored the side valleys of the Vallespir, and above all those leading up to the Spanish frontier. Armed with the Sous-Préfet's pass, they were allowed to go almost anywhere; the Gardes Mobiles whom they met at breakfast in the village inns were charmed to accept a lift to the head of the mountain road, and even to have such company on their daily patrols.

So it came about that Rosemary and Milcom got to know the Spanish frontier at the eastern end as few save the peasants and the Gardes Mobiles themselves knew it. Leaving the hardy little Peugeot at the last possible turning-place on some narrow road, they would plod with their dark-coated friends up a mule-track to the frontier-post, where the Tricolor and Franco's yellow and gold, tied to sticks, leaned drunkenly from the same cairn of stones; the Franquista guards would emerge from whatever hut sheltered them, and greet the Gardes Mobiles with the utmost warmth, begging for cigarettes. If there was anything in the nature of an inn within reach, as was sometimes the case, the whole party would repair there for a glass of wine; if there was not, they amused themselves in various ways—once by having a shooting competition with the Spaniards' rifles, firing at an entrenching-tool set up among the rocks at two hundred yards range. In the spring of 1939 that section of the frontier presented an extraordinary spectacle. On the Spanish side the slopes are gradual, and the gradients of the small mountain roads in consequence fairly easy; on the French side, on the contrary, the slopes are steep, and as a matter of policy all French roads stop some kilometres short of the frontier. So the enterprising Spaniards who, avoiding the traffic-blocks on the main roads at Le Perthus and Cerbère, pushed their cars up mountain tracks to the frontier, found on the crest that they could take them no further. They left their machines and whatever luggage they could not carry, and descended into France on foot. As a result the summit ridge at the head of all the smaller Spanish roads was strewn with abandoned cars, typewriters, and luggage—while around them, like shingle on a beach around boulders were thousands of rifle-cartridges, which the French frontier-guards had stripped from the incoming *miliciens*—one's feet sank into them as into the stones of the sea-shore. It was a formidable, a desolating sight. These rifle-bullets were the ammunition which they used for their shooting-match, the Spaniards cheerfully knocking them into the breech with stones if they did not fit very well, to Milcom's horror and Rosemary's vast amusement.

In these circumstances they came, too, to know better than most foreigners ever succeed in doing one of the finest bodies of men in the world, the Gardes Mobiles. These men are the pick of the best and most stable element in France, the substantial peasants and small farmers; they are chosen for character as well as for intelligence and physique, and the majority are married men—Rosemary used to notice how many wore a gold *alliance* on their wedding finger. They are given a very special training, in the use of arms as well as in police duties, and have a tradition almost as unbreakable as that of the Brigade of Guards; they almost always do their service in districts other than their own. With their large calm country faces under the bluish steel helmets, their smart knee-length overcoats, trimly belted, their black gaiters and glossy boots, they invariably present an appearance as impressive as it is reassuring—and before them and behind them goes the quelling influence of their immense prestige. Anyone who has seen a Paris crowd in an ugly temper begin to waver and melt at the first whisper of "les Gardes Mobiles!" realises how enormous this prestige is.

But Rosemary and Milcom saw another side of them, which the Paris visitor does not usually see. The men they met had been posted for weeks in remote villages, far from railways or main roads, among a population whose dialect they could hardly understand; and once the excitement and the activities connected with the Spanish influx had died down they were deadly bored, and quite touchingly homesick. Tramping the frontier ridges, sitting in rough uncouth one-room inns with the English man and the English girl—his daughter, they naïvely and explicitly supposed—sooner or later they talked about their homes, their own corner of France; lingering over the details of its soil, its climate, its types of poultry and wine, bringing out in slow leisurely sentences their deep nostalgia. Nothing made them so happy as when their new friends chanced to be familiar with their own district. Tenez, Monsieur knows Blois? Ah, what a city! The Loire—how wide, how noble. And the Château!—Monsieur knows the Château? And the fine fish—ah, how good

the fish is, all along the Loire. Rosemary and Milcom were
sitting drinking cognac and hot water in such an inn, one day,
after a peculiarly cold tramp over a section of the frontier with
three splendid fellows, two of whom, it appeared, came from
Bayonne,—their delight when Rosemary said that she knew
Bayonne know no bounds. They discussed the shops, the cinemas,
the bus services, mouthed the dear names of streets. The third
listened in silence to this happy exchange; at last he said hopefully—"Mademoiselle knows Brittany too?" Alas, Mademoiselle
did not. The giant sighed, patiently. "Brittany is a fine place too,"
he said. "But it is far away, La Bretagne." Mademoiselle was
almost ready to cry that she could not offer Brittany as well as
Bayonne.

They were blissful days for Rosemary. Her happiness was so
great that she could hardly contain it. She loved the country,
the fun of exploration, the long hard walks, the excitement of
seeing such big stretches of the frontier, meeting the Franco
guards, making friends with the Gardes Mobiles—all this would
have been wonderful in itself, but shared with Milcom, it was
Paradise. She made heroic and conscientious efforts to hold her
happiness in; scolded herself, warned herself that it would not
last, that she would come a fearful flop when it was over, and
so on. And she did manage to make herself the most normal
and unexacting of companions to Milcom. But her happiness
overflowed in her shining eyes and danced in her light tireless
feet, even if she managed to keep it out of her voice. They talked
a good deal; not all the time, but at intervals, between com-
panionable silences. Rosemary's knack of drawing people out
did not fail with Milcom. He talked about his work—she learned
a lot about that. He talked about the French and the Spaniards,
and the idosyncrasies of their national characters. Impercept-
ibly, too, she got to know him, and tiny things about him; his
likes and dislikes; the finicking neatness, for example, which made
him unable to endure a cigarette-end left burning on an ash-tray.
He must always stub it out, whoever had put it there. They
acquired a small stock of common experiences—and adventures
shared, jokes shared; at dinner in the evenings—he sat with the
Oldhead family now—she poked him up to the recital of special
items in the day's happenings.

Possibly James was rather careless about this situation. In
his excuse it may be said that he knew nothing about young girls,
that Rosemary's self-control was uncommon, and her technique
with people unusually good; and that his heart and mind were

so embedded in the thought of Raquel, and his devotion to her, that he was really quite myopic about any other relationship. He was still in a state of raw misery over losing her, and in his misery he clung like a drowning man to the relief afforded him, so freely and easily, by Rosemary's company. He did very occasionally recollect, as he had recollected that first night at the Thermes Jadis, that she had once professed to love him; but her ease and naturalness and gaiety in his company led him to think, gradually, that that had just been an emotional moment, an isolated outburst, which didn't amount to anything serious or lasting. The most sensitive and sympathetic and humane of men can be, and often are, complete fools in matters of this sort. The arbitray convention which assumes that love is never really destructive, or hurts seriously, under the age of twenty held in Milcom's case. The convention is false; Milcom was wrong; but it, together with his own absorbing passion, which completely preoccupied his emotional sensory apparatus, prevented him from realising what was happening. If he had, he would have done something about it, for he was both sensitive and humane, and he liked Rosemary very much; he respected her mind, he respected her enormously for the courage she had shown in that emotional moment, and he enjoyed her tireless energy, her readiness for any adventure, her gaiety and her modern gift for absurdity. This last is a quite special quality of the latest generation, and it was a novelty to him. It is new, it is amusing to a degree; it fizzes and exhilarates like champagne. James was intellectually alert enough to recognise the things on which it is based; recognition of each sort of fact, the acceptance of disillusionment, and nevertheless the resulting lively enjoyment of actual things. It startled and pleased him to realise how important sun and wind, and good plain food and natural beauty and clever modern music, were to Rosemary—how simply and rightly she let her whole being be nourished by these. What he didn't in the least realise was the effect which the unguarded and affectionate companionship of a man like himself, in conjunction with such things, was bound to have on her. So he accepted all that she gave, laughed at her lively folly, responded to her teasing ease—if his nights knew despair and wretched wakefulness, his days at least were fairly bearable. He was grateful, too, for this; it made all the difference, he freely admitted.

Actually he learned a certain amount about her, and the generation she represented, too; some of it startled him. He was quite unprepared to find that a girl of her age, educated at a rather mediocre school and by no means coming from an ultra-intellectual home circle should possess so much knowledge about international relations and foreign political personalities as she evidently had, and should be so much interested in them. He asked her once if all the girls at her school knew as much as she did about M. Léon Blum, and M. Reynaud, and M. Daladier, and what they stood for in French public life?

"Oh yes," she said carelessly—"Well, perhaps I know more *gossip* about them now, being out here. But most of us know a goodish bit. We have to read *The Times* at school, anyhow, and some of us take the *Daily Herald* as well. It's important to us, you see."

He didn't take that last point up, at the time, he didn't see what she meant. But later he learned—with a certain shock. They were sitting in the sun one afternoon up near St.-Laurent-de-Cerdans, sucking oranges—Rosemary had bought herself a pair of the local espadrilles, made of black tape, down at the little factory, and sat with her slender legs stuck out in front of her, wiggling each foot in turn and admiring the set of her new footgear; in her gay jumper and short skirt, with her elaborate curled head, she looked the very picture of the frivolous modern young who were so much contemned by the moralists in 1939. They had been talking about women in journalism, and Geneviève Tabouis and Dorothy Thompson and Virginia Cowles, and Rosemary had displayed her usual familiarity with the character and outlook of all three, to his amused surprise. At last, idly, he asked her what *she* meant to do?

"Oh, nursing, I think," she said, raising her right foot and bending it to and fro, while she admired it critically, her head on one side.

"Why nursing?" he asked. It was the last thing he would have expected to hear.

"Well, you don't have to be much educated for it—which I'm not," the girl said; "and it'll come in handy when the war comes."

"What do you mean?" he asked, startled, hardly believing his ears.

"Oh, just the war—us and Germany and everybody else—Armageddon or whatever they call it," she answered, sticking out her left foot now, and twirling that. "One will have to be *in* it, you see; and nurses are always wanted—with air-raids and things, more than ever, shouldn't you think?"

"When do you expect it to come?"

"Oh—'any moment now, chaps; any moment now'—as the Western Brothers would say," she answered cheerfully.

"You're certain it will come?" he asked, realising, confronted with her certainty, how much he himself had still hoped that it might somehow be averted.

"Oh Heavens yes. Obviously. Why? Aren't you?"

He didn't answer her question; in his almost horrified concern and surprise at her attitude, he asked her another himself.

"How long have you been thinking this—that war was inevitable, I mean?"

"Oh, I don't know—about three or four years. When did sanctions break down? '36, was it? Well, about since then. And all this performance"—she moved her hand over her shoulder at Spain—"has just pushed it along a bit faster. And then Munich—we as near as a toucher had it then."

"What did you think about Munich?" he asked her.

"Oh, lousy. It made me feel dirty all over. But what can you do? We had all the right ideas, but we had them at the wrong time, in the wrong sort of world. Well, I guess we'll have to think again," she said impatiently. "God, I hope they give us conscription, and make it snappy while they're about it."

"And do all the others at your school think the same as you do about the war?" he asked. He was at once appalled and fascinated by the pictures she conjured up, of a whole generation of youthful creatures growing up in clear anticipation of this menace, this horror, and remaining the calmly frivolous beings they to all outward seeming were.

"All the older ones, naturally; from about the Upper Fourth. I don't know what the brats think. But if you ask *me*, I think all ideologies are lousy," said Rosemary with emphasis.

He couldn't have agreed more completely. And ideology, or the ideological powers, were becoming more and more vocal, threatening. While Milcom and Rosemary tramped the Pyrenean frontier and chatted with homesick Gardes Mobiles in mountain inns, deputies and black-shirted mobs in Rome screamed "Corsica!", "Tunisia!", "Nizza!". Milcom didn't like it, he said; didn't like the look of it at all. He persuaded Mrs. Oldhead to change a large number of cheques, and to carry several thousand francs in French notes on her person always. If something broke suddenly, he said, there would be no hope of changing cheques; she had better have the money by her. Sensible Ethel Oldhead did as he advised, saying nothing to her ailing husband. Milcom changed a cheque himself, down in Perpignan, at the Banque de

Roussillon. Then he went back to his occupation of writing to hospitals, and walking and driving with Rosemary. None of the French hospitals to which he wrote, it seemed, had any record of a Lieutenant Manuel Jereda; which was disappointing. But he continued to write—and to walk. In a menaced world, in a menaced France, one person, at least, was enjoying herself a great deal.

## CHAPTER THIRTEEN

### *This Side—Prats-de-Mollo*

ONE evening towards the end of March when Rosemary and Milcom were discussing as usual where they should go next day, she said—"Why not Prats? I've never seen it, you know. The books say it's a good church."

"But we went to Prats, right at the beginning," Milcom objected.

"Only the camp, Jems—we never went to the town."

"Didn't we? All right—let's go to Prats."

"Shall we take lunch, or can we eat there?"

"Oh, we can eat there—there's a quite decent little pub in the town."

"Oke. Eight to start?"

"Yes—eight."

They set out from the tilted little square by the fountain punctually; the low sun, shooting through the gorge of the Mondony, as it did for fifteen tantalising minutes every morning, caught the higher branches of the great plane trees, lighting up the spiky balls of seed which still dangled from the bare twigs, and gilding the shabby fronts of the houses opposite. James glanced round him before kicking away a rock from under the wheel of the car—just so he had seen the square now, a dozen times, in the early light, in the keen morning air.

"I'm getting quite fond of the smell of sulphur," he said, as he settled into the car beside Rosemary; "I shall feel positively deprived of it when I go away."

She laughed. "And mimosa—don't forget that," she said gaily. He must never guess how it took the fun out of everything for her even to think of his going away. Oh well—don't let's think about it! she thought. He had gone away before, she had thought she

would never see him again, and yet here they were, driving up to
Prats together! And anyhow to-day was to-day. She began to
whistle "Un seul couvert, pliss, Jems"—it was her sort of theme-
song for him; the nick-name she had latterly begun to use was
based, though he didn't know it, on that song. James vaguely
liked being called "Jems"—it was a long time since anyone had
used a nick-name for him. He never bothered to ask why. But
the song corresponded to one that was beginning to sing itself in
Rosemary's heart, a small song that had, beside the grave shy
tenderness of youthful love, an element of joy, almost of hope in it.
Naturally, after these weeks spent tête-à-tête, she was much more
profoundly in love with Milcom than she had been at St.-Jean-de-
Luz; and, for all her realistic warnings and cautionings of herself,
she could not quite prevent a feeling that, as she put it, she had a
chance—only a 20 per cent chance perhaps, but still a chance. He
was so *nice* to her; clearly he liked being with her; it would be far,
far ahead, of course, but it did seem to her that he was getting
over the Condesa a tiny little bit. So her heart sang, and she
whistled a silly modern song, as they drove together up the
winding grey road, between the mountain woods, bloomy and
heavy with the swelling buds of spring, towards Prats-de-
Mollo.

They had coffee at Le Tech, a small village with an extremely
modest inn, and then drove on to Prats. They parked in the big
open space outside the eastern gate, where weeks before James
had seen the Spanish ponies tethered under the wall; and then
proceeded to examine the walls of the miniature city, with charming little pepper-pot turrets in pink brick projecting from the
angles.

"Where does that go?" Rosemary asked, pointing to a broad
and rather well-built road which crossed the Tech by a stout
modern bridge, and wound up into the hills beyond.

"No idea—we'll ask"—and he enquired of the two Gardes
Mobiles at the city gate.

"To the Col d'Ares, Monsieur. It is the military road. But
to traverse it is forbidden."

"Even with a pass?" James asked. The policeman requested
to see the pass, and James produced the Sous-Préfet's well-
thumbed chit. Ah well—possibly, the man said; all the same it
would have to be countersigned by the Capitaine here at Prats,
or the sentries would not let one pass. It was a *route militaire*, he
repeated.

"Do you want to go up there?" Rosemary asked.

"I thought we might. We ought to get a fine view from the top. Let's get hold of this Capitaine and see about it—we can look at the church when we come down."

The Captain was in his bureau, in the big building just across the open Place; after a little conversation he readily countersigned the Sous-Préfet's permit, and they got into the car again and drove off across the bridge. At the far end they were halted by a sentry, and again a few hundred yards further on by two more, but on showing the paper they were allowed to proceed. The military road wound up over the southern slopes in great looped curves; it was broad and well engineered, with easy gradients and stoutly-built bridges and culverts, but it had not yet been surfaced; great piles of road-metal, mostly a sort of pinkish granite, were heaped along it at intervals ready for use, but the road itself at present consisted merely of grass and greasy mud, deeply rutted, on which the Peugeot skidded and shied sideways like a nervous horse. Driving slowly and carefully James coaxed her up to a point where it flattened out on wide grassy downs, with thickets of broom and juniper here and there; it ran level for about a quarter of a mile, and then abruptly stopped. Just stopped, as if cut off with a knife; there was a sloping edge about two feet high where the foundations of the road ended, and beyond a narrow mule or *char* track, winding away round a shoulder of the hill.

James stopped the car and got out; Rosemary followed.

"This can't be the col, surely," she said.

"No, evidently not. It must be somewhere over there on the ridge"—he pointed across an intervening valley. He went and examined the drop and the *char* track, while Rosemary rambled about.

"I think we can get on," he called to her after a moment. She paid no attention; she was looking intently at the broom bushes which bordered the road. "James! Do come here," she called in her turn.

He went over to her. "What is it?"

"Look here," she said, pointing to the bushes. As brambles through which sheep have passed are draped and tangled with tufts and locks of dirty wool, so these green sprays of broom were draped with loops and strands of some stained and dirty material; it was a moment or two before James recognised them for what they were—bandages.

"Good God!" he said.

"Look—all down the road," she went on, waving backwards.

8*

"And here." She pointed to the ditch, which was full of muddy half-frozen water—at the bottom lay more of the stained and ragged bandages.

"How very horrible," he said. He looked about him, forwards and backwards; everywhere the grim remnants fluttered in the fresh mountain breeze. "A lot of wounded must have come out this way," he commented—"they're all over the place. Well, let's get on. Do you mind standing at the side and telling me if I'm clear underneath?"

She did as she was told, but the car negotiated the drop safely, and they drove on cautiously along the narrow track. It wound across the side of the hill, with a steep drop to the valley below on their left; there was barely room for the wheels to pass, but scraping the bank on their right, they proceeded for about another kilometre and a half, till they reached a high saddle of stone-strewn grass—here the track in its turn came to an end among the whitish rocks which stuck up out of the soil. Small paths, foot-paths or sheep-tracks, branched off in several directions, but there was nothing along which it was possible to drive a car.

"Now what?" the girl asked.

"I'll turn her, I think, here on the level, and then we'll walk up. Just hop out and watch for the clearance again, will you?"

When the car was turned James got out and looked about him.

"By Jove, it is a place," he said.

It was. The view was magnificent. On one side they looked across the Vallespir—with Prats lying like a toy town just below them, white and small—to the massif of the Canigou; on the other they looked down the valley along whose upper slopes they had just come, over a farther ridge, to the great hollow in which St. Laurent-de-Cerdans lies, the high southern sun was pouring into this; investing the wooded slopes with a silvery glitter—behind, close at hand, a rough slope of rock and scree mounted to a ridge where snow still lay in the hollows. They stood and gazed. The view, the height, the sense of sun and space, of being poised above the glory of the earth, halfway to the glory of the sky, filled Rosemary with a delicate passionate exáltation. This place of sky and mountains and deep valleys and toy-like towns was the most wonderful she had ever seen—and she was here with him, with him! She looked from the view to his rugged face; every detail, every defect was clear in the fierce light, outlined against that tremendous expanse of blue—and every detail and every defect she loved. She shivered a little, suddenly, under the impact of a strange sensation, something that with all her clear-eyed theoretical knowledge she had never yet experienced—the first onset of physical enchantment.

He noticed the shiver—he was very noticing nowadays.

"Cold?" he asked. "The wind is a bit nipping, isn't it? Let's go on up."

Unthinkingly, he took her elbow to start her off. She shivered again, sharply, at his touch.

"You really *are* cold," he said, surprised and kind. "Come along." It never occurred to him that cold was just what she was not.

They found a small path and followed it up towards the ridge. The air had a tonic freshness, in spite of the hot sun—and the wind was certainly keen; except for a few sheep and a herd of cows, escorted by a bull, the whole mountain-side seemed utterly deserted.

"Why do you suppose they stopped the road there, short of the col?" Rosemary asked, with careful casualness, as after making a detour to avoid the bull they regained the path.

"No idea. Perhaps there's no road to connect with it on the Spanish side—or perhaps they didn't want to connect. Or the money may have given out," James said over his shoulder—they were walking in single file. "Hullo, there we are," he exclaimed a few moments later. The path, winding round a spur, had brought them into a shallow stony valley, running up to the ridge; at the top of it, from a cairn of stones, two flags fluttered against the sky. They pushed on; the north wind, blowing down the gully as down a funnel, was cold on their faces now, and as they approached the col the usual dismal frontier jetsam began to litter the slopes beside the path—here a rifle, there a revolver; a tin hat; a machine gunner's asbestos glove, the palm sewn with metal rings; a couple of bayonets. Now they could see the Franco guards, who had emerged from somewhere to look at the new-comers, standing silhouetted against the sky beside the flags, huddled in ragged overcoats which flapped in the breeze, with scarves tied over their caps.

"I bet they're cold," James remarked.

"Yes. It's funny, there are no cars up here, or typewriters," Rosemary observed; she knew now what to expect of frontier passes.

"Perhaps there's no road that cars could get up on the Spanish side," James said again.

But he was wrong about that, as they saw for themselves a few minutes later. The guards, on being addressed in Spanish and offered cigarettes, greeted them with the usual enthusiasm, and after a little conversation led them over the crest of the ridge to see the great sight of the Col d'Ares. A well-made, well-metalled road ran down into Spain on the far side of the pass, skirting a deep ravine; the bottom of this ravine, and the slope between it and the road, was covered with wrecked motor vehicles of every description—lorries, guns and gun-carriages, cars, ambulances, motor-cyles—lying upside down, on their sides, on their noses, anyhow; this wreckage stretched as far as the eye could reach, a matter of at least four miles, and it was evident that an attempt had been made to burn it, for the cars and lorries bore the marks of fire.

"Good God!" James said, and then stood in silence, gaping. He had seen a good deal of war, but this was wholesale ruin on a scale such as he had never yet witnessed.

The Franquistas were delighted to tell him all about it. Yes, Los Rojos knew about the Spanish road and the French road, and had supposed that they met on the col; so when they saw themselves trapped by the troops of the Caudillo near Rivas, a whole division had retreated up to the Col d'Ares, with all their war material and supplies, only to find when they reached the summit that there was a gap of five kilometres between the end of the Spanish road and the beginning of the French one—five kilometres of rocky slopes down which it was impossible to drive lorries, cars, and guns. So they had run the whole outfit over the edge of the road into the ravine, where they set fire to it.

James and Rosemary walked some distance down the road, examining this scene of desolation. Then they went back to the col. The Franco guards, meanwhile, had retired out of the wind into the ingenious little shelter which they had made for themselves, a sort of lean-to under a small face of rock, constructed out of the bottoms of lorries; the upholstered seats of motor-cars had been turned into beds, and there was even a fireplace made of unidentifiable pieces of metal. They invited the strangers into this peculiar abode, and stoked up the fire—James observed with interest that one of them was reading Don Quixote, out of a magnificent eighteenth-century edition, with a coat-of-arms tooled in gold on the superb leather binding. Yes, the man said, he read it every day; it was a good book. But when James again offered them his cigarettes, one of the guards tore a leaf out of another volume, equally splendid externally, with which to make a spill. James picked up the book. It was in Spanish, a "History of

Social Progress." The guards had no idea what it was that made the English stranger laugh out aloud.

Suddenly there were shouts outside; the guards sprang up off their leather beds and tumbled out through the low entrance. James and Rosemary followed; the smoke from the lacquered car-wood which the Spaniards used for fuel had an acrid chemical pungency, making one's eyes water, and catching the throat. On the road stood half a dozen Gardes Mobiles, trim and snug in their heavy belted overcoats and gaiters; they presented the greatest possible contrast to the Spanish sentries, who had reinforced their ragged coats with every sort of garment—scarves, sweaters, jackets and waistcoats; one even had a pair of golf stockings wound round his neck and ears.

The Gardes Mobiles saluted the two foreigners politely, and as usual entered into conversation with them. Yes, they had been up here when the Spanish army came up—Mon dieu, quelle confusion!

"We had luck," the sergeant said; "right at the head of the column were fifteen auto-mitrailleuses, brand-new. When we saw what the Espagnoles were devising, we ran like madmen, and took them, and pushed them up and over the frontier, where those others could not touch them! Those at least we saved—and after, we slid them down on the snow on planks till we reached the track. Monsieur will have seen the track—without doubt it is his car which stands below on the plateau?"

James said that it was. "So there was snow there then?"

"My God, yes, Monsieur!—thirty-six centimetres of snow. And a cold—*formidable*! And figure to yourself that they had brought with them four thousand wounded, of which half were stretcher-cases."

"Good Heavens! What did they do with the wounded?"

"They? nothing at all! Took them out of the ambulances and laid them on the snow, and then ran the ambulances into the ravine with the rest, and set fire to them. We got them down, we; we sent for lorries to come to the head of the road, and we carried them down, two thousand of them. For nine days and nights, Monsieur, those brave fellows of mine have not taken off their boots! This one"—he pointed to a huge blond Norman, who grinned sheepishly—"had not enough of it, he, with carrying the wounded down; no, when they were all disposed of, I meet him plunging through the snow, giving a pick-a-back to an old peasant woman! She was pulling his ears!—was she not, Georges?"

Georges, crimson, remained speechless at this onslaught. The sergeant punched him mightily in the back, by way of reassuring him; James asked what became of the wounded?

"Oh, they were sent on by lorry and ambulance, to hospitals here and there—Perpignan, Narbonne, Toulouse; all but the very worst cases, which we kept here in Prats. Many died—those who had fever. Figure to yourself, Monsieur, the effect of being taken out of the ambulances and laid here in the snow!"

James asked a few more questions about this extraordinary episode; though he had been in the district the whole time, he had never heard of it. Few journalists, the sergeant told him, had ever been allowed up to the Col d'Ares; for whatever reasons, the whole thing had been kept extremely dark, it was clear.

Driving down the road again the bandages on the bushes told, now, a more full and terrible story. James parked the car on the Place, as before, and they entered the little town by the big arched gateway; proceeding along the narrow main street they came to a small square, where country carts were unloading hay and other produce, and went into the inn for lunch. In the sunny stuffy upstairs room, where a row of geraniums in the window caught the light and the dust alike, the Capitaine was lingering over a coffee and a *fine*; he asked how they had fared. It was very late—they had lunch rather quickly, and then set out to find the church. From the square they turned up a narrow alley to the right, which consisted partly of steep cobbles, partly of stone steps; and by a succession of such passages, all swarming with children and cats, they at length reached the relatively flat walk which contours the massive stone wall surrounding the church itself. They followed this till they came to a gate in the wall—passing through, they found themselves in a grassy space where more children played; in the centre rose the lofty grey bulk of the church, reinforced with high narrow buttresses which added to the effect of height. They went in and wandered about the dim interior, admiring the great carved and gilded reredos, the gift of Louis XIV, which is the chief glory of the place, and the leaning statue of the Virgin which is its miracle and pride. An aged and rather snuffy sacristan told them the story. Some years before, when the church was being restored, one of the masons was an ardent atheist; one day while he was at work the church was struck by lightning, and two of the side chapels were wrecked, including that which contained the statue, then vertical. But when the dust settled and the smoke cleared away, there in the midst of the wreckage, unhurt, stood the statue of the Virgin, leaning at an angle in which no natural agency could have supported it—and this and his escape so wrought upon the mason that he abjured his atheism and became a devout Catholic. The old man showed them the rather modest collection of vestments and, in a cupboard, the extraordinary papier-mâché image of the dead Christ, with real hair, which is carried in procession in Holy Week.

Emerging again into the sunshine, they walked round the east end to the other side of the church. Immediately beyond lay the graveyard, a charming God's-acre, irregularly shaped, with small walls dividing the various sections, and a pair of cypresses to give it dignity and formality; it commanded a wide view down the valley to the blue flatness of the Mediterranean plain, and up it to that great level snow-covered ridge which blocks the end of the Vallespir like a wall. Here the ridge was quite near, immense and dominating; James, leaning his elbows on a wall in the sun and gazing up at the glittering line of snow against the blue, remembered how he had first seen it—when he sat with Raquel in the inn garden at Arles-sur-Tech, and she had asked him where the end of the world was, and he had idly answered—up at Prats-de-Mollo. He remained there, dreaming, lost in the past, while Rosemary wandered about, examining the grave-stones and the wreaths of bead flowers with visiting-cards, in glazed frames; he was roused by her voice calling to him—"Please, will you come here?"

She was not in sight from where he stood; rather reluctantly, he moved a few steps, and then saw her. She was kneeling on the ground in a part of the graveyard that he had not noticed before; the stones had been removed and stood propped against the wall —the space where they had been was full of freshly-made graves. On most of them a piece of tricolor ribbon, held down by a pebble, lay on the raw earth; a few had rude crosses stuck at the head, made of two bits of wood roughly nailed together, with names scrawled on them in pencil. Rosemary was kneeling by one of these. At the sound of his footsteps she looked up—"Please come," she said again.

This time there was no mistaking the urgency in her voice, and the expression on her face made James hasten to her side; she was very white.

"Look"—she said as he stood beside her, and pointed to the wooden cross. James stooped to read. On it was written in pencil, in a thick sprawling uneducated hand:

Le Lieutenant MANUEL JEREDA
No. 38475
de l'Armée Républicaine Espagnole
Mort à l'Hôpital à
Prats-de-Mollo,
Le 17 Février, 1939.
R.I.P.

For a long moment James stood staring down at it in silence.
Mechanically he removed his hat. So this was the end—the end
of his long search, the end of Raquel's hopes and fears. And the
end of that brilliant life, the hope of a generation. Ironically, his
thought of a moment before came back into his mind—the end of
the world; yes, for Juanito Torre de Modero, Prats-de-Mollo had
indeed been the end of the world.

"Oh, God," he said.

Rosemary looked up at him then, her brown eyes blind with
tears.

"Oh dear," she said. "Poor poor Raquel." And then with a
sob—"And he was such a glorious person—so—so *noble*."

James was greatly astonished by this remark. For the first
time, then, it occurred to him to wonder how it came about that
Rosemary knew that Manuel Jereda and Juanito were one and
the same person. That was strange enough; but she spoke as if
she knew him. But before he could say anything she spoke again.

"You did know, then?"

"Yes, I knew," he said. "I told Raquel. But how did *you*
know? Did she tell you?"

"Oh no," she said, getting slowly up from her knees. She went
over and sat on the low wall beyond the new graves. Behind it,
in the field outside, a heap of bead wreaths was piled up against
the wall, thrown there, no doubt, when the space was cleared.
James followed her.

"No," she went on—"I guessed, after I met him."

"You *met* him? Where on earth did you do that?"

"Once at the Grotte de Sare—and then at the Chambre
d'Amour. The first time I wasn't sure, thought I guessed he was
a spy; but the second time I overheard him talking with the Old
Parrot, and from what they said I know that he must be Number
Seventeen. And then he gave me a letter to her."

James couldn't take it all in. "How came you to know about
Number Seventeen at all?" he asked, seizing on at least one point
to get clear.

"Oh, because I heard them all taking about it—Crumpet and Crossey and all. When there was the sabotage. And then we went to the Grotte de Sare, and this man came out of the cave, and went back when he saw the car, and came out another way. And when he saw me he went like this"—she moved her right hand towards her left armpit—"just for a second. Peasants don't do that. He was pretending to be a peasant."

"And what did you do?"

"Nothing—except talk to him, and then persuade Crossey to stop Daddy from having the Grotte stopped up." She explained about the Arbre de Noël.

"Good God!" said James. "How extraordinary! You were in on the whole thing. Well—go on. Why did you want to prevent your Father from stopping that passage. If you didn't know who he was?"

"Because he was such a splendid person. He—he really *was* like a God come down to earth, you know."

"Was he very like *her*?" James asked—he couldn't prevent himself.

"Not *so* like—at least I didn't see it that time. Except his walk; when he walked away, that bothered me—I knew he walked like someone I knew, but I couldn't get it."

"Well, and then?" he prompted her.

"Oh well, then—quite a long time after, just before Christmas, when there was all that business about the Russian planes coming in—Daddy heard about them, and he remembered that there was that way in and out, up the Arbre de Noël, so he hooshed in to Bayonne and told the French, and they sent Gardes Mobiles to the Grotte, and blocked the whole thing up." Her eyes filled with tears again. "I expect that did it, really. Oh, why did I have to notice those wretched foot-marks?—and not have the wits to keep my mouth shut? It's all my fault, really." She burst into tears. "One should never *talk*!" she sobbed out.

Awkwardly, he patted her shoulder. "You couldn't know," he said. "Actually you talk less than any woman I ever met." He paused—she was dabbing her eyes. "Do you mind going on telling me?" he said. "I don't want to upset you"—what a ridiculous phrase, in the face of this tragedy, this finality! he thought—"but I would like to hear."

"It's all right," the girl said, giving a final dab to her reddened eyelids. "I'm only being a fool, as usual! Only when I think how it's ended for him, and what it means to her, I hate myself! Because I'm pretty sure that's what made him too late to get back to Burgos before the offensive. The Parrot said the delay was dangerous, but that he must go back that once more. I suppose it was about the planes or something. And he cursed the French for being so nosy, and stopping some passage. And it wasn't the French—it was me and Daddy! Oh—damn, damn!" She wept again, unrestrainedly.

"But where on earth did you hear all this? And who is the Parrot?" James asked, in natural bewilderment. He really must get to the bottom of this extraordinary story.

"At the Chambre d'Amour." She described the *mise-en-scène*, and how she had overheard Juanito's conversation with the Old Parrot, and had gone up afterwards to intercept him. "I guessed then that it must be Number Seventeen himself; and when I talked to him, and he asked me about Raquel, I suddenly saw the likeness. He had her nose, and eyes—and she had told me that he was like her, only black."

"Yes, she told me that too," he said. "But—you say he asked about her; how did he know you knew her?"

"Because of my copy-book—I'd got it along to do some Spanish. And when he saw me that second time he was a bit suspicious, and asked what I was up to—so I showed him the book. And there was some of Raquel's writing in it—she used to set me exercises, you know. So of course he recognised that. And then he asked about her."

"Did he tell you she was his sister?" James was enormously intrigued and astonished at the whole tale.

"No—he said she was 'a dear friend.' And then he wrote me an exercise, as he called it, in the book, and said she would help me to translate it, if I would show it to her. It was while he was writing it that I got to be quite sure who he was—his profile was so like hers; and the man in the exercise was called Manuel Jereda."

"But how fantastic! It was the most tremendous risk to take, letting you know all that," James said.

"I know. But I think he was simply desperate, he wanted to see her so much. I heard him asking the Parrot if he couldn't go and see 'her,' and I realised after who he meant—he said 'as she is so near.' And when I told him that she was in Paris, he was rather upset. He hadn't heard about the Conde being let out, and her going back, either, till I told him," said Rosemary unthinkingly.

"Good Heavens!" said James. "Do you mean to say he heard that from you?"

"Yes, it does seem extraordinary, doesn't it? But I'm sure the Parrot and that wretched Duquesa kept him completely in the dark, and her too—she had no idea that he'd been coming to Biarritz; she was furious when she heard that I'd seen him."

James remembered his own doubts on this head after his visit to Pablo the barber. Well, they were laid now, once for all. But there were other points he wanted to clear up—these constant references to the Parrot, for instance. He went for that next. Lighting a cigarette—

"Who is this Parrot you keep on talking about?" he asked.

She told him that whole story, then, from the expedition up La Rhune, and the two episodes of the photographs, to her drive with Crumpaun, and the closing of the little col, and her final clinching eavesdropping under the sea-wall at the Chambre d'Amour. "Mr. Crumpet was sure the Parrot was the head of the spy racket, even without hearing that last part," she said at the end. "And so am I. What do you think?"

"Obviously. I wonder who he is?" James meditated aloud. "Oh well, it makes no difference now. But I think our Intelligence people ought to employ you in the next war," he said, bending his intense gaze on her. "I never heard such a story in my life!"

The quick colour flew into her face, warming the clear brown skin.

"It only just happened like that," she disclaimed.

"Oh no it didn't," he said. "You were very observant, and intelligent, and discreet—and you kept your mouth shut. If you had shouted about the photographs that first morning at the Bar Basque, your Father would have heard of it, and made a row with the shop, and ten chances to one the Parrot, as you call him, would never have got them from old Jacques at all." He paused. "Funny!" he exclaimed—"I remember noticing you that morning when you were looking at them—you blushed, and looked angry. I asked you to let me see them, to find out what had upset you—do you remember?"

Rosemary remembered very well indeed, as she did everything where he was concerned. His request to see the photographs was the first time he ever addressed a remark to her directly—a sacred occasion. She blushed again.

"Yes, I do," she said casually. "But look—we're sitting here talking about how it all happened, and all that; but don't you think we ought to be finding out more about him? Exactly what he died of, and all that? Someone here must know, the doctor or the nurse. And *she* will want to know."

"Yes," he said. "De Novelles must have been right, of course

—he will have been wounded on the Serge, and come out over the Col d'Ares from Rivas."

"Oh, did de Novelles say that?"

"Yes—didn't I tell you? Oh no, of course, I wasn't talking to you about him then. Yes—he was very vague, but he thought he had heard of a Teniente Jereda losing a leg up there, early on."

"Oh goodness! And of course he was in that awful mix-up in the snow. James, we *must* get hold of the Doctor and find out all about it."

"I know," he said, getting up. He threw away his cigarette. "Yes, we must do that. I'll just take this down." And he in his turn knelt by the grave and began to copy the inscription on the rough wooden cross. He heard a little click, and looked round; Rosemary was standing a few paces away—she had taken his photograph. The tears were in her eyes again.

"You don't mind, do you?" she said apologetically. "But she will want a picture of his grave, and I think she would like you in it. I'll take one without, too, when you've done."

When they had both finished and he was putting away his note-book—"What day is it?" he asked suddenly—"the date, I mean?"

"The twenty-seventh." She supposed he wanted to note it down. But instead he walked very slowly over to the wall, leant against it, and remained so, looking down at the grave and its humble cross in silence.

"Where do you suppose we could get any flowers?" he said at last.

"Here? I've no idea. There's one pretty poor shop in Amélie." He looked at his watch.

"No,—that would be too late—we couldn't get back in time."

"Must it be to-day?" he said.

"Yes." He looked up at her, thoughtfully—and then, as one who has taken a decision, he spoke.

"To-day's her birthday, and his too."

"Oh! Oh *no*." It was the same tone of pure pity that he remembered so clearly in her voice the day that she ran out after him to the little Phare at St.-Jean.

"Yes," he said. "And when they were children they used to get up early and each put flowers on the other's bed—the great excitement was to do it before the other waked." He paused again. "Well, he won't wake this time," he said, in a tone of unutterable sadness—"but I thought we might put some flowers over him for his birthday—for her."

"Yes—oh yes." She stood for a moment, her brow wrinkled in thought. "I know," she exclaimed suddenly—"I remember! Come on—let's go and get the car."

They went down again to the square outside the main gate, leaving a note at the inn on the way for the Capitaine, who was taking his siesta, asking for the names and addresses of the Doctor who had attended Manuel Jereda, and the nurse, if any. Then they took the car, and under Rosemary's instructions James drove out beyond the camp, and parked. She led him up over the grassy slopes above the road to the edge of the woods—tucked into the fringe of the trees were curious little dark green huts built of box branches, used by the Gardes Mobiles on cold nights of sentry-duty. Within the wood itself the ground was a shadowy blue with trailing periwinkles, and here and there blue wind-flowers were coming into bloom.

"How did you know these were here?" James asked, startled and pleased.

"They were just in bud that day we came to the camp, and I pottered about up here while I was waiting for you," she answered, stooping and beginning to gather the small bright things. "Were you asking about *him*, too?" she asked, pausing in her task and sitting back on her heels to look up at him, "as well as the Mexico racket, when you went to all the camps?"

"Yes, I was."

"Oh dear—how silly that we didn't both know." She bent down again and went on gathering the wind-flowers. James helped a little, but mostly he leaned against a tree and watched her slender figure bent over her task, and her tender absorbed face. What an excellent little thing she was, he thought—so quick of sympathy, so prompt and practical in action.

"You are a good friend!" he said suddenly.

The warm tone of liking made the girls heart give a great bound. She was at that moment in a rather exalted state. The sudden revelation of Juanito's death had been a considerable shock to her, and she had been greatly moved by discovering it with James, and by the story of the birthday flowers. (That one thing Raquel, in all her many trivial confidences, had never told her—she had kept that for him.) And now, too, she and James, together, were doing this last thing for them, for Raquel and Juanito. Every tender and fine and gentle chord in her was quivering under these happenings, vibrating with a sort of passionate sensitiveness, so that the beauty of the afternoon, of the place, and his presence made a sort of music in her that could hardly be borne, so deep was the bliss. She said nothing when he spoke—she bent her head lower over the flower-starred earth, to hide the colour that flooded up over her clear brown skin. She was remembering another late afternoon, up in Pierre Loti's orchard outside the Grotte de Sare, when she had sat and dreamed about Milcom, till her dreams were interrupted by the advent of Juanito. She had dreamed then without hope; now, hope was unfolding and expanding in her heart, as delicately and silently as these blue wind-flowers in the still-wintry wood. For that had been autumn, and this, some deep secret knowledge cried in her, was spring, was spring.

Tragedies are often surprising in their suddenness, trivial, even minute, in their outward form. When her hands were full Rosemary asked James for his hat, lined it neatly with a clean pocket-handkerchief, and put the blue flowers in it. "Now let's get some of the pink ones," she said.

They went out onto the slopes under the wood. Below, the smoke from the evening fires of the camp down by the river was rising very straight, the air was so still; into the last sunlight—the camp itself was already in shadow; beyond, the slopes of the Col d'Ares caught the rich light. Rosemary began to pick the single pink anemones which, out here, waved slender and free among the pale dead grasses; when she had gathered a few she took them over to him. "Aren't they lovely?" she said, confidently putting them into his hands.

He took them, and looked at them thoughtfully. The clear delicate mauve-pink of the slender-starred fragile things was precisely the same odd note of colour as that of the crocuses which Raquel had picked on the knoll under the oak trees by the Ascain road. And because he too was sensitised by the day's events, was so much stirred and moved as to be quite unguarded, he spoke of this—"They're exactly the same colour as those little crocuses that used to grow near St.-Jean, up behind that chapel, near some oak trees."

The tone of his voice, lingering very slightly on some of the words, told Rosemary a lot. She guessed that he must have found the crocuses with Raquel, for when, by himself, did Milcom ever bother with wild-flowers? Some swift recognition, some awareness, still unformulated, fell like a cold shadow across her lyrical mood of bliss. On a characteristic impulse to grasp the still invisible nettle she said, lightly, gently—

"Oh yes—and Raquel was so fond of those."

He fell straight into the trap. Still holding the pink anemones, regarding them consideringly, he said, "Oh—did you pick them with her, too?"

Now his voice and words told her still more; the shadow grew deeper and colder. She managed to say, "Oh yes—often"—and again to say it lightly and evenly.

And he, because he liked her so much, because she was such a good little friend, and so devoted to Raquel, in his unguarded mood was moved to allow himself the sweet comfort of speaking a little of what was constantly in his heart.

"It was extraordinary how much she loved wild-flowers," he said, with a sort of luxurious slowness. "She was one of the last people you'd have expected to, somehow, with the life she had to lead. But she did; she always remembered what flowers grew in every place she ever talked about—cyclamens and things. Did you know that cyclamens grew wild? I didn't. Quite little ones, pinkish—they grow near cypresses." He paused, a faint smile bringing that sudden charm to his dark face.

"It's funny," he went on—"I got to know more about what wild-flowers grow where in Spain, in Madrid of all places, than I ever knew before, just from listening to her."

The tone of his voice on that "her", the whole tone—and that faint secret smile—oh no, there was no place for hope here! A sort of deep surrender of his whole being somehow breathed from the way he spoke of Raquel then. He went on, still in that happy recollecting voice—

"She liked talking about things like that, little things and places —more than about books or people. And you know the odd thing was that I really got to know her quite well just by talking about absurd things like that. Queer, isn't it?"

. Oh no, Rosemary thought, passionately, despairingly—it wasn't a bit queer. He was only talking about flowers now, Raquel and flowers, but she had got to know quite a lot too, just from the way he talked! That was the end of that. He was Raquel's, still, body and soul; probably would be forever. She had just been a fool, a complete idiot. But for once her usual hardy capacity for lambasting herself, and for meeting any situation head-on, failed the girl. Shaken by what had gone before, overwhelmed by this sudden comprehension, which blasted all her shy secret hopes, she just managed to say: "Oh no—not really. It's the way——" She meant to say, "It's the way things happen," but that was more than she could manage; she turned her head aside, moved away across the dried wintry grass, and stooped and went on gathering the pink anemones, their fragile starry heads swimming, enormous, in the tears that slowly gathered in her eyes. Oh, stop it!—she adjured herself, shaking her head angrily, as she wandered on down the slopes; the tears splashed down on the flowers in her hands. Do stop being such an ass! But it isn't so easy to stop being an ass when one is very young and desperately in love—and has been bumped down, within the space of five minutes, from the very pinnacle of bliss to a realisation such as she faced then. By a tremendous effort at self-control she did, quite quickly, stop crying; at a safe distance from Milcom, her back to him, she wiped her eyes and powdered her face. But she could not control everything. She went on down towards the road, calling to him over her shoulder to follow, she had got enough flowers. But when he rejoined her by the car he noticed that she was very white.

"Are you cold?" he asked her, for the second time that day.

"Not a bit!" she almost snapped—and again turned her head aside. She was remembering how she had felt when he asked her that a few hours before, up on the col. She got into the car, holding the hat-ful of flowers, slammed the door, and sat with averted head as they drove back to the Square outside Prats.

As before, they left the car there and went into the town on foot. At the inn door in the little Place stood the Captain of the Gardes Mobiles, in conversation with a middle-aged man in civilian dress.

"Ah, Monsieur," the Captain said as they approached—"I hoped that we should catch you. I received your note. This is Doctor Fouchaux, who attended your poor friend."

They all went into the inn together and upstairs to the restaurant. There, over coffee, the two English heard the story of Juanito's end. Yes, it was an amputation, Dr. Fouchaux said; the right leg. It had been skilfully done, evidently, at the time, but with the jolting journey in the ambulance mortification had set in, causing fever; and then that affair up there, waiting in the snow for many hours—*que voulez-vous?* Of course there had supervened a congestion of the lungs as well. He had arrived at Prats in violent delirium. But he was always patient, courteous—stoical, *enfin*, like all Spaniards. He had one only name always on his lips—Raquel; his wife, without doubt. Rosemary and Milcom exchanged a pregnant glance. "Believe me, Monsieur," the Doctor said, "we have done the possible and the impossible, but there was no means of saving him; the case was already hopeless when he arrived here."

James assured the Doctor of his conviction that this was so, and thanked him for his information. "He left no message, no letter?" he asked.

"Monsieur, from his arrival, he was far beyond that. He was in delirium, as I have said—there was only his ceaseless talk of Raquel—and of flowers." Again Rosemary and James exchanged glances—deep ones, from heart to heart. "But never a word of complaint, though he was certainly in agony. And at the last, when I brought the priest, his mind was clear—he was sinking, you understand—and he understood, and made a Catholic end, in the Faith."

"Ah, c'est bien," said the Captain, crossing himself. James felt a moment's envy of this universalism of the Catholics, which transcends all boundaries of race and language, linking the busy living and the helpless dying in one certainty, one security, of an established order, of faith and hope. He would have liked to be able to make the sign of the Cross, at those words, with the unself-conscious inevitableness of the blunt cheerful Captain of the Gardes Mobiles.

But the Captain had another *témoin*, as he called him, of Jua-nito's last days; when Dr. Fouchaux had taken his leave a lieu-tenant, who had been hovering in the background, received a brief command, and ushered in the big fair-haired fair-skinned Norman whom they had seen up on the Col d'Ares, being ragged by the Sergeant for giving a pick-a-back to an old Spanish peasant woman. Yes, he had carried the Spanish gentleman down, Georges said—he and his comrade, on the end of a bed, as there were no stretchers. No, not immediately; the Spanish officer spoke a perfect French, and when they came to him the first time, and the second, he gave them the command to take first the com-mon soldiers who were also wounded. A real *gentilhomme*, he was. And when at the end they took him, no crying out at the bumping over the rocks—for the way was rough, Monsieur would under-stand, and long—but such gracious thanks for their trouble. Ah, a real *gentilhomme*, such as there are few now, Georges said, breath-ing heavily, and expanding in this his hour of importance and self-expression. For himself, he would have carried that officer a hun-dred miles, and gladly. He was thanked, saluted, and went out.

That completed their task of enquiry. The nursing nuns had gone back to their convent in Perpigan, whence they had come for the emergency, but it was doubtful if they could have added much to the Doctor's testimony. James thanked the Captain warmly for his kindness, and then they went up to the cemetery again. It was getting late—the sun, sinking behind the Col d'Ares, had left the valley, and blue shadows filled it; only the great ridge still caught the last rays, and burned with a steadfast rosy glow; a fresh breeze blew up from the river, whispering in the two cypresses, and rustling the ivy and small plants that clung to the churchyard wall. Together they strewed their flowers, lightly and gently, over the grave, and then stood looking down at it in silence. Rosemary drew a deep breath.

"It's a lovely place to lie," she said at last.

"Yes."

He said no more for some time, but they lingered in a quiet sadness, reluctant to go away.

"It is a most peculiar business," James said at length, "that we should find him here like this, together, when I've been combing the camps for him all these weeks. Of course I had no idea you knew, or I would have told you. But the whole thing is so extraordinary—that while I heard about him from Paquita, you should have found it all out independently, and *met* him! Twice! And then that our two separate lines should join here at last, at his grave."

"Yes," she said, and was silent for a little while. She had had time now to recover herself a little, and the account of Juanito's illness and death had as it were taken the edge off her immediate unhappiness, lifted her emotion onto a higher plane, where her personal feelings counted for less. She was thinking now chiefly of Raquel, and of James in connection with her. At last she shook back her hair with an air of resolution, and spoke.

"James, which of us is going to write to her? *Are* you writing to her?"

He so much liked the direct way in which she said that.

"Well, yes and no," he answered. "We settled not to write, of course. But she did write to me in January, when he didn't turn up, asking me to hunt for him—and I answered that, and said that I would. I haven't written since, because there was nothing to say. I was just thinking about that myself, as a matter of fact."

She looked thoughtful.

"I think you'd better write," she said at last. "I will too, later on. But she had better hear it from you. I think she would rather."

"Very well, I will," he said. He was relieved by her definiteness, and it never occurred to him to doubt her judgement—young as she was, on such matters he felt instinctively that she would be right.

And then, at that hour, quite naturally he found himself putting to her the problem that had been tormenting him at intervals ever since he parted from Raquel de Verdura—whether he had been right not to accept her suggestion that they should make Pascual arrange a divorce? He told her—with the most extreme sense of relief, of easement, that now at last he could speak of it to someone—the situation as it had presented itself to him, as he had tried to present it to Raquel. "I was nearly done, when she suggested that," he said simply. "For a bit, I couldn't say anything at all. It seemed so obvious, in one way—after the way he'd treated her he *hadn't* any rights, from her point of view. But then I'd seen him." He paused, staring in front of him, as if he were at that moment seeing the Conde. "All the same, it nearly finished me," he went on—"When you're all keyed up to something you know will be Hades, and you see Heaven open, it's a frightful temptation to walk in. And it's being such hell for her——" he broke off, his face changing. "I felt a fool *and* a cad," he went on after a second's pause. "But—I don't know. I'd *seen* him, you see," he said again.

Rosemary listened to this recital with a curiously mixed emotion—a mixture to which the poor child had become accustomed in all her relations with both the Condesa and Milcom, till these last few days. There was pain in it; and yet there was also a deep satisfaction in the thought that he trusted her enough to make her his confidante on this, of all subjects. She had listened as usual in complete silence—a silence that for him was somehow charged with sympathy by her eyes, by her questioning brow, by the expression of her big mobile mouth. When he had finished she did not speak at once—she looked away down the shadowed valley, musingly.

"Oh yes, I think you were right," she said at last. "Darling Raquel—I see how it seemed to her. She hadn't seen him. But in the end she would have been miserable if she hadn't gone back. Oh no——" she paused, and pushed up her hair. "She had to go back," she said again. "I suppose you told her that day that you sat on the grass above the cliff, before you went in to Bayonne?"

He stared at her—was there nothing she didn't know?

"Yes—but how did you know that?"

"I saw you—I was sailing with Count de Barrial and I saw her run down, in black; and you running after her—in this suit." He was in fact wearing the Lovat tweed at that moment.

"Sailing in a boat with a white sail?" he asked. He remembered the white sail—every detail of that scene was burnt into his mind.

"Yes."

It occurred to James at that moment, standing beside Juanito's grave with her, that there was something more than strange, something almost uncanny, about the way in which this child, Rosemary, who was so much more than a child in all but years, had been involved, or present, or aware at every single point of his curious tangled association with Raquel and Juanito Torre de Modero, from the moment of his first arrival at St.-Jean-de-Luz. Nothing had escaped her; she was always there—comprehending, silent, self-effacing: except when she could extend a hand in mercy or pity or help. On his Irish mind this struck with a peculiar force—for to the Irish the uncanny is also always the significant. But he made no search for the significance of this; he looked at her for a long while, in a kind of considering silence that was full of respect and liking. She would, he thought, make some man a wonderful wife, some day. Her own love, extended to him that morning below the Phare came back into his mind now—and for the first time, in all these days spent together, it occurred to him to wonder about that. Had he really been right in assuming that that was only an emotional outburst, quickly spent? Her face, as he watched it in the fading light, was still, quiet, sad—and of an odd nobility. But it gave no answer to his questioning. Anyhow, he thought, whatever the answer was, it could make no difference—not to him, and therefore not to her. Love, for him, had come and gone—or rather it hadn't gone, it would never go. He sighed and said—

"It's late. We'd better go home."

"Right you are," she said. They stood for another moment or two beside the grave, strewn with wild-flowers below its modest cross, in the little mountain cemetery; the light had faded now from the great ridge, the snow gleamed silvery in the dusk under the first faint stars which pricked the tender blue of the sky.

"Poor Raquel! Poor Juanito!" she said softly. "Come on, James."

They left the cemetery and went down the hill together.

**THE END**